NUTSHELL

(AKA **JOHN ALBEDO***)*

Black Rose Writing | Texas

First printing

ISBN: 978-1-68433-716-3 (Paperback); 978-1-944715-83-0 (Hardcover)
PUBLISHED BY BLACK ROSE WRITING
www.blackrosewriting.com

Printed in the United States of America
Suggested Retail Price (SRP) $21.95 (Paperback); $26.95 (Hardcover)

Nutshell is printed in Sabon

*As a planet-friendly publisher, Black Rose Writing does its best to eliminate unnecessary waste to reduce paper usage and energy costs, while never compromising the reading experience. As a result, the final word count vs. page count may not meet common expectations.

NUTSHELL

1

Doc Callaway squeezed the life out of the Packard's steering wheel, preparing for the danger ahead. Negotiating the first set of potholes, he misjudged the depth of a crater that bounced the automobile out of its ruts, then a bloody mound of carrion forced a counter-swerve that nearly tipped the car onto its side.

"Damnation," he murmured between clenched teeth. *Trickster deities. They're always at play, even though they don't exist.*

After taming the green Packard, he resumed an ideal speed to avoid fishtailing and continued his race to the Pettibone farm, some three minutes away. He had long forgotten the worried husband on a goosey appaloosa a quarter-mile behind, and he ignored the dust devils on both sides of the road that escorted him now to the familiar homestead.

He focused entirely on keeping his tires aligned in the two channels of rocky soil separated by a strip of tall grass, with its erratic repetition casting a nearly hypnotic spell. *Parallel tracks*, he thought. *They never meet. Never cross.* Neva Pettibone was in labor, and this could drive a convergence that was not entirely good news, in defiance of basic geometry.

On this punishing day in August 1932, half-spent with teasing clouds hoarding rain, Doc tried to forget what lay ahead at the Pettibone place. *Parallel lines can never cross. Thumbs up or thumbs down?* The air inside the Packard seemed dust-free, but he knew from the earthy aroma invading his troubled sighs that filth surrounded him.

His reputation in the community was solid, known widely as a true listener with genuine empathy. True or not, even he wasn't sure. Yet, in keeping with that persona, he never ambled from his car to the porch on a house call, no matter how trivial the malady might be. Instead, he chose to sprint, ripping away his jacket as he flew, his slight limp from a childhood injury disappearing with speed. At his destination, the dust that often spackled its way into the creases of his worried brow would emerge as ridges of dirt whenever he sighed and announced: "It's nothing serious." More often than not, he was correct.

Doc Callaway parked in the dirt yard at the Pettibone place and made his celebrated dash for the door. The west Texas wind held his discarded jacket in the air a little longer than usual, and by the time the empty sleeves slipped from the running board of the Packard, Doc was already halfway up the groaning steps of the farmhouse. He held a moistened handkerchief over his nose and mouth, not to hide from germs, but dust. In the grip of his other hand was a black leather bag of magic.

He removed the hanky from his face to open a squeaky screen door, its neglected splinters eager to pierce, then he ducked beneath the door frame to enter. He shuddered at the pop of the screen door as it slammed behind him. Tossing his fedora onto a hallway chair, Doc ran his fingers through his salt-and-pepper mane, the white hairs stiff and wiry, at war with the black ones, straight and smooth.

Glancing back through the screen door, in a quick sweep of the farm and its grim landscape, Doc wondered if there might be any pinpoints of light waiting, someday, to penetrate the relentless beige. A large sand dune covered the driveway near the detached garage where Dirk Pettibone's Model A pickup was trapped. Perched on the slope of the dune was a circle of squatting chickens, all facing inward, tails out, like feathered spokes of a wheel, an avian powwow, their beady eyes shielded from the gritty wind. At the edge of the sand dune, resting against the rotting ribs of the garage, bags of grasshopper bait sat half-buried, choking in the dirt.

Despite the wilted and windswept panorama, Doc felt the old Pettibone place was asylum as much as anything. He brushed the ridges of dirt from his brow and hurried upstairs.

.   .   .

A quarter-mile behind, Dirk Pettibone rode the appaloosa into a sweat. With his model A pickup entombed by dust, he had resorted to horsepower to fetch Doc Callaway from the city of Matherville to supervise the birthing.

"Just one... it's all we ask," Dirk prayed aloud as he rode. "Please, God, just one."

In the distance, he could see the green Packard make the turn into his property. Within a minute, he was making the turn as well. After he dismounted and tied his horse, he gazed for a moment at his home where the second-story windows above the front door appeared as the eyeless sockets of a skull. In that room, he thought, was a parade of bitter pills from the past, but now such tiny hope. The two windows seemed to shed tears of gray-stained wood left from the days when potted flowers on the sills begged for daily watering. The windowsills had been barren for at least four years now. Dirk's eyes fell to the rocky ground, somehow prying his feet from the spot, then he rushed forward, pressing fingertips to forehead where he stroked the trenches in his leathery skin, the lines seared in place by a persistent sun.

Dirk Pettibone had buried the first four infants near Crooked Creek, using oak drawers from his grandmother's old dresser for coffins, each lidded with plywood. After the fourth stillborn, with fingers itching to do something other than strangle, he found himself curiously drawn to a world beyond simple carpentry—first to ornamental woodturning, then beyond the lathe to wood carving, and finally, polished sculpture of wood.

While grieving with wife Neva over the prospect of a fruitless life without heritage, he used his skills to build replacement drawers for the ravaged dresser, complete with matching seashell pulls. As his talent grew, he was able to fashion lovely, ornate coffins for the fifth and the sixth stillborns. Indeed, he flowered in that rare privilege of discovering new abilities during mid-life as an artisan. With his farm whirlpooling into the ruin of regional drought, foreclosures being the only harvest of the day, Dirk Pettibone endured financially by creating fine pieces of furniture for the wealthy citizens of Matherville and environs, those fortunate folks shielded from the sunbaked economy.

"Please, God, just one."

. . .

As Doc Callaway rushed into the bedroom, the first thing he noticed was not Neva's labored anguish, but the homemade headboard of the matrimonial bed–a cresting wave of dark oak flowing from right to left, about to break onto a shore cluttered with seashells. The wave was carved partially in relief, but the free tips of the waves reached out, nearly touching the shells that adorned the opposite post. A broken dowel rose out of the bedpost where a shell was missing, not yet replaced by Dirk, the master artisan. Behind this seascape were rows of yellowed lilies on rotting wallpaper.

"Oh, heaven help me, Zeb," cried Neva, rousing him from the spell cast by the oak headboard. "The baby's head… I think it's already out. Can you tell? Is it breathing? Is it, Zeb? Oh, God, it hurts more than the others. Why's that, Zeb?"

Zebulon Callaway rushed to the bedside, pulled back the sheets, and lifted Neva's wet and bloody nightshirt. "Yes, Neva. The head's out. I can't tell if it's—. Keep pushing. Push! The worst is over."

"Can you tell yet? Oh, please, Lord. Help me, oh, God."

As he looked at the baby's face, Doc Callaway felt his insides sink, and he concentrated every bit of energy to force his expression into a phony calm. He rolled up his sleeves and peered above the canopy between Neva's legs to see her pleading for a drop of grace. Hopefully, the gauntlet of the birth canal had caused the aberrations of the head and face.

Neva was a handsome woman, a dark beauty, an actress in her time. In fact, her sorrow in a childless life had prompted a return to her first love–she had recently won a part in *Green Grow the Lilacs* being staged at the Dallas Little Theatre. However, when she discovered this pregnancy, she bowed out of the role of Ado Annie, and came back to the farm. And now, as she lay drenched and forever hopeful, even after six perfect stillborns, Neva Pettibone looked lusciously noble as she awaited the verdict with a gun-shy smile that took turns with grimacing pain.

"Ohhhhh….God help me," Neva screamed.

The purple blob squirted into Doc's hands, and he deftly cut the cord with the tools from his bag. It was worse than he thought. How would he tell her? Of all the deliveries he'd made over the years, this was perhaps the most bizarre. Yes, it was alive, though hopefully, not for long.

"Neva, the baby… I don't know… I don't believe it's going to make it."

The deformities would be too much to bear–for everyone. Neva's other babies had been born dead despite their apparent normalcy, so why did this creature breathe? It would only be a burden in times already too unfair and demanding. It would never know joy or happiness. It would play no role in the grand scheme, at least not a positive one. No impact, other than to decimate the Pettibone's lives. Hardworking, honest people. They shouldn't have to push another boulder up the hill for the rest of their lives. Doc Callaway knew suffering, and he knew it well. For the good of all, he had to intervene. These were the decisions, the tough ones, that medicine forced on its practitioners.

"I'm afraid the baby is a monster, Neva," said Doc, using the perfectly acceptable term for men of medicine in describing malformed babies, the subjects of teratology. "It's barely breathing, and it's already deep purple, so brace yourself, my dear."

An admonition from his youth arose in his thoughts–*A doubleminded man is unstable in all his ways*. He promptly buried the message back in its dungeon.

As Neva moaned with the ghastly sound of motherhood denied, anguish that has echoed for eons, Doc Callaway, with the powers imparted to him as a healer, slipped his palm over the baby's mouth and pinched its nostrils. Then he waited as it struggled. He craned his neck in search of a clock somewhere in the room, but there was nothing to mark time. No doubt, this was best for everyone in the long run.

With the baby still under the tent of the nightshirt, Doc's eyes alone could see it fighting back, intent on life. Then the mother's knees flattened, the canopy collapsed, and Doc Callaway lost direct visualization of the feisty newborn as well as his own determined arms that held it under the bloody gown. Yes, it was for the best. But could Neva see it move now that the tent was flat? Doc couldn't believe how vigorously the monster fought him. A few seconds earlier, it had been a lifeless purple, a heartbeat from death. Now, he felt its little arms grasping his wrist, squeezing in desperation.

Dirk Pettibone filled the doorway, in a swirl of dust, it seemed. "Doc, is it out? Is it alive?" Anxiety was scribbled on his face in wrinkles trained to expect the worst.

Frozen for a moment, Doc, in clouded reflex, felt his hand ease from the baby's mouth. He couldn't predict his own next move. Then, he lifted his cradling arms full of revulsion from beneath Neva's nightgown. *Fall thy edgeless sword*, he whispered to himself, realizing the abrupt reversal of the healing arts. His forehead turned cool with sweat. "I don't think it's going to make it, Dirk. Be thankful. The baby's badly deformed. Here, look if you must," Doc said. "Hold it while I get the placenta."

Dirk took the baby in his arms.

Doc kept an eye on the creature as it flushed pink in Dirk's hands, then he noticed the disgust on Dirk's face as the father managed through frozen jaw, "I think it's... well, Neva, it's a girl." A cat-cry, more banshee than human, came from the little blob, giving eerie alert that enough air was going into her soggy lungs and coming out again.

Neva called out, "Oh, let me have her, Dirk. Please, let me hold her."

As Doc caught the placenta, he looked at the luster of Neva's face while the baby gurgled and cried. Neva smiled at the mutated bundle in her arms as if it were the most beautiful baby on earth. The mother's glowing eyes did not seem to appreciate the same horror the two men saw.

The monster's face seemed barely human, perfectly round but with features clustered in the lower half while an over-sized forehead loomed above. Thick fur covered the entire scalp. Ears were large and low set, fixed at right angles to the head. The face was the least concern, however, from the standpoint of function.

The mother smiled as she stroked both flippers where there should have been hands, for the creature's fingers were melded together by a coating of pink flesh. Then, the mother caressed a half-length leg, stubbed at the end with a clubfoot. She lowered her head and kissed the stump. Then she touched the other leg. "Why, look Dirk, she has one perfectly normal leg. Yes, one perfectly good and lovely limb."

Neva saw only God's handiwork. Doc Callaway could tell she was embracing a living, breathing, rosy baby whom she loved more than anything in her life, replacing all other loves, past, present, and future. Lost in this thought, Doc felt his own heart grow heavy.

"I'm going to call her Ivy," she announced to the perplexed men. "For no matter how gnarly her vine, she will always cling firmly to life, and she will always grow, for she has one strong limb."

Dirk Pettibone lowered his head, then dragged the toe of his boot through the thin layer of dust that had collected on the hardwood floor. He traced the letters I-V-Y in the dirt, then sighed.

Doc Callaway dropped the placenta with a thud into an empty paint can that the Pettibone's used for trash. *Ten more seconds and I would have put an end to all the misery this baby will bring to everyone. Parallel lines do not cross.*

Dirk Pettibone sat down beside his wife and swept away the tangles of sweaty hair from her brown eyes. "Ivy, it is," he said. "I'd hazard to say little Ivy's gonna pack a wallop someday, somehow. Neva, you have a knack for knowin' things like that." Then, holding onto the seashell bedpost for support, he leaned down to the baby and kissed the top of Ivy's head. "Never knew a newborn could smile," he added.

The scene was too much for Doc who announced, "I'll be off now. I nearly missed the action anyway. Women have been squeezing out babies long before doctors were around, and without a whole lot of trouble, I might add."

He stepped to a wall sink in the corner of the room where he plugged the drain, poured water from a pitcher, and washed his hands. The birthing blood seemed to weep from his fingers into the agitated pool. After draining the red water, blood still clung to the porcelain basin, so he rinsed the bowl clean with the last drops from the pitcher. He was then irked to discover that a splatter of blood remained on his forearm. Without more water, he had to brush away the stubborn clot, but it clung instead. *Out, damned spot. Wasn't Neptune's ocean enough to wash this blood?*

The air seemed suddenly muggy, too thick to breathe, even though it hadn't rained in this county for 42 days. Not since last June. He massaged his ample nose between forefinger and thumb as if this might open his nostrils. He looked again upon Neva's peaceful face, her deep and dreamy eyes, so sultry before, now cadaverous, as if she had aged decades in a matter of minutes. When he tried to inhale, his lungs ached.

"Thanks again, Doc," the parents chimed. "We don't know what we'd do around these parts without you."

A healer, a man who understood the science of his day and who mastered the art of medicine as known in every age, Zebulon Callaway held the conviction that if Providence tagged along in the reconstitution of the sick, then it did so as a silent partner. Thus, he worked alone.

Doc made a final check of the pinkish creature that was trying to suckle colostrum from Neva's breast. He nodded toward stone-faced Dirk then headed out the door. "Bye, Doc" followed him like a ghost to the top of the stairs.

He never forgot that his nickname "Doc" was an honorary title, bestowed by his years of service to this doctor-poor county in far west Texas. For, as everyone in Matherville knew, once upon a time, Zebulon Callaway had, after only a few months, dropped out of medical school.

2

Genealogy as Overture:
Zebulon Callaway was not the poseur he seemed if one examined how he dangled from the twisted branches of his family tree. Ten generations prior, Chestwyn Callaway, an Armiger and later a Knight, for whom no noble deeds were ever recorded during life, had a profound interest in the healing arts.

Indeed, Chestwyn had championed the use of Digby's "sympathetic powder" for the Virgin Queen as she lay dying, but her ingestion of the powder, mixed into a blue elixir, had little effect. She choked on the tonic one evening, then died without clear cause the next day. Sadly, it was only later that Sir Chestwyn learned that a "sympathetic powder" was not intended for direct consumption by the patient, rather to be sprinkled on discarded dressings used to wrap and soothe the patient.

While speculation persisted that Chestwyn had hastened the death of Queen Elizabeth, he was spared reprisal and, in fact, honored by Elizabeth's successor, King James I, whose belief and usage of blue vitriol was accompanied by remarkable cures when the copper sulfate was applied according to instructions–to a discarded item of "sympathy."

While Chestwyn publicly basked in the grace of James I, he was privately drawn into a personal Hell through the waggling tongue of a disgraced lady of Elizabeth's old court, one Vanora Pugh of Wrexham. Vanora lay claim to ongoing, two-way conversations with the dead queen who lamented even from Heaven that Chestwyn had poisoned her, not through blunder, but by intent as a spurned lover. Had the House of Tudor maintained the throne, there might have been ears to hear Vanora, but the transfer of power to the Stuarts provided haven for Chestwyn, and mockery of Vanora.

Nonetheless, Chestwyn felt obligated to stop the damning tongue. Chopping off the tip of that tongue failed, as did two sequential amputations down to the stub where Vanora persisted in her garbled accusations concerning the death of her beloved queen. As such, Chestwyn took advantage of the new Witchcraft Act of 1604 that included necromancy within its provisions, and Vanora was finally silenced through a toasty fire at the stake. As the flames scorched her skin, she howled an unintelligible curse on the Callaway Clan, later detailed in a pre-mortem note: "*Innocent deaths from your guilty hands, for thirteen generations.*" While Chestwyn openly scoffed at the curse and never spoke of it again, the spell haunted him quietly. And with his death from syphilis decades later, few knew the meaning of his final words: "Oh, how wrong I was. The curse will poison twelve more."

Eldest son of Chestwyn, Archdale Callaway, was a friend of Edward Wrightman of Burton-upon-Trent, a Baptist convicted of diverse heresies and burned at the stake in Litchfield in 1611 by King James, the same year that the king's version of the Bible was published. Archdale was no champion of religious freedom or anything else for that matter, but he loved the comfort of his own skin after seeing his friend roast, and he sought refuge several years later by boarding a ship christened as the *Marigold*, bound for the struggling colony of Jamestown. So began the American branch of Callaways.

Although noble blood may run through generations, it tends to run downhill. By the time blood passed through two more generations, Hartley Callaway, an alchemist, was shamed and dismissed from his professorial post at Harvard for teaching and publishing on the transmutation of metals (Callaway H. Philosopher's stone powder for transmutating base metals as a poultice to correct aberrancies and restore harmony to the chemistry of the human body. In: *Response to the Fallacies of "The Sceptical Chymist." Proceedings of the Cambridge Society of Alchemy.* Vol. 12, pp. 207-238, 1698).

In fact, he was disgraced by the very administration that had hired him for the very purpose of teaching alchemy. The transition from alchemy to chemistry was, of course, a continuum most gradual, but for public appearances and policy, the distinction was abrupt. The open condemnation of alchemy came during the reign of Increase Mather as President of Harvard who, oddly, had a personal fascination with both alchemy and witches, as did his son, Cotton. Yet, his intrigue with transmutations and "spectral evidence" by Increase (who never gave up his day job as preacher at the original Old North Church in Boston) did not stir him to halt Hartley's dismissal. In fact, Mather did not reverse his opinion on witchcraft until the rumor spread that his own wife was about to be charged. Privately, he clung to his books on alchemy until the end. Nevertheless, with facile caprice known to most professorlings, Harvard reversed its position on the veracity of alchemy during Hartley Callaway's tenure. His ouster was swift.

The generational blood finally pooled at the bottom of the family in the veins of Hartley's third son–Charleton Callaway, the murderer.

Shortly before the Revolutionary War, Charleton was a pioneer in what would later become Clark County, Kentucky. A righteous and God-fearing man by every account, having studied the works of the great theologian and metaphysician Jonathan Edwards, Charleton entered the treacherous world of too much land, too much wealth, too quickly.

Enticed into a card game by the local banker, under the premise of learning the new fad "vingt-et-un" retrieved from the liquor-laced halls of New Orleans, Charleton was the big winner until accused of cheating with marked cards. After a vigorous thump on his head, he awoke to find another wealthy landowner dead on the floor with the grip of Charleton's belt-dagger protruding from the man's chest. Weeks later, at trial, there was no longer a bump on his head to validate his version of events, but there were five witnesses describing how Charleton had stabbed the man to death.

Just as a guilty man who draws near the gallows will often find his God, so an innocent man may lose his. As the manila hemp was placed around his neck, Charleton's hands were tied behind his back, while his feet would, by design, dangle freely. The art of hanging was a science.

Too gentle and the condemned man would survive the drop; too severe and the head would pop off. Observation of the legs at liberty allowed the crowd to stand judge over the hangman's skill. If rope length was calculated precisely to body weight, there would be perfect stillness of the legs with a neatly snapped neck. "That was a mighty fine hanging," spectators would rightly say.

On the lofty gallows, when the presiding minister asked Charleton if he had any final words, he said, "Aye," whereupon he lowered his head like a battering ram and charged the reverend and his Bible. The King James Version flew into the air as the minister fell over the wooden railing and landed headfirst on the ground below. With legs stilled, the minister was dead of a neatly broken neck.

"There you have my last word, you dregs," Charleton shouted to the several hundred who had gathered for a high time and a mighty fine hanging. "You believe this trap door 'neath my feet as a chute for slaughter–a direct passage to Hell. Yet, not for your lies against me, but for standing idle while criminals strip me of my life and my soul, each of you are standing on your own trap door. The difference be that I see my trap where you do not. You, too, will drop six feet when you die– the short and certain distance to H—"

A thud, then a popping sound, followed by the creak of a moaning trap door, played accompaniment to Charleton Callaway's stilled legs swaying six feet lower than before.

With three murders notched (that is, Charleton, plus the other card-player who was stabbed using Charleton's dagger and, incidentally, the minister), the banker and his cronies were without accusation, without remorse, and with 3,000 acres freshly added to their holdings.

Charleton's 12-year-old son Josiah witnessed the hanging from the rear of the crowd, his father transmutating before his eyes into a murderer, the very thing for which he had been falsely accused. Scourges of the town afterward, Josiah and his mother moved to Tennessee. Josiah grew up trusting no man, but a lovely young woman named Enid became his bride when she pledged her loyalty to him, even with full knowledge of the murdered minister.

Enid had come to believe early in life that there are no coincidences and no luck–that all things have a godly purpose in a grand design.

Thus, it was clear to her that the presiding minister at Charleton's hanging was guilty of something, be it past, present, or even future. If innocent at his death, then had he lived, he surely would have committed some grievous sin. Charleton's deed was, therefore, an act of God designed for a greater purpose, part of a grander scheme, invisible to humankind.

Josiah greatly appreciated this philosophical stance, in that the wondrous Enid accepted him and his dark past. However, he quietly rejected the belief himself, living a practical life in a house blessed with seven children–a house in which Enid banned the word "luck." Yes, this tiny four-letter word had insidious intent far more treacherous than outright cursing as it threatened to strip the Lord of His grand design and interventional power.

Haunted forever by his father's deed, Josiah took it upon himself to restore the nobility of the Callaway name. This resumption of honor manifest itself in a book written by Josiah describing the life of the great knight, Sir Chestwyn Callaway (Callaway J. *The Radiant and Bountiful Deeds of Her Majesty's First Knight – Sir Chestwyn Callaway*; unpublished, 1802). And where history left many blanks, Josiah filled them in. His children grew up basking in the chivalry and courage of the Great Callaway and the pivotal role he had played in English history as one of the Queen's many suitors.

Yet, Enid saw a greater lesson to be learned in the story of a different Callaway–and that would be Charlton, her would-be father-in-law and the Providential murderer. And when Josiah was not with the children, Enid would tell them the tale she thought crucial for persevering in a dark world–the story that explained how all things work according to perfect design. And it was her Bible that became the family Bible, passed generation to generation, not in random, but according to the Greater Good.

Three of their seven children died "sickly" before turning ten, and it was their youngest, Jasper, who lived to tell the stories of these two ancestors–Chestwyn and Charleton–to his son Davis who died as a consequence of the Civil War–not by direct injury, but aftermath. Davis had enlisted as an assistant surgeon in Company "A" of Gibson County, Tennessee, where the practice of quick-to-amputate medical care was standard. His role as a surgeon did not shield him, however, from DuPont's black powder used by the federal demons. The Northern powder exploded near his Southern station, imparting wounds that would later require precautionary amputation of both legs above the knee and one arm below the elbow.

After the war, Davis immersed himself in the exhilaration of medical research, publishing on the success of a new substance isolated from coca leaves, in treating the heroine and alcohol addictions of the South's survivors (Callaway D. The successful and miraculous abolition of unwelcome addictions imparted by federal aggression, through application of the newly derived alkaloid extracted from coca leaves. *Medical Letters of Surviving Sons of the Confederacy*. Vol. 2, pp. 8-14, 1868).

The experimentation turned sour, however, as Davis was largely his own laboratory. Fortune left one good hand with which to pull the trigger of his Colt .44 revolver, sending a bullet to liquefy his brain, six years after the war had ended. The note he left said simply: *'Twas not the loss of my own limbs, but the 400 limbs that I stole from others in bygone years.*

The death of Davis came two decades after he had told his second-eldest son Beck the stories of dragon-slaying by Sir Chestwyn the Great and minister-slaying by Charleton of the Greater Good. Beck, in turn, passed the stories to his only surviving son Parker Callaway, the bone setter (two of Beck's other children had died "sickly" in their teens, a terrible trend in the Callaway family).

Parker was a Kansan and a blacksmith whose keen eye for shaping yellow-to-red iron was noted by customer Andrew Still. Mr. Still was a healer, also drawn to the science of malleability, who had become increasingly devoted to the concept that all human disease could be attributed to the failure of body mechanics–errors in sinew ropes, joint pulleys, and levering bones. Andrew Still saw in Parker Callaway a potential disciple whose manipulations might better serve mankind rather than the ironworks of a horse-driven economy. As the years passed, Andrew Still became the father of osteopathy, and he grew to abhor the use of drugs and potions. Parker Callaway, on the other hand, saw great strength for healing through elixirs. As a result of this doctrinal dispute, Parker broke from Still and began an itinerant medical practice out of a purple gypsy wagon with his wife Willa, a dark-eyed beauty rumored to be a Zionist.

Willa's family closet held the skeleton of her ancestor, Shabbetai Zevi, an erstwhile Jewish mystic who, though proclaiming himself as the Messiah in the 1600s, launched a storm of controversy when he converted to Islam under duress by the sultan in Constantinople. Willa admitted nothing in this regard, but quietly sent money to her cause. She and Parker traveled together for several years through Arkansas, Louisiana, and Texas, selling a single product in four-ounce bottles– *Callaway's Vin Coca et Laudan.*

Hearing that the streets of Metzgerville, Texas were "flowing with oil up to the wooden sidewalks," Parker and Willa headed to the desolate western plains even though Willa was in her ninth month. Zebulon Callaway was born in the purple wagon, three miles shy of Metzgerville, and the joyous couple decided it was a sign of the Greater Good for them to put down roots. *Callaway's Vin Coca et Laudan* enjoyed wonderful success in the oil-rich town where almost half of the adult population became enthusiastic users and regular customers at the quickly-built Callaway store.

The Callaway family started domestic life in a tar paper shack, then a nice cottage, and finally a lovely home with indoor plumbing before storm clouds developed in the form of the Texas Pharmacy Association with its nasty emphasis on credentials. In September 1900, Parker traveled to Galveston with his 10-year-old son, Zebulon, to investigate the possibility of procuring a post-blacksmith education in pharmaceutical science at the "Old Red" building, home to the University of Texas School of Pharmacy. And if acquiring credentials proved too cumbersome for himself, then certainly he could hold out against the T.P.A. long enough for Zebulon to become a certified pharmacist.

In peculiar timing for the Greater Good, "The Storm" hit Galveston shortly after the arrival of father and son, and the building where the two were staying at 2nd Street near the beach was obliterated, along with everything in the area, by the most ferocious hurricane in recorded Texas history. While it had been raining and blowing the Friday of their arrival, no one raised the hurricane flag on the Levy building until the city was nearly submerged and there was no longer working transportation off the island. The locals had been saying, "It's only a tropical storm. Otherwise, Mr. Klein would have the flag a-hoist."

Parker Callaway's body was found on the second day, becoming merely one of the eventual 6,000 lifeless lumps in the sand. Young Zebulon sustained a crush injury to his foot, but he escaped death by following a crowd that took refuge in the sturdy home of a prominent physician. Shortly after identifying his father's body, it was explained to Zebulon that there was no way to transport bodies off the island, and no way to bury them in the moist sand. With the stench of death in the air, Zebulon nodded yes when the men explained they would need to torch his father's body on the spot. It was the same fate for most of the 6,000.

Turning from his father's burning carcass, Zebulon watched in horror as an old man not fifty feet away stumbled on a dead child buried in the sand. When the elderly gentleman pulled the corpse free, it was attached by rope to another dead child, then another. Zebulon ran to help the man, and the two of them dug six children free of the sand, all connected by a rope around their waists. Finally, they came to the end of the rope, lassoed around the waist of a dead nun. He would learn later that this was one of ten nuns of the Sisters of Charity Orphanage, all ten of them having perished with the best intent at salvation of the children with their ropes, taking 90 of the 93 orphans with them to their sandy graves.

Overwhelmed beyond words, the 10-year-old Zebulon made his way back by train to west Texas where he would never be able to shake himself free of the aftermath of the storm.

Whether it had been his traumatic exposure to mangled bodies in piles near the beach, or perhaps the fact that one of the few structures standing after The Storm was a physician's home, Zebulon decided on medical school. While he studied in college with great resolve, his mother Willa struggled to keep the one-drug pharmacy afloat. Another setback came when the Food and Drug Act of 1906 forced labeling of the contents of all patent medicines. And while the Act did not make coca leaf extract or alcohol or tincture of opium illegal, the law did make the true contents quite visible to the customers. Business plummeted, and the Texas Pharmacy Association pressed even harder against the Callaway drugstore. To help in the financial crisis, young Zebulon began working as an orderly at the Metzgerville State Lunatic Asylum.

In 1910, Zebulon was admitted to Epworth Medical College in Oklahoma City, shortly before the school was assimilated by the University of Oklahoma. Yet, the time and expense of medical school education softened his earlier resolve. Contributing to his quick departure from Epworth/OU was the fact that no women were allowed to enroll, not that Zeb was a sympathizer to suffrage and its cousin concepts. Instead, it was his simple desire for gentle companionship. Time, expense, and the desire for a bed warmed by two bodies drove him toward quicker credentialing as a man of the healing arts – a pharmacist. Women were enrolled a-plenty in the post-hurricane, re-built pharmacy school that was housed in "Old Red" in Galveston where Zeb matriculated in 1911. There, he met Hildimar Guenther, with matrimony in 1912.

"Hildy" had received her undergraduate degree with many honors at Trinity College in Durham, North Carolina, where her "fair sex entry" had been made possible by a large grant from one Washington Duke. Later, at the University of Texas, studying in "Old Red," this striking woman, who stood almost as tall as Zeb's "six foot two," dominated the number one position in the class. After Zeb and Hildy graduated, they returned to Metzgerville, re-named as Matherville in their absence, shedding the town of its Germanic origins given the war in Europe.

Although Zebulon was required to register for the draft in 1917 as part of the new Selective Service Act, he did not serve in the military due to the crush injury to his right foot as a boy, sustained during the Galveston hurricane. His limp was barely noticeable, but it was enough to exclude service, given the millions of able bodies signing up for war.

One year later, Hildy bled to death at Matherville General Hospital after delivering a healthy son, Wesley. The seeds of agnosticism had been sown for Zebulon years earlier, upon viewing the corpses stacked like driftwood on the beach at Galveston, while noting the pathetic silhouette of an impotent, decimated Sacred Heart Church nearby. After wife Hildy's death, Zebulon became a confirmed, albeit silent, atheist.

The surviving son, Wesley, offered little consolation to Zebulon, the latter having seen both his father and now his wife perish. Zeb did his best not to lay blame on the boy, but it would have been much easier had Wesley brought joy with him into the world. Instead, the boy was dark and withdrawn. He didn't smile as an infant, and he rarely laughed as a child. When he was old enough to hear the family legends of Sir Chestwyn and Charleton, he commented to his father: "Those are ridiculous stories. I don't care if the Callaways have always told them to their children, I won't be telling them to mine."

Gradually, Zebulon relinquished the raising of Wesley to the boy's grandmother, Willa, who had maintained the family drugstore through the T.P.A. siege until her son was firmly planted in Matherville with sound credentials as a pharmacist. Wesley's darkness had nothing to do with evil, or improper conduct of any kind. Serious-minded about all things, it was more like the boy had been born fully grown. This was no solace for Zebulon who, having faced too much tragedy, longed to laugh like a child.

Zebulon Callaway submerged himself in the drugstore and his customers. At first, he blindly followed the written orders of the local physicians. Soon, he discovered a problem with this mindless approach. Customers would describe their symptoms to Zeb, and he would disagree with the diagnosis, the prescribed therapeutic, or both. Often, he wondered if the physician had even listened to the patient. Dangerously, he began to voice his opinion. Worse, he was often correct. And when the referring physicians heard that Zeb had changed the diagnosis, the prescription, or both, the antipathy began to build.

Rather than back down, Zebulon saw himself as fulfilling a need, not merely a prescription. The patients were not satisfied with their doctors. Symptoms were described, but not heard. Pain was expressed, but not felt. Zebulon began reading medical texts, subscribing to journals, even attending medical meetings. The people of Matherville found great trust in their new man of medicine who never hesitated to come to their homes in the middle of the night, or their farms in the middle of nowhere.

And when formal censure by the local physicians failed to stop "Doc" Callaway, a boycott was placed against his drugstore as the doctors insisted all their prescriptions be filled at their own company store. With drug revenues slashed, Doc Callaway began relying more and more on his diagnostic acumen and his treatment skills as the town's most popular "doctor." The boycott, therefore, had the opposite of its intended effect, as Zebulon's medical practice expanded while his pharmacy languished.

Denied hospital privileges, of course, Doc Callaway became the top choice of the walking, talking sick. And it was all perfectly legal, in the strictest sense, because he never hung a doctor's shingle, nor did he proclaim himself to be a physician. He quickly defended himself by reminding enemies that "Doc" was only a nickname. Yet, Doc Callaway seemed to practice, and profit from, a great deal of medicine during the oil boom of the 1920s.

Whereas the T.P.A. had been his father's nemesis, the Texas State Medical Association soon became Zebulon's. In a Wild West showdown, the board attempted to place a figurative noose around Zebulon, calling on the strong arm of the law, but Doc Callaway stood his ground: "Dear Sirs," he said at a formal hearing, "the apothecaries of old were always in battle with physicians. In 17th century France, the physicians won, but in England, it was the apothecaries. And why? Because, during the Great Plague, the apothecaries remained at their posts, while the physicians fled like cowards to the country. The public never forgot their champions."

After his impassioned plea, Zeb Callaway was threatened with jail time if he continued practicing medicine without a license. Yet, he did not stop. Unlike the flock of quacks graduating from such schools as the nearby Eastern College of Electro-magnetico Therapeutics, Doc Callaway had real training, a real diploma, and a real license (though not for practicing medicine per se). And he rightfully pointed out to his detractors that there was not a pharmacist alive who did not practice a little medicine on the side. Indeed, the target was drawn on his back mostly because of his immense popularity.

Doc could hold the hand of a hypochondriac until the imaginary pain eased, then turn around and offer an extra dose of morphine for the hopeless cancer patient to speed the certain demise. Likewise, he could spank the bottom of a red-faced newborn and share the joy with the parents, or he could deem the child a "monster" and try to put an end to the suffering not yet suffered–all for the Greater Good, seeing himself in the role of the God in whom he no longer believed.

After skipping childhood, his detached and distant son, Wesley, seized upon athletics, especially basketball. By age 15 and a sophomore, Wesley (now called Wes) had grown well past his 6'2" father, leading Matherville High School to a state championship in basketball, all while clutching a straight-A average. In August of 1932, Wes Callaway was honored at the All-Sports Banquet sponsored by the *Dallas Morning News* as the best high school basketball player in Texas.

Wes's father did not make it to the ceremony. Doc Callaway was on duty, as always, now consumed by an oppressive vision of the future, having failed to correct destiny, allowing the birth of a monster at the Pettibone place – the baby Ivy.

3

"Latido resola me sodo," Ivy said, grinning, gap-toothed and bold. "Latido resola me sodo!" Louder now, as if shouting would help her mother get the point.

The stunted five-year-old had revealed no hint of speech until age three, and since that time, nothing but gobbledygook. The pain Neva Pettibone had felt prior to Ivy's birth, listening to her friends chatter torturous details about their children while hers were born dead, persisted now in different form. No longer did she suffer the pain of love denied, but the pain of love unspoken. "I love you, Mommy" was not to be.

Neva was dusting the piano in her dining room for the third time this week when Ivy pulled at the frayed hem of her mother's dress and gestured for them both to sit at the bench. Then, Ivy crawled into the blue hammock of Neva's frock. As the little girl reached up with both arms and cradled her mother's cheeks in her flippered hands, she repeated, "Latido resola me sodo." Neva knew communication went beyond words. Ivy had invented her own words, and Neva had learned much of the language, augmented with ill-defined gesturing. Her daughter wanted her to play and sing. Thus, "latido resola me sodo," was not the foreign phrase it had once been.

Neva brushed her fingers through Ivy's silky brown hair, although this didn't alter the look, each hair returning to its original position, each strand clipped short to avoid the need for special care. A cowlick stood stiff at the top of her head, a stubborn mast denoting Ivy's stamina in her mother's eyes.

Unlike children who outgrow odd features of birth, Ivy had outgrown nothing. Her face had altered slightly, however, with round eyes close set, turned-up nose, and a wide mouth revealing neatly packed baby teeth with a single gap in front. Her features filled more of her face than at birth, helped along by short bangs that dangled across her forehead. Low-set, saucer-like ears flapped at ninety degrees, and she delighted in her ability to wiggle them. Her fingers remained thoroughly fused, and her limp was severe from the shortened leg with club foot at its end. Neva, ever struggling to acknowledge the miracle of a living child, thanked the Lord through her hidden sadness, hourly, that her little girl was happy. Always happy. Happy and stubborn. Smiling, laughing, giggling, yet still unyielding at unpredictable moments. Ivy provided a rich and lively atmosphere at a lonely farmhouse still submerged in drought.

Preparing to play a tune, Neva moved Ivy from her lap to the piano bench, and then eased her nimble fingers to the keys of the black upright. Ivy touched her mother's scarred left hand and began to caress it with her own webbed fingers, petting the back of Neva's hand as if it were a house cat.

The mother stared at the pink scar that enveloped her own left hand like a glove. Five years ago, while pregnant with Ivy, she had dropped her wedding ring into a pot of stew, and, forgetting the pot was near boiling, reached for retrieval. Before she could pull away, the damage had been done. Second-degree burns left her with a pink, tender hand to a line well above the wrist. Luckily, there had been no third-degree burns that would have contracted her fingers into a claw. However, with her burned hand now exquisitely sensitive to both heat and cold, she required shielding, often wearing a store-bought glove over the pink glove of scar tissue. The oddity of it all was that she could no longer wear her wedding ring, the initial culprit, as it felt like a noose around the tender skin of her finger.

As Ivy stroked the pink hand, Neva thought about the waggling tongues in Matherville that delighted in pinpointing a cause for the "little monster-girl." Since the underlying premise for the majority was, "there's a reason for everything," two schools of thought emerged. Many, including several local physicians, believed the theory of "maternal impressions," wherein Neva's burned hand had simultaneously melted Ivy's hands in the womb. This theory failed to explain Ivy's other deformities, but the promoters of maternal impressions were undeterred, offering the argument that each of Ivy's hideous features could find origin in Neva's carelessness while pregnant.

Others found comfort in the theory of "hidden sin" in either (or both) of Ivy's parents as the explanation for a string of stillbirths followed by a freakish child. While it was a widespread belief that Ivy was "feeble-minded," Neva saw quite the opposite, a clever little girl who figured out how to manage in all things despite being short-changed at birth.

Neva pulled her hands from the piano keys and surrounded Ivy's melded fingers with her own. "Now, Ivy, don't move, don't wiggle, and I'll play a song for you. What would you like to hear? 'Daisy Bell'? 'Baby Face'? 'Amazing Grace'? 'Glow-Worm'?"

"Latila. Latila!"

"Okay, then. 'Baby Face' it is."

Without understanding the why of Ivy's puzzling words, Neva knew Ivy's favorite song. The mother sang as she played: "Baby Face, you've got the cutest little baby face... there's not another who can take your place... baby face... my poor heart is thumpin' you sure have started somethin'... "

Ivy couldn't sit still. She pounded the keys with her mitten-like hands, then she jumped off the bench and began to dance, hopping in circles on her good leg while clapping her mitten-like hands. Then she shifted her weight to the short leg, bouncing back to her good leg after one hop as if her crippled leg were one of those newfangled pogo sticks.

"I'm up in heaven when I'm in your fond embrace... I didn't need a shove... 'cause I just fell in love... with your pretty baby face... "

Ivy's joy seemed boundless. Neva, on the other hand, had to fight mixed tears. Her love for Ivy was piggybacked on heartache, always.

She remembered how Doc Callaway had done everything possible for Neva to experience a live birth, a healthy child. He had brought

Neva vitamin potions while pregnant, he had brought Ivy into the world against all odds, and, since Ivy's birth, Doc had been the most gallant spokesperson in town, defending Neva and Dirk against hurtful myths and superstition. Doc had countered the absurd theory of maternal impressions to a fair degree, even to the point of becoming the local expert in the budding science of birth defects–teratology.

The more stones that were tossed at the Pettibones, the more Neva noticed that Zebulon Callaway immersed himself in the underlying science to the point of obsession, to the point of writing a complete thesis on Ivy, to the point of proposing an official "syndrome" to describe Ivy's constellation of unusual findings. Zebulon had said that nothing dispels myth more effectively than nomenclature. "Callaway's syndrome," for instance, would keep the vicious folks at bay and leave mother and child alone.

The second refrain of "Baby Face" sent Ivy into a whirl, spinning wildly like a teetering top. She fell to the floor, laughing. Neva slipped from the bench to join her, hugging and tickling, then kissing Ivy over and over on the forehead. "I love you, little Ivy. You are my precious gift from God."

"Soti medo," said Ivy, which, to Neva, had come to mean, "I love you." Then Ivy kissed her mother's pink hand.

From the ground, Neva stared at the black upright piano Dirk had given her as a wedding gift. Neva's most precious possession, an antique of unknown age, the upright had two tarnished candelabra screwed into the piano's facing on brackets that allowed the candlelight to swing out over the keyboard, each ornament holding three candles. Neva loved to play the piano softly at night, after both Dirk and Ivy were in bed, the flickering light her only companion. And, during "Moonlight Sonata," she would drift away to think about what might have been.

Neva believed more strongly in God's Will than her own. Ivy had been sent to her for a reason–a reason more important, perhaps, than her own life. Neva had bathed herself in this consolation during the past five years of grief mixed with laughter. Yet, how God was going to accomplish anything through this flawed little girl was beyond her imagination.

Nothing during Ivy's development had been more puzzling than when, after three years of total silence since birth, Ivy began to speak in mashed and stirred words. Neva and the mute Ivy had been having fun at the piano on that day two years ago, same as today, when Ivy fainted and slumped onto the floor for several minutes–enough time to send Neva into a panic–and when Ivy awoke, she gave birth to her language. And from that first day, her vocabulary seemed frozen. "Soti medo" looked as if it was going to be permanent for "I love you."

As Neva held Ivy now in her arms, in the same pose as that day when Ivy's odd speech began, the mother looked at the candelabra on the piano's facing and began to sing a cappella, "Shine little glow-worm, glimmer... shine little glow-worm, glimmer... lead us lest too far we wander, love's sweet voice is calling yonder... " She couldn't remember all the words from the operetta she had heard as a child growing up in Dallas, so she tra-la-la'd through the blanks. "Tra-la-la-la-la-la, from mossy dell and hollow, la-la, gliding through the air, they call on us to follow."

With unwavering conviction that Ivy was a shrouded light meant to shine, Neva had resolved to teach Ivy one critical word–GOD. Indeed, a breakthrough of sorts had occurred in recent weeks. Forsaking the alphabet for the only three letters that mattered, Neva had written one letter–G,O, or D–on each of two dozen unused post cards she had collected in her youth. Then she presented the word GOD to Ivy every night by grouping three post cards at a time to spell G-O-D, switching the cards time after time, while maintaining the key letters in order. She explained to Ivy that God was everywhere, including all the fine places of the world seen on the flip side of these cards, destinations that Neva would never visit.

Pointing first to the written word, then moving her finger Heavenward, Neva repeated "God" over and over, while she prayed toward the cracked ceiling of Ivy's bedroom, the shifting foundation of their home apparently unveiling a direct portal to Heaven. Ivy examined the cards that spelled "G-O-D," then stared at cracks in the ceiling along with her mother, her thoughts unknown, while Neva's words tried to ring the doorbell of the Almighty.

For the first year of this exercise, daily, nightly, Neva had asked Ivy to say "God" along with her, but Ivy's best attempts sounded more like "Doti." Then, last month, after Dirk emptied his pockets of the money he'd received for fashioning an ornate armoire (commissioned by a member of the wealthy Studebaker family in Matherville), Ivy climbed on a chair and began playing with a ten-dollar bill. Pointing to the lettering on the bill, "In God We Trust," Ivy turned to her mother and said, "God." Dirk and Neva Pettibone nearly fainted. Since that moment last month, the couple had been waiting for a second coming of the word, disappointed so far. Perhaps, it had been a singular event.

Neva continued the song. "Till we steal the fire away, for fear lest it be wasted... la-la-la-la... Shine little glow-worm, glimmer... la-la... Light the path below, above... And lead us on to love."

Neva, still lying on the floor near the pedals of her black upright, took a deep breath and hugged her little Ivy, thinking back to that moment of revelation last month, recapturing the warmth and the thrill, realizing that victories, no matter how small, were key. Ivy had some measure of understanding that could not yet be measured. And Neva knew she would go to any length, spend any amount of time, do anything, to allow her little Ivy to fulfill God's purpose for her unusual life.

"Soti medo," Ivy said.

"Soti medo, too," replied the mother.

Ivy's smile wrinkled itself into a giggle.

.   .   .

For Dirk Pettibone, the many questions swirling about Ivy had a single answer—hard labor—for both himself and his daughter. He built more fancy armoires, he turned more wooden candlesticks, he sculpted more nativity scenes, working past midnight every night, finally generating enough money for the first of several operations on Ivy's clubfoot. Spare change was saved at day's end, with surgical procedures planned for the repair of her hands as well.

The first surgery on Ivy's foot had gone well, and the second would be later this fall. It had been difficult to settle on a plan for Ivy. Three specialists had designed three different strategies, ranging from non-operative casting of the clubfoot, all the way to serial surgeries to repair what the orthopedic surgeon in Dallas had called, "a most unusual case of equinovarus, a variant so severe that mere casting will not work."

A cobbler in Matherville had created a special shoe with a six-inch sole to help smooth Ivy's gait, although puny muscles in her shrunken leg added to a permanent limp. Dirk's idea for the weak leg became Ivy's burden in the form of a rigorous exercise strategy for the little girl to strengthen these muscles. He had fashioned a leather harness for Ivy, the straps weaving a figure-of-eight over her shoulders and around her waist, linking her by chain to a pole planted between the barn and the storm cellar. This way, Ivy could walk in circles for hours as Dirk tended to chores and worked his wood, all while Ivy gained strength in her slighted limb.

To the rare, casual observer, the image of Ivy chained to the pole was brutal. And, for a while, the sight of the tethered girl inspired the town's teenagers to drive by the Pettibone farm to throw rocks at Ivy as she followed her circular path. Ivy thought it all a game at first, but when pebbles met their target, she cried, a rare event. The taunting stopped when Dirk began leveling a shotgun at the teenagers, sometimes firing in the air, when they trespassed.

Dirk would have let Ivy roam free, but she had a dangerous habit of embracing animals, tame or wild. Amazingly, she had always escaped injury, as though she had a special bond with creatures that could not speak. When Ivy was only three, she had waddled into the neighbor's field where a lone bull reigned. When Dirk found her, she was stroking a hoof of the beast, laughing. Even the bull seemed amused.

Dirk had erected the eight-foot galvanized iron pole the next day, embedded in two feet of concrete, with Ivy chained to its mighty grip for her play time. A sleeved section of larger pipe with an eyebolt welded on one side was held aloft by a crossing bolt that allowed the outer casing to spin when Ivy walked in circles, her chain attached to the eyebolt.

Dirk made little effort to understand Ivy's language. After all, he'd been married to Neva for fifteen years, and he wasn't sure he understood her either. Neva had grown more and more distant with each stillborn, but after Ivy, he wondered if he had lost Neva completely. And when his heart began to sting with this thought, he would sculpt a scrap of oak into a most beautiful angel, a baby Jesus, or perhaps a wise man.

Dirk, at first, had decided he would treat Ivy like any daughter, which meant forcing normalcy whenever the need arose. Normalcy, however, seemed out of the picture after the fishing incident last summer at Groober's Pond.

Using worm bait and bobbers, sitting on a splintery dock, Ivy hooked a fish so big it pulled the tip of her pole to the water. Dirk rushed over to help, but by the time he reached her, Ivy showed uncanny strength by hoisting the fat carp into the air and landing it on the pier. Thinking he needed to protect Ivy from sharp scales or the barbed hook, Dirk tried to grab the fish, but missed repeatedly as it flipped around, splattering them both with pond water. Without a word, Ivy flew into the air and landed on the fish, pinning it with her weight first, then grabbing its head with her webbed hands and removing the hook with remarkable dexterity. She stood up, holding the wriggling glob in both arms like a pet, stroking its back while she smiled and spoke excited gibberish.

Dirk was so stunned at the little girl's strength, her lack of fear, and her skill at removing the hook despite her fused fingers, he didn't notice the mongrel dog walking down the pier behind him. Yet, Ivy saw it, and she somehow sensed the danger. When Dirk finally spotted the dog as it charged toward Ivy and her carp, he knew it meant fish for food, or even Ivy. He used his flimsy pole to strike the dog, but the beast didn't flinch after a good whack. The dog, with teeth bared, was one leap away from Ivy.

As Dirk started to rush the dog and kick it off the dock, a most remarkable thing occurred. Ivy snarled back at the animal, then she opened her mouth, rolled back her tongue, and squirted the dog in the eyes with her spit. She didn't spit outright–no ptooey through the lips– instead, Dirk saw a tiny stream shoot from Ivy's open mouth, from beneath her tongue, the stream of spittle hitting the dog squarely in the face, such that it yelped, cowered, and began pawing at its eyes. Dirk then pushed the mongrel into the water, where it swam to safety on the shore and scampered away.

Ivy closed her lips, smiling, while stroking the pet fish that was still wriggling in her arms. She gestured her father to join her in petting its slimy scales. After he had pet it a few times, Ivy walked to the edge of the pier, kissed her fish on the mouth and tossed it back into the pond.

"Ivy! Whaddya do that for? We needed that catch for supper tonight. Don't throw 'em back in the water."

"Fatime lareso."

"Do you understand me, peanut? As much as those awful-tastin' carp can catch in your gullet, we still gotta eat 'em."

Ivy shook her head 'no'. "Fatime lareso."

Dirk used his fingers to pry open his little girl's mouth where her square baby teeth guarded a secret. "And just how'd you manage to spit like that, Ivy? Your lips were wide open. You'd a-thought you spit tobacco juice the way that dog ran. And what's with your knowin' that dog was pure devilment? You usually cotton right away to critters."

.　.　.

It took a so-called doctor to work out the wonder of Ivy's spittle. Doc Callaway's exam after the fishing incident defined another remarkable birth defect the girl had been hiding beneath her tongue: "Why, I've never seen anything like it. She has enormous sublingual salivary glands! At first, I thought she had ranulas on both sides, common cysts of the salivary glands beneath the tongue. But that's not it. I've never seen anything like this."

The openings to these paired salivary glands were so large you could see them with the naked eye. By rolling her tongue back and working the musculature as she had learned on her own, Ivy could empty the glands out of both openings simultaneously to form a steady stream with the accuracy of an archer fish and the sting of a spitting cobra. Indeed, using litmus paper, Doc discovered that Ivy's saliva was highly acidic, having a pH of 2.0, comparable to that of the resting stomach.

It was the missing malformation, the last piece of the puzzle. Zebulon had been searching for a twist. Something unique. His much-worked manuscript, "A New Syndrome of Complex Birth Defects" had been rejected by the major medical journals, given that the defects were "all rather common." The whole was no greater than the sum of its parts. Finally, now, something special—*sublingual gland hypertrophy with acidic saliva comparable to gastric contents*. It was the key feature that could generate order amidst disorder through the mere power of a name. Taxonomy, above all else, could set the universe straight.

The people of Matherville believed Doc to be a different man ever since the birth of Ivy. In assuming his new role as the local authority on birth defects, and having been called to referee many arguments as to the cause of so-called "monsters," his interest had become all-consuming. Whether this passion grew from being put on the spot regularly, or whether it was the obsession itself that forced his persistent study, the fact remained that he had changed and not for the better. His kind touch had been replaced by a remote mind, a dark indifference that was unbecoming to a healer.

He read every article he could find on the individual defects—syndactyly, dysmelia of the lower limb, equinovarus, abnormal facies, short stature, delayed speech followed by sudden onset dysphasia—and he had even joined the American Society for the Study of Experimental Teratology. He learned the history of the science, dating back to the oldest written records when birth defects were regarded as prophetic, with the gods using these babies to show (*monstrare*) or to warn (*monere*) the inhabitants of Earth. He also read the history of the hybridization theory where animals were involved in the procreation of malformed babies, giving them animal-like faces, and how these children were held in highest respect since, in these cultures, animals were held in higher respect than humans. Yet, in Christendom, hybrid children were looked upon as the sin of bestiality and were in danger of being burned at the stake along with their mothers.

Such practice was not confined to mothers, Doc Callaway learned. In New Haven, Connecticut in 1641, a cyclopic pig was born on a farm, and it was alleged that the one-eyed monster must have been the offspring of George Spenser, a neighbor with only one good eye. Both George and the mother pig were butchered.

And while his audiences chuckled smugly at such foolishness described by Doc Callaway in public lectures, many of the observers in Matherville refused to budge from the theory of maternal impressions.

This deeply rooted concept had survived the scourge of science and could rear its head even among the educated. Impressions upon the mother during the early part of pregnancy could have a photographic effect on the child. Neva's scalded hand had thus fused Ivy's fingers as they formed in utero. And when Doc Callaway's listeners persisted in this claim, he was known to turn red-faced in his steamy anger, a sight unseen in the "old" Doc Callaway whom everyone knew and loved.

Another widespread opinion, of course, was that birth defects were a failure to keep Beelzebub at bay. From earliest times, children that were born with short limbs, webbed fingers, and clubfoot were considered offspring of the Devil. And while the position had softened somewhat, most of Matherville felt that someone was being punished for something even if no one knew anything about what that something might be.

As much as Zebulon tried to turn the event of Ivy's birth into a scientific smorgasbord of curiosity, he himself seemed haunted. When he read Ambrois Paré's "Des Monstres et Prodiges" written in 1573, listing the 12 causes of monsters, he could never get by number one and number two: first–the *glory* of God; and, secondly–the *wrath* of God.

As a non-believer, he considered it even more ludicrous that the birth of Ivy was wrenching at his soul. Patients and friends began to comment on his gaunt and hollow look, the uncertainty of his gait, the tremulous nature of his voice. His confidence, heretofore infectious, seemed to pale as the days passed. He believed these observations to be pure rubbish. Folks were going out of their minds. He was not obsessed, at least not in an unhealthy way, and certainly he was no different than before.

Sure, he had spent over a year reading and re-rereading the landmark work of J.W. Ballantyne. After all, Ballantyne was finally bringing sense to this lunatic world of devils and maternal impressions. In his two-volume epic, *Manual of Antenatal Pathology and Hygiene*, the great Ballantyne had described the anatomy and physiology of the fetus and, like the good scientist he was, evaluated monsters in the light of embryonic development. Most importantly, Ballantyne stressed that the study of teratology belonged to the physicians and scientists of the world, not to the clergy and not to the ignorant.

And this became Zebulon Callaway's recurring theme, in all talks and discussions and lectures at social groups, church circles, and anyone who would listen. Indeed, everyone wanted to talk about the baby Ivy and her remarkable strength and her spitting skills and her speech "in other tongues." And, everyone goaded Doc Callaway into espousing his beliefs on the subject. After all, he had become quite the expert. Yet, to many, the little monster was still speaking the language of the Devil, with or without maternal impression.

And with the Texas State Medical Association zeroing in, breathing heavy in anticipation of the kill, still hoping to charge Doc Callaway with practicing medicine without a license, Zebulon made a fatal error. After becoming enthralled as a disciple of Ballantyne, spreading the good news of scientific etiologies for birth defects, Doc Callaway re-submitted his paper, which was accepted and published– "Callaway's Syndrome: Multiple Birth Defects Combined with Sublingual Gland Hypertrophy and Acidic Saliva." The journal editors, assuming Callaway was a physician, added "M.D." to his name, even though Zebulon had not typed that degree on the manuscript. Thus, the crucial piece of criminal evidence was born–the final nail. In the past, Callaway denied he ever claimed to be a physician, so "How am I different than your Aunt Minnie who prescribes chicken soup? Are you going to arrest her, too?"

Yet now, in the *International Journal of Perinatology and Pediatrics*, Zebulon Callaway, M.D. had appeared as the author, a self-proclaimed, self-incriminating fraud. When the arrest warrant was issued, Zeb Callaway was out of town.

In fact, he was in Dallas, with his showpiece, the celebrated Ivy Pettibone, presenting her to a spellbound audience at Parkland Hospital. In front of that group of esteemed men of medicine, little Ivy performed a remarkable trick. As Doc Callaway held out a large sheet of blue litmus paper two feet in front of her face, Ivy opened her mouth, forcing a steady stream of acid onto the paper, spelling the word–GOD–the letters emerging as a wet red out of the blue background, one squirt for each letter. Some audience members gasped, others rose halfway to their feet to get a better look, but all were agog at the magic.

Basking in the glory of the applause that marked this mountaintop experience in medicine, as if he had somehow engineered this curious creature through his own ingenuity, Doc Callaway was almost able to forget the friendly tip that an arrest warrant waited patiently back in Matherville, intended to terminate his career in medicine. He had already made up his mind to yield to authority, so he expected leniency to follow his hearty promise to stay within the territorial boundaries of a pharmacist.

Something else bothered him, however, perhaps a self-induced distraction to draw him from the impending public humiliation back home. After the presentation, when the applause was nothing more than echo, as he guided Ivy hand-in-hand back to his automobile, he sensed a nagging premonition of change–unguided–but change nonetheless, a deep-seated transformation, signaled by the rumblings of his heart about to be dispossessed.

He considered himself a complex and introspective man, and this vague tugging seemed to be urging him to a new calling entirely. But what? Certainly, he had been consumed by his study of birth defects, admittedly to excess, and while he was about to be driven out of the business of doctoring, he did not want to relinquish his obsession. Yet, outside of medicine, there was no legitimate vocation dealing in birth defects, for those who wallowed in the subject.

Adding to his unrest, he had to admit to himself that he had become increasingly haunted by Paré's first two causes for monsters–the glory of God and the wrath of God. Why did Paré bother to write about ten other causes, given the total power, and conflict, of the first two? *And why, as an atheist, am I giving Paré's nonsense a second thought?*

On the long drive home, going west into the sun, Zeb talked, Ivy rambled.

"You know, Ivy, it was awfully nice of your mom and pop to let me take you to Dallas today. A whole lot of doctors might have learned something back there. Maybe they can help other little girls like you some day. And you heard those doctors who came up afterward, all of them wanting to help you. Some said they can fix your hands."

"Reti lati," she said, over and over, smiling, sometimes adding, "Dalaso dolati."

When they arrived back at the Pettibone ranch, no one was home. "Well, heck, doesn't that beat all?" Doc said to a smiling Ivy.

"Reti lati. Fatime lareso."

"Your folks had to go into town today, I know, but they should have been back by now. Said they'd be here by six o'clock and it's six-thirty already. Oh, well, I'll probably meet them on the road to town. I see that your daddy left your harness by the pole. I'll just fasten you up, and you'll be fine until they get here."

Doc took the hand of the little girl who rocked and swayed as she walked, torso always twisting in perfect rhythm – a gyroscope of sorts, maintaining uncanny balance, swooping toward the ground with each step, only to rescue herself upright, again and again. Each step without a spill was a miracle as she would nearly capsize, her mast and sails close to the horizon, only to emerge again with a wide grin as if she alone understood her own stability.

He led Ivy to the walking pole where he fit the harness over her head, buckling the leather straps across her back. Then he secured the chain that linked her to the pole, noticing her ear-to-ear grin. It would be a nice walk for little Ivy after such a long ride in the car.

"We care a lot about you, Ivy, and we want you to be a strong girl someday. Now, do like your daddy is always telling you, and walk, walk, walk. Your folks will be back soon. If I don't run into them on the road to town, I'll send our delivery boy from the drug store to check on you or I'll head back here myself. Won't be more than ten or fifteen minutes, someone will be here."

"Soti," said Ivy, as she marched forward, hobbling in her perpetual circle.

As he pulled away from the Pettibone farm, the last sight in his rear-view mirror was Ivy, waving cheerfully, chained to her pole.

4

Doc Callaway turned from the Pettibone's dirt road onto the two-lane blacktop that led to Matherville. The thrill of driving his new Cadillac Club Sedan, burgundy with white wall tires, was overshadowed by the looming fact that, if rumor held true, he would be greeted by a warrant for his arrest.

Passing through a canyon, newly chiseled into a low mesa by the efforts of the W.P.A., Doc emerged to view the city on its flatland below. He was startled by a menacing sight. A reflex slammed his foot onto the brake pedal. After stopping at the side of the road, he jumped out of the Cadillac, ran forward a few steps, then backed up slowly in fear until he bumped into the front grille. He gripped the silver-winged hood ornament to steady himself as he whiffed the muggy air, made noxious by dust. He couldn't tell what it was for sure, but a hellish black cloud was about to engulf the city. The sun, however, was still shining above the Davis Mountains in the west, and Doc craned his neck in all directions to study the situation. He'd never seen anything like it.

What if Dirk and Neva had been caught in the black cloud? He should wait here for now on the solo route to their farm to make sure they were going to make it home. On the other hand, he couldn't sit still with such an ominous cloud bank approaching. He should turn around and go back to the Pettibone place to escort Ivy into their storm cellar. Then, a fleeting thought struck him that he should save his own skin and make a beeline home. Surely, he would run into Dirk and Neva on the way.

Birds were chirping, hundreds in chorus, but when he looked around, he saw only one–a Canyon Towhee stationed on a slanted telegraph pole, this solitary bird taking on vulture-like proportions. Two jackrabbits scurried past him down the two-lane, in the opposite direction of the cloud, weaving in and out of each other's path in a helix, brown spots of fur crisscrossing the tar. The stillness was broken by a rush of cool air that slapped Doc in the face, a thirty-degree drop in temperature, at least.

Doc knew that "black blizzards" of dirt could be indistinguishable from thunderstorms, and the dark gray cumulus on the ground could well be nothing more than dust. Matherville wasn't officially in the Dust Bowl. It rested peacefully in the Pecos Valley, close to the Stockton Plateau, outside the lip of the Bowl, although well within the drought zone. No, it had to be a bizarre thunderstorm. Why would the temperature drop so dramatically with dust? The black cloud boiled over the city as he watched from his perch. It acted like a lava flow, unlike any thunderstorm he'd ever seen, erasing the ground with its darkness.

Dirk Pettibone's Model A pickup was a welcome sight as it sped toward him, sparing Doc a tough decision. Doc waved back when he saw Dirk's arm flailing out the window in greeting. The pickup stopped in the opposite lane, and both Dirk and Neva leaned toward the driver side window as Doc approached them.

Doc spoke first. "Ivy's okay. She's harnessed to her pole. I was about to turn around after seeing this monster storm. If this is dust, I've got some Vaseline in my bag to stuff up your nostrils. But a cool front just hit me, so I figure—"

"It ain't no dust storm," said Dirk, "Air's so thick the lightning only makes little puffs of light. I fear it's a thunderstorm with a cyclone buried inside, gathering from the ungodly noise."

"Get moving, Dirk" cried Neva, interrupting the weather forecast. "We've got to get Ivy."

"We'll beat it in plenty of time, Doc, but you're headed straight into it. Even that Caddy you're drivin' ain't no match for a storm like this. Better turn around and come with us."

Doc replied, "My house being on this side of town, why, I should make it okay. It's only a few minutes if I crank her all the way."

"Zeb, please come with us," Neva pleaded. "We have three days of rations in our storm cellar, and I'd venture a guess that you've never been inside yours."

"Thanks, but I'll head on. Much to tell you later about Dallas. Several surgeons say they can help Ivy, especially her hands. Might even do it gratis. One fellow says he's got a new operation that separates fingers. Calls it a Z-plasty with V-Y advancement—"

"Doc," interrupted Mr. Pettibone, "you'd better motor on to town." Dirk rolled his window up as he spoke, shutting out the words of Doc Callaway that seemed to be rambling, perhaps to suffocate the embarrassment of having left Ivy strapped to a pole with a storm approaching.

"I'll come back and check on ya'll when the storm's over," said Doc to a deaf pickup as it pulled away.

Zebulon Callaway turned to face the looming cloud. The storm was moving faster than he thought. Back in his Cadillac, he tried to floor it, but the accelerator felt like a wet sponge beneath his foot.

· · ·

The Pettibone pickup fishtailed as Dirk turned onto the dirt road, only two miles from their farm. Neva clutched Dirk's right arm as he regained control. From a birds-eye view, the road was two thin scratches in the earth, the tire tracks not much wider than tires themselves. Any straying beyond these scratches could be treacherous. The pickup bounced in and out of the ruts, the rubber tires much like four basketballs.

"Slow down, Dirk," cried Neva, "we've got plenty of time. Doc's the one who oughta be speeding."

Suddenly, two weaving jackrabbits zoomed into view from the edge of the road. Startled, Dirk stomped on the brakes, and instead of a fishtail that would have occurred on a flat road, the pickup tried to spin, but catching the edge of the rut, flipped onto its side.

Dirk was out cold. Neva was on top of him, screaming. She shook and pleaded, but Dirk didn't respond. At first, she wasn't sure he was breathing, then an agonal groan signaled that he had only been knocked unconscious.

"Ivy. Oh my God, Ivy. I've got to get to her. Dirk, wake up. Oh, God, please, *please* don't do this to me."

Crouching, then standing on Dirk's still body, Neva opened the passenger door, but its weight kept her from exiting the pickup. Securing her footing against the steering post, she gave the door another shove and it flew open, allowing her to crawl to the top and out. She slipped to the ground and began running home, over a mile away.

A Canyon Towhee, with its rusty crown and long tail, lit on the radiator of the felled pickup and, seizing the moment, began plucking dead and crumpled insects from the radiator grill for an easy meal.

In fervent and sobbing prayer, Neva pleaded with God for safety. Safety for Ivy first, then Dirk. Mostly, she begged never to be separated from Ivy again, unto eternity. She stopped every hundred yards or so to catch her breath and to look back to see if Dirk had emerged. He hadn't. Then, a gentle rise and fall in the road kept her from viewing Dirk and the pickup again. The dark cloud moved closer, and the chilly wind was stirring dust and debris that riddled her face. She cupped her mouth with her pink hand, then smelled something so odd she thought she was losing her mind—from the pores of her own flesh, she thought she could smell the boiling stew that had burned her hand five years earlier.

.   .   .

Ivy kept marching in circles, limping, chained to her pole, as the blackness approached the house. At first, a vague sense of dread. Then— Mommy running along the road toward her. A game. A new game. Ivy began to laugh. She could feel her own grin making her ears wiggle as she waved. Mommy wasn't laughing like usual when they played games. She was making strange noises—slamming-hand-in-the-door noises, cutting-her-finger-with-kitchen-knife noises. Noises of hurt, even though no hurt could be seen. Strange game.

Then, a new part of the game delighted Ivy to no end. Somehow the chain was pulling her backwards, and in a split second, she was on her rump. Ivy laughed, waving still at Mommy who was now at the front gate. Dust was everywhere, and the loose boards stacked against the barn were flying, all on their own. The broom on the porch began to fly as well. Magic. Like the man in the circus tent who made the woman float in the air. But Mommy was not having fun and that meant no fun for Ivy.

Ivy's chain still pulled against her back, stronger now, dragging her along the dirt track, in circles. Start and stop, start and stop. Round and round the pole. Legs hurt. Not so fun. She yelled at Mommy, now only steps away, "Soti medo! Soti medo!" Ivy knew that "I love you" meant something good and warm and kind, and that when she voiced this feeling, it passed through her lips as "Soti medo."

Something was wrong with the magic. Mommy screaming.

Magic lifted Ivy off her rump and back to her feet, but then jerked her into the air, flying in circles, round and round the pole. She looked down at Mommy holding the pole with one arm, reaching up with the other, trying to grab the chain. The dust and the dark made it hard to see Mommy. Afraid. "Soti medo," cried Ivy. Spinning around the pole went faster now, like the Whirling Derby ride at the Texas State Fair, and with each circle, she struggled to keep her eye on Mommy, then in a puff, Mommy was gone, and Ivy could only see the spot where she had been standing. Then she couldn't see the spot at all.

"Soti medo!"

Spinning. Spinning. Ivy's world turned black.

.   .   .

The body count totaled 75, plus four missing. A swath of Matherville was cut from the map with the only residue being the thousands of stories that every tornado unleashes. For instance, Dirk Pettibone's mangled body was found far away from the Model A pickup, a quarter mile from his home, while Neva's upright piano with the built-in candelabra was lying on its back next to him, still in perfect playing condition. Neva's body was never found, one of the four victims whose bodies were presumed lost in a tributary creek that paid its due to the Pecos River. Shreds of clothing from all four had been found on its banks.

Shortly after the storm, Doc Callaway had driven back to the Pettibone place where he rescued little Ivy who was lying on the ground, still in the harness that Dirk had made for her, chained to her pole, bumps and bruises only. With Ivy having no other kin, Doc–in his last official act as a non-practicing doctor–found a facility that would take care of Ivy.

The stories of the dead generated no fervor and little replay, in contrast to the tales of survivors and their miracles. In fact, no one mentioned the dead much at all after a few months had passed. Discussions pitted natural coincidence against the grace of God, and the living shared their versions that would dominate Matherville conversation for years. And the favorite story of all–a tale turned to testimony–was the story of Zebulon Callaway's Driven Nail.

As it was told time and again, Zeb Callaway made it safely home and into his storm cave that horrible day in 1937, right before the black storm hit Matherville. When he emerged from the cellar, a single outside wall had been ripped from his home, leaving the three walls of his library intact, and the books therein unflustered.

Resting comfortably on his desk in this library was a large and formidable heirloom–the family Bible used by Enid Callaway over one hundred years ago to explain the Greater Good to many little Callaways. The front cover of the Bible had been pierced with a six-inch nail (an eavestrough spike) that had traveled through the pages with cyclonic speed, skewering the pulp beyond midway, and coming to rest with its point pressing divinely on a proverb: "He that covereth his sins shall not prosper: but who so confesseth and forsaketh them shall have mercy." Opening the Bible by its front cover, all the pages preceding Proverbs 28:13 had been shishkebobbed.

In response, Zebulon Callaway renounced his fervent non-belief, discarded his abiding atheism, and promised a life devoted to God. The common root of seduction in any form is the heightened refusal up to the moment of assent, and so it was with *Mister* Callaway. In the weeks prior to the storm, he had started reading Bunyan's *The Pilgrim's Progress,* enjoying a good chuckle at how an otherwise brilliant man could produce such a simple-minded fantasy.

While some saw the remarkable story of the piercing nail a miracle, others couldn't help but whisper that Zeb's reaction—dedicating his life to God—was fortuitous in its timing, as he pleaded self-reformation in the courtroom and escaped conviction for the unlawful practice of medicine. And, without credentials (once again) for his new calling, but entering an arena where credentials were a luxury, Zebulon Callaway founded his own church with himself as the pastor—The Church of the Driven Nail.

The centerpiece for his church, an altar, was the Enid Callaway Bible on a pedestal, the good book encased in a wood-frame box with glass panels for easy viewing, open to the very page that had rendered Zebulon's conversion. A small red circle marked the last nail hole of the last skewered page, pinpointing the transforming verse. The extracted nail rested peacefully in the crease of the open pages. Brother Zeb, now in his forty-seventh year, did not ponder the exact words of the proverb as much as he considered the sheer power of God's hand literally sweeping away the wall of his house and hammering a nail into his heart.

Hiring a pharmacist to keep the family drugstore humming, Brother Zeb was able to maintain a comfortable life while he devoted himself fully to his new and struggling church. As Doc had studied birth defects, becoming expert in the science of teratology, so Brother Zeb now studied God's Word to replace God's Muteness in his prior life, helping him to heal the common defect of all births.

Brushed clean and baptized anew, Zebulon Callaway was able to rid himself of ghosts and ghostly thoughts, and he was able to forget that, as his last official act as guardian for Ivy Pettibone, he had committed her to the State Colony for the Feebleminded in Austin. Recently, the name of the facility had been changed to Austin State School, although a new coat of paint does not always cover the rust. "Feebleminded," like so many words that pass judgment, was becoming a pariah. A taxonomy fad was sweeping the nation–mental *illness*, for example–with the obvious implication that a distinctly opposite state of mind existed, aptly described as mental *health*. And the solid division between the two–them and us–was best defined by concrete walls.

5

Matherville was founded as Metzgerville in 1879 by Anton Metzger whose father, Ubel, discovered a spring of life-giving water in thirsty west Texas. Local Comanches, however, considered this "discovery" a peculiar claim since the tribe had soothed their throats with the bubbling water for eons. So, when the U.S. Army helped Ubel wrestle the spring away from the Native Americans, the Comanches clarified their stand on the matter by scalping Ubel.

Not that this was a deathblow to Ubel, for a scalp wound can be a mere flesh wound, and the Comanche intent was warning, not murder. Ubel developed a peculiar hairstyle with long, graying, pointed fingers that struggled to cover the shiny, paper-thin skin that betrayed every bump on his skullcap. These bumps drew the admiration of several phrenologists in the area who paid homage, and published scientific papers, through the study of Ubel's contours.

Ubel's eldest, Anton, founder of Metzgerville, leased the spring that gave rise to Crooked Creek, and later, the railroads. Settlers using the Butterfield Stagecoach Line also found water percolating from the ground, a welcome sight at Metzgerville. The entire region swelled with seekers of land.

Flooded with Germans in the early 1900s, Metzgerville was caught in the tide of changing sentiment during World War I that affected all German Americans. The influence in Texas was especially strong.

German farmers of Brandenburg in north Texas changed the name of their town to Old Glory. Men once named Schmidt called themselves Smith. Governor William Hobby even vetoed appropriations for the German Department at the University of Texas in Austin. And Metzgerville became Matherville, a re-birth of nomenclature with a decidedly English sound. No one was named "Mather," and to anyone's knowledge, there had been no intent to draw the name from the controversial minister of Boston's Old North Church.

The Metzger family domination of Matherville did not last. After the crash of '29, another German, Josef Studebaker, wrestled control of the town's largest bank from Anton's grandson, Karl Metzger. Josef spent the next ten years foreclosing his way to great wealth, power, and despised prestige. Four sons of Josef–Adler, Hardy, Bernard, Reginald–and one daughter, Gretchen, made up the next generation of Studebakers, a fivesome that sunk its claws into every sinew of west Texas, from El Paso to Midland-Odessa to San Angelo, even to New Mexico and Oklahoma. For those machinations related to hospitals and medical care, it would be son Hardy Studebaker aided by his sister Gretchen playing the key roles.

Although old man Studebaker was not related to Henry and Clement, the blacksmiths-turned-auto magnates (at least not in recent generations), Josef let the misconception thrive, as all great promulgators of legend allow for themselves, so the family never felt the need to change their Germanic name, even as they blitzed their way to greater profits during World War II. By 1950, no one in Matherville–headquarters for the Studebaker dynasty–could sneeze without Studebaker approval, opting for a "God Bless" rather than "Gezhundeit."

Yet, to ensure their acceptance as Texan-Americans, Josef Studebaker and his five children, collectively and awkwardly, became Anglophiles after the second war. Their generous donations to the city forced the re-naming of streets, parks, landmarks, even churches–not with the name of Studebaker, but with Victoria, Churchill, St. Paul's, Wellington, Buckingham, Thames, Kensington, and so forth. The Studebaker family, dividing, multiplying, spreading, even formed a walled compound for the family–Belgravia–where more than twenty homes were built with an E-footprint, in the style of Elizabethan manors.

And passing themselves off as representatives of Merry Old England, the German leaders of the town, two generations removed from forgotten German soil, established The Colony Club, dedicated to the study of English Literature and Custom. At least that's how The Colony Club worked in the beginning.

After-dinner speeches by visiting dignitaries from England soon ran thin, however, and the members gained greater delight listening to a university professor from Austin discuss how Oliver Cromwell's head was dug from the grave and placed on a spike. By the mid-50s, The Colony Club held to its tenuous English roots through the ceremonial swigging of Old Beefeater highballs in the Smoking Room.

The Smoking Room of The Colony Club, exclusive to the bluest of bloods, was where the strings of Matherville were woven, threaded, and pulled. Voters in the unofficial parliament, all male, mostly Studebakers, their in-laws, and a rumored smattering of illegitimate offspring who had duke-like status, could make or break an individual, a career, a dream.

In 1961, patriarch Josef Studebaker died of a "weakened liver," prompting division of assets among the siblings. Although choked into a corner of waning influence, the rival Metzger family rallied around a single cause where the Studebakers had left an opening, nurturing the premier hospital of the area–Permian General. Revenge cloaked in benevolence was great sport for the Metzger descendants of the oddly-coifed Ubel as Permian General Hospital became the biggest and best, a 15-story monolith, renovated with black reflective glass in the 1970s, giving the edifice a rich, oil-dipped look. Indeed, the word "hospital" did not do it justice, and Permian Medical Center was born.

In response, the Studebakers threw their family weight behind College Hospital, part of Matherville's Far West Texas University (FWTU), with Hardy serving as the invisible governor of the entire medical complex. A hospital with migrants and other poor as its primary clientele, however, proved to be a cash drain, and Hardy Studebaker sought a preposterous solution–fortify College Hospital into a full-fledged mecca where all west Texans would flock for their medical care.

And if this tactic humbled the Metzger family of Permian Medical Center by wrenching away the Blue Cross cornucopia of private patients, then so be it. There was room for two mammoths, perhaps, at the west Texas oasis of Matherville.

As part of his plan, Hardy Studebaker hoped to wax and shine each department of the medical school, one at a time. Sitting atop a pile of gold known as the Runnymede Health Foundation—which had minted its millions by corralling the profits from the sale of a smaller private hospital that left investors there plucking at their empty pocket linings—Hardy became the altruistic hero, "capturing the money from profiteers to benefit the health of west Texans" (so said the *Matherville Daily Texan*, the Studebaker-run newspaper).

Investors in the hospital sale considered themselves fleeced, yet they knew themselves mute for life, as Hardy Studebaker had already assured his place in the history of the university's medical complex, not only as the godfather, but also as the most benevolent of the four Studebaker brothers. Meanwhile, their sister Gretchen enjoyed her status as the grande dame of Matherville, married to the Chairman of the Department of Surgery at FWTU.

In the battle against Permian Medical Center, the first department for Hardy's waxing would be the discipline ignored by most every other medical school in the country—psychiatry—the bull's-eye drawn here to take advantage of the proximity of Matherville State Mental Hospital to FWTU and its medical school. In fact, only Crooked Creek came between the two institutions, while the asylum was bordered by a tributary on its far side as well—Dead Woman's Gulch, so-named after the Great Tornado of '37 that had deposited four female bodies somewhere downstream.

Matherville State Mental Hospital had been founded in 1910 as Metzgerville Lunatic Asylum. "Lunatic" was jettisoned in 1925 when Texas launched its cleansing sweep of injurious words. After the city's name change, Matherville State Asylum underwent further title changes, where even the benign, convalescing word "asylum" was deemed nasty. Name changes didn't matter, however. To the public, it was always "Matherville State," provoking images of football games and pennant-waving to the unknowing. Yet, to the locals, Matherville was inexorably linked to the new white-washed term, "mental illness."

To fortify the Far West Texas Department of Psychiatry, Hardy Studebaker had arranged for the two institutions–university and insane asylum–to be wed. And he did so in the fashion of a true Anglophile–he renovated the dreary, decaying asylum into a replica of Windsor Castle. Perhaps this was an improvement, but the ominous central tower, harboring the criminally insane, inadvertently provoked an image more along the lines of the Tower of London.

Throughout west Texas, the name "Matherville" became a synonym for the "loony bin." Texas mothers would say to their rioting children, "If you don't behave, I'm going to send you to Matherville." And if someone disappeared for a "long vacation" after neighbors noted empty Jack Daniels bottles boiling over the trashcans, then these spying neighbors would say, "I bet he's drying out at Matherville." Teen-agers invented slang accordingly: "He's going Matherville, man." Or, "She's got a far-out case of the Mathervilles." Even in self-reflection, a housewife might say, "I forgot the roast in the oven and now it's burned to a crisp. I better watch out or they'll be putting me in Matherville." Indeed, over the years, the city of Matherville took on a wrinkle to its brow that no one had really intended–the wrinkle of Perdition.

Yet, the Department of Psychiatry at the medical school gained a lustrous reputation with its gold-plated faculty. Accordingly, medical school graduates flocked to Far West Texas for their residencies in psychiatry, nearly all making quick exit from the boondocks after completion of their training, establishing upscale practices in posh, neurotic cities around the country, boasting proudly that they had "trained at Matherville."

Victory in this one academic unit hurt the other departments, however, when it came to this common scenario–mental patients, including the criminally insane, had to be admitted to a regular hospital when medical or surgical care was required. As the population of the faux Windsor Castle increased in the 1960s, the spillover to College Hospital for medical care increased as well. With clear momentum (plus state funding), the process was extended to the prison system where sick criminals were also spirited to College Hospital–"After all, College Hospital is used to handling patients in lock belts and wristlets."

Hardy Studebaker understood. He did not need the departmental chairmen knocking on his door to remind him that, "We can't compete for private patients with Permian Medical Center when the wards at College Hospital are full of mental patients and prisoners chained to their beds!"

Hardy had no trouble dreaming a solution to cleanse the wards at College Hospital. He would cross Crooked Creek to the mental hospital and re-activate its old medical infirmary, a small hospital with medical wards, an operating theater, X-ray, lab, even obstetrics–built as part of the original 1910 facility but closed during the stingy 1930s. The mentally infirm could be mended of physical ailments in their own domicile. In addition, the chained prisoners of west Texas could be treated with maximum security there as well, locked in high-security, private rooms. Lastly, the under-the-bridge indigents and illegals could call this place home for their medical care as well. And with Studebaker fingers in the legislative pie, government funding would allow a profit.

Furthermore, the residents-in-training *in every specialty* at the medical school could learn their trade on these unfortunates, all for the betterment of medicine. Better care for lost souls and better training for medical and surgical residents, all while allowing those shiny, re-decorated wards at nearby College Hospital on the other side of Crooked Creek to house the private patients filched from Permian Medical Center. It was a wickedly wonderful plan.

When Matherville State reopened its "hospital within," after decades of dormancy, the city of madness seemed to thrive once again. Neglected vegetable gardens sprang forth. The old cannery manned by the mental patients opened its doors again. From the peach orchard, originally planted in 1910, came fresh fruit and jam. Craft and hobby classes were reactivated. The beautiful gothic chapel was renovated as well, located on Churchill Lane near the three-story hospital that had no name. A basketball court was built in the church basement, home to Wednesday night soirees for the inmates. The rebirth of the maximum-security hospital seemed to have breathed rejuvenating life into the entire asylum, returning it to its glory days.

•   •   •

To step back in time, the Metzgerville Lunatic Asylum, later Matherville State Mental Hospital, had been progressive from its beginning, with a micro-economy based on homemade crafts and garden produce, thanks to the inmates. The Great Depression had caused the institution to wobble, first to parsimony then later deterioration.

Since government funding had been tied to the head count at the lunatic asylum, Hardy's father, Josef Studebaker, had used every means at his disposal to pump inpatient numbers, to the point of enticing, or forcing, other Texas facilities to ship their chronic patients, their "lifers," to Matherville State if *any* ties to west Texas could be uncovered and established.

And so it was, in 1944, during the reign of Studebaker I, that 12-year old Ivy Pettibone, with her west Texas birthright, was transferred out of Austin State School, allowing her to come home to Matherville–that is, Matherville State Mental Hospital.

6

Chase Callaway, grandson of Zebulon and son of Wesley, was lost in wonder at the scene before him, inside the walls of madness–in a church, for heaven's sake. Standing on the hardwood gymnasium floor in the basement of St. George's Chapel, Chase was wide-eyed at the spectacle of "dance night" at Matherville State Mental Hospital. The basketball court was covered goal to goal with crazies.

Edgy, fidgety, but glued to the floor nonetheless, Chase noticed that inmates outnumbered the aides 25-fold, an uncomfortable ratio should the lunatics revolt. Yet, the music, tinny and scratchy from a 45-rpm record player that sang into a bent-necked microphone, seemed to cast a charm over the dancing inmates–a spell of solace that brought sociability to lost wits.

If one stared long enough, the crowd of dancers seemed to offer rhythmic subtleties where centipede legs rippled in coordinated undulations. Yet, with one blink of the eye, the room returned to a squirming, chaotic, twisting, gesticulating whole with no hope of purposeful locomotion.

"Hey dude, where you hoping to get assigned when the propaganda's over?" asked the bearded aide-in-training who stood next to Chase, the two of them helping to form a row of five young men standing mid-court on the sideline, dressed alike in white slacks and white shirts, ice cream peddlers with no goods for sale.

"Come again? Propaganda?"

"Yeah, man, this orientation bullshit, you know, it's all propaganda. The real story is right here," said the hippie, pulling a tattered paperback of *Cuckoo's Nest* from his hip pocket and thumbing its worn pages. The fellow aide wore wire-rims with tiny round lenses balancing near the tip of his nose. His long black hair was held from his face with a leather headband. "Like, which ward, man, do you want to be assigned to?"

"The experimental ward," Chase answered. "Building Nineteen in the Quadrangle. That's what most people want, don't they?"

"Negatory, dude. Me, I want Admissions so, you know, I can intervene before the wacko shrinks really screw 'em up. Or, Maximum would do, too. I'd like to get into the heads of those farthest out. Mind-expanding, if you know what I mean. A real trip. Then again, wouldn't mind the Dungeon in the Round Tower 'cause then I'd have plenty of time to read, and what a perfect place to study Nietzche's *Zarathustra*, 'therefore must I descend into the deep'... the veggies in the Dungeon don't need a whole lot of gardening, if you're with me on that one. Abandon all hope, it's like the only mantra there, man."

"Couldn't take the Dungeon myself. Grossed me out pretty bad when we toured it today. I've got a connection who'll get me into Nineteen, I think, but the whole thing rides on whether there's an opening for a Level One aide there."

"Man, I forgot. Your people are like pure establishment, right? The old man's some sorta big shot? Gonna pull the proverbial strings, eh?"

Chase felt his jaw clinch when anyone mentioned the great Wes Callaway, M.D. "Actually, I wasn't talking about my father. My connection is a family friend. A nurse. She used to be, well, my nanny, I guess you'd say." He felt embarrassed the second he let the word 'nanny' slip. "She's worked Nineteen since, gosh, '65, I guess. Time flies. She told me that all the inmates are off their meds this summer, getting ready for a big study of some sort, so it'll give me a good chance to see raw schizophrenia."

"That's heavy, man. Good, I guess, for someone planning to be an establishment shrink. By the way, Joe's my name. Joe Davis. Here, you can take my copy of *Cuckoo's Nest*. You'll learn more from it than anything they'll teach you in school. (Chase reluctantly accepted the gift.) And read *Rose Garden* while you're at it. You don't do brain surgery with a pickaxe, man. You'll learn all about that in *Rose Garden*. Me, long-term, I'm gonna groove here as an aide for a while. A sheepskin in sociology from that diploma mill down the road was like a total waste of time. I'll probably go for Psych Aide Two later. You gotta study meds and shit before movin' up to level two, but then you're pretty much on your own. After all, I don't need much bread, man. Money corrupts, you know."

Chase smiled, then turned ever so slightly away from the hippie, hoping to end the chitchat. He was never sure why he was such a target for conversation. Yes, he stood out in a crowd. All the Callaways did. "Callaways have always been taller than a grave is deep," his grandfather used to say. Chase would have preferred to be less noticeable. Especially now, when he and his fellow aides-to-be, dressed in glowing white uniforms, had been instructed by Supervisor Dixie Barnes that they were each obligated to dance with any inmate who might ask.

Chase would have been self-conscious even without his height. At age thirteen, puberty arrived in two waves, the first being vertical with embarrassing sticks for arms and legs, along with an oversized nose and looming ears, plus smatterings of pimples that persisted until the second wave. Only Olivia, his first girlfriend and now his bride, had seen through the juvenescence at what might come to pass. Hers was the only crush on Chase at school, and she hadn't needed to compete with anyone at the time. Livvy was a dark-haired athlete with a perpetual pony-tail and smart, piercing eyes. She drew her own set of admirers, but never allowed herself a wandering glance.

Then, as if a second puberty took place in Chase at seventeen, layers of muscle were deposited on his frame. Full, sensuous lips caught up with the nose and ears, and his face was full and balanced and luminous. Heavy-lidded eyes, a little too far apart, and a thick shock of near-blonde hair only made him more fascinating to the seventeen-year-old girls who gathered around Olivia, trying to capture any crumbs of discontent.

Some girls were more "forward," as when Martie Sue Roundtree cornered him against his locker in January 1964: "I was at the game

Friday night. Second row, right behind the bench. Your derriere is sure cute in those basketball shorts. If Livvy ever, well, you know... " Chase tried to play it cool with, "How could you tell? I was sitting on my derriere most of the game. Fouled out in the second quarter. Remember?" Yet, inside, he was rattled. Insecurity plagued him always, living under the glare of his father's lights. The second puberty had not helped allay anxiety, such that he mostly wore long-sleeved shirts to hide the skinny arms that only he perceived.

Now, seven years later, standing on the edge of a basketball court littered with lunatics, Chase felt totally exposed in his short-sleeve white shirt, all eyes on him, it seemed. He felt his knees bending to make himself as small as possible, hoping to meld with his compatriots in all-white, contrasted to a world of khaki-clad men and cotton-printed women. The five mental health aides-in-training were as inconspicuous as white jellybeans in a bowl of mixed nuts.

Chubby Checker drew all sitters and recumbents from the bleachers, and in a flash, the dance floor was covered with twisting loons. "Let's twist again... like we did last summer" inspired the entire spectrum of psychiatric pathologies, arms and legs mostly out of sync, and with ghostly caterwauling adding to the soundtrack of this shindig for lost souls.

An old man with electrified gray hair had been dancing solo, prior to Chubby, hopping from left foot to right, while his hands plucked imaginary fruit from the sky. With the mandate to twist, the man clutched the fruit close to his chest, then swiveled the upper half of his rigid body, jerking like a metronome gone mad, feet frozen near center court.

A top-heavy Black woman, with hair spiraling in all directions, began twisting with such fervor that her bosom could not keep up, and the two melons beneath the green cotton print gyrated in the opposite direction of her torso as a counterbalance.

A stiff, skinny man shuffled onto the floor where, nearly imperceptible, Chase could discern micro-twisting, perhaps one inch in each direction. The man's partner, of sorts, was a bent woman twice his age who wanted to twist in one direction only, ratcheting her way around full circle. Then, she reversed direction, and repeated this until she fell to the ground where she continued to twist while her partner stared down at her, straight-faced and unconcerned. Chase estimated over 200 revelers at the Lunatic Ball, generating 200 different versions of The Twist.

Yes, psychiatry was going to be everything he dreamed. Here, in his first day on the job with real patients, he was living the movie that he had seen at age sixteen that inspired him to become a psychiatrist: *Captain Newman, M.D.* Chase could already picture himself studying the tape recordings of his patients, deciphering their codes, scaling the water tower to keep Mr. Future from leaping, and using a pentothal crowbar to pry out the secrets of Little Jim's complex about leaving Big Jim to die. And then, when beat from exhaustion, he would join his ever-devoted nurse for a few drinks, then let her coddle him on the return trip home in the jeep. Finally, like Gregory Peck, he would bury his head in Angie Dickinson's chest... Chase kicked Angie out of the jeep. After all, he was married now, and his thoughts drifted to a recent conversation with wife Livvy:

"I know you're torn, Chase," Livvy had said six months before their wedding.

He replied, "Song writing and being the emcee for The New Bloods has been the best thing in my life. I can't imagine anything better. Especially since our first record hit the stores."

"But you've heard the guys in the group complain about having to raise their own financial support, just to keep singing. It's like ninety percent of their time and energy. And none of them are married yet. What's more, you guys don't even get the royalties. The money from that album goes to Varsity Voyagers, and it doesn't count toward your support. Can you imagine being forty years old, or fifty, or sixty, and having to ask people to support you financially? God has given you so many talents, Chase, so much intelligence. Do you really think He wants you writing lyrics? After all, YOU could be the one, as a physician, with the wherewithal to financially support your friends in The New Bloods!"

The argument made sense. He had agreed. After all, the first time he had applied to medical school at Far West Texas University, he was allegedly the only applicant in history to have been offered a position on the spot, during the interview. He had declined. Instead, the Lord moved him to write lyrics for the next two years as he joined the first Christian folk group to land a single on the pop chart. And while skilled at the piano (The New Bloods used only two guitars, a banjo, and a bass fiddle), Chase did not sing or play with the group. In fact, he was no good at harmony, always slipping back to the melody, and his voice was not gifted to perform. Yet, he lived by the motto, "Store your treasures in Heaven," a quote from his grandfather Zebulon, pastor of the Church of the Driven Nail. So, he became an extra wheel for the New Bloods, serving both as the lyricist and the emcee at the group's live performances which, last year, numbered 109.

What the world certainly needed, more than another lyricist, at least as Livvy figured and to which he had agreed, was a psychiatrist working from a spiritual perspective. Not an easy feat, he knew, given that the bedrock of psychiatry, Freud, considered religion a hallmark of neurosis. Yet, medical school made more sense than music, especially for the long run.

Chase's father, Dr. Wes Callaway, applied no pressure for medical school, contrary to the assumption that doctors indentured their sons (and rarely, their daughters). In fact, Chase's father did not apply pressure *toward* anything, only *away*. He felt Chase was generally ill-suited for most any occupation that Chase considered–a piano player ("you'll become a drug addict like most musicians"), a gardener ("it's beneath you"), a landscape artist ("that's just a fancy name for a gardener"), a paleontologist ("you'll never make any money"), a lyricist ("you'll make even less money"), a veterinarian ("for people who don't know how to talk to other people"), a medical researcher ("ivory tower egomaniacs who don't know how to talk to other people").

As for medical school, his father had said: "You don't study enough. I don't see the dedication." This was an odd reaction, Chase thought, since he "set the curve" wherever he wanted it to be. Blistering grades came easy. Straight As throughout high school and GPA of 3.84 in college. The MCAT was a breeze. As for dedication, Chase felt this to be imparted from Above, not within.

The crowd at the Lunatic Ball was ambling toward the sidelines, creeping into the bleachers, when Glenn Miller's "In The Mood" sent them scurrying back onto the basketball court. Supervisor Dixie Barnes, in her starched white uniform, was pacing in front of the opposite bleachers when she was jostled by the flood rushing back onto the dance floor, knocking her winged nurses' cap to the hardwood. After pinning her cap back in place, she clasped her hands behind her back. Mixed with the players on the court, she was a few vertical black stripes short of a dazed referee. When she saw her neophyte aides watching the melee from across the court, she feigned a confident smile then marched their direction, tracing the out-of-bounds line in a squared pathway.

Chase ignored her, looking over the sea of beboppers. A teen-aged boy with an oversized head and alien face was bunny-hopping, finally throwing himself to the floor and scurrying on all fours as he barked. Two little ladies—identical twins—with gray hair cut short and ragged, their skeletal faces wearing vacant stares, jitterbugged as mirror images to each other, choreographed as if they had been practicing for years. When Chase got a better look, they weren't identical at all, yet their yellow cotton print dresses, their burr haircuts, their raccoon eyes, registered a prototype for so many of the female chronics. Dancers howled, laughed, jumped up and down, spun in circles, swooped through the crowd with arms forming a wingspan, but all of it was dancing. And they were *all* having fun in their own universe.

The Supervisor reached the aides and paced before them, hands still behind her back. "Well, gentlemen, what do you think? Surprised at how well behaved all of them are?" (Chase was staring at the barking boy on his hind legs, howling now, as Dixie spoke.)

Dixie Barnes was tall and prune-faced, her jet-black hair seemingly dyed with shoe polish and pulled back so tightly that it un-pleated her forehead. Her pancake make-up was cracked in places revealing a worn exterior, and she painted her thin lips a bright and scary red. "Well?" she repeated, in her smoker's voice.

Chase hated silence, and he felt compelled to fill the void whenever it lasted longer than a few seconds. "Yeah, the crowd is sure a big surprise," he offered, "their good behavior, I mean." More silence. He looked to his fellow trainees for support, but Dixie was staring only at him. "Uh, Mrs. Barnes, I've been wondering," he began again, "who are those guys sitting over there on the bleachers? They look awfully normal to me. I think they're the only guys in the place with their shirttails tucked in. And none of them are dancing."

Dixie reared her shoulders and raised her chin, as if she needed to get a better look, using her nose as a guide.

The hippie-aide at Chase's side kicked the answer into the conversation, "They're the drunks, dude. The alkys. Booze hounds of the establishment. What they need is mind expansion, not contraction. Just give 'em a dime bag and—"

"We refer to them as alcoholics, thank you, Mr. Davis. Or dipsomaniacs. Not alkys."

"What are *they* doing here?" asked another aide, as if these dredges were sullying the name of an otherwise classy insane asylum.

"As a matter of fact, I don't think they should be here either," said Dixie. "We dry them out and send them home. Yet, they're the same people leaving as when they arrived, so they're back again and again, taking up much-needed space we need for our *real* patients."

For the men on the bleachers, Chase could easily visualize another place and time, wearing suit and tie instead of regulation khakis, surrounded by family and friends. They did not look like they belonged here. They didn't have the vacuous eyes of the psych patients that seemed like portals to an empty soul. No, they were bright-eyed, well-groomed, some handsome, mostly cheerful, chuckling at times at the dancing on the basketball court. Chase saw bankers and schoolteachers and lawyers and dads and brothers and little league coaches and Rotarians and... and how did they *ever* end up here? In a way, their fate seemed worse than the lunatics, for these men knew exactly where they were and how far they had fallen.

He could not look at them anymore. It made him sick to think about it. He squeezed his eyes shut to force the image away, and then turned his head back to the dancing frenzy. When he opened his eyes again, there was a short, pudgy girl, no more than four feet tall, standing on the free throw line, staring a hole through him. Her skin was pale and her head shaved, with old scars coursing over her scalp, indicating a captivating backstory that he craved to know. Yet, he was learning here at the mental hospital that there was a fine line between empathy and morbid curiosity.

Chase had already figured out that inmates rarely made eye contact with the staff, but this girl was riveted–on him. He looked quickly to the gymnasium floor, hoping to find a hole where he could burrow. When he looked up, she was still staring. Her eyebrows were thick and black, nearly touching at the bridge of her nose, forming a "V" of intensity.

He was still standing with the other aides-in-training, merely one of five white jellybeans, so he hoped the young girl was staring at one of the others. He knew better. Nurse Dixie Barnes sidled into the line-up of white uniforms, standing next to Chase, while Glenn Miller continued the mood. Chase looked at the floor for another half-minute before peeking back at the free throw line. The girl was still there, staring with her "V" that seemed now to be an arrow pointed his way. In contrast to her short stature, she was fully developed as a woman, standing like a fireplug amidst a mural of jitterbuggers on a city street. The music ended. The mood was gone.

Chase froze. He knew he was a target, and he felt himself backing away as she moved slowly forward, marching as it were, like a toy soldier. Elbows straight, knees straight, stiffly, robotically, she advanced. She must be from the Children's Center, thought Chase, since she was not wearing the usual cotton print dress–instead, a T-shirt stretched tight at the bust, and a pleated, plaid skirt that did not reach the short distance to her knees. In a twisted search for comfort, Chase scooted closer to Nurse Dixie Barnes who then whispered, "That girl can be the devil incarnate. It's a good thing she's medicated."

Marching, marching, closer and closer, the toy robot approached.

Chase heard the rhythmic scratching of a new 45 record when the girl broke her military march and began to sprint directly toward him. "The Bird Is The Word" came blaring over the speakers, and the girl stopped inches away from Chase, raised the back of her fist toward his face, then sprung her fingers open like five switchblades–each sporting a red, inch-long nail. "You're gonna dance with me, mister white pants, or I'm gonna *kill-l-l-l-l* you." The blood rushed to Chase's dancing feet, leaving his brain to gasp for oxygen. He turned to Nurse Barnes for help, pleading with his eyes.

Dixie's saccharine smile through red-painted lips was accompanied by a sweeping wave of her palm toward the dance floor, pointing Chase to his destiny. He was sickened. Humiliated. Embarrassed beyond description. He was too self-conscious to dance under normal circumstances. But here? How could this happen? Yes, Nurse Barnes had warned earlier that they might be asked to dance, but he didn't believe it would really happen. No other aides had been asked, and the dance hour was nearly over.

Frozen, Chase felt his hand clutched and captured by the eager girl who dragged him to the free throw line, that familiar spot where he'd once sunk the winning shot for a conference championship (still falling well short of his father's glory). The crowd was cheering all right, but not for Chase to sink the winning goal. No, the crowd was cheering for him to *dance*, a feat that would have been easier had Nurse Dixie Barnes simply fired a six-shooter into the wooden floor where his white shoes were nailed. And the music played:

A boppa boppa boppa boppa boppa oo-mau-mau boppa oo-mau-muh-mau...

The demon-girl began pelvic thrusts that sent the crowd into a laughing frenzy while sending Chase into a nightmare from which he could not escape. His buddies, the other neophyte aides, were bent at the waist, grabbing their stomachs in the hilarity, certainly congratulating each other on being spared the humiliation. As the girl inched her way closer to Chase, she brandished her fingernails again to remind him of their full potential. Then she said, "Now, let's do the Dirty Dog."

"Oh, no. Please," Chase begged. "Not the Dog. It's the Bird. The song is 'The Bird'. The Bird is the Word." Chase, reluctantly, did The Bird.

The girl fell to her knees and began hunching the air close to Chase's left leg. He turned toward Dixie in absolute desperation. Dancing was one thing, but this girl was working into an orgiastic psychosis. Sadly, Dixie was locked in conversation with one of the neophyte aides, both trying to control their laughter. Chase could feel his forehead covered in a cool sweat, and his heart started to thump faster than the Boppa-oo-mau-maus.

As so often happens in the immediate vicinity around dancing talent, the crowd began to clear away from the couple, now at mid-court as

Chase had been inching backward. A ring of bodies, a virtual picket fence of pathology, circled the dancers. Chase did his best to wiggle and move in dispirited dance, but he felt simply cadaveric as the girl on her knees hunched the air. Her pleated skirt flew forward and back with each thrust, and when Chase craned his neck again searching for rescue by Dixie Barnes, he found relief in the nurse's worried gaze that seemed to recognize, finally, that the foul line had been crossed.

A boppa boppa boppa boppa boppa ooo-mau-mau boppa ooo-mau-muh-mau...

With a wide grin on her face, the girl reached for the bottom of her skirt with both hands, her fingernails curled beneath the hem, and with a quick jerk, she lifted the plaid cloth skyward. Underneath, she was panty-less, and for Chase, time stood still.

He was shaken back to reality when he saw the alkys across the gym rolling with laughter, some of them falling off the bleachers onto the basketball court. Others were crying like babies. Even the schizophrenics, manic-depressives, catatonics, and organic brain syndromes who surrounded him realized something had gone dreadfully wrong. Hands moved to cover mouths agape in horror. Chase couldn't move. But the girl could. And did.

Chase was afraid to do anything. Afraid of tripping a psychotic breakdown if he pulled away from the girl. Afraid of worse if he didn't. And, given his options, he did nothing. He was a statue of agony.

A boppa boppa boppa boppa boppa ooo-mau-mau boppa ooo-mau-muh-mau...

What crap for lyrics, he flashed as a desperate thought–anything to transport himself away from this place. This was *not* Captain Newman, M.D., and Angie Dickinson was *not* coming to his rescue–it was Dixie Barnes who was pulling a lock belt and wristlets from her bag of tricks on the gymnasium floor, preparing for crowd control. Before Dixie could get her security gear ready, the crowd began to split.

Chase looked through the parting sea to spot an odd little pipsqueak emerging through the opening, rocking to and fro with a severe limp that gave the impression she would topple with every step. Yet, she walked boldly, full of confidence. Her ears were like two cockleshells on edge, fanning away from her small, elfin face. With close-set eyes and pug nose, she looked more like a child's doll than human. Her cotton dress with yellow daisies on a purple background nearly swallowed her, such that the neckline was off shoulder, and the short, baggy sleeves covered her elbows. What shone most was a warm and wide smile–not mocking but melting.

This odd little shrimp was barely taller than the dirty doggin' girl who, still on her knees, let go of her skirt so that she could encircle Chase's thigh with her arms.

With her hair streaked in gray and trimmed in a bowl cut, topped with a sizable cowlick, this newcomer to the dance was clearly an adult, but at the same time, could pass for a little girl with premature wrinkles. She continued her hobbling trek toward center court.

"Fatime lareso," hollered the woman as she sliced through the mob, her voice remarkably loud. Her nonsensical babbling continued more in a whisper as she grew closer. Chase noticed that as soon as each inmate on the dance floor spotted the odd little creature, they backed away in respect, sometimes smiling, sometimes giggling, while some bowed their heads politely.

When the girl who was wrapped around Chase's leg spotted the potential foe, she loosened her grip, then jumped to her feet to meet the challenge.

"He's mine, you nasty thang–you slimy bitch," yelled the girl, again flaunting her fingernails and furrowing the "V" of her forehead. The limping woman in the daisy dress stopped an arm's length from her adversary, muttering incoherently.

Chase could not tell exactly what happened next, but the little lady who had teetered onto the dance floor opened her mouth and seemed to roll her tongue back on itself. The next thing Chase saw was the dirty-doggin' girl screaming and rubbing her eyes as she tore from the crowd, being chased by Nurse Dixie Barnes who was dragging the leather lock belt and wristlets at her side, along with two white jellybean aides.

The crowd lost interest, and Chase stood breathless, face to face with the little runt who had saved him from the worst humiliation of his life. "Thank you," he said, several times. "My name is Chase. Chase Callaway."

She seemed to be surprised at his name, her eyes widening, followed by a squint of scrutiny. She then resumed her gibberish, but what struck Chase odd was that she nodded her head as she spoke, apparently understanding that he had introduced himself. *Private languages are a hallmark of schizophrenia,* he reminded himself. *Could she understand plain English, yet not speak it? I guess that's not so unusual,* he thought. *I hear perfect pitch in my head, but I can't sing it.* He searched for words of gratitude that the woman might recognize. "I didn't know what to do out there. I was really at a loss. Thanks again."

The peculiar inmate continued speaking in her own language, grinning as if she were an old friend, long lost, presuming that Chase understood every word. Unlike most other inmates with eyes that stray, she locked her gaze on him and never wavered. When she extended her hand to shake, Chase saw that it was a flipper–her fingers fused into a paddle.

Slowly, he lifted his right hand to touch hers, and she enveloped it with her other hand, another flipper. Both her thumbs were scarred, and it appeared they had been surgically separated from the still-trapped fingers. He forced a smile, then felt his left hand rising to join in, all hands together now, at mid-court.

"Soti medo," she said with her sing-song voice. Their four hands, in macabre fusion, levitated, while Chase felt pins and needles go all the way up his arm. He had never shaken hands with a crazy person before. *I must be hyperventilating to cause these goosebumps.* The tingling stopped within seconds and a peculiar warmth followed. His smile was no longer forced.

"Soti medo," she repeated. And for no reason he could explain, he echoed the phrase in a phonetic volley back to her, the best he could, as if he understood what it meant: "Sodimeedo."

. . .

At home that night, Chase's wife Olivia asked the inevitable question: "Well, honey, how was your first day at work, with actual patients, I mean? Anything weird happen at that place?"

"No, Livvy. Nothing much really."

7

As with the Jesuits who boast that, after molding the first seven years of a boy's life, they'll deliver the man, so the destiny of Chase Callaway was perhaps written those first seven years.

When Ramona Callaway first observed her son reading at a 9-year-old level at age 37 months, it was no surprise, merely an expectation. After all, she'd been Mortar Board at the University of Texas where her bachelor's degree in Harp Performance was followed by a masters in classical art history where she focused on modern myth genesis of the "great mother goddess," based on incorrect assumptions about the Minoan Snake-Goddess figurines. Then, intrigued by the artwork that accompanied texts prior to Gutenberg, she sought her Ph.D. at Far West Texas University where her dissertation was titled, "Psycho-sociologic Underpinnings of the Symbolism in Medieval Illuminated Manuscripts." It was at Far West that she met and married the basketball legend and pre-med major Wesley Callaway. During the early years of marriage, she taught art history at Far West, but when her first child, a daughter, was born with cystic fibrosis, she retired. A healthy son followed, and she saw early on that her unfulfilled dreams might be realized through Chase.

Her young son, at age five, complained one day that the artist in a young adult book entitled, *Great Men of Medicine*, had failed to draw the adjustment knob on Robert Koch's microscope. Ramona checked with Wes, and the child was right. She was hopeful, at first, that her prodigy might have an eye for art, for fine detail at least, but what followed began to vex her. Chase insisted that his mother write a letter to the artist, or publisher, or whoever might understand, to set the problem straight. And when she didn't carry out this wish, explaining that the books had already been printed and no one would notice anyway, Chase was troubled. And he remained so afterward, resurrecting the issue time and again, finally resulting in Ramona's surrender. She wrote the letter. From the publisher came a response promising to make the correction in future printings.

Then, with his first record player at age six came a quirky habit that Ramona did not understand at first. Chase would listen to the same 45rpm record 20 or 30 times every night. Finally, she discovered that he was trying to write down the lyrics. Some tunes, such as The Four Lads' "Istanbul (Not Constantinople)" spelled crushing defeat for the first-grader who wrote "His stand bull knot con stand tin noble," reminding Ramona that all genius requires tutelage.

One by one, for each record in his collection, Chase wrote down the lyrics, including his favorites—"How Much Is That Doggie In The Window" by Patti Page, "I Believe" by Frankie Laine, and the Mills Brothers new version of "Glow Worm." This odd practice took a new form when Ramona enrolled Chase in music lessons whereupon he sat for hours at the piano bench, punching keys, creating and capturing the words that the notes prompted.

About this same time, Wes and Ramona noticed that their son was staying up much of the night reading, unable to sleep. By age seven, he was devouring everything from *Sports Illustrated* to Greek mythology. Over and over, he read Charles Kingsley's 19th century fantasy, *The Water-Babies,* never revealing to anyone how he desperately wanted to live and travel underwater, where peace seemed to border on hibernation, a place where the coughing and gagging and crying of his sister Annie and her cystic fibrosis could not be heard. The Victorian illustrations reached out and pulled him into the pages as a water-baby trying to impress the girl Ellie, and he memorized every detail of each picture while communing with the fairies Mrs. Doasyouwouldbedoneby and Mrs. Bedonebyasyoudid.

Wesley's answer to the boy's insomnia was to prohibit reading after 9:00 p.m., but Chase would lie awake and stare at the bunk above, counting the springs overhead and creating designs from their drab interlocking pattern. Sleep would not come, so Ramona bought a spinning bedside lamp advertised to help children ease into slumber. The lamp had a celluloid cylindrical shade, a translucent drum covering a bare bulb. The top of the drum was a louvered metal disc that captured the heat of the bulb and prompted the cylinder to spin. Wildlife escaping a forest fire was the design embedded in the celluloid, so when the heat of the bulb set the scene in motion, the yellows, reds, and oranges would parade around Chase's bedroom walls in conflagration.

The eerie patterns that revolved in the darkness kept the young Chase up most the night as he studied the predictable sequences of blazing stripes that brushed across the wall and his hanging pictures of Paul Bunyan, John Henry, Pecos Bill, and Johnny Appleseed. And as the flames licked at these legends, Chase could feel the warmth of his future.

In the next experiment in slumber, Wes Callaway offered his son a red sleeping pill–a tiny gelatinous football, and in Chase's mind, a magical ruby. When he took the pill, he fell asleep within minutes. Although this trick by the father, using a placebo to usher sleep in the son, worked only a few times, with insomnia returning as a permanent plague, Chase took note that his father had shown care and concern. Chase realized that such thoughtfulness could be recreated at a moment's notice, through the simple proclamation of an ailment. Sore throats brought a yellow pill, ear aches a green one, and so forth. Relief, therefore, became color-coded.

Wes and Ramona disagreed often, and he could hear his name being tossed to and fro through the thin wall that separated his bedroom from theirs. Listening to muffled debate, Chase understood his mother to be on his side, his father against, no matter what the topic.

As early as kindergarten, Chase began asking his mother, "Why can't father be more like Hector's dad? Hector's dad laughs and stuff. And he doesn't criticize everything Hector does, and he doesn't talk to Hector or his mom like they're dumb heads or anything." Ramona was troubled by the subtle gap between father and son, but she could do nothing other than nurture the obvious talent in Chase. Meanwhile, her attention was mostly diverted toward Annie, with her severe form of cystic fibrosis.

Talent can be amorphous in its early days, and no one could put a finger on aptitude when Chase was still young. His piano skills were only average, but Chase's music teacher (and Sunday School teacher), Jewell Pollard, predicted a bright future for Chase when he sang his newly invented words while playing "Chopsticks." His story-in-verse was called, "The Only Lonely Panda in a Tree at Waikiki," and the entire plot was revealed through six repetitions of the tedious melody.

"Ramona, I'm afraid I don't know how to, uh, categorize what I heard from Chase this week at Sunday School."

"How so?" asked Chase's mother, while he stood in the same living room, apparently invisible to them both.

"It's not his piano playing, and it's certainly not his voice. It's the unusual lyrics he wrote for that tune. He was supposed to play 'This Little Light of Mine' for the class, but he snuck in this crazy song."

"You sound a bit worried, Jewell."

"Not at all. I've simply never heard a seven-year-old dream up such... well, let's just call them *imaginative* words. Frankly, everyone was spellbound, and I'm talking about the adults that were helping me with the class on Sunday. I must admit, some of us were almost wiping away tears when we heard about that panda, alone, all by himself in the palm tree. And when the panda finally discovers that he's a champion underwater swimmer, and when he saves the little girl, Nellie, from the giant clam, why—. I don't know where a boy goes with unusual skills like that. It's not like the world needs another poet."

Jewell Pollard didn't leave it alone after this one conversation. She organized a coterie of hard-praying women from the church with outstretched wings to serve as shelter for Chase, for they sensed "something" was on the way. Indeed, the women's circle prayed every week that the youngster's destiny be earmarked for God. This effort trickled down and anointed the head of the impressionable boy once he learned of the targeted prayers.

Jewell's husband, Jack Pollard, was musical director at the Church of the Driven Nail, and he joined in the confirmation that Chase's talent was "not in music per se," rather in the words that made songs sparkle.

The Pollards encouraged him to write more rhymes and limericks, and they scheduled him to perform for clubs and social groups in Matherville, with Jewell playing piano to Chase's musical poetry. Gradually, Chase's original stage fright disappeared. Over the years, as Chase continued tinkering with lyrics and song, he would credit the Pollards with every success.

Ramona and Wes Callaway, bewildered parents, were at a loss to explain the talent of their son. Neither had a penchant for word play. What they saw was not necessarily natural talent at all, but unnatural persistence. After Chase had locked onto a song or a thought or a dream, he never let go until completely drained. After prompting her son toward stellar achievement in the early years, Ramona reversed her tactics as her worry mounted, wondering if it might not be best for Chase to *relax*.

And this is where Sukie Spurlock came in as the family's horticulturist, among her many roles. Ramona thought a garden might serve as the ultimate source of equanimity, helping to put brakes on Chase's overactive mind.

Sukie Spurlock was Chase's auxiliary mom. Three-fourths Black and one-fourth Comanche, Sukie was coated in beautiful caramel skin, and her head was topped with a shock of wondrous hair with a color that Chase's parents always referred to as "prematurely gray." That term fell short, in Chase's mind. Indeed, it was more accurate to recognize that Sukie's hair was pure silver.

Officially, she was the maid and cook for the Callaways, and the nanny to Chase and his older sister Annie. Yet to anyone familiar with the blurred social boundaries created by noble women in service, then it should be noted that Sukie opened her Christmas presents with the family–grandfather Zeb, Wes, Ramona, Annie, and Chase. Indeed, Chase's sister Annie cried for days when she fully understood that Sukie was not a blood relative.

Sukie taught Chase to love all creatures made by God, lesson one being her swat to the seat of his pants when she caught him at age six pulling the legs off June bugs. *All creatures* made by God were included in the ban on torture. "Lorda mercy, Chase, don't *ever* let me catch you harmin' those little ol' bugs again."

The love of God's creatures came easier with fur. Chase loved his pets. With permission from Dr. and Mrs. Callaway, Sukie had taken Chase to the Matherville Pound to pick out his first dog, but they returned instead with three kittens and two mutts. Chase ignored the brouhaha from his father who finally caved to the notion of five animals made possible by Sukie's subtle influence: *"Doctor, why you know best, of course, but if you coulda seen the look on that little boy's face, why I'll swanny. He said you'd never allow it, of course, but I... I told him you knew how much love was in his little heart and how it seems sometimes he just has no place to put it all. And, oh, how mostly he wanted to see the smile on his sister's face when he brought those little friends home."*

Despite the unexpected victory, Chase was preoccupied for weeks by the haunting memory of the sad-eyed dogs and the frightened cats that he'd left behind at the pound.

Chase didn't need an alarm clock. His bedroom was positioned directly above the kitchen, and the dawn of each day was announced by "Amazing Grace," sung by Sukie in a faltering soprano that penetrated the floor, all the way to Chase's slumbering ears.

One day, Chase awoke to screams–screams that he would remember for the rest of his life. As he came to learn, Sukie's husband, at age 39, had dropped dead that morning of a heart attack while working at a construction site. Dr. Callaway had broken the news to Sukie in the kitchen, which then turned into a wailing hell directly beneath Chase's feet.

After Sukie's two children, a son and a daughter, grew up and out, she continued to live in her own home, with her days (except Sunday) at the Callaways, nearly a full-time part of the family. "Amazing Grace" continued to announce every new morning for Chase, although the first few notes always startled him as a potential shriek of agony.

Sukie loved to grow vegetables, and this is where she did most of her parenting, as she and Chase tilled the soil together, each year adding another section to the garden for a new and exciting vegetable. Annie participated when she could, but her cystic fibrosis held her prisoner most days behind her bedroom window overlooking the garden.

Indeed, it was while hoeing beets that Chase first learned of original sin. A week earlier, Chase had achieved neighborhood fame by throwing a dirt clod toward a sparrow in flight, hitting the bird square, against all odds, and sending it to the ground in a death spiral. Chase became a wunderkind to the other kids on the block, and he reveled in the glory. Yet, when Sukie learned of the miraculous feat (Chase's best friend Hector ratted him out), on a day when Sukie and Chase were quietly hoeing beets, Sukie went far beyond punishment with this simple story:

"I was just a little girl, not more than seven or eight, about your age, don't you know. And I was out hoeing, like we're doing today, all by myself, accountable to no one, nobody. And I never–never in my life up to that point–*never* served as witness to a mean thing done by anybody no matter what their color. My mama was a saint, and so was her mama. And the three of us lived together growing up. Once, as I was digging the weeds away, from cabbage as I recall, all of a sudden, this frog jumps into my furrow and sits there a-looking at me, his ol' neck a-puffing in and out. And you know what I did? Do you know what came over me? Why, some sort of devil deep inside of me comes a-bubbling up and... and I took my hoe and I chopped that poor little frog plum in half (Sukie's voice cracked at this point). And I didn't stop there, honey. No, I didn't. I chopped and chopped until everything in that spot was nothing but red and green. It was a bloody, awful thing."

Her eyes glistened, and she lowered her head in shame before continuing her dramatic recitation, full of expression and voice inflection, enough to hold spellbound any but the hardest of hearts.

"And I knew the second I'd finished him off, that I'd done an evil, evil thing. I dropped that hoe, that awful instrument of death, and I ran into the house a-cryin' to my mama and my grandmamma. I can still see the disappointment on their faces. And I cried 'til I couldn't cry no more. I didn't know what in the world had come over me. I had no reason to be afraid of that little frog. I had no reason to wish him poorly now. Just a harmless little frog. And that little frog probably had a family, don't you know. And they were probably a-wondering what mighta happened. And I couldn't ever rid myself of that thought. You see, Chase, that's what people are like. They got a mean seed deep inside. *All* of us do. And that's why we all need the Lord to lift us up from that ugliness. Lots of folks cover it up with all sorts of good deeds and whatnot, but the seed is still there. Ain't no way to be rid of it without the Lord and his forgiveness."

Sukie always ended her stories with a simple saying. In this case, it was: "Be nicer than you have to be, even when no one's looking."

Perhaps such instruction had more impact on Chase than did his own grandfather, Brother Zebulon, pastor of the Church of the Driven Nail. Chase loved his grandfather without reservation. Oddly enough, Wes Callaway referred to his own father as "a semi-nut case on occasion," a moniker to which Wes added some strange comments upon discovering that certain members of the Driven Nail had started "speaking in tongues," a term that meant nothing to Chase.

Whereas Wes was always at the hospital or the clinic or making house calls, Grandpa Zeb was always ready to play. And play they did, mostly basketball. Even though it was Wes who'd been the star, Chase rarely saw his father shoot a basket. It was Grandpa Zeb who installed the goal so Chase could practice and practice, hopefully perfecting the shot that made his father–"Fadeaway Callaway"–famous as the captain of the team that took Far West Texas University to its only small college national championship.

After the goal was set up by Grandpa Zeb, Chase practiced for hours on end, or until his father shouted at him from the second-story bedroom window, "Chase, for crying out loud. It's almost midnight. Stop that racket and come to bed."

Grandpa Zeb took Chase with him on his evangelistic outreach missions, too, where the grandson played a "catalyst" role at tent revivals. The way Grandpa Zeb explained it to him went like this:

"Most people don't want to be the first to come forward, Chase. I can preach the finest I've ever preached, and I can inspire most everyone to get one foot in the aisle, but then, on occasion, nothing happens. Yet, if one person, just one, sees another body move forward, even if it's a little boy like you, why there's a veritable deluge. So your job is to listen for the cue. If people are moving to the front on their own, then you hold back. All's well. But if they're frozen, then my signal to you will be the words 'driven nail'. If you hear me say 'driven nail' three times in a row, then you walk on down the aisle like you've never seen me before in your life. Of course, we would only do that once in any one location, and I'll only use it if I have to. It's for the greater good, son."

Chase obliged. It never occurred to him to do anything else. At age seven, stories of chopped frogs made more sense than his grandfather's sermons. On these summer excursions, Chase would be washed in the blood enough times to leave his skin raw. And, in moments of circular thinking, knowing a good cleansing was around the corner, he'd wonder about the dark inner seed in himself, the one that kills frogs and sparrows and pulls the legs from June bugs. Conveniently, he didn't have to feel guilty for very long about anything. After all, he'd be washed in the blood all over again very shortly, a wash and dry cycle that worked remarkably well.

Chase believed that God spoke to him once, almost audibly, without help from the Church of the Driven Nail. In the second grade, while walking to school down a shaded alley, an inner voice told him to stop in his tracks. At that moment, the sun came out from behind a cloud, allowing a bar of light to pierce the tree limbs above, brightening the very spot where he stood. A rush of excitement filled him, not so much with joy, but with expectation, a destiny. It was his first taste of euphoria. When he followed the bar of light up through the interlocking fingers of the trees and toward the sky, he felt the source of the message was coming from well beyond the sun. The date in the alley–April 4th– became stamped in his memory, a seed of prophecy, and this day would be the day, perhaps in one year, perhaps fifty, when the rest of the message, the full revelation, would be delivered in a twinkling. It would be the day when he would finally understand the reason for God's teasing whisper.

Thus, by age seven, he was the man he was to be.

8

Over the course of the next 15 years, these are the words Chase Callaway heard and remembered long enough to become a matter of record in his own psychoanalysis.

First, from girlfriend Livvy...

"No one will blame you for taking that shot. You were wide open... Of course you can face everyone... No, you're not a ball hog, Chase, why do you keep saying that?... Is your mother upset about you turning down those academic scholarships? I mean no one from Matherville has ever had that many. Duke, Rice, Vanderbilt... Sure, a basketball scholarship to Far West is nice, but... You didn't say anything about my being elected pep club president today. Yes, I know you have a lot on your mind."

From sister Annie...

"I'm sorry my room smells so awful, Chase. You hardly come in here anymore... Remember when you were little, and you snuck in here and kissed me when you thought I was asleep, and how you told mother you were trying to catch CF, so that you could go to Heaven to be with me. Hey little brother, no dice. You didn't take harp lessons like mother had me do, so you don't have a ticket. Angel prep school, that's what I call it around here... Why is it, Chase, that we don't talk like we used to? Is it 'cause you know I'm getting close to the end? It's going to be over soon, you know. And I'm okay with it."

From mother Ramona…

"After you lost at the state finals, I thought you'd re-think those academic scholarships rather than playing basketball… Yes, I realize you grew up dreaming about attending Far West. I'm not going to argue with you… Oh God, I don't know how to comfort Sukie through yet another tragedy… No, your father's never seen it happen. First goes her daughter at twenty-seven. And now her son, only thirty-one. That's the amazing thing. For a sister *and a brother* to get breast cancer and both die from it. Sukie's all alone now… You know she's going back to nursing school what with our Annie gone, God rest her soul, and you on your way to college… No, she's not really that old, a little over fifty, maybe. That white hair makes her look older… Your grandfather has really been the one encouraging her. He says that after she gets her LPN, he's arranged her to have a job at the mental hospital… Yes, it will be hard for me without Sukie. She's become like a sister to me, plus both of us losing children and all."

From father Wes…

"Your mother will never be able to forget that you didn't go to Annie's funeral. I don't care *how* sick you were. There are no excuses for that. *None!* Not unless you're dying, too."

From Dr. Raphael Delgado, father of Chase's childhood friend Hector…

"No, I've never regretted becoming a psychiatrist, but I wouldn't base my career decision off a movie, if I were you. The actual practice of psychiatry is nothing like they made it for Gregory Peck… Oh, Hector is doing fine, I guess, as well as can be expected. Seems like so many kids these days are dropping out to find themselves, so they say. He fell into the wrong crowd last year after he switched his major to philosophy and met some real kooks. I sure wish you and he could have stuck together like when you were kids. Seems like just a blink of the eye when you boys were running around the neighborhood wearing your coonskin caps and Superman capes... Anyway, one thing for sure, you'll get top notch training if you stay right here in Matherville. It's the best department at Far West med school... You need to forget about that basket you missed at the state tourney. In five or ten years, no one will remember... Your dad's jersey is the only one in a glass case at the Far West field house. You can't hold yourself to that standard. You have your own life to live."

From father Wes...

"I never could understand why you took that shot in the finals at state last year. Coach told you to pass off to Smitty. Why would you try that shot yourself?... So what if you were wide open? Smitty's the shot-maker... No, this *isn't* the tenth time I've brought it up... The reason I don't read medical journals when I get home is for diversion. I've been practicing medicine all day, and I'd rather read *Sports Illustrated* or *Field and Stream*... Advice about getting married? Well, to be honest, you've never asked for advice before. Why now?... Okay, here's my advice. You know we think of Livvy as our daughter, and frankly, she deserves better (crooked smile), but, well, remember there's going to be times when you think you made a mistake, and you might even think you can't stand the sight of her. Ignore that because it goes away. Too, don't forget she'll have moments she thinks the same awful things about you, so remember there are two in a marriage. Also, make sure you've got a liner beneath your sheets, to protect the mattress, of course, from the menstrual flow. Women don't always know when it's going to start... Yes, I've heard of menstrual huts in New Guinea. Why is it that you always have to be such a wiseacre?"

And perhaps it is important to point out what Chase's father *didn't* say during these fifteen years–and that would be: "I love you, son."

From his histology professor in college...

"I've never seen a student come through here who's made a hundred on every test. More importantly, your drawings are *par excellence*. The study of tissues under the microscope is a challenge for us teachers. The only way we know what your mind's eye really sees is what you draw. And it's not artistic talent that does it, but it's seeing what others don't, recorded in your sketches. You are appreciating fine details and relationships under the scope. I want to encourage you to consider a career in histology, as an academic microscopist. Of course, if you absolutely must sell out and go to medical school, then you should strongly consider pathology, our counterparts in the world of the abnormal."

From Livvy...

"You've sat on that bench for three seasons, Chase. This isn't high school anymore. College ball has changed, dramatically. To be honest, I'm not sure that your dad would even start now. There are eleven Black players and you, the token. And you're only there because of your father's name... Don't get upset. Yes, I realize the team could be headed for its first national championship in years... Okay, go ahead and stick with it this last year, to be part of something big, as you say... Now, we need to settle some things about the wedding plans."

From Jack Pollard, music director of the Church of the Driven Nail...

"One of my good friends in California is putting together a new concept, Chase, a Christian folk group. Not gospel, where they're singing only to believers. Instead, music for everyone. Like The Weavers, or for your generation, Peter, Paul, and Mary. Or the Mamas and the Papas. But with Christian lyrics. Naturally, you came to mind. My friend is with a non-denominational group called the Varsity Voyagers, a college outreach mission, and they're planning on a rigorous performance schedule. Gonna cut some records, too. Could be quite an opportunity. They're not only looking for a lyricist, but they also want a front man, an emcee, someone who introduces the group and delivers the message. Chase, I think you're their man... Yes, I understand that you and Livvy are getting married soon... Yes, I know you've already interviewed for medical school... No, you won't make much money at all, but then again, remember the importance of storing treasures in Heaven... Yes, I suspect Annie would have wanted you to consider a spiritual path... Great. I'll tell my friend you might be interested."

From Livvy...

"Varsity Voyagers? Chase, don't the staff members have to round up their own financing? Won't you have to ask people to support you?... Yes, I know it's always been your secret dream to write songs... You know I love you, and I'll follow you anywhere. Yet, you have so many talents that seem to be leading you to medical school. And to be offered a position right there on the spot *during your interview*... Okay, I admit it. I was wrong about Varsity Voyagers. Who would have guessed it? One of the first songs you write for the Voyagers is a hit. Unbelievable, really, that "One's a-Changing–the World's Re-arranging" made it onto the pop charts... It's wonderful, Chase, that you feel such peace. I know you've been bothered by all that tent revival stuff you did for your grandfather... I admit it, maybe this could be your life's work... but you're gone so much of the time... I can't believe Varsity Voyagers doesn't count the record royalties for your support money. You don't have time to keep going out and raising support like other staff members if you're on the road all the time. You guys are raking it in... I've got to agree with your father on this one, Chase. Can you imagine being gray-haired and still going around asking your friends for money? I'll support whatever decision you make... I'm sure you wouldn't have any trouble getting re-accepted to medical school two years since your first offer... You should be relieved now that you've made your decision. No more fretting, please. Med school is the right choice."

.   .   .

So, Livvy became the primary breadwinner, working as a high school gym teacher and softball coach. Chase, trying to help the best he could with their shaky finances, went to work as an orderly at the Matherville State Mental Hospital at the same time he entered medical school.

Out of 150 green freshmen, he was surprised to discover that one of his new classmates was his childhood chum, Hector Delgado. In the orientation session, Chase thought he had spotted Hector, but the shoulder-length hair and full beard made it tough to tell. Later, in the hallway outside the main auditorium, Chase lay in wait.

"Hector? Is that you?"

"Chase, old buddy." Hector's pensive face, lost in deep thought, brightened as he recognized his old friend, and he surprised Chase with a hug.

"The last time I talked to your dad," said Chase, "he believed you might be gone for a long, long time. And by gone, I mean *really* gone."

"Well, I was gone, man. Went to Madison, you know, for the anti-war effort. Majored in philosophy until I figured out that it does more harm than good. Turned on, tuned in, and dropped out for a coupla years, but yeah... I'm back. And feeling much more in the groove. We should grab a cup of coffee some time and get caught up. I hear you dropped out for a couple of years, too. Some sort of religious singing group? You didn't join a cult, did you?"

Chase shrank a bit as he sensed a mocking tone. "Well, we actually had a crossover hit, made it onto the charts. Still not sure I made the right decision to give it up." Chase was trying to read Hector's reaction, but with the full beard, it was tough. What did stand out, however, was the fact that Hector had developed nervous twitches in his face, a tic with his right eye blinking every few seconds while the corner of his mouth jerked upward in response. *Too many drugs,* guessed Chase.

"Listen, I gotta get going, Chase. We really need to sit down together. And I mean soon. You know. Cup of coffee. Deal?"

"Sure. Get caught up. Absolutely." He started to offer a time to meet, but when he saw a hippie girl sidle up to Hector, Chase backed off. Headband, long straight hair, wispy blouse, cool and cute. She looked Chase over, up and down, then said to Hector, "Gee, Hec, you didn't tell me all your friends were so straight here in Texas."

"I'm pure establishment," said Chase, trying to turn a joke.

Chase waited for an introduction, but Hector turned away, calling over his shoulder, "Don't forget, Chase. Coffee."

Chase felt the urge to lock down the time for coffee, knowing how such promises can lie idle. The girl's arrival had brought an end to the conversation, however. Chase admitted to himself that Hector's bizarre trip into the counterculture was unsettling, forming a wedge of sorts, real or imagined. Still, he and Hector had been inseparable as kids, so a few minutes over coffee could be an opportunity to share a message of faith. How easy it had been to deliver this message to a group of eager faces in a crowd of strangers while serving as emcee for the New Bloods in concert. But my, how hard it was to talk to a friend.

After the first academic test was administered to the med students, including a practical with the microscope, the results for freshman histology were posted by name. There was only one perfect score–Chase Callaway.

Classmates were stunned. Chase was already a known entity by most students, not for academics, but as the only white basketball player at Far West and a bona fide BMOC who then, remarkably, went on to chart a record as a Christian lyricist. His perfect grade was even more irritating in that Chase didn't talk smart, he didn't act smart, and he didn't one-up other students with medical trivia in the snack room. Some had seen his face on the back cover of the New Bloods album, set apart in a small corner, away from the group itself, but clearly a contributor to a hit record wherein he didn't sing a note. How *dare* he be smart as well?

Chase was as surprised as anyone at his top score. Not surprised that he'd answered every question correctly, but surprised that twenty other top students were not up there with him. In fact, he was embarrassed. Yet, at the same time, he felt a powerful rush within. A rush of unused, untested talent. A rush of purpose. His father, after all, had struggled to make it into the top half of his med school class years ago. Now, here was Chase, sitting in the Number One slot. The rush was transforming, and perhaps divine.

By the time of the second test, an innovation crept its way into the school of medicine – computers – and the grades were printed by dot matrix, correlated to social security numbers rather than names, helping to secure anonymity. When a lonely nine-digit identifier stood alone at the top, the entire class had Chase's number.

That evening, his phone rang.

"Chase, this is Larry Fremont, you know, in your class this year. I was president of the Christian Student Union as an undergrad, so I know–we all know–of your work with the New Bloods."

"Sure, Larry, I know who you are. It's hard to get around and talk with everyone in our class when there's so many."

"Chase, I'm sure you'll agree that medical school is going to strip us, or at least try to strip us, of our spiritual connections, so I started a Bible study, and we're planning to meet once a week. I'd like to invite you to join. It won't be easy finding time…"

The idea rattled around Chase's mind as he tuned out Larry's voice. "Let me think about it, Larry, and I'll let you know. I don't have a sense yet as to how much time this medical school business is going to take." Chase knew exactly how much time medical school was going to take, for he had been transformed by his class-topping test scores. Chase never called back, and never raised the subject again with Larry.

Alone at the top. Originally, he had planned to study only hard enough to graduate in the top third of his class, but his own scores had prompted him to rearrange his priorities, literally overnight. He had once seen how a malpractice case had nearly destroyed his stone-cold father, and Chase had no intention of ever having to deal with something like that. He would learn it all. He would master it all. He would not make mistakes.

The time commitment was not his only concern when it came to a Bible study, however. Deep inside, he knew that vocal Christians were outcasts, of sorts, especially in medical school, and he was enjoying new and diverse friendships that had escaped him during high school and college days. Two of his new friends were Jewish, of all things, here in the middle of Nowhere Town filled with Germans. And the thought of the attractive hippie girl, so smug while mocking his "straightness," bothered him.

Certainly, opting out of the Bible study was a minor transgression, entirely forgivable, easily washed clean, another walk down the aisle of repentance. However, a single Bible verse in the book of Mark began to haunt him – "*But he that shall blaspheme against the Holy Ghost hath never forgiveness, but is in danger of eternal damnation.*"

What did it mean, exactly, to blaspheme against the Holy Ghost? Although he had long ago forgotten about this verse, it flashed into his mind the very moment he decided to opt out of the Bible study. In the same flash, he recalled that his grandfather Zebulon had told him the verse meant "the denial of Christ after one has already accepted Him." Had Chase denied Christ by saying "no" to a simple Bible study? *Of course not!* Peter had denied Christ three times, for gosh sakes, so his grandfather's stance on this topic was clearly erroneous.

The day after the Denial, Chase awoke energized. He'd experienced the same feeling every morning for the past few weeks, ever since his top score on that first test. It was the feeling that his life was charmed. At breakfast, he announced to his wife, "I think we need a pet, Livvy. A dog. Or maybe a dog and a cat. Raise them together. I had so much fun as a kid doing that." Startled at first, Livvy agreed after a short discussion. "I'd rather get them from the pound, Chase, like you did when you were a boy." He agreed. "Let's go this weekend."

As he drove to class that morning in his metallic blue Chevy Malibu, he couldn't shake the thought of having a dog to chase around their tiny house, or romping through the park nearby.

In a split second, from nowhere, a large Labrador ran into the street and stopped directly in front of Chase's blue tank. He could see the dog's soulful eyes looking at the driver, stunned that it had miscalculated the car's speed. The thud was definitive. Chase knew the dog would die.

Jumping from his car, hoping to save a life, Chase couldn't even comfort the Lab as it returned a vicious, snarling bite when he tried to stroke its head. "Oh, God, I'm sorry. I'm so sorry." It bared its teeth as blood poured from its mouth along with an unearthly hissing sound. When it breathed its last, Chase felt that his own wind had been sucked from him. He was devastated. He dragged the dog to the side of the road, leaving a red stripe on the pavement, betraying the slaughter. The dog had a crumbling leather collar around its neck, so it had once belonged to someone, but no tags, no identification. He looked around for help, but no one saw him alone on the access road to the highway.

Frantic, but helpless, there was nothing he could accomplish by sticking around. He would be late to class, so he drove on, miserable that he had left the dog in the weeds by the road, and he could think of nothing else the rest of the day. He intended to call the highway department or animal control or someone, between classes, but he was interrupted at each break by someone wanting something. On the trip home that afternoon, he drove to the spot where the accident had occurred. The carcass was gone. He couldn't face Livvy. For some reason, he had connected their conversation about adopting a dog that morning to the canicide moments later. Why did he feel guilty? It was an accident.

Before traveling the final few blocks home, he called Livvy from a pay phone near the scene of the missing carcass to explain what had happened. Crazy as it might seem, he simply didn't want to tell her face to face that he'd killed a dog. He wanted her to know, but he didn't want to see her disappointment as he confessed. He wanted the sadness in her eyes to be over and done with it before he saw her. Understandably, Livvy sounded distant on the phone as he told her the story.

When he walked into the house a short while later, Livvy was red-eyed and teary. He knew how she much she loved animals, so he wasn't terribly surprised.

"Hector Delgado's mother called your mother," she managed, "then Ramona called here."

"Oh, yeah, quite a coincidence. Hector's in my class. Philosophy was a dead end, I guess, so he's into medicine now. I told him we'd get some coffee and get caught up. I thought it might be an opportunity for me to share—"

"Hector hanged himself," Livvy said. "He's dead."

Chase staggered to his study where he sat motionless for hours, leaving his wife outside. He retraced his steps over and over. Only this morning, he had been dwelling on his golden touch, with good fortune at every turn. A charmed life, indeed. Oh my, how he'd suppressed sister Annie's death to the deepest and darkest chambers of his mind. He didn't even attend her funeral, sick in his head more than his body. And what about the death of Sukie's husband? Then her children? He had been sad, of course, at all these things, but somehow, his gut had repelled any wrenching pain. Agonizing grief had failed to penetrate. Until now–until this cascade of anguish poured over him in a matter of hours, yet with a sense of permanence as if to say that tragedies were the new norm. *If you are going to ignore the tragedies in your life,* an inner voice told him, *then God will ramp things up until He gets your full attention. Carpe diem? Really? What if each day is filled with horror, as it must have been for Hector? Are we to seize the horror?*

9

The shadow cast by her perpetual motion grew large, then small, then large, then small, forever bobbing and dipping. The wax and wane of her silhouette fanned across a beige plaster wall, a forsaken canvass, branded with faint interlacing cracks. Framed pictures were banished from the ward as potential weapons, so the artlessness was open to interpretation. It was nighttime in the Day Room at Building 19 of the Quadrangle, and Ivy Pettibone was walking in circles as she had done day and night, for years.

Scant furnishings adorned the Day Room–an upright piano in one corner and a couch against a wall. Snuggled up to the couch was a floor lamp with one bare bulb covered by a wire cage. This lonely light served as the projector bulb transmitting Ivy's shadow on the walls as she navigated her loop.

A narrow wooden bench stretched for eight feet along the wall opposite the couch and could hold six inmates at a time, even though no six could ever tolerate such proximity. Two made a crowd. Most of the inmates spent their days in the Main Hall of 19, and few cared about trespassing in the Day Room where Ivy held her circular court.

Chase stood half-bent in the nurse's station where he rested his elbows on the ledge of a Dutch door, the lower half locked, the top half open but ready to swing shut to block madness as needed. The other two aides were herding the inmates from the Main Hall into the sleeping areas—40 men in one barrack, 40 women in another—in preparation for lights out. Nurse Sukie Spurlock, Chase's former nanny, was logging charts at her desk.

"Am I seeing things, or is there a rut in the linoleum where she walks?" Chase asked, straining his eyes in the dusky light.

"Shouldn't come as a surprise," Sukie said. "She's been making that trip for nearly thirty years now, as I understand it."

"Unbelievable. And it's like she never stops talking, whatever it is she's saying."

"No one has any idea what that girl's talking about."

Chase added, "And it looks like no one except Bertie comes near that circle."

Sukie looked up and smiled. "That Bertie, she's a devil. Mean as a snake. But Ivy, she can take care of her own."

Bertie was pacing in the Day Room, hugging the far wall from Ivy's circle, while keeping a close watch on her longstanding adversary. In return, Ivy's eyes were fixed on Bertie. Jabbering non-stop, Ivy smiled between her nonsense words.

Standing over six feet tall, with stringy dark hair, Bertie's shoulders were huge and rounded, giving her power and fierceness that predicted victory in any combat. The giantess was three or four times the size of the diminutive creature who limped in circles. Bertie tugged at the neck of her cotton print dress where the collar seemed to dig into her skin. She grumbled her curses while snarling at Ivy.

Ivy kept unbroken vigil on Bertie during each circle, straining her neck as far as possible in one direction, then a quick flip around to the other side as the roundabout continued.

"Do they ever tangle?" asked Chase.

Sukie sighed. "Not often, that is, if everyone's on their meds. Bertie always starts the fracas. She's learned to dodge Ivy's crazy spittin' most the time, you see. And even if Ivy's spittle hits her, she'll charge Ivy sometimes anyway, blinded for the moment, just for the heck of it. Don't let Ivy's size fool you. She's a pistol. And she can sense when Bertie's on edge. Of course, everyone's been on edge since the meds were stopped."

"How much longer is everyone going to be drying out?"

"At least three more months," Sukie said as she left her desk and joined Chase at the half-door where she hollered: "Bertie! Ivy! You two be gettin' on to bed now. It's almost curfew."

"Three months off all meds... wow," he said.

"Takes that long, they say, to get every little bit of chemical and whatnot out of your system, so they can tell if the new drugs work better. We're liable to see some mighty tense times around here. The way these folks are usually doped up, you don't see mental illness like they did in the old days."

Chase couldn't wait. Raw schizophrenia. Raw manic-depressives. Raw organic brain syndromes. Raw psychosis. Raw everything. It was exhilarating. Leaving Sukie at the half door, he returned to the aide's desk and pulled Bertie's metal chart from the rolling rack. He began writing his observational notes in green ink, the color for the evening shift. Every little sentence, he thought, was adding critical information to the research of Dr. Wendall Latimer, Chief of Psychiatry and Director of Matherville State. Who knew but what Chase's key observations could serve a pivotal role in the research? With careful penmanship, he wrote:

Bertie seems more agitated this evening than last, which was more than the night before. She refused her insulin that Nurse Spurlock tried to give her until told she wouldn't get to go to the cafeteria for dinner. So, she sat with her arms folded on the bench in the Day Room for two hours without moving, pouting, then when everyone lined up for the cafeteria, she told Nurse Spurlock she was finally ready for her insulin. Tonight, Bertie seems increasingly irritated, pacing in the Day Room.

    C. Callaway, P.A. I

Chase wanted to elaborate, but he was told that Level One Aides were to keep their comments brief. He was also told (by the other aides) that no one ever read anything written by aides, but he refused to believe that. After all, Captain Newman, M.D. had to be a veritable Sherlock Holmes of the uncharted mind, seeking out clues from everything and everyone. Every notation made in a patient's chart was a clue.

"Sukie, do you think the doctor ever reads these notes we aides make?"

"I'd say so, dear— oops. Can't call you 'dear' anymore." Sukie smiled over her shoulder. Chase knew they both were struggling with roles sharply altered from their days in the vegetable garden. "Chase, you must know I have quite a time trying to remember that you're on your way to becoming a doctor. You know how mothers are with their children, and you'll always be one of my babies. Now shush my lips. I'm not gonna talk that way anymore."

Sukie's smooth skin was still flawless, her silver hair unchanged. One word described Sukie–calm. Chase had never known a soul so much at peace.

To ease the awkward new roles, with Sukie as his supervisor, Chase reached for basic conversation. "Sukie, how long has it been since you left our house to work here?"

"Six years, I believe... that's right, six years. After you left for college, there wasn't that much to do for your folks anymore. Your mother tried to keep me on, even asking me to move in with her at your house to spare the expense of mine. But I had a life outside your household. Church friends and all. Too, I had lots of bills left over from both my children, may they rest in peace. I'd always wanted to be a nurse, to get my LPN and all. Still, no matter where I rest my head at night, your family is my family."

Chase slid Bertie's chart back into the rack and took out Ivy Pettibone's record, opening the metal lid with his left hand, staring at his ring finger and the shiny band of gold that still looked out of place there.

"I never did properly thank you, Sukie, for getting me assigned here to Building Nineteen. It looks like all the action is going to be here for the next few years. I probably won't get much time clocked in after the third year of med school begins, with the clinical rotations and all. For now, it's great study time 'cause there's not much to do on the evening shift. Still, I get to work with all the patients before they go to bed."

"Well, I didn't do much in the way of getting you assigned here. I said something to Dixie Barnes, like you asked, but your dad knows Dr. Latimer, and your grandpa Zeb had some strings he pulled as well. But about your schedule, Chase, you don't need to be working all the time. Your folks will help out with you and Livvy for a while. She looked so pretty at the wedding, by the way. I'd never seen her without the ponytail. And I did consider it right honorable to be sitting there as part of your family."

"Glad you made it," he said. "Yes, I plan to work three nights a week max, and some on weekends. Livvy is trying to get her schedule to fit mine. That way, we'll be off together. I don't want to ask the folks for money anymore. It's time to grow up."

Sukie smiled, and for a moment, they were in the garden, together again, tilling the soil and adding a new vegetable to the repertoire every spring. He didn't miss living at home, but how he missed "Amazing Grace" in the mornings.

Sukie loved to give advice. "A good marriage is one where you *both* give and give and give until you can't give no more, *without* expecting anything in return. My Glenn was as good as they come, and we had— " Sukie's eyes widened. "Now, Bertie, you leave Miss Ivy alone."

Chase scooted from behind the desk and joined Sukie at the door. Bertie was teasing Ivy by placing her toe inside the circle of worn linoleum, as if she were testing the water of a swimming pool, then pulling her toe back out again as Ivy approached with her next lap.

"Berrr-tie, you come over here and talk to me now, girl," said Sukie.

Like an enormous bunny, Bertie hopped with both feet into Ivy's circle for a showdown. After that, things were a blur–Ivy spitting at the behemoth to no avail, then Ivy diving to the floor where she bit Bertie's ankle–Bertie's arms swinging wildly, hoping to find a target on Ivy–Bertie hopping on one leg holding her injured ankle–Ivy jumping onto Bertie's back whereupon Bertie began spinning like a pro wrestler before tossing Ivy to the ground. By then, Sukie was at the scene trying to separate them, well before Chase realized that he should have been helping. He joined Sukie at the melee, embarrassed that his response had been so slow.

Ivy jumped up and began slapping at Bertie's head with her flippers, shouting her gibberish, while Bertie answered with a constant stream of profanity, her hands covering her face. Sukie calmly reminded them both about the seclusion rooms if they refused to separate. The word "seclusion" seemed to freeze the fighting inmates.

Bertie stood up, her head bowed in deference, then she reached out with an open palm to shake hands and make up with Ivy. When Ivy smiled and lifted her arm to return the gesture, Chase found the moment charming. Then Bertie closed her fingers into a fist and cold-cocked Ivy with a right hook that sent the little woman flailing into the couch against the wall.

Chase gulped as he realized he was about to wrestle this 300-pound woman into restraints, but Bertie took off in a dead run. She headed for the row of seclusion rooms that formed a long hallway between the men's and women's wings of Building 19. There, at one of the rooms, she leaned against the steel door and waited politely for Chase to find the right key to unlock the isolation cell. Then, she walked proudly into her punishment, plopped onto the mattress, and sat with her legs crossed, her back against the stark wall, giggling to herself.

Back in the Day Room, Chase found Sukie tending to Ivy's bleeding lip. He was surprised to see tears in the eyes of the tiny woman who had been so vicious in her fighting moments before. When Ivy saw Chase, she smiled and began talking incoherently. Grinning with confidence between phrases, maintaining eye contact as she spoke every nonsense word, Ivy seemed to have all the answers while remaining oblivious to the fact that no one understood her.

"It's only a little cut, Ivy," Sukie said, "and I'm gonna hold some pressure here for a moment more, then you'll be all right. Yes, you will."

"Mesola redoti," she said to conclude her message, speaking directly to Chase. He nodded as if he understood.

Chase headed back to the nurse's station where he recorded the events in Ivy's chart first, carefully recounting the moments before the fight. When Sukie returned to the station, Chase said, "Wow. Things go from quiet to crazy here in a matter of seconds."

"Don't ever forget–here, things are *always* crazy."

Moments later, he asked, "Do you know anything about Ivy's weird speech. Hasn't anyone figured out what she's saying after all these years?"

"Sure, lots have tried. They had a speech pathologist studying her, I recall, as recent as last year. Not to teach her to say normal words. Ivy's way too old for that. Still, the researchers love to study the chronic patients, tryin' out this theory and that."

"I just finished reading *I Never Promised You a Rose Garden*," said Chase, "and they really broke down the language that girl used, but I was surprised that it didn't help her at all. In fact, the girl knew exactly what the substitute shrink was trying to do by analyzing her word origins, and the patient said something in her own head about, 'you don't do brain surgery with a pickaxe'. So maybe figuring out the language isn't all that important."

"I suspect the way people talk in this place might be a way to build walls around themselves. I've seen a lot of craziness these past six years, but much of the time, you'll see that these folks aren't always that much different from you and me. They laugh. They cry. They feel. It's more like they never had the right plaster to build a proper shell that a person needs to protect herself from the world."

After lights went out in the sleeping areas, Chase opened his *Gray's Anatomy*. He could get two more hours of good study in before shift change, then off to bedtime with Livvy. Then he closed the text as quickly as he had opened it, drawn to learn more about little Ivy who had saved him from humiliation a few months ago at the Lunatic Ball.

Chase pulled out the file drawer marked with the letter P. With 40 women and 40 men on the experimental ward, all of them chronics, it took seven file cabinets to hold their old records. Chase found *Pettibone, Ivy*, and lifted the three-inch-thick manila folder from the file, although noticing that Ivy had four additional folders, even thicker than the one he held.

"That's only the most recent ones, Chase. When the current metal chart gets full, it gets emptied into that file cabinet, as you know. Just read the summaries when a new resident rotates on the service. It'll be easier to put the story together. Those records only go back five or ten years, however. When someone's been here as long as Ivy, why she's liable to have boxes full of those things in Medical Records at the Administration Building."

Indeed, as Chase began to leaf through Ivy's manila folder, he saw that most of the pages were nothing more than daily vital signs and notes by the aides or nurses. Physician entries were rare, and then only a few sentences. There were sections, however, tabbed by specific years, with a concise summary for each section, as Sukie had described. When Chase opened the 1967-69 tab, he found a summary by a psychiatrist who concluded that Ivy was a chronic, undifferentiated schizophrenic. In the 1965-1967 section, the summary by a different psychiatrist concluded that Ivy was a paranoid schizophrenic. In 1963-1965, she had organic brain syndrome. And, in 1961-1963, she was a hebephrenic schizophrenic. And that's where this manila folder ended.

How could her diagnosis change with each and every psychiatrist? Her problem wasn't multiple personalities, it was multiple psychiatrists.

"I call Ivy my little scissortail," Sukie said, breaking Chase away from his introduction to psychiatric taxonomy.

"How so?"

"The scissortail is a gentle bird. That is, until someone invades its territory, like you just saw with Bertie entering Ivy's circle. When an invader comes into its area, the scissortail will attack a bird twice its size or larger, even a hawk, if that's what it takes. Ivy, she doesn't take guff from anyone. Yet, at the same time, she's the sweetest little thing on the ward. Always helping the aides and nurses with the other patients. You won't see that very often. Most of these lost souls live in a world of one."

Chase was only halfway listening to Sukie as he perused the pages until he found a more complete summary dated 1964. Someone with an M.D. degree, perhaps a resident assigned to the task, had written a story of Ivy's stay at Matherville State up to that time, a full three pages out of several thousand in the folder:

This week appears to be the 20th anniversary of Ivy Pettibone's arrival at this institution where she presented as a 12-year-old with multiple birth defects, after being orphaned at age 5 in the Tornado of '37. She was housed at the Austin facility initially where she carried diagnoses such as "idiocy" and "feeble-mindedness," as was common at the time, until her normal level of intelligence gradually came to be appreciated despite unintelligible speech. With several IQs measured over time ranging from 90 to 107, understanding the sharp limitations of such testing when language comprehension is in question, her attending physicians were prompted to re-classify her, as justification to remain in the institution could no longer be based on mental retardation. Since then, she has defied a consistent diagnosis. By early accounts in Austin, it seems her behavior was "age appropriate."

Prompted by such diagnoses as "hebephrenia" and "mania," Ivy was assigned to a great variety of treatments appropriate in their day, but no improvements were ever noted, perhaps because her symptomatology was measured largely by her unintelligible speech, rather than distorted ideation or behavior. Electroshock, insulin shock, and Metrazol convulsive therapy were tried in Austin and continued after transfer to Matherville. She was also chosen for the hydrotherapy experiments, followed by sleep and sensory deprivation, and even the cryotherapy stratagem in ice water, which forced a short stay at College Hospital for a cardiac arrest that occurred without apparent harm or sequelae. No treatment ever seemed to improve her "manic condition" and "inappropriate laughter," and certainly no improvement in her speech, but she did demonstrate increasing outbursts of rage.

In contrast to her prior docile demeanor, Ivy's quick temper resulted in attacks on other patients to the point she was considered for prefrontal leukotomy during the era when it was at peak popularity after the Nobel Prize went to Moniz. Although some of the records and details have been lost, it is recorded later that Ivy was placed in the operating theater, with the great lobotomist, Walter Freeman, MD, about to insert his ice pick through the orbit into the prefrontal area of the brain when the procedure was terminated abruptly.

There's an untold story there, said Chase to himself, and I wonder if it has to do with her unique gift of targeted spittle. He continued to read:

Then, from the observation made by the nursing staff that Ivy had no aggressive tendencies if invasive therapies were withheld, the decision was made to back away from further attempts at lobotomy (leukotomy).

Ivy was then transferred to Building 19 to be enrolled in the various psychotropic pharmacologic studies being performed there.

Her transfer to 19 prompted a review of her old records dating back to Austin where it was revealed that her birth defects had prompted a case history that was published in the medical literature. She was also the subject of considerable surgical planning to address her physical deformities. Of many operations considered, only one was performed on her club foot, and only the initial separation of her thumbs was accomplished for her syndactyly. She was left with a severe gait disturbance as well as webbed fingers of both hands.

Additional review of her five-year stay at the Austin facility revealed a most unique history surrounding electroshock treatments wherein the EST Director admitted no major behavioral problems whatsoever in the patient. Indeed, the EST specialist had great enthusiasm for the procedure as a panacea for a wide variety of neurologic conditions. He felt that Ivy suffered from a lack of neural connectivity between Wernicke's Area of speech comprehension near the superior temporal gyrus, and Broca's area of speech generation in the posterior frontal lobe, left hemisphere–these two areas being a good distance apart in the brain. Remarkably, Ivy was given EST solely on the premise of forging a union between Wernicke's Area and Broca's Area. Ivy could clearly understand the speech of others, but much like a stroke victim, she could not generate intelligible speech. Over 20 EST treatments were delivered with the simultaneous repetition of normal one-syllable words before and after the shock. In the end, she was unable to repeat any of the words suggested to her. No neural pathways had been forged...

Chase closed the folder as he neared the end, realizing he had only a fraction of her medical records.

"Sukie, can just anyone review those old records at the Administration Building?"

"Well, you have to be employed here, of course, or you gotta have a really good reason. Considering that the Director is a classmate of your father's, you shouldn't have any trouble. I'm sure Dr. Latimer would love to meet you regardless of the reason."

"Did you know they had Ivy on the launching pad once for a prefrontal lobotomy?" Chase asked, in disbelief that the procedure was still being done so recently.

"Yes, I heard something about that," said Sukie as she thumbed through papers at her desk. Sukie's eyes were usually all-knowing, overflowing with hidden wisdom, something that could chill an ornery boy to confess things, such as pulling the legs off June bugs. But now, as he tried to open a discussion about Ivy Pettibone's psychiatric history, Sukie didn't even bother to lift her eyes from the desk.

10

From the shelves behind her bathroom mirror, Livvy took her packet of birth control pills and twisted the dial until the next pellet fell into her palm. Would eight more years of the pill be safe? After all, eight was the plan. Then, she and Chase would start their family–two children–at the end of his residency in psychiatry. With a sigh of resignation, she swallowed the pill, chasing it with a half-glass of water, hoping she was not tempting trouble with blood clots or cancer. She adjusted the straps of her nightgown and sprayed herself with Shalimar.

Livvy had studied relationships and why they failed and why hers wouldn't and how open, constant communication would make the difference. And she knew her heart was overflowing with unselfish love, even before having met Chase, as a firm believer that there was only one person in the universe meant as a match for her devotion. She felt gifted with the ability to make any sacrifice to meld man and wife.

Growing up in Matherville, Livvy had been the only child in her grade school class with parents who had divorced. Even though the schism occurred before she could remember, she had trouble explaining two homes to her friends who had no other reference for a divided family. Embarrassed by the novelty, she finagled her way out of hosting slumber parties and birthday parties, forever seeking the company of friends on their own turf. Then, as a high school student, she watched her two older, married sisters struggle and separate and threaten and cry and curse and reconcile in predictable cycles, such that Livvy committed herself to a world of daisies and daffodils.

Given her mother's aphorism, born of failure, that "communication is a two-way street for one-way minds," Livvy planned to keep things exciting in the marriage. To that end, she dreamed up a newlywed covenant wherein the Shalimar cloud would let Chase know she was in the mood. Chase joked that he would be equally subtle by coming to bed after fumigating himself with English Leather.

Contrary to the spirit of their pact, however, Livvy was not in the mood tonight. Indeed, she felt guilty immersed in her Shalimar mist given her rattled state of mind. She was afraid. Perhaps, she reasoned, this was even more justification for perfume.

Earlier in the day, she had attended the traditional "Spousal Lecture" at the medical school for the freshmen wives (and three husbands), featuring the wildly histrionic speaker, Dr. Everett Meeker, Chairman of the Department of Psychiatry. The pudgy orator with gray lambchop sideburns had stomped back and forth across the lecture hall floor on an annual basis for years, whipping the microphone cord around like a lion tamer, screaming, "Damn umbilical cord," and threatening the audience of spouses with five to eight years of living hell.

Dr. Meeker had described the psychological fractures imparted by the unnatural acts of poking and prodding body orifices of people that were once called fellow humans, now called patients. He had planted his face directly in front of one of the three husbands sitting on the front row, and shouted, "How are you going to react knowing that, as part of the standard physical exam, your wife will be massaging another man's testicles, then sliding her finger from scrotum to groin to check for hernia? (pause) And *then*, ramming her finger up his anus?" The husband was wide-eyed and speechless.

Meeker told horror stories of various manifestations of suppressed and repressed anxiety in medical students—impotence in the men while rotating on gynecology, loss of libido in the females after working in the death-plagued neonatal ICU, hypersexuality with the altered brain chemistry of sleep deprivation and caffeine abuse, self-destruction in the sons of doctors unless the paternal star was aligned properly; and, of course, rampant alcohol and drug dependence, not so much for the old college buzz, but to maintain appearances when "one's insides are rotting away."

Dr. Meeker told of emotional walls that would be built by their loved ones in the struggle for personal survival, walls that would demarcate and alienate the doctor from the world, and how those walls could leave spouses on the outside, alone. Alone in the rest of the world. All in all, the lecture made Olivia Callaway sick to her stomach.

As she slid between the sheets, Livvy glanced at the clock, hoping that the slow-moving hands might pull Chase away from work for an early return. He was working his usual evening shift tonight, so he'd be another thirty minutes. Nonetheless, she would be ready. In fact, she needed to strike a pose. First, with lights left on, she pulled the bedspread up to her waist and decided to cover her chest with a copy of *Life* magazine to give the appearance she had fallen asleep while reading. From a bedside basket, she picked the latest issue, with angelic Tricia Nixon on the cover in a story about her love interest with a Harvard law student. No, on second thought, she pulled out an older edition of *Life* with Ann-Margret as cover girl with her tousled, bedroom hair aglow.

Motionless, prepared to feign sleep, Livvy couldn't fight the image of the mad psychiatrist who had railed relentlessly at today's lecture. Why did the medical school allow that sort of thing? And to think–he was considered a national expert on the medical education process! Oh, those poor wives of the guys going into surgery. The shrink had claimed that psychological research shows only a single stressor greater than a surgical residency – wartime military. And for those choosing general surgery with its high patient mortality due to abdominal operations and trauma, the divorce rate was 50% nationwide, *during* the five years of residency, not even counting the years afterward. However, at Matherville, the shrink claimed, the divorce rate had been 75% over the past few years for general surgery residents. Many residents didn't even bother to marry, thus avoiding the snare. Thank goodness Chase was only going to be a psychiatrist, and hopefully, a sane one, unlike today's wacky orator.

Still, she worried. Chase was sensitive. Sometimes, too sensitive. He couldn't turn left while driving if cars were following, uneasy making strangers wait. And if the wait was too long, he would turn right to avoid causing a jam, only to backtrack to make the left he had intended. Livvy was shocked the first time he did it, but now she saw it as a unique part of her husband.

And when it came to medical school, he had cringed at the thought of sticking someone with a needle. In fact, this seemingly minor dread had swayed him against medical school in the first place. He'd even noted, regrettably, that Captain Newman, M.D. injected Little Jim with pentothal *intravenously*, so even psychiatrists weren't safe from having to stick needles into another human.

Livvy felt a small twinge of guilt about it all. After all, it had been her unrelenting, albeit gentle, encouragement for Chase to leave the New Bloods and reconsider medical school. In her heart, she knew it was the right thing for Chase to do. He would get over his silly sensitivities like the needle sticks. All medical students, surely, had to feel queasy at first. It simply made no sense for him to waste his intellect on song lyrics. Yet, she had to admit he seemed on top of the world each time he emceed a concert where the New Bloods sang his songs. He told her once that he could listen to those songs constantly for the rest of his life and never grow tired... or old.

Livvy opened her eyes and scanned the bedroom, remaining still and listening for the sound of Chase's car door slamming shut. She wondered if lying on her side might be more alluring. No, she was fine on her back with Ann-Margret's cleavage covering her own.

She made goals, and she kept them. Her father, a local high school basketball coach (Chase's coach, in fact), had taught determination. In high school, Livvy was the entire female track team, her event being cross-country where she placed third at the state meet. Across town, her mother ran a popular floral shop, and she taught Livvy the business end of beauty. Now as a gym teacher at Matherville High, Livvy made sure she stayed in shape herself by running at least three miles a day, still finding time to serve as her mother's right hand at the shop. For Chase, this meant day-old flowers were always available to freshen their small home.

Now that Chase had made the leap to medicine, she knew her responsibilities would increase as well. She had seen warning signs once, early on, although the problem seemed fleeting. The summer after high school graduation, Chase decided to get the jump on college by taking Psych 101 and Introduction to Statistics by correspondence. He was transformed. And not for the better. While his two instructors were so impressed that they invited him to tour their departments at Far West Texas and encouraged him to enter their respective graduate schools, Livvy didn't share the enthusiasm.

When Chase studied that summer, he went into a trance. He wouldn't even answer her phone calls. Hours later, when they'd be at a movie, he couldn't concentrate on the story. He could barely recall going to certain movies that summer, and sometimes there was no memory at all. For instance, he denied they ever saw *The Sandpiper* together. Yet, later in the year, after he'd decided to kick back and coast in college, he could recall the tiniest of details and much of the dialogue of the films he loved, such as *Doctor Zhivago*.

Those odd symptoms of obsession disappeared after that one summer. Then, near the end of college, Livvy noticed that he was starting to lose his happy-go-lucky attitude the closer he got to medical school. And when he latched onto the Varsity Voyager opportunity, this seemed related more for his peace of mind than a calling. Then, after two years of bliss, she had tugged him away, back to the real world.

Livvy buried most of her quiet remorse for disengaging Chase from the New Bloods. Although now, after hearing the crazy shrink today, guilt was rearing its ugly head, accompanied by fear. She would have to work harder, that's all. She would have to be a tigress in the bedroom. She would have to make sure Chase was well fed, well rested, well balanced, and never at wont for anything. Chase was her calling. He was her life project. And she was prepared to sacrifice anything and everything to make their marriage work by inspiring Chase into full bloom. In short, she was prepared to lose herself.

Livvy heard a faint thud, but it was still too early for Chase. She hadn't heard the car door slam outside, nor had she heard the front door creak open. Perhaps she had been so lost in her thoughts that she was not listening for the specific sounds of Chase's arrival. Then, she remembered a string of burglaries that had occurred in Matherville this past week, all at night, all near their part of town. In the silence, she felt her pulse pounding in her ears. Her face flushed and beads of sweat formed. She was slipping quickly into panic.

When she saw the silhouetted figure at the foot of her bed, she started to scream, but then she was overcome by a deluge of English Leather.

"Oh my, you scared me. I should have known it was you."

Then, as Chase unbuttoned his shirt, a secondary stench from the swamp of the insane asylum took command of the room and obliterated the smell of his cologne.

11

With full penetration, she let out a yelp. Blood oozed from where he'd stuck her, and Chase started feeling woozy. He pulled out. More blood followed. With his thumb, he tried to put pressure on the stick site, having forgotten to release the tourniquet.

As darkness crept in from the edges of his field of vision, leaving only a tunnel, he saw a hand–probably Amy DeHart's–reach in to release the tourniquet that was choking his classmate's arm for the phlebotomy practice session.

His next image, after unknown seconds in black-out, was the ceiling of the module, eclipsed partially by Amy's worried face. Her blonde-streaked hair hung in curtains around her shadowed expression. "Are you okay, Chase?" she asked. He felt her hand jostling his shoulder.

"Yeah... I think so."

Group laughter followed. Not from Amy, but from his module mates delighted to see the spotless Chase Callaway flat on his back in total humiliation.

"I think the reason you didn't get blood return was you forgot to loosen the plunger on the syringe," Amy said. "That rubber seal on the plunger seems to stick against the plastic sometimes. You were in the vein, I'm sure."

"You idiot," said classmate C. C. Chastain, "don't *ever* pull out the needle with the tourniquet still on."

The room seemed to be regaining its light, as if the sun were emerging from a cloud. Chase reached for the countertop and clawed his way back into his swivel chair, the five-legged support that had failed him as he swooned.

Will Glendenning, another classmate, put his hands on his hips with a chuckle that was forced well beyond its natural ebb. "I can't wait to tell my wife. Maybe she'll stop saying, 'Why can't you be more like Chase Callaway?'." Glendenning held his pose, standing with one foot on the seat of his own swivel chair, elbow on knee, his hand stroking his chin with the smug confidence imparted through his own flawless phlebotomy technique.

Modules harbored sixteen students, chopped into study groups of four. The alphabet drove these unions, so Callaway, Chastain, DeHart, and Glendenning were cast together, while Will Glendenning, as the alphabetical misfit in a room of Cs and Ds, had been added as a last-minute replacement. A guy from New York had dropped out of med school on day three, accepting a fellowship to study film with Stanley Kubrick. Two additional students had dropped out of the class as well. And, of course, there had been Hector's suicide. And the year had barely begun.

Chase, Amy, Will, and C.C. had jelled right from the start, so they began their own study group. Amy's husband was working on his master's degree in journalism, Will Glendenning's wife was in law school, and C.C.'s girlfriend was always pleased to have him out of the apartment. So, the foursome rotated in the three homes of the wedded. Group study time was more confirmatory than anything else, as intense memorization was an individual pursuit. Together in the same room, however, they could cross-examine and pose more complex clinical themes beyond the rote memorization of the basic sciences that dominated these first two years. And they could get drunk as well, which added greatly to illusory intellectual prowess (though Chase was mostly an amused spectator with a one-drink limit).

"Yessireee," continued Will, "the next time my wife says, 'Chase does this, or Chase did that', I'll just remind her of this moment. Flat on your back. Cold-cocked." Realizing that he might be making too much of the moment, Will Glendenning retreated, patting his classmate on the back. "No big deal, Chase. It'll be a breeze next time."

C.C. Chastain wasn't ready to let go. "I've heard of the draw-*ees* fainting when blood is drawn, but not the draw-*er*."

Amy was the only one who thought to put a blood pressure cuff on Chase's arm, and she announced to the group, "110 over 70. Everything's fine."

Chase was humiliated. It had been a self-fulfilling catastrophe. For years, he had dreaded this moment–the first time to puncture another human with a needle–and now he had failed in spectacular fashion. His heart had been whispering this for years. Now, it was true. He had no business in clinical medicine.

"Damn good thing you're gonna be a shrink," said C.C., verbalizing Chase's own thoughts about himself. "You could really hurt someone if you actually had to do something."

Chase's early reign as Number One in the class only magnified his mortification. If the bottom student in the class had fainted, no one would have bothered to shrug a shoulder. Yet, for squeaky-clean Chase, SS #942-00-1049, top dog on dot matrix test scores, to faint... well, surely, the rumors that he was a total wuss would add juice to every conversation for weeks to come, if not months, if not years. Medicine was loaded with pokes and prods and cuts and sticks, and the mighty Chase would surely fall flat in the third year when book-learning could no longer save him... nor could his charm, nor his reputation, nor his dad's reputation, and wherein skills during the third year would be measured with new yardsticks.

.   .   .

One month later, word spread through the class that another student had dropped out.

The foursome from Module #116 was seated at their corner table in the "Coke room," a wide hallway lined by a sentinel row of vending machines, square-bodied soldiers that seemed to stare beyond the tables and chairs into a landscaped courtyard on the other side of a huge plate glass wall.

"Your turn to deal, Will," Chase said. "I didn't hear why he quit. Did any of you?"

"Nope." Will shuffled the cards and began to deal, a straw dangling from the corner of his mouth.

"I heard he was rotating on Patient Contact and his MS-3 asked him if he wanted to watch a surgery," C.C. Chastain began, as he scooped a strand of his light-brown hair off his forehead. "When they opened the patient's belly, it was full of dead bowel and pus, and most everyone in the room gagged at the stench. But our man–Note Group member #67, I might add, since every friggin' one of us has to transcribe more and more lectures every time these shitheads quit–anyway, he beelines to the Dean's office and quits on the spot. Another MS-1 bites the dust."

In this new age of technology with pint-sized recorders, the lecture halls were mostly empty. Instead of students filling the chairs, tape recorders played while professors fumed at the vacant seats. And one of the devices, each lecture, was the official listener for the Note Group. In this organization that enrolled most of the freshman class, students rotated turns in transcribing the lectures, so that any one student was assigned this burden every hundred lectures or so. It was important to have large numbers in the group to minimize the number of times one had to transcribe tape recordings into typewritten pages. C.C. Chastain had distinguished himself by being elected President and Omnipotent Ruler of the Note Group, and he kept the spurious bylaws registered firmly in his own mind. Non-participants were, in C.C.s estimation, scumbags. And drop-outs were worse.

"Quitting like that is a good demonstration of the boiling frog theory," Will offered.

Amy looked up from the bite she'd made in her ham sandwich. "The what?"

"The boiling frog theory."

"What's that?"

Will continued, "If you're trying to cook frog legs, but you toss your live frog into boiling water, it'll jump out pronto and escape. But if you let it swim in a pot of cool water where it thinks it's happiest, then you turn up the heat oh so gradually, it feels okay, then turn it up a little more… more relaxed, then numb… turn it up more, then before you know it, you're dining on some mighty fine frog legs."

"Translated for you concrete thinkers," C.C. added, "they desensitize us gradually in med school, over time. If they turn up the heat too quickly, we're history. They trick us, in other words, into thinking we're happy. And for you, Chase, I'd say you're in a world of hurt, seein' as your water's already boiling."

Chase forced a nervous laugh, ignoring the reference to his recent fainting episode. "I'm not sure there's much science behind that theory. Not to mention some questionable culinary issues. Don't they remove frog legs before they cook 'em?"

"How cruel is the metaphor for the shallow mind," said C.C. "So I repeat, how do you *gradually* turn up the heat on someone who passes out when he draws blood? And my second question is, what do you plan to do after you quit, Chase? And thirdly, since the Note Group is already down to critical mass, I'll friggin' clobber you if you do quit."

Will Glendenning plunked his Coke can on the table when the fizz started coming out his nose. He was choking, laughing, something. No one could tell for sure. "Excuse me. Shit, oh dear, it's all over my shirt. Anyway, if any of us hits the pavement with four tires spinning and headed for the exit, I'm betting it's you, C.C., what with your Broadway musical thingy you got going. So don't start pointing fingers."

Chase scanned the other three classmates at the table as he recalled Sukie Spurlock's admonition to "Be nicer than you have to be, even when no one's looking." Sukie sometimes added a modifying dangler at the end: "… because you never know how big of a cross that other person is carrying." Chase was committed to supporting others, part of being a good psychiatrist. He had already learned that both C.C. and Will considered their mothers "certifiable," but Will talked about it flippantly, as if his mother were a colorful eccentric in Lost Mine, Texas. C.C. talked about it as if his mother actually wore a straitjacket. Amy, on the other hand, had a great relationship with her mother, despite her parents' divorce.

Yes, it was still early in the first year, yet Chase Callaway had already implemented the philosophy of Sukie, a far simpler approach to life than the convoluted and ever-shifting rhetoric of Grandpa Zebulon.

Chase felt he had a unique talent in the ability to empathize. People were, by their very natures, self-absorbed. Most people, that is. He would be different.

Amy set her sandwich on the table and picked up her cards, fanning them into a perfect array. *Drats.* She was holding the queen of spades. "No one here is quitting, but I've got a question for you guys. Let's go 'round the table, each one of us, and admit what we'd be doing if we weren't here in the Bastille."

The concrete cell block, called the Basic Sciences Building, had central windows that pulled the light from an open courtyard, providing most of the natural illumination in the building. As for the outer shell of concrete, only thin slits of glass allowed a peek to the open air, wide enough for crossbow archers to aim at barbarian hordes, but too small for escape.

C.C. Chastain opened his mouth first, in response to Amy's "what if" question. "Do I really need to friggin' answer that? Surely, I've mentioned that my song-writing partner and I produced the first undergrad-written musical ever performed at the University of Oklahoma School of Drama."

"No-o-o. Really? Why don't you tell us about it for the hundredth-friggin' time?" Will pleaded with his eyebrows funneled into mock interest.

"Screw you. We've got the financing and we've got the connections, and we're scheduled to go off-Broadway next year. If it flies, man... I, the esteemed El Note Group Presidente, will not restrain myself from telling you bozos I'll be vamoosing, giving my adios to Matherville and my regards to Broadway. Then I'll be the happiest freakin' frog on the planet."

"So, why are you even here?" asked Chase.

"This is Plan B, man. Back-up. Our musical is a comedy based on the comic strip, *The Sorcerer of Siam,* and we're waiting on the cartoonist's permission. Or, actually, we have to come to an agreement where he gets reimbursed 'cause he has all the rights."

"I saw the show last year at the university theater, so I have to admit, C.C.'s *very* talented," said Amy, also an OU grad, nodding in C.C.'s direction. "And it sure will be fun if it makes it to New York. I'd love to see it there."

"Me too," said Chase. "I've done some song-writing myself–well, lyrics, that is."

"I wouldn't call that Christian clatter 'songwriting' exactly," C.C. said. "I'll grant you... that song you wrote, the one that made it on the charts, it's pretty okay. But the guy I'm working with is phenomenal. A true professional. Now, who's got the friggin' two of clubs? Lay that sucker down."

Chase laughed, as always, at the bite-less bark of his new friend, C.C.

C.C. Chastain was a fiery, rapid-talking, musical genius, of sorts. Trained as a classical organist and pianist, he had once performed with the Tulsa Symphony at age 12. And in college, he had played keyboards for a rock group that cut a few records that sold well, regionally, that is. He was in no way embarrassed by his height–indeed, he had nicknamed himself The Hobbit.

"How 'bout you, Amy, what would you do?" Chase asked.

"Or, what would you *rather* be doing, a better way to ask it," added C.C. "Especially, if you had your future income guaranteed."

"I'd *rather* be doing this. I'm not like you guys. I don't have other talents."

C.C. jumped at the chance. "Well, shit, Will doesn't have any talents either. Don't let that stop you."

Will gave C.C. a go-to-hell look, but everyone knew C.C.'s barbs were harmless. Indeed, it was the very absence of mocking jabs that meant you were no friend of C.C. Chastain.

Amy continued, "I enjoy business, I guess. I put myself through college by working as a distributor, of sorts, for the Wurlitzer company. I had juke boxes all over fraternity and sorority row at Oklahoma."

"Is that where you got to know C.C.?" asked Chase.

"Well, not through the juke boxes. C.C. was in the same fraternity as my husband, Kyle, there on University Boulevard. When it came time for med school, I couldn't get in at Oklahoma, probably because I'm a woman, and C.C. couldn't get in probably because his grades were lousy. So here we are. Together again."

"Easy girl," said C.C.

"Easy about what? That I'm a woman? Easy that only five percent of med school classes across the country are women?"

"No, you libbers have that issue by the balls already. I hear they're aiming for twenty women next year, and thirty the next."

"So you're defending your grades in college?"

"Correct. They weren't lousy."

"Well, C.C., in fact, they *were* lousy by med school standards. I mean really, what did you have, a 3.2 GPA? I didn't say you weren't smart. You never studied. All that variety show stuff, your rock band, and then the *Sorcerer of Siam*. I'm merely calling a spade and spade. And, by the way, here's the queen of spades, just for you, sweetheart."

"Damn, you gave it to me last time," C.C. groaned as he picked up the punitive queen. "Anyway, back to my favorite subject–me–having great talent is a great burden, and that's all I'm gonna say."

"Life is tough," said Chase to C.C. "But to answer Amy's original question, you'd think I'd already done my dreaming with the New Bloods for the past two years. Instead, what I've wondered is this–what if I have a talent that I've never explored? Any of us, for that matter. You know–hidden talent. What if I have the talent to be the greatest trombonist the world has ever seen, but I never bothered to take trombone lessons? Or, maybe it's sculpting, or high-diving, sword-swallowing, I don't know... it's so frustrating to think there are so many things out there in the world. How would you ever know? I wonder about past centuries, past societies. I mean, think about all those people who lived meaningless lives as serfs and slaves and stuff, but if they lived today, they might be Super Bowl heroes, or movie stars, or Nobel Prize winners. Now apply that same concept to the future. Maybe one of us has the right talent to come up with the cure for cancer, but the technologic platform that fits with your particular brand of genius hasn't been developed yet. So, you're a chronologic error, a mismatch, just like the serf who would otherwise have been a movie star if born in the right era. We're all golden keys, perhaps, but our corresponding locks might be in another time, another dimension."

At this point, Chase realized the other three card sharks were staring at him silently, mouths wide open, and that their game of Hearts had grown cold.

"Well, I'm glad you got that out of your system," C.C. said. "Now, if you're back from visiting whatever planet you've been on, Chase, let's return to the question at hand."

Amy, pretending to look at her cards, said, "You seem awfully quiet, Will. What about you? What would you do if you weren't in medicine?"

"Hell, he's not going into medicine in the first place," interrupted C.C. "He's going into pathology."

"Bite me, C.C." Will gazed through the glass wall in the direction of the neglected courtyard in the center of the building where the weeds had overtaken the flower beds, and unruly shrubs looked as though they were back in the wild. "I always wanted to write detective novels, or mysteries. I guess that's why I'm going to sub-specialize in forensic pathology."

"Oh, brother, I've heard it all now. Then again, who *hasn't* wanted to be a novelist?"

"C.C., it might surprise you to know that I was an English major, and that I've had several short stories published."

"Published where? In your high school newspaper?"

"I never knew you wanted to be a writer, Will," Amy said. "Have you ever mentioned anything about that to my hubby? Kyle was always waffling between medical school and journalism."

"Really?"

"Oh, yes, he waffled long and hard. Finally decided against medicine, I think, just to avoid his daddy's footsteps."

C.C. Chastain brightened at the mention of 'daddy'. His father was a prominent physician in Tulsa, and he knew that both Chase and Will were following those precarious footsteps as well. "You might recall what our favorite shrink, Dr. Meeker, says about father-son combos in med school. He says if the relationship is good, the son will be a good doctor. But if the relationship's bad, watch out below! So what is it? Will? Chase?"

Chase spoke quickly to bring the topic to a close. "My dad's fairly distant, but still a good role model. That's pretty much all there is to it. I can't imagine that it matters as much as Meeker says."

Everyone at table turned toward Will. Chase was glad to have escaped the probing by C.C.

"My dad apparently wanted to be a pathologist," Will said. "Maybe I'm trying to live out his dreams, I don't know. Forensics would be a combination of detective work and medicine, so it just seems right for me. My dad ended up being a GP. Couldn't get a residency in path, or something like that. Never gave it up. He's dead now, but he had his own little lab in the basement, still there by the way, where he played around with different colored dyes to stain tissues on microscope slides. I grew up with a scope in my room, always looking at everything under the sun. Used to squash bugs under a cover slip and look at them magnified. It's an amazing world at that micro level. I don't really want to be a GP. I mean, who wants to treat runny noses for the rest of their life? To be honest, I thought I might be the one to pass out the first time I drew blood. I don't want to do any of that stuff. I want to diagnose things, solve mysteries, looking under the microscope."

"Solve mysteries? Gimme a break, Glendenning," C.C. said to Will. "Kinda weird your dad couldn't get a residency in pathology. What's up with that? I mean, it's not like they're competitive or anything, like surgery is. Maybe it was different back in the dark ages. Did he ever think about doing pathology later on?"

"No. Not that I know of."

C.C. Chastain led with the jack-of-hearts, then said, "Maybe your dad simply preferred to be a Dr. Frankenstein down in his basement lab. Interesting hobby. Creepers. Oh well, my dad is hero-supremo to me. He's my best friend, so I'm not worried about that lunatic shrink Meeker and what he has to say. And since I seem to be taking all the tricks at Hearts here, I think I'll go ahead and shoot the moon."

"No one in my family is in medicine," said Amy. "And I sorta like it that way. Keeps me free to choose."

"Choose what?" asked C.C. "Pediatrics or... uh, hmm, let me see... pediatrics?"

"Why in the world," Amy asked, making a fist with her right hand, "from the initial interview, to everyone you meet in medical school, including professors *and* classmates, it's assumed a woman is going into pediatrics? Why, for instance, are all the gynecologists *men*? Does that make any sense? And why are surgeons nearly all men? Is the establishment really telling us that women can't sew?"

"Easy does it, *Mizzz Steinem*," C.C. replied.

Amy continued, "As I was saying, I'm sorta glad I don't have anyone in the family who's in medicine. I heard at the spouse lecture that Dr. Meeker told a grisly story about a surgeon who rose above his father on the academic totem pole. Then, when the son became Chairman of the Department, he shot himself."

C.C. rolled his eyes. "You know what I've decided? I think Meeker is totally full of bullshit. I think he makes up half the crap he tells us."

"I don't know, C.C.," Will Glendenning added, "I've heard Meeker's a bigwig, known for his publications on the psychiatric dynamics behind medical education. He thinks we ought to be including psychological testing as part of the selection process for med school. More important than the MCAT, he says. Keep the mad geniuses and con artists out, I guess."

"Well, Mr. Would-be Novelist," said C.C., "you might be impressed by his publications, but I for one, want to know the meat inside, not the flesh. Why's he so histrionic? He's a freakin' performer, for gosh sakes. An entertainer. No different than me, I might add. He's puttin' on a show. He's got such a reputation to uphold that I bet he spends all year making up these stories for one reason and one reason only–to scare the crap out of next year's crop of MS-1s. What great sport that must be, scaring the bejesus out of the new recruits. And their wives, to boot."

"You're too young to be such a cynic," Chase said, still snickering at C.C.

"Too young? Cynic? I'm a realist, old buddy. And a realist sees right through the bullshit. C'mon. Do you believe for one minute that a female medical student regressed so much during her third year rotations that she curled up in fetal position in the lap of a lesbo professor and asked if she could nurse? Gimme a break. This Meeker guy is making this stuff up, I'm telling you. He gets his rocks off performing for you gullible fools. Are you gonna defend his baloney? Especially you, Mr. Psychiatrist. After all, Meeker is going to be one of your bosses someday, if you stay here in Matherville, that is."

Chase laughed, nervously now. "C.C., don't you think you're just a *little* jaded? I do think, even if you don't, that medical school is horrible stress for some people. You may or may not know it, but Hector

Delgado was a childhood friend of mine. Even though he had lots of problems during college, he was back on track and his future should have looked pretty darned good. There's more going on than meets the eye, for some people at least."

"Thank–you–Doctor–Freud. Hector's future? Looking pretty good? Right up to the moment he killed himself? A leopard doesn't change his stripes, and the crazy ones were crazy when they got here."

"A leopard doesn't have stripes," Will said. "But you're probably right that the shaky ones bring their problems into med school with them. And whaddya think about Meeker's research on the No-Conscience personality? Supposedly, he's gonna write a book."

"It's hard to believe that five per cent of the population, not counting prisoners, have no measurable conscience," Chase said. "Zero. That they fake emotions that they've observed just to be socially acceptable. And it's harder to believe that it works so well. Shouldn't it be more obvious?"

"Yes, seems like it would," said Amy.

Chase continued, "And I really have trouble believing Meeker when he says it's even more common among medical students. Seven per cent? C'mon. The highest rate for any of the professions? That means ten-point-five students in our class are what Meeker calls 'narcissistic pretenders'."

Will chimed in, "And C.C. is the zero-point-five–he's only got half a conscience."

"Screw you, Glendenning. Like I said earlier, most of what Meeker has to say is pure BS. Thank goodness I'm going into surgery where I can get away from all that mumbo jumbo. Like my dad. Unless, of course, the *Sorcerer of Siam* takes off, then you'll never see my ass in this backassward part of the country again."

Amy played the queen of hearts.

"Damn, I can't believe the queen was still out," C.C. said. "I lose again."

Amy replied, "It's hard to follow the cards when your mouth is running."

Chase drifted away in thought. Because he and his father had never really "clicked," then Wes Callaway had no psychological power over him, neither good nor bad. Furthermore, Chase would not be following his father's footsteps. His father had been a practicing surgeon early on, but had abandoned surgery and returned to general practice after suffering a malpractice suit, a misadventure his father never discussed. The ice in Wesley's veins had helped him become the basketball superstar he was at FWTU, and that ice did not seem to thaw after his sporting days were over.

Yet, vaguely, Chase remembered his father having said, on a solitary occasion, "The *only* decision I regret in my life was not finishing my surgical residency to become board-certified. It was no big deal at the time. Not in the 1940s. However, those boards sure got big later on. And it came back to haunt me."

"Haunt" was a powerful word for the ice-blooded Wes Callaway. Chase couldn't recall his father ever claiming to be upset, regretful, angry, jealous, bitter, sorry, guilty, frustrated, vengeful, or sad. His father did not mention negative emotions at all. In fact, he didn't mention *any* emotions. He showed them, muted perhaps, but he simply didn't name them. Yes, "haunt" was an immensely powerful word when spoken by Wes Callaway, son of Zebulon, father to Chase.

12

At a table in the Coke Room, alone, with bouncing knees banging against the undersurface of the tabletop, sat Porter Piscotel. Balding prematurely, his prominent brow emerged like a bony eave overhanging thin slits for eyes. His fingers drummed, both hands synchronized like a pair of 4-cylinder engines. As a former member of The Corps of Cadets at Texas A & M University, Porter felt uncomfortable out of the uniform he had worn daily for the past four years as a member of this elite group.

Porter felt that most of his medical school classmates were neither mates nor of his class. He grabbed an empty soda can in his left hand, massaging the metal until it collapsed. With his right hand, he started turning the pages of his biochemistry text, pretending to read while he listened to the nonsense at the table nearby, where three classmates and a female, of all things, were discussing what they'd rather be doing than attending medical school. It was unsettling. And all things unsettled needed to be sliced into one of two categories—black as distinct from white.

The female looked more like a model who ought to be perched on a revolving platform while pointing to a shiny new Grand Prix at the Texas State Fair. Women diminished the guts and glory that medicine had to offer. They had no place here, and it was even worse that the three guys had accepted this female as one of their own. In fact, the entire module #116 was a little too chummy, in Porter's view. Partying on Saturday nights, planning their skit for the end of the year Gridiron Show, they never seemed engrossed by the challenge of medicine. Their lack of dedication was clear.

Especially annoying was hot shot Chase Callaway. Smiling incessantly, laughing at everything, Callaway posed as a friend to everyone. There wasn't a trace of commitment to medicine about him. In fact, rumor held that Callaway wasn't even planning to be a real doctor. Psychiatry, it was. What a joke. Porter knew all he needed to know about the subject, having suffered through the required course in psychology as an undergrad. There, he learned of the Milgram studies on obedience, performed at Yale, where unwitting participants were duped into delivering "lethal" shocks to the professor's confederates, all in the name of science. People were sheep, and that was that. Only the chosen few were born to lead. And it galled Porter that every time he checked test scores, Callaway's number was at the top of the list – S.S. #942-00-1049.

Porter studied constantly. After all, he had proven himself early on as valedictorian of his high school class at Tyler, Texas. Well, not Tyler actually, but nearby Arp where 62 were in his graduating class, 61 beneath him. Then, as an Aggie, he had distinguished himself as a "fish" in the Corps, such that he was placed in charge of the Aggie Bonfire his sophomore year.

His cadet unit had been the most formative and exciting experience of his life. He loved daily formations, marching to class, the uniforms, and the richly embedded traditions. His favorite mottos were: "Where Leaders Are Forged" and "Guardians of Tradition." As a junior, he had been selected as one of the "top 80," thereby earning his place as a Ross Volunteer–an honor guard drill team that was often in service to the Governor of Texas. The selection process had required above average grades in addition to passing a stringent review board–but most importantly, willingness to represent The Corps as a "Soldier, Statesman, and Knightly Gentleman." And had it not been for bunions on both feet, he would proudly be serving his country right now in Vietnam, carrying his M-16 above his head, while wading chest deep in rice paddies.

It was during his Aggie experience in the Special Operations Training Unit where men learned varied skills such as repelling, land navigation, and weapons qualifications, that he also learned CPR, sparking his desire for a career in heroic medicine. Now, here he sat, in the hallowed halls of the Basic Sciences Building, listening to the pansies at the next table whine about boiling frogs and how they'd rather be doing something else.

Porter couldn't wait to attack the hospital wards his third year. These first two years of medical school as an MS-1 and MS-2 were nothing more than ground school–book learning, boring, and of little practical use. The thrills were yet to come, and thrills occurred in the trenches, not in the lecture halls. And while the gutless wonders at the next table were dreamily writing songs and skits and having fun on Saturday night, Porter volunteered in the emergency room at College Hospital, helping, learning, excelling, and networking with every resident physician in the medical center.

As for the first two years of med school, test scores meant little. Sure, after being valedictorian at Arp, it was hard now to accept that he studied constantly, only to see his scores consistently fall smack dab on the hump of the bell curve. In three more years, however, when it came time to select the top students to the prestigious Alpha Omega Alpha Honor Medical Society, the third-year grades from the clinical years would count double the basic science grades. His plan was to be selected, if not with the top 5% at the end of the junior year, then in the next 5% tier during senior year.

Porter didn't trifle with silly emotions. Rather, he was bound by an overriding sense of duty. His father, a veteran of the Normandy invasion as a paratrooper in the 101st Airborne, had died of a heart attack the day Porter graduated from high school, merely half an hour before the ceremony and Porter's valedictory. In cap and gown, and with his mother, Porter left the festivities to follow the ambulance to the emergency room where nothing could be done for the purple carcass that used to be his father.

Afterward, his mother was devastated, unable to cope with the loss of her husband and, too, the emotional loss of her son. After months of solitude and a private battle with alcohol, she found solace and substance by cleaning homes in nearby Tyler. Porter was privately ashamed by his mother's reaction to it all. The demeaning work was bad enough, he thought, but the fact that she *enjoyed* it, took pride in it, bothered him.

Porter worked his way through college as a hospital orderly, suffering the smug condescension of nurses who didn't understand how hard it was to excel as a member of The Corps and, at the same time, study pre-med. He looked forward to the day when nurses would show him respect, standing and offering their chairs when it was time for him to do his chart work.

It was for a brief period as an orderly that Porter slipped toward introspection. Thinking about his father's death drew him inward to ask, "Why are we here? What am I about?" Yet, there was no joy in this self-examination. In fact, a vague restlessness that had no specific name seemed to swell every time he asked, "Why do I think that way?" Or, "Why did I do that?" He found that a life examined was overrated. Fortunately, he discovered an antidote to this growing miasma–to boldly forge ahead, lifting his feet above a quagmire of sentiments that dragged average people down. This assertiveness brought him a profound sense of peace. It opened doors. It made others react. It quieted dissent. It set the agenda. And it kept the muck beneath his feet.

This talent of assertiveness was not working well in medical school, however. At least, not so far. At A & M, he had supreme confidence, and he showed it in many ways. He could, for instance, raise his hand during class and ask questions that indicated he already had command of the subject matter, such that he could challenge the teachings without offending the professors. With a rehearsed and feigned style of innocent humility, his long-winded and challenging pontifications were well received at A&M by the faculty, and his grades were well above average.

So far, however, as a medical student, he was having trouble drawing upon his well-honed technique. Swallowed into the belly of an equally bright body of students seemed to paralyze his right arm, keeping it at his side, rather than reaching for the ceiling of the lecture hall to flag down the professors. Other classmates were raising their hands and exposing their own stupidity, asking questions that had already been addressed in the lecture. He could easily trump such embarrassing displays. So, why couldn't he assert himself like he had done so ably in college? And why didn't hot shot Chase Callaway ask questions? How could Numero Uno sit there in lecture, if he bothered to show up at all, never raising his hand, yet turn around and ace the tests? If Porter were making grades like that, he knew he'd have his hand reaching for the sky so often, it would—

"Hi. Saw you sitting there by yourself, and I thought I'd introduce myself. I'm Chase Callaway. I don't think the modules on this side of the building ever get to know you guys on the other side. Here we are mid-semester, and I'm still meeting new people."

S.S. #942-00-1049 had a hand of friendship jutting toward him.

Porter jumped to attention, knocking the crumpled can of soda to the floor where it rattled forever. He bent over and made a brief overture to stop the noise, extending his arm toward the can, then back again, then toward the can once more, then deciding to let the can spin to a stop, whereupon he pulled himself erect. "Porter Piscotel. My pleasure." Porter shook hands, staring at Chase with one eye, while the other eye watched the pansy card players head out the door for the next lecture in physiology. "I'm in Module #124. Other side of the building. Like you said. Sides don't mix it up much."

Silence followed. Porter waited for Chase to make the next move. Ordinarily, Porter would have taken command of a new situation like this, but he had been caught off guard.

Chase dropped his gaze to the pumping handshake, and Porter offered quick release, embarrassed that he had forgotten to stop the greeting. After jerking his hand away and burying it in his pocket, Porter shifted his weight from side to side, adding, "Everyone seems to be impressed with your test scores so far. Where'd you go to undergrad? Ivy League or something?"

"Naw, I stayed here at Far West Texas. I'm a true patriot for the hometown school. How 'bout you?"

"Texas A & M. I'm an Aggie."

"Oh, really? That's good." More awkwardness followed as both struggled to keep the conversation alive. Chase finally said, "I guess physiology is starting. We'd better move toward the lecture hall. Or do you skip and use the Note Group? That's what I do most of the time."

"I go to all lectures. Can't shake my training in The Corps."

"The what?"

"The Corps. At A & M. I was in The Corps. Lots of discipline there."

"Oh, yeah, that military thing they do there?"

Porter fumed inside at "military thing" as he walked down the hall toward the lecture, ignoring other pleasantries being offered by Chase. Once inside the auditorium, Porter hustled his way to the front row where he sat alone. Ten minutes into the lecture he looked toward Chase's customary seat near one of the exits and saw that #942-00-1049 had already escaped the classroom, having judged himself to be above it all.

Note group, thought Porter. *He's a lazy note-grouper. It figures.*

When the lecturing professor made it to Starling's Law of cardiac physiology, Porter was overcome by the urge to break the ice and establish his role as a force by asking a probing, insightful question. It was now or never.

Starling's Law... hmmm... with increasing pressure due to the left ventricle of the heart filling with blood, thus increasing the diameter, then the contractility of the heart muscle increases and— but wait... that puts it in conflict with Laplace's Law! Laplace states that the tension on the wall of a hollow viscus increases with increasing diameter of the viscus, leading to rupture, like when the cecum selectively perforates with colonic obstructions. So... then... there must be a major conflict in principles of physics! Both cannot be correct.

Overwhelmed with his perceptive analysis, Porter felt his hand reaching for the sky.

The professor continued, "Of course, any simpleton should be able to figure out that the incredible contractile strength of the sturdy cardiac muscle fibers easily overcomes the minimal effect of Laplace's Law. Otherwise, the left ventricle would rupture with any increase in the end diastolic pressure."

Porter jerked his hand back to his side and felt his face flush even though no one in the room had known his intent. He would never attempt a hand-raising again, at least not during this two-year tour of duty in the Basic Sciences Building. He would simply wait his turn until he reached the wards where he already felt at home after his years as an orderly. It would not be a long wait, all things considered.

At the end of the lecture, he found himself walking down the opposite hall from his bunker for reconnaissance at module #116, foreign soil to him. As he walked past, he was not surprised by the spectacle–the same four clique members, laughing and talking and playing cards, having skipped lecture, relying totally on the Note Group translations. Besides hot shot #942-00-1049, there was the musician, the detective novelist, and the female. A motley crew, indeed.

And the unnamed emotion that coursed through every capillary of his circulation prompted him to quicken his pace, straighten his back, tighten his fists, all without recognizing anything about himself, other than the sense of relief that enveloped him now, rededicated to hard work and excellence, knowing his father could look down from Heaven and smile.

Indeed, Porter Piscotel knew himself to be a man destined to cut a wide swath in the world.

13

Eighty tentacles, outstretched and undulating, were attached to 40 khaki-clad bodies. The limbs groped at Chase's face and backed him into the corner against a treasure-laden, padlocked cabinet. Wiggling fingers, tattooed by nicotine, fluttered in his face. The men were gray–their hair, their skin, their breath.

The ravenous inmates, perfumed by the lingering incense of urine-soaked underwear, closed around him in a mob that reminded Chase of those horror movies where the walking dead move robotically with antenna-like arms and zombie eyes. Although he had repeated this ritual twice a shift for nearly a year now, it still carried a tiny vestige of fear when he was the only aide in the men's Day Room as the clock struck Time. Inmates knew the Time. They watched the second hand ticking away, anticipating relief to the point of rapture, their raison d'être. Chase's apprehension always peaked at that brief flash of time when he turned his back on the craving crowd to unlock the cabinet.

He felt their breath on his neck, their spooky fingers brush against his white shirt, then he pulled the key from his belt loop ring, jiggling it into the padlock. If the inmates had been shouting for him to hurry, Chase could have relaxed. However, the 40 men voiced nothing. Near total silence. The only sound was the shuffling of feet on the concrete floor as bodies pressed together, the sound of khaki ruffling khaki as the strong pushed the weak out of the way, accented by the collective coughing of polluted airways making room for new ashes.

The padlock clicked open, and Chase swung the doors back revealing the precious contents of the cabinet–a plain, wooden cigar box. Flipping the lid open, he confirmed the fruitful output from the prior shift of aides–several hundred cigarettes, freshly rolled and stacked like logs. A murmur arose from the crowd, muted enthusiasm, as the gray words emerged, "Gimme... gimme... "

When Chase turned to face them, the 80 arms pleaded with grotesque contortions, yet he knew that no one would reach inside the box. These men were disciplined, some would say "institutionalized," but well-behaved, nonetheless. They waited patiently for Chase to lift the cigarettes one by one from the box and feed them. He struck only one match, lighting a mere three cigarettes for those men standing closest to him. From there, the inmates formed small huddles to light each other's smokes until all the cigarettes were burning. It reminded Chase of a hellish version of the Christmas Eve candlelight service at his grandfather's church.

With no smiles, yet no sadness, the smokers wandered back to the benches in the Day Room, or the bathroom, or simply stood in the corners, and relished the moment. And what a glorious time it was, every four hours around the clock during the day, one cigarette always waiting to serve as a beaming reminder of normalcy. Then, as always, Chase noticed the one would-be smoker who stood alone, still without his smoke.

Walter was unmoved, staring at Chase. This was the norm. Creepy, but expected. Walter routinely stood behind the crowd, towering above all, waiting for his cigarette, dead last, after the others scattered. Not that he was being polite. Walter simply abhorred physical contact, or even proximity, with the other inmates. He was the only patient in Building 19 who had once been an inmate in the 3rd floor Tower for maximum security. That was back in his spry youth, however, when sinew still coated his six-foot-six frame. Nowadays, Walter was skeletal, weighing no more than 160 pounds. His gray hair was thick and long, mostly standing in a high flattop, bringing his effective height to nearly seven feet. Without the hair, his head would have been nothing more than a skull, for his eyes seemed absent, lost in dark grottos.

Walter used real words when he spoke, but they never made sense. Chase tried to avoid engaging because Walter became terribly frustrated when his listeners failed to respond appropriately to his rants, which was always. Yet, if cornered by Walter, Chase tried to offer him a listening ear, pretending to understand. Chase had studied the old medical records, and Walter was one of the few inmates for whom the psychiatrists had consistently written the same diagnosis for the past 40 years–paranoid schizophrenic.

"May tag central agitator," growled Walter through his yellow, twisted teeth. "Central agitator, yes. Man cannot make a heavier-than-air machine for the Lord Keeper of the Great Seal has chained the book to the library. May tag. Central agitator."

Walter shouted these inanities as he walked toward Chase and stuck a bony forefinger in the aide's face, with an earnest and frustrated appeal for Chase to do something about "it," whatever "it" was. Walter's mouth formed an oblong O, reminding Chase of "The Scream," when adding a gray flattop to Munch's image. Walter continued, "The book cannot float if it is chained. May tag. May tag. Agitate. May tag central agitator."

Walter had been repeating the agitator phrase on a regular basis lately, growing more and more restless every day, perhaps due to the research requirement to stop all meds. Chase wondered if complex theories should be tossed aside, and Walter simply taken at his word. In paranoid delusion, perhaps the inmate believed himself aligned with the central agitator in a Maytag washing machine. Perhaps, this was merely an issue about laundry. What did Chase know? He was a lowly Psychiatric Aide I, preparing for Aide II status so that he could distribute medications and, more importantly, qualify for a raise. Still, as a budding Captain Newman, M.D., Chase was obliged to pry away at the clues.

"Here you go, Walter. Enjoy." Chase offered a cigarette to Walter, trying to play it cool even though Walter gave him the jitters. No matter how many times he went through this exercise, Chase breathed a sigh of relief after rationing tobacco to Walter, the mother-killing and mother-mutilating monster (if his 1931 medical records were correct). On the bright side, Walter hadn't killed anyone in more than 40 years.

Walter refused the cigarette Chase had touched, then grabbed another from inside the box while grumbling at unseen disturbances in the universe. He predictably refused to get his light from other inmates, so Chase provided the flame. After his first puff, Walter announced, "The sky blows high in the air. Hydraulic connections shake trees to upward keep and splinters burn. So easy a child can do it." When Chase said, "Oh, really?" Walter cursed him and walked away.

Chase set the cigarette box back in the cabinet and locked the treasure in place for the next four hours. He left the Day Room and entered the main hall that connected the men's and women's sides of the building, usually called the TV room, an understated name given its great size comparable to a medieval banquet hall.

At the other end of the building, in the distant doorway of the nurses' station, he spotted wife Livvy, holding up a basket of goodies, standing next to Sukie Spurlock. Olivia was the best wife anyone could hope for. Faithful attention and encouragement, relentless pampering, no selfish demands. And, yes, she made him want to be a better person.

He smiled and waved as he headed to the nurses' station. The TV room was one of two connections that extended across the entire width of the building. The other crossbar was the row of seclusion rooms.

Chase kept his eyes on Livvy as he walked, ignoring frozen bodies planted along the way–some perched next to the bricked-up fireplace, others gazing out chicken-wired windows, a few on the couch staring at the TV with stone-faced psychosis, entertained by "The Sonny and Cher Comedy Hour." As he passed the women's Day Room, Chase glanced in, spotting Ivy Pettibone walking in circles. He shook his head to clear it from the madness and returned a smile to his wife.

"Hey there, Livvy. Thanks for the food."

"Any excuse I can get. Otherwise, I'd never see you." Then she wrinkled her nose and frowned. "Gosh, it takes a few minutes to get used to that smell, doesn't it?"

"Ah, but you do get used to it," said Chase. "A real potpourri of bodily fluids, including sweat and blood and puke."

Former nanny Sukie Spurlock opened the lower half of the door for Chase to enter the nursing station. "The smell is more than that, I think," she said. "Yes, bodily fluids, but don't forget tears. Somehow the aroma gets into the walls and floor and ceiling, then it's the combination of it all blended. It's the stew of madness."

Livvy handed him the basket. "Gosh, you put ribbons all over it, Liv. You didn't need to go to all that trouble."

"Don't you love a man in uniform, Sukie?" Livvy said as she kissed him on the cheek. "Even if it's an ice cream man's uniform."

"You kids are too much. A blessing to me, for sure. And I know you're tired of hearing it, by the way, but you best be thinking about having some children, don't you know. It's been nigh on three years since the wedding, and your folks are sure looking forward to some grandbabies. And so am I."

"Now, Sukie," Chase said, "don't start in on that again. You know we've got a long time before we're able to support a family."

Sukie eased back to her desk to continue charting and advising. "Chase, you aren't gonna be out there working like a real doctor for years. Do you really want to be the only gray-haired father at your kids' junior high graduation?"

Livvy plopped onto the edge of the desk used by aides, where Chase had settled to eat his chicken breast, cheese, and apple. "We might not wait for Chase to be completely done with residency. For kids, I mean. He'll get paid some as a resident, so maybe in several years."

"You best not be waiting too long, Livvy."

Chase never admitted to anyone that the taste of sister Annie's death had a way of lingering, forcing him to wonder about the chances that he and Livvy might have a cystic fibrosis baby. So, whenever the talk moved toward the making of a family, he diverted. "For right now, Sukie, the only thing we're fertilizing and growing is our garden. That takes all my free time as it is, which says a lot about my free time. It's not easy trying to grow anything out here in the land of sand and gravel. But everything I learned about growing vegetables, I learned from you."

Sukie grinned but said nothing. Chase knew his diversion was not slipping by unnoticed. Finally, Sukie said, "Why, Chase, it seems like yesterday we were out there planting those beets and cucumbers and tomatoes. I still remember having to drag you by the ears to get you out of that garden. There was always one more blade of grass to pull, or one more drink of water to give those plants. Or, you'd have to scrape away the dirt around the carrots to sneak a look at that beautiful orange color."

"Oh, believe me, he's still that way," Livvy said. "You'd think those things were human."

"Well, I always told Chase when he was a little boy that there's no quicker sign of God's sweet presence than watching a plant sprout from seed. I'm halfway surprised that you didn't grow up to be a truck farmer, Chase."

Livvy added, as if Chase were no longer in the room, "Of course, vegetables or not, he tends to go overboard on just about everything. I think he studies way too much. The *weird* thing is that he's scoring the highest in the class, way better than what he did in college, and now he's got a reputation to uphold."

"No, the weird thing is," said Chase, "after all these years, I've realized I've got a variation of what you might call a photographic memory. Not in the usual sense, but a memory for photographs."

"What's that supposed to mean?" Livvy asked. "I've never heard you talk about that."

"Photographs seem to stick with me. For some reason, when I see them and register them for only a moment, it never leaves me. That's why I did so well at histology in college, and then in med school. I remember every detail of the image. Same for anatomy. Same for biochemistry when I look at the structure diagrams. It's not a photographic memory per se, it's a memory for photographs. Sure enough, the only course where there were fuzzy concepts and fuzzier pictures, little more than cartoons, was neurophysiology, and what happened there? I wasn't number one."

"And shame on you for it," Livvy mocked. "Good grief. You still got an A."

"Barely. And if I'm going into psychiatry where the concepts are so nebulous, and there aren't clear photos of brain function—"

"You *still* got an A."

"But it wasn't completely clear in my head. It was fuzzy. I'm a good test taker, that's all."

Sukie was fanning her face with a patient's chart. "Chase, dear, you gotta slow down pouring over those textbooks. You've got your pretty little bride here and you've got a life to live and you're gonna be the best at whatever you do anyway and—"

"I get it, Sukie. I get it."

"And while we're on the subject of *living life to the fullest*," Livvy added, "Claudia and Will want us to come over for dinner Saturday night. Amy and Kyle will be there, and C.C. and Suzie. You know Claudia originally wanted to get together tonight, but you were working, and she never wants to do *anything* without you there, Mr. Storyteller."

Indeed, Chase had taken center stage at the group's parties, recounting story after story–tales from the lunatic asylum–ad nauseam, no embellishment needed. Yet Chase had a voice deep inside, at the same time, that would whisper, "Don't mock lost souls." The astonishment and laughter of his audience kept him charged, and he even took notes at work to invigorate his repertoire for the parties.

"You know," Chase said, "there's another party, also Saturday night, two of the modules getting together, mine and #115 next door. Maybe we should quit being so cliquish and do more with other classmates."

Livvy squirmed as she glanced at Sukie to judge her level of attention, which was focused now on paperwork. "Well, okay," whispered Livvy, "but you know that means some of your classmates will be using. I don't really care what they do, Chase, but it's still awkward since we don't."

Chase was relieved that Livvy didn't mention Quaaludes and other recreational drugs in front of Sukie. "That group is really entertaining, you gotta admit. And I'm starting to feel like we're not part of any group outside the three couples—"

Loud piano music broke into the discussion–not "music" in its true form, but a cacophony of key-banging.

"That's little Ivy," said Sukie. "You can recognize her playin' instantly."

Chase rose from the desk and stuck his head out the open Dutch door, spotting Ivy at the lonely upright piano in the corner of the Day Room.

Sukie shook her head and smiled. "My how that little lady can pound away. She must be celebrating that Bertie's back in seclusion."

"Is that the only time she's plays the piano?" asked Livvy.

"Oh, heavens no, but certainly when she's happy. I do think that girl hears beautiful music when she plays. Music that the rest of us can't appreciate. Just like her speech."

Chase added, "If her fingers weren't stuck together, maybe she could've played just fine. Who knows? When I looked through Ivy's old charts, I saw that they sent her at least twice to the Surgery Clinic to separate her fingers, but the operation never seemed to happen. Her thumbs were released as a child at the Austin facility, but the attitude around here has been that she's good enough with her thumbs free. After all, she doesn't know any different. If her fingers had been separated, however, she might have managed some sort of sign language. Syndactyly surgery is best done in childhood, or else independent mobility can be lost for good."

"Her what surgery?" Livvy asked, sliding off the desktop and pulling the strap of her purse over her shoulder. "You've been reading. No surprise."

"It's called syndactyly when fingers are fused like that. Older methods of repair didn't work very well. The scarring caused as much problem as the skin webs. But I looked it up, and they have procedures now that work a lot better."

"Lord knows the surgery residents are always on the prowl for new cases when they rotate through," Sukie said. "So it's odd that no one's done anything about Ivy."

Livvy said, "I'm parked in the fire lane, so I better be off. I'll see you when you get home, hon." She swept back a strand of dark hair that had slipped from her ponytail. "And you can leave the stink here if you don't mind."

"Yeah, see you in a little bit," Chase said without turning around from the Dutch door. He continued to watch Ivy in the Day Room, banging away.

"What should I tell Claudia about Saturday night? She's called twice already."

"Okay," he sighed. "Tell her we'll come for a while... but that I need to leave early to study. Then, maybe we'll go to the other party, or maybe I *will* study."

Livvy must have left through the exit door in the nurses' station as Chase heard her tires crunching the gravel in the fire lane.

"You know, Sukie, I want to try something. I'm going to teach Ivy to play a song on the piano. Or at least I'm gonna try."

Sukie looked up from her charting and spoke after some hesitation. "Chase, you shouldn't let your bride leave a room without giving her a kiss. And if it's too embarrassing in front of me, then you blow her a kiss with your eyes."

Chase nodded without turning to look at Sukie, a bit surprised at her concern, then he entered the Day Room. Ivy seemed to sense his presence. She stopped clobbering the keyboard, then turned and smiled. In her oversized purple dress decorated in tiny yellow daisies, she looked like a little girl playing grown-up, and her cheerful wrinkles didn't spoil the illusion.

Ivy scooted to one end of the bench and patted the seat beside her to demonstrate where she wanted Chase to sit. He figured, perhaps, by using her thumbs alone, she could learn "Chopsticks." So, he sat down and began playing and singing his childhood opus, the song that Jewell Pollard had deemed (age-adjusted) creative genius–"The Only Lonely Panda in a Tree at Waikiki."

Ivy rejoiced in the tune, laughing hysterically, hebephrenically. She seemed to understand the lyrics Chase had written for "Chopsticks."

Zanda the panda
Alone in a land-a
Where bears do not live
But a storm... blew him out to sea

In a palm tree
He did land
Don't you see
Forever alone at the top

He cried, boo-hoo, boo-hoo. He wanted bamboo, he only boo-hoo'd
Boo-hoo, bamboo, boo-hoo, I want to go home. I want to go
home...

She gleefully rocked her head from side to side, waiting until Chase finished the song. Then she sang her own version while Chase played, translating Chase's lyrics to her own:

Ladoti solati
Me soti falati
Solaso Dolati
Doti! Fa-la-la-la...

After he had played through "Chopsticks" a few times with Ivy singing her version, he leaned over and held her hands in his, sliding down to her thumbs and placing each in the "Chopsticks" position. Under his direction, holding her thumbs as if working a marionette, Ivy played a recognizable tune, perhaps for the first time in her life. And with it, came her version of the lyrics, over and over.

Dr. Meeker, Chief Shrink at the nearby med school, had warned the students that the most foreign feeling they would have to overcome, especially during their third year of clinical rotations, was the handling and manipulation of other people's bodies. As he held Ivy's hands in his, they did not feel foreign at all. In fact, there was a strange kinship. Her hands were remarkably warm, oddly enchanting, nothing like the goosebumps and tingling he'd experienced on the dance floor, the night of the Dirty Dog.

He flipped through the file of photographs in his brain, pinned in place after reviewing a surgical text on Z-plasty repairs of syndactyly. He then began tracing the Zs on her hands, trying to outline how a plastic surgeon might give her fingers their freedom.

Ivy thought it was a game, muttered a few strange syllables, then laughed and began dragging her fingers over the skin of Chase's hands. She quickly zeroed in on his wedding ring, turning to him with an amused expression that he ignored. He was still deep in thought, wondering if he should try to arrange the completion of Ivy's surgery. Or, at least, provide her with another trip to the Surgery Clinic.

He had scrutinized Ivy's mannerisms in the cafeteria, how she carried her tray and how she handled her silverware. She did remarkably well at mealtime. However, he had also watched her trying to turn pages of picture books at the patient library, and this was a fumbling concern, every bit as awkward as smashing the piano keys. Would there be any point in trying to arrange a repair? He recalled, a month earlier, seeing her come to the aid of a palsied inmate who had spilled ice on the cafeteria floor. Ivy scooped up the chunks, both hands working like shovels to clear the mess whereas the shaky "normal" hands of her fellow patient had failed. Was he tampering with nature? Conceivably, Ivy might *want* her fingers to stay exactly as they were.

In psychiatry, he would not be touching patients. Arm's length was the rule of the day. Yet, as he continued to hold Ivy's hands, he felt something more unique than anything he had seen on *Captain Newman, M.D.* Touching a stranger, a mentally deficient stranger, was something new. He'd forcibly slapped lock belts and wristlets onto agitated lunatics, of course. And he'd tossed his fair share of inmates into seclusion rooms. In gentler moments, he'd even steered a wanderer back onto the asphalt path while herding the inmates of Building 19 to the cafeteria. Yet to hold a stranger's malformed hands in a moment of kindness was unique, and the image came to him of Christ who had washed the filthy feet of the disciples.

"The dance tomorrow night has been cancelled," warbled a noise over the intercom speaker located directly above the twosome at the piano. It was a man's voice coming from the central office, transmitted hospital-wide, to all wards, all buildings. "I repeat. The dance for this week has been canceled. The record player has gone missing so there will be no more dances until it is located."

Ivy was staring into Chase's eyes when the announcement was made, and she slowly lifted her face to the voice, pulled her hands away from Chase, and pointed with her fused fingers at the cracked ceiling where beige paint was curling around the grille of the speaker. "God," she said, nodding her head at Chase as if to let him know who had just spoken. It was the only intelligible word he'd ever heard from Ivy, yet there was no way of knowing what it meant to her.

This prompted Chase to think about the frustrating binary notion of Paradise vs. Perdition, prompting debates among members of his grandfather's church regarding "the age of accountability for salvation," "those who had never heard of Christ," and other stumbling blocks that forced Catholics to adopt Purgatory (desperately grasping at *Maccabees* for justification, a reach outside the Protestant Bible, according to Zebulon).

As Chase considered Ivy and her eternal fate, he questioned how the rules of salvation could possibly apply to her, or to her millions of brain-altered, kindred spirits over the centuries. If mentally deficient humans had a free pass, as one hoped they should, then the likes of Walter were "in," while the good person devoid of the good news was "out." Was it a logical conclusion that it was better to spend life on earth in a lunatic asylum than to live outside in a world of temptation, risking an eternity bathing in brimstone?

As he rested one hand between them on the piano bench, his palm landed on the edge of her housedress, and he felt what seemed to be gravel in the large pocket of her daisy dress. Peeking inside the pocket, he saw a collection of tablets and capsules, perhaps 50 or so, forming a rocky bottom.

"Ivy, you've been squirreling away your meds again, haven't you?"

Ivy giggled, then she reached inside her pocket and fished out a handful of pills, dropping the many colors into Chase's palm as if she were sharing her candy. Since patients were off their anti-psychotic meds for now, the pills and tablets were mostly for pain or sleep, prescribed routinely for nearly all inmates, needed or not.

"Soti medo," she said with a wide smile.

Chase patted her on the shoulder, awkwardly. "Here, I'm gonna take these pills back to the nurse. And I'm sorry about the dance, Ivy. I know how much you like the Hokey Pokey."

"Mesola redoti."

Later, when Chase turned the stashed meds over to Sukie at the nurses' station, he barely noticed Supervisor Dixie Barnes sitting in the corner, her nose buried in a hospital chart.

14

The freshmen year ended with both good and bad punctuation. The final histology exam had included a practical–an interpretation of 20 microscope slides of normal tissue for which the students were asked to identify the source organ. That said, it was the five bonus slides that threw the students into an uproar.

Tissue sections on glass slides, being two-dimensional extractions from three-dimensional organs, are created through traditional cutting angles. The knife that samples skin, for instance, does so in a perpendicular direction, and the same goes for the GI tract, bronchi, and all tubular structures. Expected patterns allegedly allow rote memorization and perceptual regurgitation for students. However, these five bonus slides had been nothing short of academic trickery–cutting the sections at 90-degree angles to tradition, such that the tissue source became exceedingly difficult to identify. Furthermore, there was no multiple choice. Students were asked to write the name of the organ in longhand.

Dermal papillae floating in squamous epithelium was easy to recognize as originating from skin. Paneth cells were much more subtle, yet those students with a clever eye called the small intestine origin correctly. However, the most brutal cut of the five unknowns was through the medulla of the kidney where tubules were seen, for the first time, in perfect cross section as opposed to the longitudinal orientation in the teaching set. Rather than pipelines aligned as if by a magnetic field, the slide showed a sea of random glands, or tubules. Only 12 students correctly identified the medulla of the kidney as being the source ("kidney" without "medulla" was given half-credit). In the end, only one student identified all five bonus slides correctly–Chase Callaway.

For Chase, it was the simple recognition that everything they had studied all year under the microscope had been two-dimensional representations of three-dimensional structures. Even though his eyes had been looking at two dimensions, his brain saw all three.

A group of protesting students stormed the office of the course director with a petition calling the slides unfair, demanding they be dropped from final grade calculations. Chase had gently declined to sign the petition, prompting this response from the organizers: "You selfish sonuvabitch. We can't believe you're not with us on this."

He had never been the object of group wrath before, and he couldn't understand why–if he'd done nothing wrong–his refusal to join the protest had caused such a horrid feeling inside, an emotion so nebulous he couldn't put a name on it.

As counterbalance to the politics of disgruntlement, the end of the first year held a happy note as well. The faculty spoof skits, at a celebration called Gridiron, had been a major challenge for freshmen thespians over the years. Usually, the MS-1 skit was booed by the upper classes until it had to be stopped. However, C.C. Chastain wrote a rock opera, lyrics by Chase Callaway, then they used the new videotape studio at the medical school to film the opera instead of the traditional live skit format. C.C. Chastain's filmed masterpiece was called the "greatest skit in the history of Gridiron," and C.C. had been hoisted to the stage for a sustained, standing ovation.

Chase reflected on that moment (even years later), and how it brought more joy than anything in medical school so far, including his own lofty class rank, even though his role in Gridiron was primarily to bask in C.C.'s glory. Still, he had to acknowledge in himself a greater passion for arts than science.

The twinkling of that night was now one month removed, but he held it close to his heart, and it offered a place to travel mentally. Indeed, he was traveling through the lyrics of the Gridiron opera now as he sat with Ivy Pettibone in the hallway of the Surgery Clinic at the loony bin, with patients and their escorting aides lining both sides of the bleak corridor, waiting.

Ivy was babbling her special words while Chase scanned the opposite row of inmates as they rocked back and forth in their chairs, sometimes swarmed by their own tics, hands exploring forlorn faces, pulling at hair, plucking at skin, others cackling, while still others, like Ivy, babbled. All-knowing winks passed between the aides. "Makes you feel normal, doesn't it," said the communicating eyes.

Whispering rumors came in waves, flooding the hallway, that the surgeons were late to clinic due to an emergency–that they were waiting on X-rays on Elsie Steiner from Building 7 who was on her way to the operating room again because Elsie had swallowed another fork. Others said it was a table knife.

Then, emerging from the steps that led to the operating suite upstairs, three young men in short white coats marched down the hall toward them, one in front, two behind. Chase was surprised that he recognized the leader, Thad Thompson, who had been a basketball star at Far West Texas when Chase was in junior high. He had been one of Chase's heroes. Thad's two henchmen also looked like jocks, but perhaps it was their swagger.

Dr. Thad Thompson announced to the crowded hallway, "Okay, folks, we gotta move fast with clinic. We're going to the O.R. as soon as anesthesia gets here from over at the med school. We'll be working three clinic rooms for the next thirty minutes, so you aides, listen for the names of your patients. If you don't move when your patient's name is called, you're off the list."

Chase was pleased that, after a brief wait, the name Ivy Pettibone was called by Dr. Thompson.

"This is Ivy," said Chase, easing into a corner of the exam room. "She's has syndactyly, incompletely corrected. Thumbs only so far."

"That's a pretty big word there, buddy. Syndactyly."

As Thad took Ivy's hands in his own, Chase continued, "I'm an MS-1. Well, actually, I'll be an MS-2 in the fall, that is. And I remember you from your basketball years. I played at Far West, too, but I was at the other end of the bench."

Attention turned from Ivy to Chase. Thad stuck out a hand to shake. "MS-2, huh? Picking up some extra coin?"

"Well, yes. Plus, I've been thinking about going into psych."

"Psych? You gotta be kidding. Hell, you can't go into psych, partner. You're speaking the King's English. You gotta speak Hindu or something like that to go into psych."

Chase laughed nervously, not at all tempted to explain the distinction between Hindu and Hindi. "All the more reason we need good people in psych," he managed.

"I guess. Really, though, you oughta hold off 'til you rotate through everything your third year. Don't let anyone push you to a specialty early on." Turning his frat-boy face back to Ivy, Dr. Thompson said, "And what about you, sweet lady, what can we do with these pretty little hands?"

Ivy smiled and babbled her usual.

"Well, that's very interesting. I'm glad you told me about that," replied Dr. Thompson, feigning comprehension without mocking.

Chase watched every move of the surgeon as he navigated Ivy's hands, asking her to squeeze and open, squeeze and open, and questioning whether or not she understood him. "So, Miss Ivy, if we could get your fingers to look like everyone else, would you like that?" Ivy nodded "yes." Up to that point, Chase hadn't determined if Ivy even considered herself different, or if she had an opinion about her own melded fingers.

Dr. Thompson turned to Chase. "Problem is… first we gotta get court-ordered permission since she has no legal guardians according to her chart. Then, the surgery has to be done by Plastics. Ortho will lay claim, but you'll never get them to show up here except for emergencies. And, as you may or may not know, the beauty surgeons tend to fill their schedules with cosmetic procedures at College Hospital. They only hold clinic here once every three months. But your time wasn't wasted, buddy. A referral to Plastics has to come through us in general surgery, so I'll fill out the requisition, and we'll see if we can't get these hands fixed. How's that sound, Miss Ivy?"

Chase was impressed by Dr. Thompson's confidence, his smoothness, his polished concern, be it genuine or not. After a lifetime of delay for Ivy, Chase had expected the process to be much harder.

"What did you say your name was again?" asked Dr. Thompson. "You look familiar, but I don't remember you from the old basketball days."

"Chase. Chase Callaway."

"Callaway?" The surgeon looked up from the chart. "You Wes Callaway's son?"

"Yes."

"Well, hell, why didn't you say so? Listen, after you take Miss Ivy back to her ward, why don't you come on back and watch some real medicine? None of that psych stuff. We've got a good case lined up. Strangulated obstruction, I think. She's got SBO at a minimum, but her white count's so high, the bowel might have infarcted. We'll be cutting skin in about fifteen or twenty. Are you game?"

Chase didn't understand the lingo, but he got the gist, and he was game if he could be excused from work. Sukie was leaving early this afternoon, so he'd have to clear it pronto. "Yeah, that'd be great. If I can get free, I'll be there."

"Well, if it works out for you, come back to this spot, then head up those stairs at the end of the hall, go to the third floor, and tell the nurses who you are. They'll direct you from there."

. . .

"Give the kid a stepping stool so he can see men at work, Jerri Ruth," ordered Dr. Thompson. "Chase, stand up there and look over our shoulders. And don't touch anything, or else you'll contaminate the field. Can you see?"

"Yes, sir."

"You don't have to call me 'sir'. Hey, do you guys realize we've got a celebrity in the room? Our observer today is Wes Callaway's son, the only retired jersey in the history of Far West. His dad, that is. Chase is a med student, MS-2."

Chase felt uncomfortable when the other two masked surgeons turned around and stared at him with expressionless eyes from the window of skin between their green masks and green caps. Both nodded silently and turned back to their work. Chase leaned toward the operating field and saw writhing intestines in the middle of the green square defined by the drapes.

"Do you see the point of obstruction?" one of them asked. "Not yet," another surgeon replied. Chase could not tell which of the three surgeons was talking. Detached voices simply hovered above the patient. Dr. Thad Thomson ran the length of the intestines through his hands like a limp garden hose.

"If you don't mind my asking," Chase said, "are any of you guys in private practice, or what?"

Laughter filled the room, and Chase felt his face flush.

"Hardly, buddy. I'm top dog here," Dr. Thompson said, "even though I'm still a resident. Chief Resident. Rick is a third-year resident, and Larry here is our 'tern. The med school covers all the surgery done here at the asylum, but you'll never see the faculty on this side of the creek. Only the residents. Of course, we like it that way."

"Hell, you'll never see the faculty anywhere," said one of them, followed by laughter.

"Nope. We're on our own over here."

Chase couldn't believe it. These guys were only several years ahead of him, and they were cutting on people, by themselves!

"Here it is!" cried Dr. Thompson. "Look, Chase, can you see it?"

"What is it?"

"The point of obstruction. She's got a single fiddle string adhesion in here, a band of scar tissue that formed after her last surgery when we removed some silverware from her stomach."

Dr. Thompson had the intern hold the guts out of the way, then he pulled up on the abdominal wall, looping his index finger around a thin string of glistening white tissue. "This little baby is causing all the trouble. Watch this." He took some scissors, and with one snip, the band popped.

"We're done."

Chase couldn't believe it. Done? One snip of the scissors? In one snip, the patient was cured? In one snip, the patient's life was saved?

"Do you think that loop of bowel is still alive?" asked Rick, the third-year resident.

"Absolutely," replied Dr. Thompson, with complete confidence. He laid the loop out on the green drape for all to see. "This is the area of bowel, Chase, that wrapped itself around the fiddle string. If it were purple, and no peristalsis, we'd resect her in a New York minute. But it's pinking up real nice now and it's got good contractions. We're done, cowboys."

The intern fidgeted a bit before he spoke up. "It's still lookin' kinda purplish to me, Thad. And I'm remembering her white count was 30,000 pre-op."

"Larry, that's why they call me 'Chief' and why they call you a 'tern."

Chase was mesmerized at the certitude of Dr. Thad Thompson. While the surgeons sutured the abdomen closed, Chase was consumed by one question for himself–could a person go from fainting when having to draw blood, all the way to cutting people open and making brilliant pronouncements like Thad Thompson had just done? Although Chase had collapsed with his first blood stick, something different had transpired today. He didn't get faint at all. And, he enjoyed the surgery. The green drapes had covered the patient, so it didn't seem like they were cutting on a real human being. Of course, general anesthesia made things vastly more palatable. This lack of pain infliction seemed to make all the difference in the world. Chase was surprised by his own blasé response to the cutting and sewing, and by his own comfort in the operating room.

Later, in the recovery room, he looked at the patient, Elsie Steiner, whom he recognized from the cafeteria lines. At her best, she was haggard and gray, but now with tubes coming out her nose, her bladder, and the IV lines, plus her surgical bonnet, she looked like death. Yet, these gritty surgeons had swept in and fixed her with one tiny snip of the scissors.

Chase began thumbing through her surgical chart, realizing very quickly that he didn't understand the jargon or the abbreviations. In fact, it was unreadable.

"Here, hon, if you're gonna stay here all day and read, why don't you sit your sweet bohunkus on this." Nurse Jerri Ruth pushed a chair underneath him.

"Thanks."

In a jiffy, Chase gave up on the medical language in the chart and reached instead for Elsie's psychiatric chart that dealt with her long-term illness.

"So, you work on Nineteen, huh?" asked Jerri Ruth.

"Yeah. Thought I wanted to go into psychiatry."

"Oh, heavens. You wanna be one of those weirdo shrinks? You look too darn normal from where I'm a-sittin'." She was bustling about Elsie, checking and fiddling with tubes and things that had no meaning for Chase whatsoever.

"You know, five years ago," said Chase, "the number one student in the class at Far West went into psychiatry, and they haven't stopped talking about it yet at the med school. 'What a waste,' they all say. Well, he went to Harvard for his residency and is on faculty there now."

"Hon, smart and weird go hand in hand. Don't let that Harvard stuff fool you."

"I suppose."

In Elsie's psych chart, Chase discovered the woman had been admitted to Matherville State in 1952 with "organic brain syndrome" after a near-fatal drowning accident. It was sickening to learn that she had been a normal human at one time. A mental disorder was easier to accept if the person had been "born that way," or if genuine craziness had been creeping up on a person since childhood. But to be normal, then suddenly you're at this place for the rest of your life... ugh.

"You'll find these post-op crazies don't have much pain. That's one area where they're lucky, I guess. We rarely have to give the schizos anything for pain after major surgery. They'll be running around the next day. We give 'em sedatives so they don't rip out their stitches. Elsie here, she'll be on the surgery floor for a day or two, then we'll send her to the Dungeon for another week of recovery since they can restrain her down there, full time. Can't keep patients restrained full-time on the regular wards. Then, tubes out and stitches out, she'll be good as new after that. Back to the Quadrangle where she'll be free to swallow some more flatware."

Chase knew the Dungeon was the basement ward of the Tower, although he'd seen its insides only once during orientation week. The round Tower, the Windsor Castle copy-cat, was female maximum-security on the first floor, male maximum-security on the second, and criminally insane on the third. At the basement level, however, Hell's preview of coming attractions, the so-called "Dungeon" held vegetative and combative patients so far gone that the rule of thumb was 4-point restraints, 24 hours a day, all patients, all the time.

Chase closed Elsie's chart and looked at her again in a different light. He'd learned that she had three children who visited her regularly, eight grandchildren, and that she'd worked in her youth doing radio commercials in Chicago. Later, she'd been a writer for *Vogue*, before marrying a wealthy west Texan. Then, while on a cruise in the Mediterranean, she had fallen into the sea while making the transfer to a lifeboat tender, hitting her head against the boat on the way down, deprived of oxygen for seven minutes. Now, she was a lifer, a "custodial." And the psychiatrists had nothing to offer her. Nothing, after twenty years.

Yet, the surgeons–in one second–one snip of the scissors...

.   .   .

Five days post-operatively, Elsie Steiner died in the Dungeon, an undistinguished human shell, securely strapped by all fours to her bed rails. The aides on duty denied any change in her status ("She was writhing about, moaning and crying, but exactly like every other patient in the Dungeon, for gosh sakes."). No autopsy was requested, a senseless act that would have likely revealed intra-abdominal sepsis due to dead bowel–dead bowel that had been pronounced as "absolutely" alive by Chief Resident Thad Thompson while the lowly intern questioned viability of the trapped loop of intestine. Easily correctable with prompt recognition, fatal without, Elsie's death came as solace to the family who had suffered greatly, perhaps more than Elsie, during the past twenty years.

The news of her death was lost in the buzzing hive of Matherville State, unbeknownst to all except the microcosm on Elsie's original ward where she was remembered by the aides as a kind spirit whose only oddities had been partial paralysis, a variety of jerking tics on her good side, muteness, and a peculiar taste for forks, knives and spoons.

The news of Elsie's death never made it to Chase Callaway who was eager to meet with his grandfather to discuss the turbulence in his own soul as he struggled to redefine his career path. From the inspiring victory he'd witnessed through the operation on Elsie, Chase Callaway was in the middle of an about-face.

15

As a bibliophile, Zebulon Callaway divided his collection into three parts, each section devoted to a different discipline. On the east wall, theology–concordances, Bibles (archaic and modern), study guides, and core treatments of "other" religions. On the north was science–medical and pharmacology texts, monographs on various scientific topics, plus biographies of the great men in all such fields. On the west–a smorgasbord of novels. The remaining south wall was windowed floor to ceiling, each panel dissected into small diamonds of glass, hinting at opulence beyond expectations for a country preacher.

Family lore put forth that the south wall of windows was shattered and ripped away from the house by the Great Cyclone of '37, leaving the three walls intact. Indeed, the winds had wrenched open Zebulon's home and his heart, even though his books were untouched. Chase only knew his grandfather as a minister, while the notion of a "prior life" was completely foreign.

Grandpa Zeb sat at his ball-and-claw writing desk, his back against the east wall where the bloated shelves loomed over him. From Chase's vantage on the other side of the desk, it seemed as if the volumes, overstuffed, might belch theology at any moment.

At 81 years, Zebulon was still an imposing figure, having lost little in height, perhaps gaining in mass. Although Chase had seen pictures of him with a full head of salt-and-pepper hair, only white tufts remained, sprouting above each large ear. His crisp and eager eyes, close set and surrounded by darkened skin, transmitted the vibrancy of a young man still. Chase could remember, years ago, his mother commenting that Zebulon had an "Mediterranean" look, and somehow this comment centered on Grandpa Zeb's nose and eyes, but Chase never understood exactly what she meant.

Though officially retired as founder and pastor of the Church of the Driven Nail, Zebulon was still the figurehead of a flock of five hundred. Successors had been hard to find, and Zebulon, reluctantly, resumed the throne each time the pulpit was abandoned by the replacement, three times and counting. Parishioners urged Brother Zeb to stay to the end (his own), since his mind was as sharp as ever. Yet, when Chase last attended the church, over a year ago, his grandfather seemed to have lost some zeal. He spoke in a muted tone, more honest and convincing than Chase remembered, as if he had been empowered by second thoughts that were more pleasing than the first.

Second thoughts of a secular nature drove Chase now. He struggled to explain his dilemma.

"It all happened when I escorted a patient to the surgery clinic and the surgeons invited me to scrub in on their next case. The next thing I know, I'm watching these guys, not much older than me, do the most amazing things. They opened this woman up, cured her with one snip of the scissors, and closed her up again as good as new. And there's the catch, for me at least. She wasn't *really* as good as new. She was as bad as ever. She was the same old hopeless case of organic brain syndrome that she'd been for twenty years. No one could do anything for her. Seems to me that surgery is a heckuvalot more fun... getting to watch instant success."

Grandpa Zeb didn't budge, except for scratching a two-day growth on his chin. "Your father found out it wasn't nearly as much fun as he thought it'd be."

"I wouldn't know about that, Grandpa. He never talks about it."

"He's simply not much of a talker. Never was. He chose surgery because he knew he had good hands. Told me once he'd watched all the guys above him on the totem pole, and he could operate circles around them. Being so cocksure drew him to quit surgical residency early. In the end, he paid dearly for not finishing."

Chase had heard bits and pieces of the story, but his father was not one to dwell on the past, nor did he like to scrutinize the present. Chase asked, "What happened with his quitting surgery, anyway? I never understood."

"Quitting residency or quitting surgery later on?"

"Both... I guess."

Zebulon paused for a moment, lifting gold-rimmed glasses from his long nose, then he eased the rims back to the same spot. "The residency answer is easy. Your father had mouths to feed–yours and your sister's. And your sister's medical bills were crippling. Your dad only made fifty dollars a month as an intern. Even as a resident, it wasn't enough to live on back then, especially if you've got a little girl with cystic fibrosis. Anyway, board certification was no big deal in those days, so as soon as he felt comfortable doing the procedures a general surgeon does–I believe he had only eighteen months left to go–he quit and set up shop at Permian Medical Center. Well, the other docs there were a might jealous, your dad being the biggest name in Matherville, what with his basketball days and all. Within months, he was the busiest surgeon around. Made those board-certified boys pretty angry."

Chase interrupted, "You're talking about grown men. Wasn't there plenty of work to go around?"

"Sure, but that's not the point. First of all, don't confuse grown men with adult behavior. I believe you'll find more childish jealousy in medicine than anywhere. Or maybe it's magnified since folks don't expect it. Anyway, you wouldn't recall, but back in my days as a pharmacist, they used to call me Doc Callaway. The real docs in town nearly hung me from the nearest tree for overstepping the boundaries. And, like had happened to me, your father prompted envy way out of proportion to the actual threat. I suspect he was doing a better job than any of 'em, by the way. An absolute perfectionist, he was."

"Still is."

"Yes... still is. Anyway, the pressure for surgeons to get their boards got greater every year. At one point, he applied to the American Board of Surgery to take the test based on the operations he'd done in private practice, but they answered that he had to complete a formal Chief year. He couldn't go back, what with Annie's condition and all. The Board wouldn't even let him try the written exam. Well, a short while after Annie died came the malpractice suit, and that was the straw that broke the camel's back, as they say."

"One malpractice suit shouldn't cause someone to hang it up, should it? Especially, someone like dad. I don't mean this disrespectfully, but he's not one to be bothered by psychological complexes. The world's a pretty simple place to him."

Zeb laughed under his breath, then said, "True, very true. I nearly fell out of my chair once when your dad, a real live medical doctor, told me that one of my parishioner's sons had probably turned homosexual because of teen-age pimples that chased the girls away. Why, I was embarrassed to call the man my own flesh and blood, saying something that silly."

Zebulon's smile prompted Chase to do the same and soon they were both chuckling. It felt good. Grandpa Zeb was the only person on earth who could poke fun at the great Wesley Callaway.

Grandpa Zeb continued, "But you're right. One malpractice suit usually won't break a doctor's back, although it does happen, for sure. No, the reason your dad's back was broken, you see, is because he believed that the lawsuit was a deliberate set-up."

"A set up?" Chase was floored. "I've never heard anything of the sort."

"Remember, don't let on that I told you anything. Nothing could ever be proven. Recall what I said about childish jealousy? Well, one surgeon who'd been the top man before Wes went into practice, a guy plenty rich already, couldn't stand to see Wes's name on the O.R. schedule board with the biggest number of cases every morning. So, one day, *allegedly* I'm telling you, this guy who will remain nameless happened to be in the pathology lab when your dad was in the O.R. Your dad sends down two frozen sections on a woman, a breast biopsy from each side.

"Turns out, one side was cancer and one side wasn't. The pathologist asked this surgeon I'm talking about if he'd mind calling on the intercom to Wes in the operating room. According to Wes's summation of the events, the guy flip-flopped the reports on purpose, so your dad does a radical mastectomy on the normal side, leaving the cancer in place on the other. Next day, imagine how your dad felt when the report came back, opposite what he'd been told. Had to take the patient back to the operating room and remove the other breast. The woman was only thirty-five, and the lawyers brought in national experts at the trial who swore that it's mandatory for surgeons to remove the cancerous breast during the same surgery as the biopsy, or else the cancer will spread. In short order, they made your dad look like a murderer. The patient, by the way, is still living last I heard, but sometimes I think your father died the day he lost in that trial."

Chase saw his father in a new light, one where Wes actually *felt* something. "But why was *he* the one found guilty? He was merely operating based on what he'd been told."

"Ah, there's the catch. The character who called him on the intercom denied reversing the sides, and no one in the operating room could remember. They could only recall your dad in the O.R. saying, "Okay, let's go ahead with the mastectomy on the left.""

"That's awful."

"Of course, your dad couldn't prove a thing. It was his word against the other surgeon who'd been the messenger for the pathologist. And, I can't say for sure myself what might've happened. I don't recall your dad *ever* making mistakes like that, however. Wasn't like him. Of course, he was subject to the 'captain of the ship' standard."

"The what?"

"Ooo-boy. You better learn that one. Captain of the ship. It means that no matter what happens in the operating room, the surgeon is responsible. Anesthesia screw-up, or the nurse doesn't count sponges right, or your bumbling assistant cuts a major artery by accident, it doesn't matter. The surgeon's goose is cooked."

Chase felt something stir in the pit of his stomach. "That doesn't seem fair."

"Fair isn't part of the equation, Chase. The others might be sued as well, but the captain is always sued. Yeah, after your dad's lawsuit, especially reading his own headlines in the Matherville newspaper every day during the trial, ugly as they were, after all those years as a hero, then all those years in service to the community… well, it just about killed his spirit. Crushed him. His heart hasn't been in his work since. For sure, he didn't ever want to cross paths with the saboteur surgeon again. Better to stay away from the operating rooms. He retreated into his comfortable little office practice, staying away from the hospital, treating sore throats and the like."

"I never knew." Chase put his hands on his knees and pushed himself upright in his chair.

Grandpa Zeb folded his arms across his chest and cleared his throat. "So, you asked for my advice? I'd be cautious in your choices. The most important thing is to maintain balance. Cling to your spiritual life first, then family, then profession. You've never really balanced your life, Chase. Body, mind, and spirit. For you, each has taken its turn, one at a time, but they need to mesh."

"What do you mean?"

"I mean, it was your body first, what with your basketball. Then, it was all spiritual when you were with the New Bloods. And now, with the demands of med school, it's all about your mind. I'll tell you something now that might seem meaningless, but think of it, will you, years from now? Don't confuse knowledge with wisdom. Wisdom comes with equanimity. It comes with meshing body, mind, and spirit. Wisdom reveals that one has *less* knowledge, not more. Here, let me give you a book to read."

Grandpa Zeb walked to the scientific wall of his library and pulled out a volume called *Aequanimitas*, then he handed it to his grandson. Chase leafed through the pages while his grandfather continued.

"Sir William Osler was the most famous physician of all time, and he wrote this book way back in 1904. Human nature hasn't changed one bit, however. One of the first essentials in achieving equanimity is not to expect too much of people with whom you work. That's the part your father forgot. He expected all his colleagues to be worthy gentlemen. He didn't count on scoundrels. Of course, I never gave this book to him. Whatever I said or did, he generally did the opposite. Chase, you read this book, now, I'm telling you."

"Of course, grandpa, you know I like stuff like this. In college, I studied philosophy for fun. That's why I don't really agree with you about my lack of balance. I read non-medical stuff, plus I'm polishing up my French, I still garden, I still write lyrics on the side... "

"And how much time do you devote totally and absolutely to what Olivia wants? What do you do to support her dreams?"

Chase was silent. *Her dreams?* Creeping conviction made him realize that he hadn't truly considered Livvy to have dreams of her own. Having kids, eventually, sure. That was about it. His dreams were big enough for both of them, and Livvy had pledged her full support.

"Balance, Chase, balance."

Chase tucked the book at his side, navigating his eyes around the room as he spoke, "Okay. Balance."

"Just so you'll know, Chase, when I die–but understand, I'm as healthy as a horse–I want you to have all these books. Three walls. Three walls balanced."

"Don't talk like that, grandpa. You aren't going to die. Not anytime soon. Besides, I bet you haven't read all those novels, have you? How could you, after all, if you've read the Bible four times cover to cover?"

"Don't bet on it, Chase. I'm getting through 'em all, I am. Turns out most of these great novelists, many of them agnostics by the way, were quite taken by the Lord. Sometimes I think they knew the way of the Lord more than some of these Christian authors. Lots of truth in the classic novels. Lots of wisdom."

"And your favorite?"

"Dostoevsky, I suppose. *The Brothers Karamazov.* I'd venture to say that, in one book, old Fyodor quite rightly boiled all the books on these three walls into a single tome."

"I've read a few of these already," boasted Chase as he stood up to get closer to the west wall. "Steinbeck's really good, and Faulkner. Dickens, of course. And Tolstoy. I see you've got Kafka here. I read *The Metamorphosis* in college. Weird. I even read some of these Greek plays in high school. And here's Thomas Hardy." He pulled out the book by Hardy and began flipping its pages.

"Yes, Hardy planned to become an Anglican minister at one point, but Darwinism hit the scene and turned him into an agnostic. His ashes are buried at Westminster Abbey, but his heart was taken back to be buried near his home. I'm talking about his real heart, literally, not a metaphor."

"Losing faith because of Darwin and evolution? That's ridiculous. I'll bet there's more to it than that." As Chase spoke those words, his eyes photographed a phrase from Hardy on one of the pages. This out-of-context snapshot of words struck him as odd, forming a perfectly clear picture in his brain as if he were looking at a histologic section of kidney under the microscope. He would ponder the image later.

Zebulon was still rambling. "Darwin himself started on the path to becoming clergy, that is, after he gave up on medicine. Watching surgery back in those pre-anesthesia days took a strong stomach, and it made Darwin sick. Anyway, I suspect it's better to have never believed in the Lord at all, than to have believed once, but turned away."

Chase thought about Zebulon's words for a moment, but could not decide if they were true. "Well, lots of books to read. I'll have a go at them someday. No time now."

"Well, they'll have more meaning for you later on anyway. Most folks prefer non-fiction because they want facts, facts, and more facts. Like I'm saying, though, facts are a far piece from wisdom. I'm not sure how factual non-fiction really is. On the other hand, I think some of the great novelists have seen the truth. And they know folks won't believe truth when it's presented as such. So, the great novelists hide the truths they've discovered under the guise of fiction. Odd, isn't it, that non-fiction might be twisted truth, while fiction is the real thing?"

Chase loved his grandfather, but the pontifications were getting worse with age. "Yeah, I guess so."

"Do you remember about Diogenes, Chase?"

"Of course. Always looking for an honest man. Used a lantern."

"Yes, but it's better to believe the myth than the man. He was a repugnant human being. Anyway, the myth says he held out his famous lantern *only* in the daylight. Does that strike you as odd?"

"Well, I didn't remember about the daylight. That doesn't make much sense."

"Oh, it does, really. Think about it. We consider evil as lurking in the darkness. We're on guard for it there. But when it's hidden in broad daylight, why, that's where we get tricked. That's where we need Diogenes' lantern. And that's what the novelists are telling us, the great ones, I mean, in the classics. They're writing in code, shining a lantern, of sorts, trying to see if there's anyone out there who might see the truth."

As Zebulon joined Chase at the west wall, his grandfather had drifted so far from the intent of Chase's visit that there was no return. Chase would have to bring up his quandary again next time. After all, he had another two years before he would have to decide on a specialty. It would be a critical decision for sure, every bit as permanent as marriage. He held tightly to his grandfather's gift, *Aequanimitas*, and waited for Zeb to wind down before leaving.

"Now consider this," continued the old man, now thoroughly pedantic. "Diogenes was the son of a banker, a minter of coins, and they both were charged with adultery. Of coins, that is. They adulterated the coins with base metals, a long way from honesty, eh? The father went to prison and Diogenes escaped to Athens where he became a lunatic by most standards. It wasn't beyond him to cough phlegm in another man's face, or to squat and empty his bowels before a public audience."

"Whoa, you're losing me now, Grandpa."

"Yet, read the words attributed to Diogenes sometime. Kernels of wisdom every time he spoke, a two-sided coin of course, depending on how you look at things. Very odd. Can such wisdom come from a madman? That's my question. Can wisdom come from a madman?"

As soon as he felt an opening for escape, Chase apologized for having to leave, then offered his hand for a good-bye shake. On the way out of his grandfather's house, Chase met Sukie Spurlock, on her way in.

"Why, fancy meeting you here," Chase said. "Nice of you to come visit Grandpa."

"Oh, yes, I drop by every now and then to see if he needs anything. You know, a little clean-up here, a good meal there, and lately, I've been helping him get the family papers in order."

"Family papers?"

"Genealogy and the like. You know how folks get when they grow old."

"Well, watch out. Grandpa's on a roll. I guess I got him started, but he's off on a big tangent now, all about Diogenes."

"Ooh, how that man can preach up a storm about most anything."

16

Turning points are usually defined in retrospect. Yet somehow, Chase knew that the sophomore lecture, "Introduction to Pathology," would eventually qualify as such, not to steer him toward pathology, but to lure him further toward its animated cousin–surgery.

Chase sat spellbound through the entire pathology lecture, forsaking the truancy option afforded by the Note Group. Indeed, he hung on every word.

The lecturer drew from history, pointing out that Vienna had been the wellspring of most everything medical. While Freud was still a medical student at the University of Vienna, a professor of surgery at that venerable institution, Theodor Billroth, constructed the model for surgical education that would eventually be adopted in the United States. Chase was intrigued to learn that there was no such thing as a distinct discipline of pathology back then–the surgeons *were* the pathologists. They did it all, from clinical diagnosis to treatment to final diagnosis under the microscope. When the co-mingled worlds of pathology and surgery became too much for one person to handle, pathology broke away as a splinter group. And like all fissuring groups in medicine that spawn new specialties, the child proclaims the parent incompetent. By the turn of the century, surgeons were deemed largely unfit for the microscope.

The lecturer went on to reveal that surgeon Theodore Billroth not only interpreted his own pathology slides, but also was an accomplished musician and close friend of Johannes Brahms. When Billroth died, he was co-authoring a book with Brahms on the physiology of music.

If this musical interlacing nudged Chase toward the precipice of a major decision, the final push came when the pathology lecturer stated, "Medical practitioners today are lost souls, searching only for named diseases with recognizable taxonomy. Indeed, they are treating mere words written on a report and, let me assure you, those words may or may not have anything to do with the patient's condition. *(Chase's classmates later condemned the professor as being a megalomaniac. "That's why weirdoes go into pathology in the first place.")* To understand cancer, you must know its face. Its face is not a word. Cancer is a living entity that can outwit and overcome its host. You cannot understand the enemy if you don't recognize its face. For many physicians treating cancer today, the disease is a total stranger. *(A committee of protesting students even wrote down their objections to the megalomaniac, requested censorship of the anti-clinician sentiment, and submitted their petition to the Dean's office.)* It's like contemplating travel to a foreign city. You can read and read and read the words all day long. You can even look at snapshots of various angles of the city. However, the photographer chooses those angles. That's not reality. Photographs do not tell the whole story of the city. You only get the true feel for the city by going there, and better yet, living there. When you return, the photographs have an entirely different meaning, for they are now in context. *(The Dean replied to the students that they were listening to an emeritus professor considered one of the premier pathologists in Texas, if not the entire country, and that they should concentrate on their studies.)* The scientists who find the cures, perhaps one or two among you, will realize it's necessary to travel through the barrel of the microscope, into the tissue, inside the cell, and wallow in its molecular structure, in order to make a difference! *(Two-term Note Group president, C.C. Chastain, announced afterward that the student assigned to transcribe this introductory lecture would be reassigned to another one, since "There's no need to waste time transcribing crap like this. They can't make up test questions on this sort of garbage, so don't sweat it.")*

With photographic memory–that is, a crystalline memory for images–Chase excelled in pathology, the dark side of histology, where tissues go bad. Accordingly, he was offered a three-month fellowship working in the pathology lab at Matherville's private hospital, Permian Medical Center, a job starting next June that would exhaust the final free summer of medical school.

During the school year, however, he continued as an aide at Matherville State, enjoying the promotion to Psychiatric Aide II, with its attendant responsibility of passing meds, and more importantly, with a generous pay increase to $3.50 an hour, almost twice minimum wage.

Chase, C.C., Will, and Amy continued their daily Hearts games in the Coke Room, and life was neither complicated nor particularly burdensome. As MS-1s, they had done nothing but study "normal," a mere extension of college. Yet, the "abnormal" was captivating for MS-2s. All was new. All was horrid. All was spectacular.

Like Chase, module-mate Will Glendenning had become enchanted with the universe revealed by the lenses of the microscope. In fact, he and his wife Claudia invited Chase and Olivia to spend a weekend in Lost Mine, Texas, at the Glendenning home where an adventure in microscopy lay in the basement. There, Will's father, long deceased, had once worked as a would-be pathologist, thriving in his private laboratory, testing various dyes borrowed from nature to stain slices of tissue mounted on thin glass rectangles, allowing contrasting illuminations under the microscope. For his real job, Dr. Glendenning had been a general practitioner.

And, while Livvy and Claudia visited the town's only tourist attraction (the abandoned silver mines and a one-room museum), Will and Chase poured through the relics in the Glendenning basement laboratory as Will recounted the history of science in Lost Mine as it had transpired there in darkness.

Dr. Glenndenning's research had targeted a type of free rover cell, branded as the "mast cell," part of the immune system. The intrigue lay in its beauty under the microscope. Mast cells were huge, and each one looked like a gumball machine with tiny colorful spheres in the cytoplasm, the zone outside the nucleus. Since most of the important cellular machinery was thought to reside *inside* the nucleus, home to DNA, it was odd that the cytoplasm would be so jam-packed with these tiny water balloons that were allegedly filled with heparin and histamine, at least according to the correct answer on the MS-1 histology exam last year.

Will explained: "My dad would not have answered that question correctly, as the standard answer was wrong, or more accurately, only a small part of the story of the mast cell. He used to say, 'what is commonly thought is commonly wrong'. Even the experts are wrong. He said experts are nothing more than smart people stuck in mental ruts that lead them down a single path—toward grant funding."

That night, as they brought their bedcovers to their chins, Livvy was both curious and restless. "So, Will's dad was a total fanatic about those mast cells?" she asked, hoping to label the obsession as misguided and to steer Chase toward some sightseeing in the Big Bend area.

Chase replied, "Yeah, but it's amazing what he was able to do in his own lab. He tried out different stains to understand what mast cells really do. The way those colors attach to different parts of a cell tells you a lot about function."

"To be honest, Will's house kind of gives me the creeps," Livvy said. "It's like a giant mausoleum or something. And did you see all those books about death and dying in the library? And what about that stuffed bird his mother has in the cage? Her beloved pet, of all things."

"Shhh. I think the kitchen is right below us," Chase said. "But yes, you wouldn't believe some of the things in the lab. There was a human calvarium, you know, a skullcap, turned upside down for a bowl. Will told me his dad used it as a candy dish. His father would sit for hours looking into the microscope, reaching for the skullcap beside him, munching on candy corn, without ever looking up."

"This house is too spooky for me. Will's mother seems nice enough—stuffy, but nice."

"I wouldn't use the word 'stuffy' around this place. Eccentric, maybe."

"Chase, I'd hoped to see some more of the country, Big Bend for instance, while we're here—"

"I'm sure we'll have the chance to come back here with Will and Claudia again. Frankly, I think Will likes as many people around him as possible when he's near his mother. A dilutional effect, if you know what I mean. Keeps his mother off his back. Really, I need to head home in the morning and start studying. If I'm going into surgery, I need to ace every course."

"Surgery? When did you make that decision? And since when did you not ace a course?"

.   .   .

Chase continued working at Matherville State, mostly on weekends. Still at Building 19, he was constantly frustrated by the invisible brick walls that kept Ivy Pettibone's hands away from surgical repair. Ward nurse Sukie Spurlock relayed the same news over and over: "The plastic surgery residents said they didn't have time on their schedule, that Ivy should return to the clinic at a future date. Of course, it's a different set of residents on rotation the next time around, so we go through the same thing over and over. Too bad the general surgeons won't do it. They're here full time. Anyway, we'll try again next clinic. And, of course, we'll need a new court order for permission."

So, Ivy kept walking in her circle, or banging on the piano, able to hit many of the "Chopsticks" notes with her thumbs, singing the song Chase had taught her, in her own language. Whether or not she cared about the delays, no one knew.

Although not at Building 19 as often during the school year, Chase was still pleased to offer his input on patient behavior when the research trial was launched with Substance #558 in the winter of 1972. Many of the patients seemed calmer, and Chase tried to use his new medical vocabulary as he charted: "slightly obtunded" or "lethargic" or "seemed to have malaise today." His contribution to science was, in his own mind, valuable.

Ivy seemed immune to pharmacologic intervention, however. Perhaps she was in the placebo group, thought Chase. Then again, her behavior, other than the circles, was not particularly abnormal in the first place, so how could one tell? *What do these anti-psychotic meds do if there's no psychosis?*

The staff routinely checked open mouths of patients after distributing medicines to assure swallowing, but in fact, Ivy had learned to lodge her pills behind her super-sized salivary glands. After each open-mouth inspection, Ivy would slip away and, in secret places, stash her pills, be they routine sleepers or the study drugs. So, little wonder that Ivy was unaffected.

As the year wore on, Chase became more and more consumed by his studies, and he began forgetting plans that Livvy had made. His absent-mindedness spread to other commitments, culminating in the grievous act of forgetting his own mother's birthday. To patch this growing defect, he started using a personal calendar with important days circled in red, each event described inside the circle. Of course, April 4 was always circled, though blank within, denoting the hope born from the teasing epiphany of his childhood predicting "something big."

The role of the red circles expanded to serve as reminders of those tasks appropriate for a balanced life–visiting his grandfather once a month, dinner with Livvy's parents every two weeks (alternating her mother and father), inviting Sukie Spurlock to dinner the fourth Tuesday of each month, even personal tasks of equanimity, such as times to exercise, times to play foosball with his three closest friends, times to read non-medical books and magazines, times to meditate, read the Bible and reflect.

On a red circle dinner with Sukie, Chase mentioned, "I never really understood why you left our house, Sukie. Of course, no kids there anymore, but still, mother had lots for you to do. I know you're probably making more money now than what my folks used to pay— " Chase shut himself up. The more he talked, the more Sukie sounded like a hired hand. This was not the case. She was part of the family.

Sukie smiled at both Chase and Livvy, the three of them still seated at the modest dinner table, in repose after a starchy meal. It was almost as if she could read Chase's mind as to why he had silenced himself. "Well, children, I'd always wanted to be a nurse. And, of course, when your sister was alive, Chase, I *was* a nurse, without the degree, of course. Pounding that dear girl's back four hours every day to dislodge phlegm, making sure she took her medicines, and making sure her oxygen tank was all filled up, helping her in the bathroom, yes, I was a nurse, don't you know. After Annie passed, your mother and I would sit all day, it seems, talk or no talk. Ramona didn't do too well at first, but we had so much in common, your mother and I did. Not to look at us, of course. In Matherville, there's a big difference between skin colors. Both of us, though, having lost our little ones, well, it made us best friends, closer than many sisters, I suspect. Anyway, I needed to chase down that dream of mine. And, of course, your Grandpa Zeb pushed me pretty hard in that direction, too. He paid for my schooling, did you know? And supported me until I got that L.P.N."

"Grandpa Zeb paid for nursing school?" Chase blurted out with more force than he intended. "I mean... well, that's great."

Chase saw a change come over Sukie's face, her smooth caramel skin bunched up in pleats on her forehead, making her look a full fifty-five years old. "I think he wanted to help me because, well, he was mighty grateful for my taking care of your sister, and then, of course, support for your mother afterward."

"That's strange. I never knew." Chase considered for a moment that Sukie had more to tell, but if anyone on the planet was completely honest, it was Sukie. Of course, honesty and full disclosure were not identical concepts.

Sukie patted her lips with her napkin, and said, "You know, I love your family like it was my own. I don't know why my children had to pass when they were still so young. And I don't know why Annie had to have such a dreadful disease, and such a horrible death. But I do know the Lord has his reason for every single, solitary thing that happens in this world. And you remember that fact about faith, both of you, as you go on about your lives."

Chase wanted to explore the Grandpa Zeb connection further. Perhaps, the next red circle evening would tell him more about the Sukie he didn't know.

.   .   .

During the second semester, the MS-2s were thrilled, finally, to don white coats and carry black bags, pretending to be doctors for "Introduction to Clinical Medicine," a course where they would learn to perform histories and physicals.

In their first official foray into the jungle of the hospital wards, an internal medicine specialist, Dr. Daryl Crim, told Chase's group of six students that they would be visiting three patients with interesting findings on physical exam. The rest of their classmates, it turned out, were hooked up with interns and residents, so Chase took this to be some sort of sign. He and his group were with a *full professor*.

In the first patient's room, Chase was one of three students who could *not* feel the thyroid nodule said to be present in the young dark-haired woman. He was embarrassed at his failure. In the second room, he was one of two who could *not* hear the elderly man's heart murmur. He was flabbergasted. In the third room, he could *not* feel the obese gentleman's abdominal aortic aneurysm. He was the only one in the group with the inexplicable deficiency of not having appreciated *any* of the three physical findings.

Common knowledge among medical students held that the geniuses of the first two years often became the buffoons after hitting the wards the third year. The mighty fell hard. The first became last, and the last became first. Clinical skills were a different pot entirely than the basic sciences. Stories were plentiful about Numero Unos becoming Numero Zeroes when it came time for actual patient care. Chase felt his destiny gobbling him up in carnivorous delight.

When the fiasco was over, the professor told the shamed Chase Callaway to meet with Dr. Meeker, Chief of Psychiatry, that very afternoon. *Oh, no. Not only did I flunk physical diagnosis, they think I'm crazy, too! No, that's not it. I get it now. They already know I'm going to be worthless on the wards, so they're going to tell me I should reconsider psychiatry where I won't be able to hurt anyone.*

Usually histrionic, Dr. Meeker spoke calmly. "Have a seat, Mr. Callaway" was a sharp contrast to the entertainer that had scared the bejesus out of Livvy at the start of med school with his "Spousal Lecture."

"Thank you, by the way, for taking time to fill out that long questionnaire," said the psychiatrist. "This helps us with our research. Everyone in your class will eventually fill it out. You've probably heard about the new computer lab that the university has recently opened, and they're telling us that the computer will be able to pick up things missed by the human eye. We'll see, I suppose."

Chase exhaled an audible sigh and sat down across the desk from the shrink, relieved that he'd not been asked to lie on the nearby couch.

Dr. Meeker popped up from behind the desk and began pacing in front of his office windows. Rays of light intermittently blinded Chase as the psychiatrist eclipsed the setting sun each time he passed across the Venetian blinds. Then, Dr. Meeker lifted a small placard from his desktop and showed Chase the squiggly lines on one side. "What kind of flowers would you choose to place in the vase in this picture, Mr. Callaway?"

Omigosh, this nut is going to start Rorschaching me here on the spot. "Uh, I, well, I'm having trouble seeing the vase. No, I see it, but I also see the profiles of two women looking at each other."

Dr. Meeker seemed to smile, though Chase couldn't really tell for sure since the psychiatrist's lamb chop sideburns almost covered the corners of his mouth.

"Mr. Callaway, I'd like you to be part of a longitudinal study."

"What?" His mind raced to Ivy Pettibone squirreling away her study meds.

"Yes, you know of my fascination with the medical education process, I'm sure, from my lectures. Well, I'm interested in following a cohort of students long-term, based on a variety of parameters."

"Parameters? What parameters?"

"For starters, the image I just showed you. Your cognition allowed you to see two possibilities. That's very unusual when pre-conditioned to see only one. Left to their own devices, people will see either a vase or two women talking. However, if I tell you in advance what you're going to see–well–99% will perceive only that image. You're in the one percent that could still see two options."

"O-kayyy. I'm confused. I thought I was being sent here because I couldn't appreciate any of the physical findings today on rounds—"

"Quite the contrary," Dr. Meeker said as he leaned across his desk and waggled his finger near Chase's nose. "You were sent here because you *could* appreciate the findings."

"But—"

"You *could* admit you didn't detect the abnormalities. You *could* be honest with yourself and your colleagues. A serious deficiency in the world of medicine is the inability to say, 'I don't know' and the variations thereof. Not so much to patients and families where the need for confidence may supervene, but to oneself. Mr. Callaway, my research focuses on *self-deception* in the medical education process–how it is learned, why it is learned, how much of it is brought to the table before starting medical school, and why others are highly resistant to self-deception. I'm especially interested in that last question, why some students refuse to deceive themselves, and that's where you come in. I'd like to know if we can identify, early in the process, those students who are seemingly immune to self-deception."

"I'm having a little trouble following you, to be honest." Chase squirmed in his chair as Dr. Meeker opened a side office door revealing a half-bath, whereupon the shrink unzipped his trousers and began urinating as he continued to speak.

"Let me shoot from a different angle," he continued, while Chase scanned the room for a hidden camera. "Medical students have long been tested on pure memory skills. Not true for cognition, especially as it relates to abstraction and generalization. I have a theory saying, in brief, that medical education tends to subvert cognitive skills, rather than enhance, through preconscious distortions of reality. Now it's easy to think of this as a defense mechanism. When we pull normal kids off the street and tell them that, in four years, they'll be doctors in charge of other people's lives, the pressure is so great that students go through a metamorphosis, or as I call it in the book that I'm working on, 'the transforming power of an assigned role.' This is fairly complex." Dr. Meeker shook free the remaining drops of urine and zipped up again, without missing a beat.

"The name of my book-in-progress is *The White Coat: Guard or Prisoner*, and it's based on the study out of Stanford where they built a mock prison and assigned volunteers to be guards or prisoners. Intended as a two-week experiment, it had to be cut short after six days because the role-playing guards had turned too sadistic and some of the prisoners were having emotional breakdowns. It's a fascinating study that could re-write how we think of assigned roles. And no role is more abruptly *assigned* than when we stick young men and women in white coats and start calling them doctor before they've even graduated from medical school. That's why I've been calling you "*Mister* Callaway," in case you didn't notice. Unwittingly, some medical schools are starting this ritual even before students start their first year, an institutionalized rite of passage when there's been no passage whatsoever at that point. And my principal concern is that this sort of premature assigned role is a deterrent to certain aspects of cognitive skills."

Dr. Meeker finished washing his hands, and then, seeing no towel, began to shake his hands furiously for a natural air-dry.

"From the writings of Osler and others, we've known for over a hundred years that when we professors turn you loose on the public, you don't know near what you should. So, we tell you to fake it. Not in those words, of course. We cloak it in the word "confidence," but we're really saying and teaching 'fake it'. Even during these first two years in medical school, where my colleagues have directed the role-playing sessions with actor patients, we're basically telling you how to fake empathy for your patients. The gestures we've taught, the facial expressions to use for superficial empathy, for deep empathy... we're teaching you to act."

Dr. Meeker paused to catch his breath, then turned to Chase and put his air-dried hands on his hips, as if waiting for a response.

"Well, sir, I don't feel personally that I'm faking—"

"And that's why you're here, Mr. Callaway. The first hint in identifying subjects for my research study comes from our small group sessions last year, where you were pegged as one of the students with natural empathy. Fine. No instruction needed. Quite a few of your classmates fit that bill. But today, you passed a much more rigorous test that now qualifies you for the longitudinal study."

"The vase and flowers?"

"Not exactly. One of the trends I've monitored is that students with natural empathy are also people-pleasers, so they're *more* likely to go along with whatever the professor is saying. With cognitive preconditioning, if the professor says there's a thyroid nodule, then the people-pleasing student feels it. It's exceedingly rare for a student to be a naturally empathetic people-pleaser, then turn around and make a tough stand, saying 'I don't know' or 'I don't appreciate it'. In other words, it's difficult to have thin skin *and* a strong spine."

"I'm not sure I understand."

Dr. Meeker shifted a few steps away from the window allowing another beam of light to hit Chase in the face, effectively blinding him. *Was that intentional?* Chase put one hand up to block the light, only to see Dr. Meeker in silhouette shaking a finger at him in rhythm with three quick sentences: "There was *no* thyroid nodule. *No* heart murmur. *No* aortic aneursym."

"What?"

Dr. Meeker continued, "Every student in your group today had been selected for their natural empathy from our sessions last year. Yet, you were the only one in your group who boldly stood up for what you felt— or *didn't* feel, I should say. Cognitive preconditioning is incredibly powerful. It's been studied in the lab to the hilt. Now we're taking it to the clinic. The pressure to feel and hear and diagnose is huge during medical education, especially when you've got a full professor telling you something's there.

"My pathology colleagues say it's true for them as well, that is, you can precondition people to see the exact opposite of what they're really looking at under the microscope. Mr. Callaway, just like our role-playing sessions last year, the patients you saw today were actors. They had *nothing* wrong with them. Many students admit they can't feel the thyroid nodule because the lumpy neck anatomy makes for a difficult background. Yet, how many can withstand the pressure of not appreciating *any* of the three findings? Not many, I'll tell you that. Dr. Crim and I have been publishing our work on this subject for the past several years. This is our fifteenth year to run the study."

"So, Dr. Crim was in on it?"

"Of course."

Chase was gushing with relief. He wasn't crazy after all. He wasn't going to be a bumbling fool on the wards.

Dr. Meeker locked his hands together behind his back. "Yes, the power of suggestion is incredible in medical education. After all, you're trying to fit into that white coat. To have the conviction to stand in front of your own peers and a distinguished professor, and admit you didn't... Well, all I can say is you are part of a most interesting group of study subjects, the very cohort forming the basis of my research."

Chase heard it all as a ringing endorsement of his personal integrity, his future abilities, and his upcoming clinical skills that were sure to blow everyone away on the wards next year. He sat straighter in his chair and could feel a smile forming on his face no matter how hard he tried to look serious and distinguished.

"It's all rather convoluted, Mr. Callaway, but the conclusion is deceivingly simple. The wall, the one that *must* be built between you and your patients, by definition, excludes true empathy. (Chase cocked his head, unsure if he had heard correctly.) If the wall is too thick, the physician is happy, the patient is not. If the wall's too thin, the patient is happy, the doctor is not. Building just the right thickness is a talent few have, and fewer develop. I'd like to believe it's the students who are relatively immune to self-deception–those who resist the White Coat Complex–who are best at this skill. That was my original hypothesis, at least."

"And?"

"Well, our research is pointing the opposite direction. It looks like my own preconceived notions were flat wrong. It's looking more and more like true empathy coupled with an immunity against self-deception creates a wall that only *appears* to be the right thickness, but is actually quite fragile. The test you passed with flying colors today may, in fact, be a harbinger of trouble, or at least conflict."

Chase felt his head shrinking. "How... how could today's test, or my track record these past two years, lead to anything but–frankly–success?"

Dr. Meeker paced quietly for a moment, then sat down at his desk. "It's not a hundred percent by any means, but what we're seeing is an idiosyncratic outcome in a disproportionate number of subjects."

"Idiosyncratic?"

"Yes, an unexpected, peculiar outcome."

"What sort—"

"It's as though we're missing a third parameter that defines the final result. Beyond empathy. And beyond resistance to self-deception. Turns out that 37% of our qualifying subjects have gone on to brilliant careers at some of the top medical centers in the country. But the others, well... clinical depression, drug addiction, self-destructive patterns of all sorts, even the ultimate self-destruction of suicide, you name it. And these students were often near the top of their classes."

"How could that be?" asked Chase, continuing the conversation to keep up appearances, yet having switched off the psychobabble.

"Like I said, we're missing the third parameter. That's why I'd like to offer you long-term therapy, no charge of course, as part of the longitudinal study. Not so much therapy, I guess, as much as touching base with me periodically. To see if we can unlock the final part of the mystery."

Oh, my gosh, thought Chase. *I'm sitting here in the office of the proverbial head-shrinker who's talking crazy, acting crazy, taking a piss in front of me... what's next?*

Chase finally managed to respond. "Dr. Meeker, I don't mean to be disrespectful. But the things you've mentioned, drug addiction and the like, those things are a matter of will power, and too, I think people build their own nests. I'm one of the top students in the class, if not *the* top. Frankly, I'm the sanest guy I know. We've got some nut jobs in my class if you really need subjects. We've got one guy who beats up people in bars on Saturday nights, and he uses another classmate, a shrimpy little guy, who plants himself at the bar and then pours beer on someone to get the fight going. Then we got a guy who sleeps in a coffin and wants to be called 'Count'. These are future doctors of west Texas. I'd say if you're looking for some real pathological personalities to study, I can point you in the right direction. And, too, ask any of the people I've known my entire life. They'll tell you I'm the most normal, boring person they know. Well, almost everyone. Other than Will, my classmate, who can't get over the fact that I eat my cafeteria food one section of the plate at a time—"

"Mr. Callaway, stop. Please stop. There is no reason to be offended. No reason to be frightened. Therapy is no disgrace. I'm simply offering it to you. It's not a requirement of the study. Our research protocol simply requires that we contact you on an annual basis, indefinitely, to see how you're doing. And, for you to take a short quiz each year on the satisfaction in your chosen field. The therapy is not mandatory, by any means. I am simply searching for the third parameter. As a matter of fact, we're worried that our third parameter could simply be the observer effect that you know from Psych 101, our interference with the natural process by informing students that they are candidates. As our old friend Heraclitus said, 'no man steps in the same river twice'. We upset the order of the universe merely by trying to study it."

Chase politely declined the offer of therapy, though he agreed to the yearly follow-up questionnaire. He left with his head still spinning. Confused, irritated at ludicrous assumptions, offended that excellence and empathy could be so horribly twisted by a psychiatrist, Chase knew for sure now that he was making the right decision about his future specialty. Surgery, with its green drapes covering the patient, provided the greatest conceivable distance from intrusive, if not abusive, psychiatry.

A nagging feeling began to bother him again as he drove home. The feeling was a vague, amorphous thing, like a hand belonging to someone else. This foreign hand was pulling him from family and friends. The foreign hand was leaving him increasingly detached from Livvy. The foreign hand was *changing* him, for it brushed away joyous images and dragged him into recalling the dog he'd killed last year, on the same day that Hector Delgado hanged himself. Hector had majored in philosophy as an undergraduate, prompting a bad turning point according to Hector's father. A dog. A philosopher.

The vivid image popped into his head again. It was the cluster of words his mind had photographed in his grandfather's library on the recent visit. From Thomas Hardy's *Far From The Madding Crowd*, completely out of context, came these picture-perfect words: "...taken and tragically shot at twelve o'clock that same day–another instance of the untoward fate which so often attends dogs and other philosophers who follow out a train of reasoning to its logical conclusion."

Dogs and other philosophers? Untoward fate?

Out of the countless books on his grandfather's shelves, he had he pulled out this particular volume, his eyes falling and fixating on one phrase, a sentence that paralleled a most horrible day, second only to the death of sister Annie.

He knew that "dogs" and "philosophers" were metaphorical in the novel, and his conversion of likeness to literality would be labeled "magical thinking" by the psychiatric community. Yet, what if dark forces, in fact, were at play in the universe that were so formidable they could trump willpower, outwit empathy, confuse clear cognition, ruin excellence, fool logical conclusions, and wreak havoc in a person's life?

17

Chase's mini-fellowship in pathology, the summer after his second year in med school, at the black tower of Permian Medical Center, affirmed his waxing desire to become a surgeon. The experience also dissolved his already-waning fear that a weak stomach might prohibit the same. He proved to himself he could perform horrific, brutal acts on the human body by day, and still eat spare ribs by night.

As part of executing a routine autopsy, he would dissect the scalp and pull the rug over the face, then cut open the skull with a vibrating saw. The brain would plop into his hands after he carefully cut the optic nerves and brainstem. Then, after turning to the chest, it was nothing more than garden pruning as he wielded loppers to snip the ribs and create a window to the heart. Examining the heart was a ritualistic dissection that he enjoyed the most, exposing each chamber in sequence, followed by sausage slices along each coronary artery. And, he could fashion the liver into perfect one-centimeter thicknesses as deftly as any professional butcher, drawing praise from the most experienced pathologists. Indeed, he had the knack. Other than repugnant odors, especially in those who had died of peritonitis, Chase genuinely enjoyed the dissections, and his stomach was strong. Much stronger than he had thought. Much stronger than the MS-1 who had fainted the first time he drew blood.

Chase found even greater intrigue in the transfiguration of surgical specimens. Three-dimensions became two when the tissue appeared on the glass slide resting on the microscope stage, one dimension having been lost in space. He learned the limitations of frozen sections; he learned how mistakes can be made in tissue processing; he learned how "floaters" from one person's biopsy can travel through bathing fluids and end up in another person's cassette and how the expert can *usually* recognize this when it occurs. And he listened in naïve mystery when the pathologists argued about a final diagnosis.

A ghostly edifice haunted him during his summer months in the pathology lab–the intercom box where frozen section results were called to the surgeons, for this is where the alleged sabotage against his father had occurred many years prior. The gun metal gray of the intercom box seemed harmless as it rested on the wall, though its round speaker reminded him of a Siren's mouth luring mariners to crash their ships into the rocks. Chase considered the deluge of news it had delivered over many, many years to temporarily deaf, anesthetized patients upstairs in the O.R.

When Chase thought of his father's ordeal, he couldn't imagine such sedition by one doctor against another. Innocent mistakes were much easier to accept. Doctors were men of integrity, so Chase had to question whether, indeed, his father had made an appalling error years ago–that, in fact, his father had amputated the wrong breast after a correct report. On the other hand, Wes Callaway never blamed others for anything. This fact made the allegation of sabotage quite possible, and made the little gray box on the wall take on oppressive proportions each time Chase pressed its button and shouted a diagnosis into its mouth.

.　　.　　.

In the fall of 1973, on the first morning of the third year in medical school–the launch of clinical medicine–the entire class met for an orientation session offered by the Dean before splitting to their separate rotations. In their white coats, the students were not the total frauds they had been as MS-1s and MS-2s. They were only partial frauds–MS-

3s acting as though they were real doctors. Chase, for one, still felt like a total fraud.

He was being honest with himself in that he didn't know very much about clinical medicine. Yet, he was captivated by the fact that some of his classmates didn't seem to be hampered in the slightest. Students whose names he barely knew during the first two years were strutting around, tossing their black bags and medical lingo about as if they'd been doing it for years. Some classmates had already looped their stethoscopes around their necks, as if they knew what to listen for. One classmate was so bold that he asked for clarification on the proper procedure should he disagree with his intern or resident. *How could a lowly MS-3 be so cocksure and nervy?* Some students had even altered their physical appearance as if protean efforts externally would transform their shaky and awkward interiors. For instance, the Texas Aggie, Porter Piscotel, had changed his thinning hairstyle to a straight comb-back, parted down the middle. And remarkably, he was smoking a pipe (more accurately, his lips were supporting an unlit pipe).

After the Dean covered the essentials, including parking procedures (nothing available for MS-3s) and vacation time (no changes after assignments made), the neophytes scattered in small groups across campus to their respective rotations. Chase started on the psychiatry clerkship to settle any lingering doubts about his career. Given the various outpatient options as to the location of his clerkship, he chose the familiar grounds of Matherville State where the training program was so closely tied to the medical school. Plus, this gave him the opportunity to drop by Building 19 on a regular basis to visit Ivy Pettibone and play a few rounds of "Chopsticks" on the piano.

However, having been exposed only to the "chronics" at Matherville, Chase thought he might give psychiatry one last chance by witnessing some legitimate therapy for the "acutes." His module-mates followed him ("Chase knows the ropes, so we'll be sitting pretty at Matherville State."), although each MS-3 was assigned to a different resident physician in psychiatry.

Chase's resident had a sour disposition and never smiled once. Wearing a neatly trimmed beard and wire-rimmed glasses, the resident seemed to be a finely groomed hippie trying to adopt a physical likeness to Sigmund Freud. So, it was little surprise that when Chase admitted his past life as songwriter and emcee for a Christian folk group, the resident psychiatrist, without cracking a smile, asked Chase if he was aware that religion was an outward manifestation of neurosis.

Chase's resident had adopted an interesting technique for therapy—he confronted every single patient to the point of rage, as though this shrink considered himself a failure unless the patient screamed. As a fly-on-the-wall observer, Chase felt himself squirming in his seat as the resident attacked one patient after another with his oh-so-soft and tender voice. When one muscled fellow (a patient being held under court order for trying to kill his wife) stood up during a therapy session and threatened to beat the therapist to a pulp, Chase felt like joining in. Nonetheless, the patient was restrained and locked in seclusion for a week, while Chase went home every night. Meanwhile, Captain Newman, M.D. was confirmed as a myth.

Chase still had to shoot for an "A" on the rotation. Fortunately, the grade on Psych had nothing to do with knowledge or interactive skills, but everything to do with the MS-3's "project," a written treatise on a topic chosen from a short list. Chase picked "The Case for Outpatient Treatment of Chronic Mental Illness." At the end of the rotation, Dr. Wendall Latimer, Chief Psychiatrist and Administrator of Matherville State, called Chase to his office to review his work.

"Doctor Callaway, I don't usually meet with the clerks on the rotation, leaving that up to the course coordinator and my colleagues at the med school."

"Yes, sir..." Chase had mixed feelings about the title 'doctor' as this common moniker for MS-3s seemed to be a half-mocking, half-joking tagline. Still, he liked the sound of it.

"Since you've worked here as an aide, and since I know your father—we were classmates, you know–well, that's not why I called you here... let me back up a minute."

Chase stiffened.

"First of all," continued Dr. Latimer, with a half-smirk, "I should mention that I was across the creek at the undergrad Student Union yesterday, and I saw the names of you and your classmates on the chalkboard, advancing through the foosball tournament brackets. I believe the four names I saw were all on the psych clerkship right now."

Chase shrunk two sizes and tried to blend in with the paisley fabric of his chair. "We, uh, my classmates and me, we've managed to get over there, during lunch breaks, of course. We got surprisingly good at foosball back in the day, playing doubles, *especially* during those first two years when we had more time and now, well... you wouldn't think there's that much skill involved, but you can actually get to the point where—"

"Let's put the foosball tournament aside for now. That being said, it's always hard to evaluate students on this rotation where, primarily, the MS3s are only observing." Dr. Latimer seemed to be hiding a leftover smile after his foosball exposé. "That's why we rely so heavily on your project."

"Yes, sir."

"And I must admit, your project is probably the best I've ever seen. If placed in the proper format, it's ready to submit for grant funding. And you didn't miss the potential of a grant, either, with your research on sources for federal and state funding. Your basic ideas are so original–your renderings for those Z-shaped floor plans allowing individual apartments for our patients so that the counselor can view them, while the patients still maintain a sense of privacy. And, well, your ideas for a garden for each patient, your selection criteria for patients who would be allowed to have pets, your group living arrangement for certain patients, singles for others, and how this might be affected by the new drugs on the horizon that are going to allow more outpatient management. I could go on and on. I'm really astonished. I was quite sorry to learn that you had decided against psychiatry. I know your father must be enormously proud of your class standing and your work here, even going back to your time as an aide."

Doubt it, thought Chase. Then he said, "I'm still filling in as an aide occasionally, and what I've been most impressed by over the years is that the chronics are usually well-behaved, and generally self-sufficient. Because they're institutionalized, though, they can't make decisions for themselves. They certainly don't need to be in a dreary warehouse with communal sleeping and communal baths. There's no reason they couldn't live nice quiet lives in small groups. I know some of them still need to be locked away. But when I watch patients like Ivy Pettibone, it's always like, 'Why does *she* need to be here?'"

"I agree, Chase. In fact, I've recently returned from a meeting where a landmark experiment was described by a fellow named Rosenhan. It's going to be published in *Science* in a few months. In brief, pseudo-patients volunteered to go into mental hospitals, and the psychiatrists and staff were unable to distinguish the sane from the insane. In fact, quite normal behavior was charted in pathologic terms consistent with the label assigned at the time of admission. When the article comes out, I encourage you to read it. It is, as your generation would say, mind-blowing. And it speaks to the need for community mental health facilities, as you've described in your project. For a third-year student, this is above and beyond. And with that, let me wish you good luck in the finals," said Dr. Latimer in closing.

"The what? I didn't think there was a final test on this clerkship."

"No, I mean the finals of the foosball tournament."

Chase felt his face turning warm, and he hoped the flushing wasn't obvious in the dim light of the Chief's office. "Oh, yes, the finals. Amy DeHart and I are in the finals for doubles. She's very coordinated. The undergrads are trying to get us disqualified. They're saying the tourney wasn't open to medical students." Chase hoped his protracted explanation might ease the embarrassment, knowing that he and his classmates had been practicing over four hours a day at the Student Union rather than wasting their time listening to the psych residents torment the patients.

Chase ended up with an A+ on Psych, plus a small trophy for the Far West Texas University foosball doubles championship.

. . .

On the remainder of the clinical clerkships his third year leading up to Surgery at the end, Chase's evaluations were nearly identical. Each course coordinator – Pediatrics, Ob-Gyn, Internal Medicine, Neuroscience – commented on Chase's quiet nature, paradoxically magnifying the surprise when he eventually began to speak, leaving his superiors–housestaff and faculty–bewildered at his mastery of the subject. And if the course had a written exam (Surgery was the only clerkship that maintained an oral exam), it was Chase who usually set the curve.

For most students, there was a large element of subjectivity when it came to grades for the clinical rotations, and many of Chase's colleagues played the subjective angle to the hilt. Bringing lasagna to the hospital at nights to the residents on call usually did not impart a good grade, but unbridled enthusiasm for working beyond the call of duty usually did, even when raw knowledge lagged.

Chase's module-mates did well on the clinical rotations, keeping jealousies in check, although Will Glendenning struggled to get over the harassment he attracted through the misfortune of having been born with a look of fear stamped on his face. After Will was caught reading a detective novel during a lecture on renal failure, he received a B-minus on the Internal Medicine rotation, though he didn't seem to care. The Ob-gyn department tried to recruit Amy right out of the third-year clerkship, and C.C. Chastain was a hyperkinetic, comical whirlwind that the residents loved, awarding him with straight-As on every rotation.

However, the MS-3 chrysalis-to-butterfly award went to Porter Piscotel. Porter out-dazzled every other student in the class with orgasmic reactions to each "fascinating case," salivating eagerness to take on greater patient loads than the other students, staying late, arriving early, rounding on Sundays, and shouting out the answers to questions while classmates were sipping their coffees. And while this approach drew accolades and grades of "A" on each and every clinical rotation, it drew God-like proclamations on the Surgery clerkship where Sam Dinwiddie, a hulking Chief Resident known mostly for his brawn, announced to the world that Porter Piscotel was the "best third-year student I've ever seen–bar none."

Chase marveled at the stories of Porter that swept through the class ("How does Porter find the time to read the material, much less memorize?") and was thankful that he didn't share any clinical rotations with the frenetic Porter. Chase was becoming more and more convinced that surgery was the place for him, and the competition for residency slots was fierce. In addition to everything else, he knew he had "good hands." He had been the best typist in his class in high school (65wpm; 0 errors); he played the piano well; and, he already knew how to dissect the human body. So, it all boiled down to his final rotation of the year–Surgery–long after Porter had left his superlative mark on the residents and faculty.

Each student was assigned five weeks of vacation during the third year, and Chase's time came immediately prior to the Surgery clerkship. Livvy suggested one week in Dallas, one in San Antonio, and several weekends at Big Bend. Instead, Chase spent every day of the five weeks reading and highlighting all 2,000 pages of the surgery text, devouring more information about human disease than he had acquired heretofore.

By the time the clerkship began, Chase had more book knowledge than the surgical housestaff, including senior residents. Most were dazzled at his encyclopedic recitations on any topic, but the impact seemed lost on Chief Resident Dinwiddie who was annoyed by most medical students, and particularly, those with schooling. Chase didn't care. Dinwiddie would be in private practice before Chase began his internship.

During the fourth week of the ten-week surgical rotation, Chase had the rare opportunity to serve as first assistant to the new Chairman of the Department, Thatcher Nolan Taylor (known quietly to the underlings as T.N.T.). Most on campus considered T.N.T. the most distinguished and most respected professor in the medical school, and a gentleman of the first order–"totally different than the usual surgeon." Although a native Texan, Dr. Taylor had trained at Johns Hopkins, and rumor held that he had recently been offered the Chairmanship of the Surgery Department at that august institution. He had declined with this alleged statement: "If I became Chairman back East, it would be hard to look out my office window and view Gretchen's domain." Thatcher's wife Gretchen, prior to becoming Mrs. Taylor, was a Studebaker of top order, daughter of patriarch Josef and sister of Hardy, the family member who silently governed the medical school complex.

Rarely did a third-year clerk ever get promoted to first assistant with T.N.T., but near the end of a gallbladder removal, the scrubbed intern was called to the emergency room, away from assisting Dr. Taylor.

Offering Chase the opportunity to "sew a little," Dr. Taylor watched Chase bumble his way with a needle holder and forceps for the first time–an unnatural act that could reduce the most nimble hands to a bushel of thumbs. While Dr. Taylor placed twenty perfect and identical stitches, Chase only placed three. After the case, the scrub nurse whispered to Chase how rare it was for Dr. Taylor to let any medical student practice sewing on his private patients. And furthermore, she noted that Chase's sutures, although few, were perfectly tidy, indistinguishable from the master's. She had never seen such perfection from a med student.

"Chase, I'd like to talk to you about your career plans. I hear you're interested in surgery," said Dr. Taylor a few days later when Chase was called to his office. Tall and tanned, with blonde hair turning gray, Dr. Taylor seemed more like an aging tennis pro than a surgeon. Certainly, he had an aura. "Have you given some thought to academics as opposed to private practice?"

"Not really. I'm planning on private practice... I suppose."

Despite Dr. Taylor's remarkable affability, his thin lips formed an inverted U that suggested scorn or melancholy until he spoke, whereupon his face realigned into creases of warmth and wisdom. "Let me say this. Of all the students I've seen this year, I'd put you as our first choice for the program here at Far West. I hope you'll consider us."

Chase was caught off guard, yet not completely surprised. "There's so many in my class interested in surgery, like Porter Piscotel," he said, wishing instantly he could retract the mention of a specific student. After all, the program finished four each year so there was plenty of room for two gunners.

"Porter's on a different track. He's headed for academics. I've got a spot lined up for him back East. You know, it's funny in academics– geography is everything. You can be a clumsy fool in the operating room, and believe me, some of the biggest names in academics shouldn't even be allowed in the O.R. But if you've trained at one of the key medical centers, you're golden. You're validated. Anointed might be a better word. On the other hand, you might be one of the most talented surgeons around, but if you train at a state program, you'll always play second fiddle. And if you train at a private hospital, you can forget academics altogether. That's why I always check with our top students here at Far West to see if they're academic-bound. If so, I strongly encourage you, saying it bluntly, to get the heck out of Dodge. Matherville is no place to launch a career in academics, not if you're upwardly mobile, that is."

As Dr. Taylor spoke, Chase was enjoying the newfound relief that he would not have to compete with Porter Piscotel as a resident at Far West. Chase knew he could cripple Porter intellectually, but he also knew he didn't have half the energy, and he certainly couldn't gush perpetual enthusiasm. If he tried to mimic Porter, he'd only be faking. And no matter how sincere Porter might be in his zeal, Chase believed knowledge was the core attribute for a physician in any specialty. Given equal hands and equal judgment, the surgeon with the most knowledge would supervene. Or, so Chase believed.

"...it's very much like our private high school here in Matherville where we encourage our top graduates to attend the Ivy League schools. So, if you're interested in academics, Chase, I would suggest one of several programs back East, or a few on the West coast, and I'll help you go anywhere you want. If you're interested in private practice, however, let me offer you the first spot here at Far West."

Chase signed on the spot, even though internship was still more than a year away.

. . .

Porter Piscotel became the first student in remembered history at Far West to decline his five weeks of vacation during the third year. The shocking word of his personal sacrifice spread to all the wards and all the hospitals on campus. As a result, he achieved MS-4 status, senior medical student, five weeks early, ahead of the rest of his class. And for his first senior rotation, he became student-intern on the Surgery clerkship—one notch on the totem pole above Chase and his classmates as they were still lowly MS-3s in their final weeks.

Porter had no qualms whatsoever about assuming this leadership role. He felt no compunction to maintain humility with his old classmates, an attitude not born of malice, but oblivion. In short order,

Porter was besmirched by his former classmates and beloved by the surgery residents.

"*Doctor* Callaway, what is the proper treatment for cystosarcoma phyllodes of the breast?" asked Chief Resident Sam Dinwiddie during a mastectomy.

Chase recited the textbook copy for this rare tumor line for line. With the comfort imparted by reading the entire text before the surgery rotation began, he had the freedom to study up on the latest published literature as well: "…so even though it says in the books to do a Halsted radical every time, it looks like this particular malignancy rarely travels to the lymphatics, so the lymph nodes might not need removal. In fact, pathology subdivides these lesions now, and it appears some of them are completely benign, making the name cystosarcoma a misnomer."

"What operation am I doing right now, *doctor*?"

"Uh, a Halsted radical mastectomy."

Porter Piscotel was scrubbed in on the case as first assistant to Dr. Dinwiddie, while Chase was second assistant. Chase thought he heard Porter snicker.

Dinwiddie was burning through the patient's breast tissue with the electrocautery, but then he stopped and let the smoke clear before saying, "So, you're saying that our surgical texts are wrong? That the operation I'm doing right now, this very goddam minute, is wrong? Is that what you're telling me?"

Chase felt the size and hulking presence of Sam Dinwiddie bearing down, and he felt his own throat tighten.

"No, I didn't mean that. A mastectomy is certainly needed most of the time, but I still don't know why the lymph nodes are removed. Sometimes, I think, by the time medical texts are published, a lot of stuff is obsolete. Not to mention the errors present to begin with."

"Errors, you say?"

Chase knew he was in treacherous waters, but given the continued silence in the room, along with Dinwiddie remaining a preoccupied Goliath, he decided to fill the void with his own voice. After all, Dr. Taylor had assured Chase the top spot in the program already. Why not brandish some intellectual weaponry in front of the Piscotel-Dinwiddie team?

"Well, yes," Chase said. "For instance, when you look at the diagram of Duke's classification of colon cancer in the Big Blue text—"

"I memorized that diagram back when you were probably in junior high school. What about it?" asked Dinwiddie.

"Well, for starters, the drawing is inaccurate. The muscularis layers are drawn incorrectly. Then, the layers are mislabeled to boot. And finally, the caption describes the tumor invading into the muscularis mucosae as being the key to staging when it ought to say the muscularis *propria*. But the amazing thing to me is that not only did that chapter's author let it slip through, but also the editor. So, I went to the library and looked in the previous editions. The mistakes have been there for many years, multiple printings."

A long silence followed with the Chief Resident motionless, staring at Chase. Then, Dr. Sam Dinwiddie lowered his head and began separating the patient's skin from underlying breast once again, the humming cautery filling all nostrils with burnt offering. "I'll be interested to check that out," he muttered, "I doubt you have the right story there. Too many eyes have seen that diagram. So, back to the case at hand. You were in the process of telling me that I'm doing the wrong operation here? That I should, at least, leave the lymph nodes behind?"

This time, Chase heard a grunt coming from Porter who was busy chasing bleeding vessels with a hemostat, lunging at the skin flaps, clamping here and there until Dinwiddie would pronounce, "Good, Porter, good."

"You were saying..." prompted Dinwiddie.

"I didn't mean to say the *wrong* operation. It's just odd that the text says this type of tumor doesn't go to lymph nodes, then the very next sentence in the book says to remove the lymph nodes. You're doing exactly what the book says, for sure." More silence, before Chase continued. "So, I found some European literature that indicated that simply taking the tumor out with a rim of normal tissue might do the trick. And several articles in the pathology literature describe a continuum from benign to malignant, and what we might be calling malignant—"

"Good God Almighty. Why are you quoting pathology garbage in an operating theater? Did you happen to read the *surgical* literature for this case? Jesus H. Christ, reading the *European* literature. Reading the *pathology* literature. This is a *surgical* clerkship, *doctor*, and we're operating in the U.S. of freakin' A."

.　　.　　.

One week later, Will Glenndenning dropped out of medical school during the surgical clerkship, his final rotation of the third year, shortly after scrubbing with Dr. Dinwiddie. Chase was disturbed by the abrupt exit since Will was one of his best friends. It wouldn't be the same without him. At one time, they'd even toyed with going into pathology together until Chase confirmed his preference to dissect living organs, while Will wanted tissues certifiably dead.

"I quit, Chase. I can't take it anymore. I wasn't particularly thrilled about clinical rotations in the first place. I just wanted to do pathology. I've got it all arranged. I'm going to enter the Ph.D. program in pathology. It's designed for researchers. Actually, it's molecular biology, but you get your doctorate at Far West in molecular either through the biochem department or pathology. Same subject, different departments. You can't practice medicine with a Ph.D., but I should have gone directly to research from the beginning. I don't need an M.D. for that."

"But Will, just one more year, and it's the easiest year at that. You've already done the hard stuff."

"I'm not letting the likes of Dinwiddie ride herd on me for one more minute. That sonuvabitch. He's yelling at me the entire case to pull harder on the retractor. I bet he yelled it a hundred times. He needed to see the gallbladder and common duct better, and you know how slippery that sweetheart retractor is. Hard to control. He's the one having trouble, of course, but when he cuts the common duct by accident, it's my fault, and the asshole throws *me* out of the operating room for what *he* did. Hell, I was pulling so hard with the sweetheart that the liver capsule got a little tear. I couldn't pull any harder, safely that is. Chase, you don't belong with these surgery assholes. Seriously, you don't have the right personality. These guys are jerks. They're blamers. No other rotation treats students like they do. And they're not selective. They're rude to staff, too. They're even rude when they're talking about docs in other specialties. C'mon, what's the deal with calling internists 'medicine queers'? They're rude to everyone. You remember the boiling frog theory? Well, this freakin' frog is boiling all right. I'm outta here."

"Will, calm down. Not all the surgeons are like Dinwiddie. You're over-generalizing."

"Bullshit. Even your precious Dr. Taylor gets mad in the operating room. I saw him throw a clamp against the wall last week. What's that about? What's with these guys?"

"Just don't do anything rash until you've cooled off."

"It's a done deal, Chase. I've already quit. I start classes next week for my Ph.D. When you're a surgery intern, pulling thirty-six hours on, twelve off, for an entire freakin' year, I'll be home every night making love to Claudia. You keep saying that surgery needs people like you, but that's bullshit, Chase. They'll eat you alive. You're outnumbered in a big way. Or else they'll turn you into one of them. And from where I'm sitting, that's no compliment, buddy."

"I really wish you'd hang in there, Will."

"I'm sick of it. Claudia's sick of it. She's in her last year of law school, you know, and she loves what she does. She's sick and tired of hearing me complain, and I don't blame her."

Chase nodded, acquiescing at the mention of Claudia. If Claudia had decreed this abrupt departure from med school, it was truly a done deal. She could be harsh on Will, sometimes to the point that everyone in the room felt the heat (especially Chase, if Claudia happened to be comparing Will to Chase). Claudia knew what she wanted in life, and she wanted Will's undivided devotion most of all. Livvy and Claudia had become close friends, but sometimes the pecking bothered even Livvy. And now this—dropping out. The more he listened to Will rant and rave, Chase figured this wasn't about Sam Dinwiddie, M.D. at all. Will was either crumbling to Claudia's demands—or, there was a tiny chance that the reverse was true—that Claudia had been the engineer of the train to med school all along, and Will was making his first real stand.

. . .

As the third year came to a close, selections for Alpha Omega Alpha Honor Medical Society—top 5% of the class—tapped Chase Callaway as First Vice-president, a designation as the "Number Two" spot out of 144 in the class (6 drop-outs to date). His B-plus on the Neurology rotation had cost him the top position. *Fuzzy anatomy of the brain*, he thought, *was always my nemesis. Can't picture the brain's regions without well-defined borders.*

Chase didn't care about missing the top spot, or so he told himself. What he did care about, however, was the fact that many of his classmates didn't believe that he should be in the top 5% at all–this, in spite of his unique A-pluses on several clinical rotations and his number one position after the first two basic science years. The chief critic was one of his closest friends, C. C. Chastain.

"Maybe top seven, sure, but I don't think you deserved number one or number two," said C.C. "I can think of six or seven guys, myself included, and one girl, I'd put up there before you. Sure, you've got that photographic memory, or memory of photographs as you call it, but you were way too quiet on the rotations. And it was the same quiet as the jokers who didn't know diddly squat. Couldn't tell if you were really that confident and relaxed, or stupidly lethargic."

"I didn't like being a know-it-all even when I knew it all. The faculty seemed to appreciate it without any trouble after they saw my test scores on every rotation. Classmates never saw those scores, including you."

"That's my point. Test scores don't take care of patients."

Chase thought about stopping the discussion right here, but he couldn't resist a good tangle with C.C. Chastain. "Of course, basic sciences counted, too," said Chase. "Remember? Top score in anatomy, physiology, histology, pathology and tied for number one in pharmacology–who was it? Who did that?"

"So what? The guys with the lowest A's got the same points for AOA as your top A's did."

"My point exactly. My A-pluses didn't count any more than a regular A. Like the A-plus I got on Pediatrics where my attending said my formulation written on cystic fibrosis was the best he'd ever read in his forty years as a professor. How does that figure in? If anything, the point system hurt me."

"I'll grant you some leeway there, but I'm tellin' you, some people think you got pushed up a few slots only because of who you are. Or, better said, because of who your father is, you know, famous at Far West and all that."

"Thanks, C.C. I appreciate your candor and your shaky appreciation of my talent. I'm sure you'll make it into AOA when they drop down to scrape up the next 5% in the fall."

"Shoulda been in the first 5%. I mean really, think about it–I had straight As on the clinical rotations while you had your one B-plus. Hell, just because I didn't study the first two years like you did… But, hey, if anyone has a right to complain, how 'bout old Porter Piscotel? He was clearly the stand-out in our class if you only count the MS-3 year, at least according to the rules of crazy-ass enthusiasm. They say there's always one student in each class that shines big time on the wards after a lackluster performance at the Basic Science Building. I thought it would be me until I saw brother Piscotel in action."

"Well, the fact that Porter didn't get to leapfrog over a bunch of people to get AOA goes to show you that the medical school still places value on working knowledge above bluster and bravado."

Chase took C.C.'s critique in stride, but he was quite surprised when Livvy reported similar grumblings coming from the spouses of those who didn't quite make the cut.

"I don't know why you're so incapable of seeing how jealous people are of you, Chase. You're such an idealist. You told me once that you've never had a drop of jealousy in your life, so maybe that's why you don't see it. Still, your naïveté worries me sometimes. You don't seem to notice that people gun for the gunners."

"Funny. I had several classmates tell me that they had no idea I was one of the gunners until AOA was announced."

"Well, now they know. And you've probably got twenty or so classmates who think they should be in your shoes right now."

Chase shook it off. His focus was on becoming a surgeon. Even his famous father's reaction bounced off:

"The best students don't always make the best doctors… I was nowhere near AOA… I think a person can study too much… I'm not sure you have the stamina to be a surgeon… It'll be five long years before you're making any money, to speak of…. You know, general surgeons are big shots during residency training, but when you get out, you're at the beck and call of every other specialist… The public thinks you're the same as a GP–people have no idea that abdominal work has some of the hardest technical procedures possible, with the highest complication rates, but it's 'oh, you're *just* a general surgeon'?"

Wes Callaway seemed more annoyed than proud. While Chase was accustomed to somewhat reserved, often ambiguous, criticism from his father for his choices in life, he had never seen the Great Wes Callaway so agitated, seemingly fearful, in his ramblings. Inside, Chase felt a surge of power and a longing, more than ever, to become a surgeon.

18

The fourth year of medical school was a fleeting respite, a sanctuary wedged in between the yoke of the third year and the onerous responsibility of next year's internship. MS-4s could frolic in illusory self-confidence while looking over a steep cliff and perhaps spitting upon the lowly MS-3s. And, MS-4s could revel in the misconception that this peaceful year mimicked what life would be like "on the outside," once residency was over. Specialty choices had been made, these decisions often grounded in a fog of baseless passion while seemingly irrevocable.

Chase claimed the year for himself, that is, in the name of balance. His garden grew, his lyrics flowed, he read primers in Greek and Hebrew and, anticipating more in-depth study of *Daniel* and *Ezra* in the future, he dabbled in western Aramaic. He secured time for Livvy, anchoring their relationship as never before, serving as a companion by day and offering Edenic restoration at night.

Livvy's favorite movie for the year was *Alice Doesn't Live Here Anymore*, while Chase was content that *Cuckoo's Nest* had finally made it to the screen. He attended varsity basketball games at Far West Texas. And he began attending church once again, opting initially for the Matherville Methodist congregation as opposed to the emotionalism that seemed to typify his grandfather's church. Yet, midway in the year, Chase learned of Arminianism within Methodism, and that salvation could be lost under said doctrine, so he returned to his grandfather's church where a fall from grace was nearly impossible.

Given humane working hours, and thus, the absence of dogged exhaustion, Chase was plagued again by the bane of his youth–insomnia. This time, however, he prepared himself with an antidote–reading the classics to the point of near slumber. Chase borrowed novels from the west wall of Grandfather Zebulon's library. *Scarlet Letter, Call of the Wild, Lord of the Flies...* Zebulon had hundreds, and Chase hoped to consume them all. He calculated one per month for the rest of his life to cover the west wall alone. More books could be consumed, he knew, if he could bring himself to skip researching the author, stop transcribing important passages, and quit writing summaries about the symbolism and themes. Someday, he would have even more free time to attack the north and east walls.

This year was not only the final lap of medical school, but also his last stretch as a part-time aide at Matherville State and his last chance to earn what was now $4.50 an hour. Surgical interns calculated their earnings at $2.50 an hour (based on 100-hour weeks), and after five more years of surgical training, the chiefs earned $4.00 an hour. While hourly concerns bothered his colleagues, Chase never dwelled on personal income. He rested firm in the assurance that good things come to those who wait. The personal economics of a career in medicine never once took space in his head–not in his choice of specialty, not in his location of practice, not in any decision–*not* because he didn't care about worldly comforts, but because he took it for granted that his talent would translate accordingly.

Only one thing bothered him at all during this time–ostracism. Chase had made friends with an eclectic group of self-styled intellectuals in his senior class who, along with two psychiatry residents, had formed a Philosophy of Medicine club. He discovered, shortly after induction, that the deep thoughts from his new friends were engendered through hashish first, and secondly through Quaaludes (a.k.a. 'ludes). Because the topics at club meetings so enraptured Chase, he enjoyed inclusion to the group, but stopped short of the chemical hors d'oeuvres. Although comfortable with his own decision to abstain, especially since Livvy attended the co-ed meetings, it was clear that his refusal to partake impacted the others. He was, reluctantly, a killjoy.

"Chase, you and Livvy might as well take off. We're done with Al Schweitzer, and we're moving on to the 'ludes now," said Dr. Savinski, a second-year resident in psychiatry.

"You do mean methaqualone, don't you?" replied Chase, hiding his dismissal through jest. "Remember, use the generic if you want to impress."

Livvy saw no purpose in the meetings. In silence on the way home, Chase sensed that his wife was on the brink of announcing her split with these amateur philosophers. To fill the dead air, he offered, "I never knew Schweitzer's cousin was Jean-Paul Sartre's mother, did you? And what about all of Schweitzer's work on the historical Jesus? Amazing. I only thought of him as treating tropical diseases in Africa."

After a few seconds, Livvy answered, "Golly, gee. I wonder if Albert Schweitzer did 'ludes, too?"

Still, the fact remained, Chase did not like being "excused" early. His new friends realized (and gently mocked) his Christian beliefs, but they still accepted him in their lot. That said, they did not want an abstainer in their midst, possibly passing judgment, while they were having fun.

"Chase, I don't have a problem with them doing whatever they want, but I really don't feel comfortable with that group. They're smug. And why in heaven's name they like you, or why you like them, I can't imagine."

•   •   •

The next weekend, while on duty at Matherville State, Chase was observing Ivy Pettibone, walking in her relentless circles, bobbing up and down with each step, rocking her shoulders as a counterbalance. She'd been at it for 30 minutes when she broke ranks and headed toward the piano, a signal for Chase to join her. Aides and nurses had commented that while she frequently banged on the piano keys with her fused fingers, she only played "Chopsticks" when teacher Chase was present. Practice had made perfect, and with thumbs at 90-degree angles to the keyboard, her performances were nearly flawless.

Chase sat down beside her on the bench and held each of her hands in his. "Ivy, I haven't forgotten about getting your hands fixed. While I won't be working as an aide here much longer, I'll still be around. Pretty soon, I'll be training to become a surgeon, like the guys you've met in the clinic when I've taken you there before. I'll be one of those doctors, and I'll be in a much better position to get you scheduled with the surgeons who'll operate on your hands. That is, if you still want that done. So, I've got to ask you now, whether or not you still want your fingers to be separated, like mine, where they can wiggle?"

Ivy nodded her head 'yes' as she mumbled "Reti lati," followed by other cryptic words, a big smile in place.

As Ivy began playing "Chopsticks" and singing her version of the Panda song, Chase did his standard sweep of the large pockets of her daisy dress, looking for stashed medications. While Ivy continued to play and sing, Chase emptied more than 30 candy-like capsules and tablets from her hoard. Already "counted" in the med log, there was no way to track as to whether or not the drugs had been consumed, and it struck Chase that about half of the pills were Quaaludes, prescribed routinely for inmate sleep. And with an impulse that he didn't understand–perhaps, a twisted longing for acceptance–he plucked the 'ludes from the stash and turned in the rest of the pills at the nurses' station.

With ethics teetering, Chase considered the fact that the philosophy club's shenanigans were wrong only if he joined in. So, when Livvy was out of town the next weekend on a shopping trip with her mother, Chase attended the high-minded, low-principled club meeting, serving the pharmacologic dessert by himself in the form of pilfered 'ludes. The gratitude was fleeting, and Chase felt like a stranger in his own skin the moment he saw the 'ludes disappear down the eager throats of the highly-educated. Indeed, he felt horrible, and he vowed that he would never degrade himself like that again. *Saturday night movies with Livvy from now on*, he thought. *How stupid of me. How did I ever think I needed to be accepted? Anywhere? By anyone?*

On his next night shift at Matherville State, with inmates tucked into their beds, Chase was engrossed in reading *Heart of Darkness* when a new face appeared at the window above the Dutch door. A young woman with piercing green eyes rested her elbows on the ledge, cradled her chin in her palms, and asked for a sleeper. Her frizzed red hair was electric, oscillating away from her face in all directions.

"Quaaludes," she said, smiling. "Got any? You know 'ludes, don't you?" (Chase panicked inside, as if she could see right through him.) "Sweethearts of slumber?"

He regained his composure and found himself puzzled by her youth. Building 19 was a ward for lifers. New patients were a rarity. Young patients even more so. With her non-blinking eyes and her ornery smile, she transmitted a look that gave a measure of advantage to inmate over aide, a chilling reversal he had felt only on the maximum-security wards, where the charismatic criminal sociopaths could be intimidating. Chase was nervous.

"I'll check to see if you have a doctor's order for 'sweethearts of slumber'. What's your name?"

"The impotent chart will speak Viola using its metal tongue, but I am one who is no longer... I am Sister Jeanne des Anges, avenged accuser of Urbain Grandier."

Chase didn't need to double-check the diagnosis in the chart. He had seen her type before, complete with grinding jaw and puckering lips, the side effects of her anti-psychotic medications. Classic paranoid schizophrenia. "How 'bout I just call you 'Viola'?" He held his nervous laughter in check as he confirmed that she had a standing order for Quaaludes. On the face sheet in her chart, he also noted her stated occupation: "Channeler of All Antiquity."

Chase handed her the sleeper, watched her swallow, checked her empty throat, then charted each step while resting the metal plate of the chart on the Dutch door ledge. "That ought to bring you slumber, sweetheart," he said, trying to bury his apprehension with a quip.

She reached for his scribbling arm and gripped it with amazing force. "Do not mock me. I watched Urbain Grandier receive his just reward, burned alive for witchcraft in the public square after he demonized my nuns and all the women of Loudon centuries ago. Oh, those empty

words: 'Father, forgive them, for they know not what they do' as his
skin sizzled. How Heaven must have moaned that this French devil
would draw from Christ in the end, as do all devils draw." Her
frightening scowl transformed within seconds to a seductive smile.

She gave Chase the creeps even though he had been dealing with
crazies like her for years. Her fingernails clawed into his skin, and when
he reached to peel her fingers away, she drew close to his face and began
whispering with a hissing sound: "I interpret tongues-s, and there is one
here who s-s-speaks in a language long-forgotten and ill-under-s-s-
stood."

"Oh?"

"Yes. Ivy. The crippled one." She raised her voice to a near-shout.
"The Siren sounds, but no one's alarmed."

"Oh really? Siren?"

"Demons live in the cobwebs of her fingers, screaming to escape.
Their voices speak a poem to you. Do I interpret? Yes. I, and only I."

"A poem? For me?" Chase knew to steer clear from the psychoses
of others, but he felt himself curiously drawn to this madwoman. He
was both fascinated and afraid. Although he tried to maintain eye
contact with the unblinking girl, he lost the staring contest. Finally, he
managed, "Well, what do the demons have to say for themselves?"

Viola cocked her head to one side, her voice dropping to a low,
guttural sound:

> *"Death's kind door is nigh ajar*
> *Tongues of fire lick from afar*
> *The curse hath slumbered since heels did hang*
> *The dog awaketh to feel the pain."*

"Heels did hang" and "dog" reverberated as he once again recalled
that fateful day three years ago when he had killed a dog the same day
Hector Delgado hanged himself. Dogs and other philosophers—the
words from the Hardy novel. He could hear the sound of his own
heartbeat. *Ridiculous*, he thought, *this is how horoscopes and fortune-
tellers work—if you offer up nebulous nothingness, something is bound
to fit somewhere, somehow.*

"Those words mean nothing to me," Chase said, somewhat surprised to hear his own voice quivering.

Viola waggled her finger toward Chase's nose. "Your lie is not white. You are reincarnate," she said, "and the curse tippy toes from mountaintop to mountaintop, thirteen times, larger and taller than you can imagine."

Enough was enough. After all these years with wackos, achieving a nice comfort level, only to have one finally get under his skin. "Viola, it's past curfew now, and you're supposed to be back in the sleeping quarters. And, by the way, my life is charmed, not cursed, so I'm sorry to disappoint."

Viola laughed, muttering "charmed" repeatedly as she backed away, never taking her eyes from Chase, as she began to conjugate, "Charm. Charmed. Was charming. Have charmed. Had charmed. Would have charmed." Then she spoke another rhyme, getting louder with each line:

"Hickory Tickery start the clock
Boughs will break; locusts flock
Bullets melt in the name of gunnery
Horror smokes after sex in the nunnery."

As she turned toward the sleeping area, she called over her shoulder to Chase, "Good night, Urbain. The centuries are but seconds when I tippy toe." Her manic laughter continued for a few moments, echoing from her bed where the methaqualone eventually quelled the psychosis.

. . .

Chase never saw Viola again. The encounter had been surreal. After all, the residents of Building 19 were usually there until death. A one-night stand at 19 was nearly impossible. So, on his next shift at work, Chase followed the asphalt path to the administration building on his break where he learned that Viola had been an overflow patient from Admissions that one night only. After transfer from 19 back to observation the next day, she had gone AWOL. No pursuit had been launched since her commitment had been voluntary.

Returning to Building 19, Chase could still feel Viola's rhymes bouncing around his head when he spotted a fellow aide getting ready to leave the ward. Joe Davis was the hippie who had gone through orientation with Chase years earlier. He had been full-time, mostly at 19, with the same tenure as part-time Chase, both now Level II aides. Joe had one foot out the back door.

"You're late, Chase. I need your help inside here."

"Sorry. Had to check on a patient."

"Well, I'm eventually going to take my full fifteen on break, too, but not right now. I need help with Walter. He's restless, man. And per usual for the past two weeks, he's refusing his meds. Of course, he might be on placebo as part of that new study. Anyway, he's got the TV on test pattern, and the tube is speaking to him, like, you know, only Walter can hear. I'd leave him alone, but his racket is waking up the clientele."

By the time the two aides reached the ghostly Walter, the inmate was standing on the couch, waving his arms, screaming and arguing with the hissing sound of the television test pattern. Walter didn't notice the two aides, as he was fixated over the snow on the screen. He was silent for short intervals as if listening to what the tube had to say before lashing out again with gibberish: "Agitate, agitate. May tag. A kaleidoscope has no Z-axis. No Z-axis. Agitate."

"Oh brother," said Chase. "You're right. This'll take both of us."

Even though his six-six frame was nothing more than skin wrapped around bones, Walter made Chase nervous. During his prime, Walter had been in maximum security in The Tower. It had taken him decades to decompose enough for Building 19. With Joe at his side, however, Chase felt prepared. Two aides could overpower nearly any lunatic on a chronic ward.

"Walter, listen to me," Joe said, turning the television off. "The other patients are complaining. They can hear you clear over on the women's side." Walter stepped off the couch, but kept his glare riveted on the dead television. "It's past curfew," continued Joe, "so let's hit the bed now." Then Joe touched Walter softly on the shoulder to break an apparent trance.

Chase didn't have time to react. Walter grabbed the TV and lifted it above his head as if it were a feather pillow, shouting "Death to all chordates," then he smashed it onto Joe's head, knocking him to the ground where the aide groaned once before rolling face down. The picture tube shattered as it hit the floor beside Joe.

Walter turned slowly toward Chase, bellowing more gibberish: "Fan the phlogiston. Death to all chordates. Agitate. Agitate. The Z-axis is the road to the central agitator. Only phlogiston will burn." Chase started to back away, but he bumped into the couch, his getaway now blocked, whereupon Walter thrust his boney hands forward like two arrows from a crossbow, and grabbed Chase's throat in a death grip.

Chase couldn't breathe. Walter was yelling louder and louder, the same words over and over, shaking Chase's neck until his head barely felt attached. Chase fought back, kicking and kneeing and roundhousing his fists against Walter's face. Yet the blows bounced off, having no effect. Even with a direct hit, Walter didn't flinch. Chase felt himself wilting to the ground, his knees giving way. A peculiar resignation overcame him as tiny spots in his eyes swirled, then blackness eased in from the edges.

A split second before losing consciousness, Chase imagined that the squeezing vice around his neck was easing. And crazy as it might have seemed, Walter's growl suddenly switched to the yelping sound of a wild animal, as if its leg had been caught in a steel-jaw trap.

19

When Chase first opened his eyes, he was dazed, disconnected. He thought it odd that he was not at home, waking up next to Livvy. Then he saw the small wire cage around a solitary light bulb that hung like a reluctant drop from the beige ceiling. The nightmare took shape as reality, then replayed in his brain. The assault by Walter became all too real. Chase massaged his own throat where he could still feel Walter's fingers encircling him as though the Grim Reaper himself had tried to choke him into the next life. His body was afloat, then he realized that two aides were lifting him onto a gurney.

"What happened?" Chase asked.

"Walter went nuts. That's all," said one of the aides. "Well, more nuts than usual. You came out better than your friend, luckily. The other aide, he got taken to College Hospital to have his head sewed up and some X-rays. We're only taking you to the infirmary here. I suspect that crazy sumbitch will be transferred from nineteen to our neck of the woods in Maximum."

No ambulance was needed for Chase, as the nameless hospital within the walls of Matherville State was less than a hundred yards from Building 19. Winding asphalt paths connected all buildings on campus, allowing a smooth ride. The outpatient infirmary was on the first floor of the hospital, along with the lab, the clinics, and X-ray. Merely the thought of being a patient at Matherville for a few hours made Chase cringe.

Outside on the gurney, flat on his back, Chase looked at the night sky where he tried to identify the patterns his grandfather had taught him years ago. He could only spot the Great Square directly overhead, not a constellation any more than the Big Dipper is a constellation, but instead, an asterism. He identified Vega as the brightest star this time of year, toward the north. Bumps in the path kept him from further study above. He massaged his neck throughout the trip, hoping to press away the memory.

"How— How did I get free? Do you guys know? The last thing I remember, Walter had me down for the count."

One of the aides replied, "That little gimped-up girl, you know, the one that spits when she's mad? I guess she heard the commotion, best we can tell, and she must have fired her personal water pistol at old Walter, hitting him smack dab in the eyes. At least, that's the way it looked to us. By the time we got there, Walter was over in the corner, rolled into a ball, rubbin' his eyes. That little gal, what's-her-name, why, she was standing over him with hands on her hips."

"What a little spitfire," the other aide said.

"Hey, good one, Stuart. Spitfire."

The aides lifted the gurney's wheels above three concrete steps that led into the hospital, then they rolled Chase inside.

"Hey, wait. Who called you guys from Nineteen?" Chase asked. "Joe and I were the only aides on duty when Walter went berserk."

"Supervisor must've seen something," said one of the aides. "We're from Maximum, so we get all the emergency calls from the operator. Our voice pagers just said, 'Stat to Nineteen' and we don't ask no questions after that. Four of us ran over, and the other two put the crazy dude in seclusion. Come to think of it, though, the supervisor didn't get here 'til later."

Chase considered the improbability of Ivy making the call. Even if she could work the old-fashioned dial on the phone at the nurses' station using her thumbs, she certainly could not communicate anything intelligible. Maybe the operator recognized trouble when she heard Ivy's loony speech, since patients were not allowed access to the telephones.

"This is slightly embarrassing, to say the least," Chase said as the aides helped him shift from the gurney to a flat, wood-framed exam table in the infirmary. He could not believe that he'd almost been killed by a skinny rail of a madman who looked as though he'd break off at the waist if you twisted him just so. And then to be saved–by Ivy? His life had been spared, remarkably, by a tiny wisp of a woman who happened to be an inmate at a mental institution. Random thoughts seemed to congeal to form a single, powerful idea–*Ivy Pettibone does not belong here.*

A nurse thanked the aides and then provided Chase with a pillow. "There, we'll keep an eye on you for a little while," she said. "Got to make sure you don't have a delayed onset of laryngeal edema. Do you need anything?"

She had begun taking Chase's blood pressure, plugging her ears with the stethoscope before he could answer.

"Nothing, really," he hollered. "I don't think you have a cure for humiliation. I don't know how I'm going to explain this to Sukie, I mean Mrs. Spurlock, when she takes over the morning shift."

Chase saw the nurse's eyes dart from the mercury level in the sphygmomanometer and fire directly toward him. She removed the scope from her ears as her eyes widened. "Did you say 'Sukie Spurlock'?"

"Yes."

"Didn't you hear?" said the nurse.

"Hear what? I only work part-time, and I haven't been here since last week."

"Sukie was fired."

"What!"

"Fired. She admitted to stealing narcotics."

.   .   .

Chase's stint in the infirmary lasted until sunrise, then he hurried to Sukie's house in what was commonly called the 'colored section' of Matherville. Sukie was in her bathrobe when she answered the door, her eyes still half-closed.

"Sukie, what's going on?"

She raised one eyebrow in an arch intended to deliver shame, not to receive it. "I guess you've heard," she said.

"Last night. I was on duty and Walter— oh, never mind. The nurse at the infirmary told me you'd been fired. What's that about? You *couldn't* have done anything wrong."

She paused before answering, "No, Chase, I didn't. Now let's talk about you and your friends and the fondness for Quaaludes."

"What?" His mind flipped to Ivy's 'ludes. Surely, that couldn't matter to anyone. After all, half the aides slipped drugs out of the asylum routinely, explaining why so many hippies worked there in the first place. It was also why so many became Level II aides, to dispense (and steal) meds. "The only thing I can think of— Are you talking about— Once— one time, I took a few of Ivy's stashed Quaaludes. One night. One time. But they weren't for me. I gave them to some of my classmates. They—" He shut his mouth, realizing how absurd his rationalization was sounding.

"Chase, you picked a mighty bad time to be givin' dope to your friends. Livvy told me about that group. Come on in the house. Sit yourself down."

Chase felt himself sinking into a swirling haze of confusion, guilt, remorse and frustration.

Sukie waited to speak until he'd fallen into an overstuffed chair where he stared mindlessly at the handsome faces of Sukie's dead children and dead husband, framed in pictures, faces that smiled forever, perched atop her old Victrola phonograph.

She continued, "The pilfering all over the hospital had gotten plum out of control, so they've been watching all the wards. Watching closely. Actually, they'd done it in years past, but held off on taking action for some reason. I suspected the stealing was happening at our place, and I figured it was your buddy, Joe Davis, adjusting the med counts. Dixie Barnes was tracking the narcotics, but it's hard when we've got so many patients stashing, no matter how close we look to see if they've swallowed. Sad to say, the very night you picked to take some of Ivy's stash, why that's the very night Dixie had set up her sting."

"A sting? You've gotta be kidding."

"There's nothing to kid about, child. Dixie put the stash in Ivy's pocket herself that night, Quaaludes mixed with other meds, without my even knowing it. When you found the stash and turned over the drugs to me that night, all the Quaaludes had been removed. I charted what you gave me in the log, so when Dixie saw my notes, it was either you or me that had stolen the narcotics. And not only for that one night. Dixie figured, like anyone would have figured, that whoever she caught was guilty of all the stealing, all along, at least at building Nineteen, don't you see?"

"And you took the blame? For me? Sukie, I can't live with this." Chase felt like he'd pulled the switch to electrocute his own mother.

"I'm believin' you when you tell me it only happened once, Chase. I figured it was Joe Davis all the other times. I'm no spring chicken, so don't fret for me. I don't really have to work, if you know what I mean."

"But— But—you can't do this. I won't let you do it. I'll go in and talk to Dr. Latimer today. He'll understand."

"Chase, I wouldn't advise it. It could ruin your life. It's not gonna affect me like it would you. This wasn't a one-time sin from where they're sittin'. They could easily expel you from med school, and who knows what else. They told me I'd committed a felony, but nothing would be said or done as long as I resigned. They went easy on me, if you think about it. They're not going to be so kind to other folks. They've got stings working all over the hospital."

Chase was devastated. He couldn't believe it. The guilt was overwhelming. Sukie had been a second mother to him, and now this. It was too much. Too stupid on his part. He would have to figure a way to clear Sukie's name.

"What about my folks, Sukie. I don't want them thinking you did something wrong." Silently, he thought, *Nor do I want them finding out it was entirely my fault.*

"Don't you fret about that. The official position is that I quit of my own accord. If they hear something different, you tell 'em it's a silly rumor."

Now he felt even worse. Not only had he saddled the most honest person on the planet with a crime, but also he was dragging her into an ongoing lie as well.

Yet, despite his self-loathing, after a half-hour of debate with Sukie, strategizing ways for both of them to be cleared, he reluctantly agreed to let her take the fall. At least, for now.

So, when Grandfather Zebulon called Chase a few days later to "drop by for a talk," Chase assumed the worst. The secret was already loose, and the knives of reproach were certainly being sharpened.

20

"Chase, given that you're the only Callaway to carry on the family line, it's time we talk. I just now got off the phone with your father, so he already knows."

Chase dropped his eyes to the ground in a contrite manner that broadcast pure guilt. The grim expression on his grandfather's face said it all. Chase had rehearsed a statement for Grandpa Zeb, and he formed the opening words with his lips, inhaling enough air to take him all the way through the first long sentence about Sukie, and what he'd done to ruin her career and her reputation. As his first word began to tumble out, his grandfather continued.

"There's no easy way to say this. We all must face it someday, and all of us will feel cheated out of a few additional years. Those who drop dead suddenly have it easy. What I'm trying to say, Chase, is this–I've got cancer. Prostate cancer. They say it's high grade."

The words were shocking. And yet, diversionary. Chase struggled with the mixture of dread and relief that struck him simultaneously.

Chase managed, "Is it early? I mean, can they get rid of it?"

"Don't know. Surgery is next week. They'll tell me my odds after that."

Chase shared what little he knew about prostate cancer treatment, and Zeb seemed grateful, although Chase felt he had not helped much, if any.

"I'm still not sure I buy into the castration part," Zebulon said.

"They talked about castration already? Well, that's done sometimes to get your testosterone levels as low as possible, but they only do that if they're worried the tumor might have spread." Chase wondered if his grandfather had more advanced disease than he was admitting.

Zebulon replied, "Of course, I haven't really kept up with the latest treatment fads. I did read a curious thing that cancer cells in culture are immortal, dividing to infinity, whereas normal cells will divide a fixed number of times, 50 or so, then quit. Now, isn't that a kicker? Our days are numbered, indeed, even at the cellular level. Anyway, it's hard to believe it's been almost forty years since I quit doctoring."

Chase concealed a smile at the word "doctoring," knowing that Zebulon had, according to family lore, greatly overstepped his bounds years ago as a pharmacist. On occasion, Chase would still hear an oldster refer to his grandfather as "Doc Callaway." Yet, Chase knew few details.

Zebulon continued to hold forth, reminiscing how he had undergone a radical change from being a healer to being healed, emotionally that is, through his conversion experience. Here, Chase knew the details by heart, having listened to Grandpa Zeb's testimony countless times as a boy. The recitation was so smooth that Chase's thoughts drifted away, and he surveyed the three walls of books that had intrigued him for years.

Then, Chase heard his grandfather say, "But that's not all," forcing the young Callaway to pull his eyes away from the bookshelves and stand at attention. "They say bad news never travels alone," his grandfather continued, "and I've got something awful to tell you now. On tonight's news, and in the papers tomorrow, you're going to hear a horrible story about Jack Pollard."

"Jack, the choir director? *Your* choir director?"

"Yes. Jack hung himself this morning."

"What! I can't believe it." Chase hadn't seen the man in years, but the news still crushed him. "I— I don't know what to say. I'm sorry. I know how much you've depended on him over the years. And if it hadn't been for Jack, I wouldn't have known about the New Bloods. He changed the course of my— And poor Jewell. She had an even bigger impact, on me at least. Does anyone know why he did it?"

"Nope. Didn't leave a note. Jewell's been mighty sick of late, however. She hasn't been to church in some time now. No one seems to know what's going on with her. Jack wouldn't talk about it. Other than that, I haven't the slightest. Understand, however, even when men seem to be walking in the narrow path of the Lord, why, some of them may be secretly harboring enormous burdens and resentments. Resentments toward God."

"What do you mean? Why would you say that?"

"Jack hung himself from the cross—you know, the big wooden cross at the altar at my church."

Chase pictured the ten-foot cross of rough-hewn timber that loomed over the primary focal point of the church, that being the glass-enclosed Bible and its tornado-driven nail that had pierced the pages. "That makes me sick. I don't get it. I can understand most things about depression from my psych studies, but the one thing I can't get a handle on is suicide by people who seem so normal and all."

"We'll never know in Jack's case. I only wanted you to be aware. It's going to reflect poorly on the church and on me, I suppose. But that's not important. I don't think Jack had a mean bone in his body. He meant no harm to the church per se. By the time a person gets to the point of suicide, at least in those well-planned cases, my guess is there's no feelings left for anyone or anything. All hope for any change has truly vanished. The future no longer exists. Your world has constricted down to the point that you are the only thing in the universe, and you can no longer escape yourself."

"The ultimate selfishness, huh? Like a black hole, where no light can escape?"

"Hmm... selfishness falls flat, implying a choice. Absolute self-absorption is more like it. It's the opposite of what we call salvation, others call nirvana, or for that matter, any higher state of mind where you've learned the secret of happiness is getting outside of yourself. Most folks who find happiness find it outside of themselves, in contrast to all the hoopla in your generation over *finding yourself*. We're a whole lot better off losing ourselves than finding ourselves. And the poor soul who gets totally swallowed up in himself, why, it's bound to cause despair.

Zeb continued. "I am sad, very sad, for all those good folks at the Driven Nail who now must sit there, Sunday after Sunday, looking at that big old cross, and picturing Jack swinging from the crossbar, heels hanging directly above where he stood for years as the choir director. I suppose we oughta remove that cross, the more I think about it. Frankly, Chase, I'm more upset about Jack than the fact that I've got prostate cancer."

.　　.　　.

The thought of Jack Pollard's heels swinging from the cross plagued Chase daily throughout the final year of medical school. *How could a person become so indifferent to God, so self-obsessed, that he would commit suicide in such spectacular fashion?* Several times, Chase considered sending Jewell Pollard a sympathy card, or writing a note, or something. Given a total loss for words, however, coupled with the rationalization that the Pollards were "remote" from his childhood, he did absolutely nothing besides fret over Jack's death.

On the plus side, the bad news had deflected the heat regarding Sukie's horrible fate. Chase renewed his commitment to maintain a healthy balance in his life. Internship was around the corner, a huge threat to balance, so he redoubled his efforts to stay "outside" of himself.

For starters, he made sure that he and Livvy visited Sukie Spurlock more often. After Livvy learned the appalling basis for Chase's sudden preoccupation with pleasing Sukie, however, Livvy visited her privately without Chase even more frequently. It took Livvy almost three weeks before she could say a decent word to Chase after learning of the Quaalude scandal. Yet, in the end, she agreed that nothing could be done, other than helping Sukie whenever and wherever possible. Still, she worried about Chase and his faltering judgment.

Graduation day finally arrived. Chase spent the entire ceremony in cap and gown lost in thought, ignoring the monotone speeches, and instead, reminiscing about the past four years. He stared at the program in his hand and the three asterisks beside his name–two for achieving the M.D. degree with Highest Honors and another asterisk for Alpha Omega Alpha Honor Medical Society. He thought back to the second round of AOA selections, where his group of seven AOAs who had been picked during the junior year were given the unique opportunity to sit in judgment of their own classmates, another seven students to be awarded the honor.

C.C. Chastain had been selected to the club in this second go-round, as had Amy DeHart, the voting done by all AOA members on campus, residents and faculty, in addition to the student inductees from earlier this year. A mild controversy had arisen over Porter Piscotel who, even with his straight-A third year, plus his straight-A fourth year, had landed in 32nd place due to the stubborn mediocrity that had stained his first two years of basic science. Porter Piscotel was nowhere close to the 14th spot where the final cut-off was to occur.

"I move that we dispense with tradition and leapfrog Dr. Porter Piscotel into the 14th slot," one of the cardiology professors had announced. "That guy has more energy than any medical student I've ever seen. Frankly, I'd like to replace my entire housestaff with a team of Piscotels."

"You can't leapfrog Piscotel," argued a tradition-rich dermatologist. "It's not fair to the fourteenth man. If you make Piscotel fourteen, then you're forced to boot out the rightful person in order to stay within our chapter by-laws. We've always done it the same way, and we've always followed the rules."

"Then let's elect fifteen."

"By-laws are by-laws. Considering the dropouts from this class, we're only allowed 10% total, and that's 14.4 students, 7.2 as juniors, 7.2 as seniors. Top five percent as juniors, next five percent as seniors, in this case, rounding down."

"Well, round it *up*."

"Again, you're dealing with the same issue if you elect fifteen, which is unfair to the bona fide number fifteen."

The debate over protocol raged, with traditionalists shocked that anyone would suggest leapfrogging, while other faculty members echoed the superlative sentiments about Porter Piscotel.

"It doesn't really matter in Porter's situation," said one of the surgery faculty members.

"Why not?"

"Because Thatcher Taylor has secured a surgical residency for Porter back east, and that's all he'll need for success in academics. AOA won't matter."

"AOA isn't merely a ticket to a top residency, it's a badge of honor for life."

"Nevertheless, Piscotel won't suffer. He'll be fine without AOA."

And with that, the AOA members–faculty, residents, and the seven students already elected from Chase's class–voted to stick with protocol and leave Porter Piscotel at the undistinguished class rank of 32nd. No leapfrogs.

Chase shook himself free of the AOA memory and looked again at the graduation program in his hand. The Dean was still at the podium, announcing the winners of various individual awards. When the overall top student in the class crossed the stage for her award, Chase tried to ignore C. C. Chastain, sitting alphabetically correct in the next seat, as his friend whispered: "Told you that you'd never be Numero Uno."

Pride goeth before a fall, Chase thought to himself. Yes, pride was the most insidious of the deadly sins as it was the only transgression that was often considered a virtue. After all, one certainly never hears, 'You won't succeed unless you have more gluttony in your work.' Chase recalled the story about Benjamin Franklin who once had introduced 12 self-created commandments, called "virtues for uniform rectitude of conduct," whereupon one of Franklin's friends confided that Ben should have added a 13th–humility–given that Franklin was "generally thought proud."

Yes, Chase needed to be content with his three asterisks. After all, he was lucky to be graduating at all. Had it not been for Sukie Spurlock, he might be standing, not before the Dean dressed in a black robe, but before a judge in similar garb, begging for a lighter sentence.

Medical school would be a clean break with the irrelevant, the esoteric, and the senseless. It was over. From now on, everything he learned would be of practical, if not critical, use. And, he would tackle his surgical residency while maintaining balance. Even though surgery interns were on-call every other night, sleeping at the hospital, he would devote his off-time to Livvy and to cultivating their marriage, staying outside of himself, ever mindful of the April 4th epiphany in childhood, portending a defining moment at some point in the future.

After the ceremony, Dr. Thatcher Nolan Taylor, Chairman of the Department of Surgery, treated the entire graduating class to a soiree at Matherville's prestigious Colony Club. Chase and Livvy were ecstatic to see the inside of the legendary club, with its white-washed exterior and its wood-paneled interior. And when Dr. Taylor introduced the couple to his wife Gretchen, saying, "Chase might prove to be the best resident we've ever had," the newly-minted *Doctor* Callaway beamed brighter than any silly trophy given to Numero Uno during medical school graduation. Livvy squeezed Chase's hand a little tighter as Dr. Taylor smiled.

Then Dr. Taylor added, speaking to his wife, "You know, Gretchen, Chase is Wes Callaway's son."

"Very nice," she said, nodding graciously. From her unchanged expression, Chase doubted that Mrs. Taylor was a basketball fan.

A rush of cool air seemed to pour out of the dark and empty fireplace with its tall opening, large enough to swallow a man whole. Chase imagined what an impressive sight the fireplace must be in the winter, with flames forming a leaping display for Matherville's high society.

Chase heard an irritating squeak and looked to the left of the fireplace where a stately wooden door with ornate jambs and lintel had eased open, apparently on its own.

"That's the so-called secret door to the Smoking Room. The latch is broken," said Dr. Taylor, obviously noting Chase's wide eyes. Dr. Taylor stepped forward and pulled the door shut. "They barely let *me* go inside there," joked the surgeon. "Josef Studebaker, Gretchen's father, was one of the founding members of the club, and he's the only reason I was allowed in the Smoking Room. Even then, ol' Josef–may he rest in peace–made sure the marriage was going to last before I was invited inside." Dr. Taylor chuckled while his wife Gretchen poked him in the ribs, both acting like high school sweethearts.

As Chase stared at the elaborate carvings of scrolls and seashells in the lintel above the door, the words of crazy Viola, the paranoid schizophrenic, wormed their way into his thoughts:

Death's kind door is nigh ajar
Tongues of fire lick from afar
The curse hath slumbered since heels did hang
The dog awaketh to feel the pain.

21

"It's only for a year" was the anemic battle cry for the new surgical interns–subtle defeat woven neatly into a pattern of inevitable triumph.

Anticipating the worst, Chase went overboard to brutalize internship with preconceived notions, hoping to desensitize himself. Still, he underestimated the impact. The surgery 'tern never went to work and came home on the same day. Billed as a marathon of "36 hours on–12 off," the truth was closer to "40 hours on–8 off," and those "off" were for sleep – catatonic sleep – glorious, dreamless, without interruption, at home, in one's own beloved bed.

Sure, there were minutes, sometimes hours, of rest during the night in a hospital, but Chase discovered that a call room tends to poison the quality one's sleep. Slumber as balm for the bruised mind simply did not work very well because the telephone as a roommate always snores.

"I'm not willing to pay the dues" was the anti-battle cry of those medical students who, albeit drawn to the exciting discipline of surgery, chose paths more softly traveled into specialties with humane call schedules and reasonable expectations. And every time Chase heard this feeble cry from non-surgical friends, he swelled inside with a shapeless passion that validated, or forced, his mettle.

Once, after a long shift, with nerves frazzled, he overheard a cranky, middle-aged nurse complain about having to "work a double." It was a common complaint among nursing staff and one that never really bothered him, until now. This time, he was tired.

"Each and every time I come to work," he said, "I work a quintuple— that's *five straight shifts*."

The nurse didn't hesitate, apparently having fielded this complaint previously. "You chose this for yourself, *doctor*. You've got a payoff coming someday with the big bucks. For now, you made your nest. You lie in it. Don't complain to me. I'll show you my paycheck, if that'll make you feel better, 'cause it's peanuts compared to what you'll be pulling in when you're a real doctor."

He never criticized a double-duty nurse again.

Gradually, Chase came to understand why Dr. Meeker, the histrionic psychiatrist, had described surgical residency as the "next-to-worst" occupational stress that life had to offer, second only to troops in combat. And while the metamorphosis into surgeon might well have been a distant second to enemy fire, the toll on the wives was more insidious.

In contrast to wartime brides who envision their heroes overseas fighting for virtue, where absence can make the heart grow fonder, the surgical wives saw their beleaguered heroes brush past them in a dash to hibernate every other night, which was, in fact, *every night* that they were at home. Such predictable and regular neglect took its toll by biting away at love piecemeal.

Making matters worse, surgeons-in-training (and Chase was no exception) were tense, frustrated, insecure, fearful, overwhelmed, plus they made demands, both spoken and unspoken, for emotional support to flow in one direction, toward themselves. They complained to their wives (surgical residents at Far West were *all* men) about their relentless burden of "sins of commission," rather than the cozy lifestyle of the medicine interns where "sins of *omission*" were feathery in comparison. For the internists, disease was often running its natural course, where medical intervention might or might not alter the downward spiral, with mistakes assimilated by the whirlpool. The sins of the surgeon, however, killed people outright.

The ever-listening wives were not allowed to suffer, or even commiserate. They could not possibly understand. They were not allowed to hurt, and they were not allowed to be lonely. After all, their husbands were living a nightmare. So, the wives stood by and watched the stress, the sleep deprivation, and the "sins of commission" chip away at the granite men they thought they had married.

Livvy knew the divorce rate at the Far West surgical program was currently running at 75%, and she was consumed by making sure that she and Chase would be in the surviving 25%. Despite best intentions, however, even with Livvy's fingers clawing at the cliff of normalcy, their life slipped into surrealism. Chase would come home after dark, fall asleep first in his plate of food, then a second time in their bed. Livvy knew the lives of patients were at stake, but the only lives she saw in danger were Chase's and her own.

Chase's sworn program of balance was gone in a flash. There was no hope of balance. Survival became the solitary goal. "It's only for a year," he reminded Livvy. "Next year, the call schedule changes to every third night, and I'll be on easy street."

To offset the negatives of a back-breaking schedule, Chase reveled in the art and skill of surgery, as he had hoped and planned. Patients rolled into the operating room with disease, and they rolled out hours later, free of disease, most of the time. He mustered a great guffaw whenever people reminded him that he had once planned a career in psychiatry. His worry about whether he had "good hands" disappeared quickly. Chairman Thatcher Taylor was a meticulous surgeon to whom all aspired in principle, yet few had the patience or compulsion to make each snip and stitch perfect. Chase was an exception. Perfection was key. Unlike most surgical departments, surgical speed in the O.R. was downplayed by the faculty at Far West, in deference to Dr. Taylor's perfectionism, and it made sense to Chase. Technique was everything.

An open-heart scrub nurse whispered to Chase during a coronary bypass, "I've been scrubbing these cases for seven years now, and I've never seen an intern close the leg so nicely." Chase lifted his head only long enough to see her raise an eyebrow as accent to her compliment. Then, he went back to closing the skin of the leg where the vein had been harvested. "Plenty of interns have been faster, sure. I can tell you, however, no one has done such a beautiful job." Chase hoped that

Thatcher Taylor, at work repairing the stilled heart in the open chest, overheard the nurse's hushed praise.

Chase considered going into thoracic surgery. The residency was a measly one year of training beyond general surgery–six months of lung surgery and six months of open heart. Yet, he was struck by something odd–the cardiac cases were not fun (for the surgeons, that is). The heart surgeons didn't seem to enjoy themselves. There was no joking, no kidding. The atmosphere was tense. Always. Even airline pilots holding a few hundred lives in their hands could banter while on automatic pilot. But there was no automatic pilot while the patient was on the heart-lung machine.

Chase wondered, however, if the brooding persisted in private practice because, here at Far West, there was a vainglorious surgeon who likely set the tone–Chief of Cardiac Surgery, Brick Dagmar, whose bellowing condescension kept all surgery residents on their heels, or on their butts.

During this time when Chase was contemplating yet another battle cry– "Gee, Livvy, thoracics is just one more year"–Dr. Dagmar announced new national standards that required thoracic surgery training to be two years beyond general surgery, rather than one. Eager to "get out" and "get started," Chase dropped the idea, and settled into general surgery where the residents played their radios, told good stories, and joked around–perhaps to escape the fact that, while tension in the O.R. was minimal compared to heart surgery, the post-op complication and mortality rate for patients undergoing abdominal surgery, what with mischievous bacteria, was higher than cardiac surgery. Indeed, death after complications from abdominal surgery occurred long after the intraoperative banter of general surgeons had faded away.

Dr. Thatcher Taylor called Chase into his office halfway through the intern year. Tanned, even in the dead of winter, Dr. Taylor sat with elbows resting on the arms of his chair, fingers interlocked as if in prayer. "Chase, unfortunately, we must decide years in advance who's headed to thoracic surgery, since we want that individual to spend the third year, the research year, at Mass General. I've heard through the grapevine that you're no longer in the hunt. I'm sorry to hear that if it's true, but I wanted to make sure before we filled that slot."

"That's right, Dr. Taylor. I don't think cardiac is the best path for me. However, since you mentioned the research year, I've been thinking about something, if it's okay with you, of course. It's different than anyone has ever done in the program, best I can tell. I know that most the guys go to the animal lab, either here or somewhere else, for the research year. But I was wondering about doing a year of pathology. I understand that path was once required for surgeons to rotate—"

"Chase, that's an excellent idea. You may or may not know that I spent one full year in pathology myself. A few practicing surgeons are still around today who did rotations on pathology, but there aren't many of us left who did a full year. It wasn't that long ago that candidates going for their surgical boards had to interpret microscope slides as part of their certification. Today, I'm afraid it's a lost art among surgeons. Talk to me next year about arranging that. As you know, I encourage our residents to spend the research year at another medical center, out of state usually, so that you get a feel for what the rest of the country is doing."

Chase gushed relief. He had considered that Dr. Taylor might nix the idea. After all, whenever he had mentioned his plans to explore the roots of surgery–that is, pathology–his co-residents had said things like, "What do you want to do that for?" "You won't be operating at all during the research year. Even operating on rats beats looking through a microscope." "What a waste of time." Chase was more worried when colleagues said, "Dr. Taylor will never let you do something like that." Yet, Dr. Taylor hadn't merely endorsed the plan, he had been enthusiastic. Chase was thrilled that he might get the opportunity to give the microscope a final twirl.

. . .

Like any internship, the year had highs and lows. The highs occurred whenever Chase "got to do the case," and the lows were all other waking minutes. Sanity was maintained only through the restoration provided by weekends, wherein either a Saturday afternoon or Sunday afternoon was "off." To escape, over the course of the year, Chase read *The Hobbit* and Tolkien's trilogy, then he planned Asimov's *Foundation* trilogy to follow the next year. No world, no planet, no universe was too far away for Chase.

Further restoration came with two precious weeks of vacation. During week one, Chase slept, read, slept, scribbled lyrics, slept, read, and slept some more. During the second week, later in the year, he and Livvy drove to Kansas City where she enjoyed shopping at The Plaza (fantasy shopping, that is, with actual purchases postponed for five years when discretionary income would appear). Chase tagged along, for the most part numb, but thrilled to have a change of venue. Watching Livvy cruise through department stores at full steam was great respite from gunshot victims vomiting blood and alcohol into his face, draining perirectal abscesses in the emergency room, or patients going into septic shock after surgery and dying despite all efforts.

Shortly after returning from Kansas City, Chase endured a new low during teaching rounds with Brick Dagmar, the cardiac surgeon whose words spilled out like boiling oil upon the residents. The focus was on a young male patient who had undergone an exploratory laparotomy for a stab wound to the abdomen. Although a cardiac surgeon by trade, Dagmar served as the attending physician on general surgery cases as well, proving to everyone that you could not only be a jack of all trades, but also a master of everything.

When Dagmar pulled off a 4X4 dressing from the patient's abdomen and saw that the stab wound had been packed open for secondary healing, as opposed to closing the cut with sutures, he spun around and thundered, "Who left this wound open?" From the back of the group, Chase managed, "I did. I considered it contaminated."

Dagmar brushed through the gathering of residents and students then jammed his stiffened index finger into the intern's chest as he bellowed, "I told you at M&M conference just last week, to *close these stab wounds primarily*. Did I not make myself clear? Did you not listen to me?" When no response came from the dumbstruck intern, Dagmar jammed his finger again into Chase's sternum. "Knock, knock. Anyone home?"

Fury welled, and Chase wanted to grab the finger and yank it off. Instead, he replied with a quiet, humble voice, trying his best to avoid sounding smug, for he was about to humiliate Dagmar by twisting the facts back to the truth: "Sorry, but I was on vacation last week, Dr. Dagmar, so you might have told everyone at conference, but I wasn't there. I didn't get the message."

For a moment, Dagmar was stunned by the challenge. His red hair seemed to stiffen, his heavy-lidded green eyes squinted in ferocity, and the red blotches on his face coalesced until the skin everywhere was flaming. In protecting himself with an apology, the insolent intern had simultaneously accused Dagmar of making a mistake. And when in doubt, Dagmar used a treasured weapon–he glared. Forever, it seemed.

The students and residents were like statues placed in a circle around the bed of the wide-eyed patient whose stab wound had become a centerpiece. Finally, Dagmar stirred, thrusting his finger into Chase's chest for a third time. "No. I'm *certain* you were there, so it must have been the week before when I made myself so patently clear. I'm not going to tell you again–stop packing these stab wounds open! Sew them up."

Dagmar turned to the other residents at the bedside: "And the next time I see a stab wound packed open, heads are gonna roll, and you can start checking out other programs for your training." He glared again at Chase who was fuming inside, although returning the stare with perfect stoicism.

It was generally held that one's relationship with Dr. Dagmar was established on Day One and would last the entire residency. Certainly, Chase felt a sense of doom for his future, but he was not going to quake at the knees when Dagmar had been dead wrong. His respect for Dagmar plummeted, especially after confirming with his friends that the dictum had been issued while Chase was on vacation. The story became the stuff of legend, and residents would often recount how close Dagmar came to throttling Chase's neck. "Heads are gonna roll" became an all-purpose catch phrase.

One month later, Chase was serving as first assistant to Dagmar while he, the cardiac surgeon, performed a mastectomy on a patient with breast cancer. Chase's job was to use special hooks to hold the skin flaps at right angles from the body. And when Dr. Dagmar accidentally cut through the flap–"buttonholing" the skin and jeopardizing its blood supply–he yelled at Chase: "Hold those hooks at right angles, for god sakes, do you see what you made me do?"

Chase spent every minute of the two-hour case holding the skin flaps at perfect right angles, but Dagmar chewed on Chase all four times that buttonholes appeared. Chase had been a pillar of stone the entire time, while Dagmar grappled with the mastectomy, a procedure he rarely performed, but one in which the traditional teaching had been "thin skin flaps." *Nothing worse than a blamer*, Chase thought. He did not care one bit about Dagmar's glowing reputation, nor did he care about the mothers who thanked God for Brick Dagmar after he corrected their babies' malformed hearts. For Chase, Dagmar was a playground bully.

On Christmas Day, Chase was the intern rotating on thoracic surgery. The entire team was planning to go home after morning rounds to celebrate with loved ones. But a wits-end Matherville woman altered housestaff holiday plans when she stabbed her husband in the heart with an ice pick on merry Christmas morning. The chief cardiac resident easily repaired the hole with a single stitch. However, the anesthesiology resident-in-training had placed the endotracheal tube in the esophagus rather than the trachea (confirmed as being "perfect" by the anesthesia faculty), and the problem was discovered only after the chest was opened whereupon the lungs were found to be sagging and still. The cardiac resident yelled at the anesthesiologist, the tube was replaced in the correct spot, but in those several minutes without oxygen, the patient's brain became mush. At the same time, the patient's 30-year-old heart was fine.

"Too bad the kidney transplant program isn't open for another month," said the cardiac resident. "His kidneys are perfect."

"After he dies, we'll be charging the wife with second-degree murder," said the police detective who was waiting for the surgeons as they walked out of the ICU around noon. "Until he dies, though, it's only assault with a deadly weapon."

Chase thought it an odd twist of fate that the anesthesiologists got off scot-free. The ice pick was not going to kill the man. The lethal blow came from the sleep doctors.

"You can't look at it that way, Chase," said another intern. "You gotta figure, hell, the guy had a hole in his heart. Whaddya expect?"

"Yes, a tiny hole, fixed with a single stitch. Might have closed off even without the stitch."

It was almost the exact reverse of the "captain of the ship" policy where the surgeon takes the blame for everything, no matter who is at fault. In this case, the wife was "captain," and she would be spending a long time in jail, perhaps well-deserved, but decades as opposed to a few years, because the anesthesia resident had slipped a tube down the wrong pipe. Malpractice potential? "Whaddya expect? He was stabbed in the heart!"

Yes, a faculty member had been glued at the resident's side for the misplaced tube, but procedures in medicine were often one-person acts, and it didn't matter how many faculty members were in the room. Chase had to consider such a "sin of commission" as a daily partner in his life from now on. Yet, who actually paid for these sins?

That said, the ice pick victim had not died yet. Dr. Brick Dagmar, at home with his family, telephoned the order that intern Chase Callaway was to stay by the bedside and manage the victim's care as long as the brain-dead man still had a heartbeat. For the next 12 hours, Chase adjusted cardiotropic medications, fiddled with the ventilator, inserted monitoring lines, and struggled to keep the man alive, even though everyone knew the situation was hopeless. Chase grumbled that it should be the anesthesia resident who ought to have a spoiled Christmas if someone was required to stand bedside. And to make matters worse, Chase had been on call the night before with little sleep, and was scheduled to be off Christmas. Now, he was standing vigil for who knew how long? Dagmar had trumped the call schedule, handpicking low man on the totem pole for Yuletide duty.

Chase phoned Livvy every hour throughout Christmas day to offer an update, but he didn't tell her the horrible turmoil within–that he actually hoped the man would hurry up and die, get it over with, so that Chase could have a merry Christmas. Although Chase tried his best to keep the man alive, in spite of his urge to walk away, the ice-picked man died shortly after midnight. As instructed, Chase called the police to let them know that the wife was now a murderess.

Livvy was waiting up for him when he got home. His Christmas present to her was a set of earrings. Her present to him was a gold chain so that he could wear his wedding ring around his neck. Somehow, during internship, the iodine in the surgical scrub soap had interacted with the gold in his wedding band, causing the skin beneath his ring to welt and scale and itch in a perfect red circle of contact dermatitis. No poultice seemed capable of halting the process. He'd even tried coating the interior of his wedding ring with clear fingernail polish. When that failed, he had tried leaving the ring off, letting the skin heal, but then it would turn angry red as soon as he started wearing the ring again. Finally, he had no other recourse than to stop wearing his wedding ring entirely.

. . .

As the intern rotating on plastic surgery, Chase tried to stimulate interest among the residents in a "great case" of complete, bilateral syndactyly he knew about, across the creek at the mental institution. However, he did not get far with the plastics residents, senior or junior. The surgery schedule was "very tight," "the hospital at the asylum is substandard," and "after all, syndactyly repair is not on our checklist of cases for board-certification." Still, Chase thought of Ivy often, even as he visited her less and less, with his free time vanishing.

After serving as the rotating intern on pediatric surgery, then a month on internal medicine, Chase finally made it to general surgery. His first appendectomy went smoothly. Cutting into a living, breathing human was not the barrier it might have been. After all, the surgery was done through a square patch of skin, bordered by green towels, and the process seemed quite natural, no different really than the incisions he had made in the autopsy suite. He had come a long way since fainting as a first-year student drawing blood.

The Level Two surgery resident, of course, had made the diagnosis of appendicitis (not Chase), prompting the tough decision to orchestrate surgery in the middle of the night by calling the operating room, anesthesia, and notifying faculty. The Level Two resident then talked Chase through the procedure step-by-step. The fact that the appendix was completely normal didn't bother anyone. After all, Chase had learned, even as a medical student, that some cases of suspected appendicitis are going to be tricks–symptom complexes that mimic appendicitis. In fact, a 10-15% normalcy rate had been calculated as a desirable goal. No test could assure the diagnosis, leaving surgery to serve both a diagnostic and therapeutic role. Even the normal appendix must be removed once a patient has been opened, of course, to protect against the possibility of a replay should the decoy illness come again, or should a true case of appendicitis evolve. Although this first appendix was technically "normal," Chase was quite pleased with himself as things went smoothly, plus resting in the comfort that his patient would never have to be operated on for appendicitis again.

Then, on the second post-op day, the healthy 18-year-old boy who had been freed of his appendix, stepped out of his hospital bed aiming for the bathroom, took a few steps forward and dropped dead, a few feet shy of the toilet.

"Chase, you deal with the family," said the Chief Resident, "you're the one who knows them best, and you're really good with that sort of the thing." After the news, the wailing mother fell to the ground and clutched Chase's leg as she screamed for God to deliver her from the horror, begging Chase to recant his lies. The father looked as if he'd be comfortable murdering Chase with complete justification.

"Pulmonary embolus" was the verdict from the autopsy. "Couldn't be helped," said the chief resident in a cavalier manner. "Must've had an underlying thrombogenic disorder. If the surgery hadn't got him, something else would." If there was any guilt, it diffused like a drop of poison rendered harmless in a large vat of wine, equally spread among the team–chief resident, junior resident, and the knife-toting intern.

It can't get any worse than this, thought Chase, another battle cry dangerously close to a mantra. *Maybe surgeons should stop bragging about how many cases they've done or how fast they go "skin-to-skin." Maybe we should focus on improving things. Maybe we should have waited until the next morning to examine the kid again. Watched to see what his white count did. Maybe we need to improve the way appendicitis is diagnosed. Surely, some sort of X-ray test, or a better blood test, or something, would help. Why don't we check pre-op for thrombogenic disorders? And why do we simply accept the fact we're going to take out normal organs now and then? Fortunes of war, and that sort of thing, we say. Still, why do we accept things like they are?* Chase contemplated the case for months, as he did for everything less than perfect.

Unexpected and unexplained tragedies were part of the profession, however. A month later, a group of fifteen doctors and nurses surrounded a bed in the recovery room, always a bad sign, and Chase caught a glimpse of a beautiful young woman connected to a ventilator. Creeping to the back of the audience, Chase asked the obvious question of a bystander. The answer came as a whisper: "Brain dead."

"What procedure?" asked Chase.

"Wisdom teeth," was the answer.

"Thank you, Lord," Chase said to himself. "Except for the grace of God, there go I." Then he felt remorse for even thinking such a thought. "I" was the ultimate selfish reaction–no concern for the poor patient or her family. Chase realized his knee-jerk reaction had been the overwhelming gratitude that the disaster *had not happened to him.* Something didn't feel right. A shell had formed. While Chase knew himself to be highly introspective, he didn't understand his own response. Somehow, he thought, chronic sleep deprivation, or something, seemed to be altering, not only his personality, but also his values. He was running through a mine field, tippy-toeing in combat boots.

A 32-year-old woman had undergone a Halsted radical mastectomy at age 28 and now had metastatic breast cancer. Two weeks after witnessing the Wisdom Teeth case, Chase was assigned to perform a pre-op history and physical on the unfortunate young woman. Although she was on the surgical service, the scheduled procedure–an abortion– would be performed by the gynecologists at the request of Chase's surgical attending who said, "I can't believe she was so foolish to go out and get pregnant after breast cancer. She must have some sort of death wish. If terminating this pregnancy doesn't shrink her metastases, we'll take her back to the O.R. and remove her ovaries and her adrenals."

In his pre-op time with the patient, Chase learned that the diagnosis of her metastatic disease was new, made shortly *after* the discovery that she was pregnant. He was bothered that a woman so close to his age could get breast cancer. However, he recalled Sukie Spurlock's children, both a daughter *and* a son, who had developed breast cancer as young adults.

Then the patient said, "I know I'm going to die with this cancer, so why not let my baby live? My mother could take care of it, and my husband. We don't have any children. Crazy, isn't it? When we tried, we couldn't, and then when we tried *not* to, it happened. I wish my baby could live. I'd feel like part of me would still be around for my husband. He agrees. So what if it shortens my life? I'm going to die regardless."

Troubled, Chase asked the attending surgeon if the abortion was absolutely necessary since the mother wanted to have the baby. And from what he could tell in the textbooks, the admonition to abort pregnancies in breast cancer patients was based on dictums, not data. Hormone-related theories swirled about without real proof. Why couldn't they let her deliver?

The answer was swift and intense. "Dr. Callaway, as surgeons, we are charged with eradicating cancer. Leave the emotional baggage to the psychiatrists. In the past, we performed adrenalectomy and oophorectomy on all young women with metastatic disease willy-nilly. Today, we have the luxury and sophistication of being able to measure estrogen receptors, and to perform our surgery only where appropriate. This represents a major advance in surgery. So, are you suggesting that we allow the hormones of pregnancy to skyrocket in this woman who has an estrogen-sensitive tumor?" The faculty surgeon stopped short of saying it, but the tone was there: *"What kind of assassin are you?"*

The next day, the abortion was performed. Legality had never been a concern with "pregnancy terminations" as related to standard treatment in metastatic breast cancer, but the new Supreme Court ruling made it even easier. The Ob-gyn intern used the new suction device invented to make the procedure Hoover-quick and easy. But when the intern inserted the cannula, the introductory spear perforated the uterus, and the collection bucket quickly filled with most of the woman's small intestines, vacuumed briskly along with a fetus that was swimming somewhere in the mess.

The attending general surgeon flew into action, belittling the intern and his gynecology attending as he readied the patient for emergency abdominal surgery with Chase serving as first assistant. The surgeon connected the remaining 18 inches of jejunum to the remaining 8 inches of ileum. "If she makes it out of the hospital, she's going to spend the rest of her short life on the shitter," said the attending. *And childless,* thought Chase.

The intern who performed the super-suction curettage was marked for life. The attending Ob-Gyn allegedly did his best to blame everything on the intern, even though "captain of the ship" landed guilt squarely on faculty shoulders, along with a million-dollar settlement. The defense attorneys tried to point out that no matter how much supervision a faculty member claimed to have, major damage by a "sole agent" could occur in a split second, and there was nothing a faculty member could do to stop it. No matter how much assurance was given to patients at a teaching facility–in this case, College Hospital– that "I'll be right there guiding everything," an errant intern or resident could kill or maim while faculty gawked helplessly. This persuasive line of reasoning by the defense was said to have reduced the original demand for two million dollars down to a paltry million.

The winds of novice care at College Hospital swirled everywhere. No one was immune to disaster. One of Chase's fellow interns, while starting an internal jugular IV line in the emergency room, under careful instruction from the junior resident, hit the carotid artery instead, apparently dislodging an atherosclerotic plaque and causing the patient to suffer a major stroke. Another surgical intern, while retracting the renal vein during abdominal aneurysm surgery, ripped the vein in half, and the patient bled to death on the table. It wouldn't have mattered if an army of attending surgeons had been present when these things happened. Things simply went south sometimes–part of the "learning curve." Chase was taught to adopt a philosophy of medicine best explained by its mantra: "Shit happens."

Perhaps the potential for such disaster explained why the general surgery faculty personally performed all operations on their private patients at College Hospital. And no one was stingier with allowing interns and residents to sew than Chairman Thatcher Nolan Taylor,

M.D. Dr. Taylor performed his own cases from beginning to end, including the final stitches. The assisting resident could hope for a minor role in the skin closure, at most. Upon discovering this, Chase was even more grateful for the three stitches he'd been allowed to place for Dr. Taylor while still a third-year student on the surgery clerkship. Those three stitches had charted his career.

. . .

Surgical education was undergoing many changes, and one such change was in the taxonomy of training. "Interns" were now to be called PG-1s (post-graduate year one), but they were still referred to as "terns." First-year surgery residents were the recipients of numerical upgrading to PG-2s, called Level Twos, or the diminutive form–Two. The term "junior resident" would be supplanted, then, by a simple number. That said, no one was called a "Five," so Chiefs remained Chiefs.

Chase was thrilled to become a Two, not only for the unique experience of "every third" night on call instead of "every other," but also because of the dramatic leap in responsibility.

For the first time, a Two became the senior resident on call, in-house. At night, you ran the codes for cardiac arrest, you dictated management of crises on the wards, you made the diagnoses coming from the emergency room, you called the shots. And, you dragged the Chief (or the Attending for private pay patients) out of sweet slumber at home to operate *based on your impressions, not his.*

Your word was golden. You were charged with synchronization– announcing the need for surgical intervention, calling the operating room for availability, phoning the anesthesia resident for same, then orchestrating the entire scene to perfection, including the Chief's driving time, so that induction of anesthesia took place in the operating room at the exact moment the Chief burst through the swinging double doors. And if the diagnosis was wrong, all eyes–those of surgeons, anesthesiologist, scrub nurse, circulating nurse, even the lowly "tern" who would be up all night with post-op care–shifted to the *junior* resident who had destroyed sleep for everyone in the room. The jump from PG-1 to PG-2 was, in fact, the widest chasm in surgical training.

The most colorful rotation for PGs at any level was the time spent at the maximum security hospital across the creek at Matherville State where the residents treated not only the inmates of the mental institution, but also the incarcerated criminals of west Texas. For College Hospital at Far West Texas to have a chance at competing with Permian Medical Center for private patients, it was of critical importance that anyone in shackles, and those of unsound mind, be admitted to the unnamed hospital that was part of Matherville State Mental Hospital.

This hospital, built in 1919, renovated by Josef Studebaker in the 1930s, was a step back in time. Two operating rooms had been constructed, but only one was currently in use. The other, now a storage room, had once been a "theater" where avant-garde procedures, such as prefrontal lobotomies (first done through craniotomies, then the nose, and finally the eye socket) could be viewed from three rows of bleachers. It was rumored that the most famous lobotomist in the country, Dr. Walter Freeman, had visited Matherville to teach the local doctors how to perform the simple procedure, using a single instrument–an ice pick.

It was also a legend that a famous series of sham surgeries had been performed in the unnamed hospital as well, all failures. These sham procedures had been designed and predicted to cure psychological ills where bodily delusions were the central feature.

One such historical case that landed in the textbooks concerned a schizophrenic woman obsessed with the idea that a snake lived inside her belly. While the Freudians argued their position on the matter and tried to block the planned surgery, the frontier psychosurgeons argued that their approach could result in an easy cure. Surgeons sometimes claimed to be "internists with knives," and in this case, they tried to be "shrinks with knives." Furthermore, surgical cures were much easier to pitch to families than "psychotherapy" and "pharmacology," neither of which had accomplished much for mental health at this point in time. So, this particular woman underwent a sham surgery to remove the snake.

Under general anesthesia, an incision was made into her belly and, for a convincing photographic record, a live snake borrowed from the city zoo was held above her open abdomen for proof of removal. Indeed, the operation worked brilliantly, the patient felt cured, and the surgeons, giddy with excitement, wrote a manuscript half-prepared for publication. However, a few months later, the wily patient announced that the snake had been a female, and that said snake had delivered a nest of babies before extrication. Now, the patient was dealing with five snakes in her belly. This not only multiplied the variables for the Freudians, but also put an end to the sham surgeries.

The ambiance of the surgical suite at the Matherville State hospital could not be found anywhere short of a time machine. The spidery limbs of the O.R. lights, the black linoleum on the floor worn so thin the underlying white hexagon tiles peeked through, and the unthinkable *windows* (anathema in current guidelines for infection control) that were filled with translucent glass bricks—it was a journey to 1930 with no plans for renovation.

The walls outside the O.R. were decorated with shadow boxes crafted by a previous generation of nurses who had chosen to display foreign objects ingested by patients and prisoners, and then surgically removed by the doctors in training who rotated through Matherville State. One shadowbox was filled with flatware, another with pencils and pens, another with a "sharps" theme (razor blades and knives mostly), and even one large shadowbox filled with springs and links all taken from a single patient who had tried to eat his entire bed frame.

And in this surrealistic environment, each resident functioned one PG step above his official capacity. The "tern" did the work of a "Two," and the "Two" did the work of a Chief, and the Chief acted like an attending. As for the faculty, the true attendings, they never set foot in the building.

On his rotation at the Matherville hospital, Chase was caught up in the carnival atmosphere, including the jokes and commentary about patients after they were asleep. How could one not participate? When you're revising the colostomy and the ureteral ileostomy on the half-man, Renaldo, who had undergone removal of the lower half of his body—a "hemi-corporectomy"—after a self-inflicted gunshot wound to the abdomen destroyed his lower aorta, how could one not comment on the bed sores at the base of his body stump? Or the bag for feces that hung below his left nipple? Or his bag for urine beneath the right nipple?

How could one not tell stories of Renaldo transporting himself with circus-like skill, racing around the ward on his knuckles? Merely climbing into his bed was an artistic wonder.

And if the old schizophrenic, Cephus, has an abscess cavity drained from his chest, yet he keeps tearing his incision open with his bare hands exposing a cavity that leads directly to the beating heart, and if Cephus has to be restrained from reaching inside the cavity and fiddling with his own heart like a toy... how could one not joke to evade the staggering depths to which a human can decay? Yes, removing swallowed razor blades and sticking the prizes in shadowboxes was entirely within the framework of an eccentric world of surgery gone mad.

In the midst of it all, now a "Two" instead of a 'tern, Chase managed to convince the new plastic surgery residents to cross the creek from College Hospital and evaluate Ivy Pettibone in the surgery clinic. To his surprise, they scheduled a repair of bilateral syndactyly on Ivy, to be done in two weeks. "We'll do both sides at the same setting, even if that's not the norm. With splints and dressings on, her function is going to be much the same that she's used to with her syndactyly, plus it's so hard for us to get over here to operate. Bottom line–bilateral repair."

Chase was thrilled that, after all these years, it was finally going to happen. He worked to get an updated court order for surgical consent, then he reviewed hand anatomy and the planned surgery, as he had done in the past.

However, on the day Ivy was scheduled, the plastics team called to cancel. The Chief Resident in Plastics had an opportunity to perform a facelift on a private patient. The junior resident was left in charge, but he had not prepared for Ivy's case by reading the night before. "All those Z-plasty maneuvers are terribly tricky, and you've got to watch out for the nerves and vessels, and I think it would be better to wait until the Chief is free." Yet, "free" was never to be. The schedule for the plastics residents at College Hospital never seemed to allow another opening.

Chase promised himself he'd never give up. It was a matter of keeping his word. In his mind, it had become payback for a debt he owed Ivy after she had saved his life. Granted, the memory of playing the piano at Ivy's side and making promises to fix her hands was starting to fade. He had to keep his memory fresh. *I'll be back as an upper-level resident some day when I have more authority. Ivy won't mind. She's waited over 40 years already, and to be truthful, I think she's fine with her fingers. It's me that wants it more than her anyway.*

.   .   .

As Chase's confidence in his own operative skills grew, so did his ability to handle the emotional challenges in surgery, a world that included the horrors he'd seen at Matherville State. The walls he built for himself became thicker and thicker. He could joke with the best of them in the O.R. He could operate while quoting lines of classic literature or snippets from old movies, or reciting lyrics from most any song written after 1955, or in a pinch, he could always mock the empty aphorisms spewed by colleagues in other specialties as they misdiagnosed surgical problems. He was becoming a Master Surgeon, and he knew of nothing that could stop him. However, wife Livvy saw it differently.

She saw happiness decline as his confidence grew. She saw laughter turn quiet while abilities soared. She saw a different Chase Callaway being born again.

Often, deep-rooted changes are linked to single events, but the metamorphosis of human being into surgeon was so subtle, so insidious, occurring over so much time that nothing seemed to be changing at all. Livvy had to think backward over long periods of time for full perspective. Months told her nothing. Years told her everything.

Livvy had to resurrect their years in medical school, and earlier, to hear Chase laughing from the gut, or to see him writing lyrics, or to feel him touch her with true affection. And the more she worried about such change, the less Chase seemed worried about anything. One great hope kept her head aloft–it was time for the "research year," when life would revert to normal, at least for 12 months.

Disturbingly, no plans for the research year had been made. Despite Dr. Thatcher Taylor's enthusiasm last year for Chase spending a year in pathology, when the time came to finalize plans, Chase was on his own. Dr. Taylor's nationwide contacts were surgeons, not pathologists. "If you were planning a year in the animal lab, Chase, I could get you in about anywhere."

Chase petitioned thirty different medical centers around the country, explaining his intent and his hopes. Pathology departments at leading universities and hospitals responded that they no longer accommodated fellowships by surgery residents. In fact, they had not done so "for many years." And there was "no funding" to support such a year. "Nothing available" seemed to be the universal answer.

Chase had not yet heard from his first choice–one of the leading medical centers in Southern California near Hollywood. Stargazing held secondary intrigue only. Primary was the fact that his old medical school classmate, C.C. Chastain, was practicing emergency medicine in several coastal hospitals near L.A., while forging a career in the music industry. Chase admitted to Livvy that he relished the thought of turning their old medical school spoof-opera collaborations into something more.

It was this obsession that haunted Livvy the most. If Chase was so gung-ho surgery, then why was he fantasizing about a return to his musical roots? And the more he talked about going to Southern California, the more Livvy worried, given that the chances appeared nil. After all, 28 of 28 responses so far were rejections. Only two responses were left. If no one would take him at this late hour, he'd be stuck in Matherville, possibly back on the wards, with the research year postponed. Then the 29th rejection came in the mail, this one from Boston. Its one sentence rebuff seemed to tap into an alter ego.

Chase spilled forth in an ugly catharsis that Livvy had long suspected: "Does a surgeon's life really get any better once you're out of residency? I'm not so sure it does. And I'm not so sure I'm cut out for this. I'm a worrier. And I worry about patients who aren't doing well. I love doing the procedures, but I worry over things that might turn out to be the proverbial 'snake under every rock' because very often, there *really is a snake* under that rock. The busier you are, the more complications there are. My mood moves in the same direction as the complication rate, up when things are going well, down when something goes wrong. And with general surgery, it seems like something is *always* going wrong. Too many freakin' bacteria in the damn GI tract... "

He had held it in for almost two years, and Livvy saw that California was not simply a one-year respite. In Chase's mind, it could mean a new life. Perhaps, even a new life in music rather than medicine. She felt a twinge of guilt as, years ago, she had encouraged the latter. They would wait for the letter from Los Angeles.

"...and if I don't capture this year for pathology, like it's looking right now, then I'm going to be stuck in the freakin' dog lab here at Far West for my research year, probably delayed since the solo spot in the lab this year is already taken. And to boot, I don't like dog labs. I don't want to kill mongrels, all to publish nothingness in the medical literature, just to create a curriculum vitae to impress myopic academics who don't give a damn about actually eradicating diseases like great men in the past used to do. They only want fat CVs to brag about. Twenty-nine freakin' rejections, and here I sit in Matherville, Texas with dust, sand, and gravel up to my nose. The Bard said it best–life is a tale told by an idiot, full of sound and fury, signifying nothing."

Livvy was alone at home two days later when the 30th letter arrived. She felt a duty to end the torture, to open the letter, to soften the news somehow to spare Chase the pain. Then, they would need to have a heart-to-heart to discuss the possibility that Chase might have selected the wrong specialty, exactly like everyone who knew him had suggested years earlier when they said, "You don't have the right personality to be a surgeon... " And that personality was best summed up by adopting the mantra that covered all bad outcomes: "Shit happens."

When Livvy opened the letter, she thought she was hallucinating... that she could no longer read plain English. After 29 rejections, it had to be another "No." She read it again and again: *"We would be very interested and most honored to have you spend one year with us. The pathology faculty has agreed that a surgery resident in our midst would be highly beneficial to both parties–you and us."*

Livvy was beside herself. She couldn't wait to see Chase smile, ear to ear, for the first time in two years. Without another thought, she drove to the unnamed hospital at Matherville State and paged Chase from the clinic. As it turned out, he was around the corner in the lab, so Livvy approached him with the letter outstretched in her arms as if she were getting ready to release a dove of peace.

As she entered the laboratory, she saw Chase talking to a wide-eyed blonde, a lab tech in a white skirt and white jacket, perched on a barstool, her legs crossed while she held a rack of blood tubes in her uniformed lap, smiling as she chatted. When she spotted Livvy, her smile faded, prompting Chase to turn around.

Livvy didn't offer a hint as to the reason for her surprise visit. She silently handed Chase the letter. And waited. She did not acknowledge the lab tech, but noticed from the corner of her eye that the girl was sliding off the stool while tugging at her skirt.

Livvy felt pure joy when she watched Chase's eyes widen as he recognized the return address on the envelope. After all, she would not have rushed to the hospital to tell him of a rejection. Then, as he read the letter, he started laughing, almost crying. "I can't believe it. I just can't believe it. Out of thirty places. Only one pulled through. And that single, solitary one was, by far, my first choice. I can't wait. My first choice. I'm going to call C.C. Chastain right now. This is going to be fantastic. I mean, this might sound crazy, but I've got lyrics running through my head already."

Livvy took one of Chase's hands in hers and said, "This is answered prayer, Chase."

He gave her a quick hug, and she expected a full kiss on the lips. Instead, he let her go, spinning around to the lab tech to explain the reason behind his enthusiasm, as if she were somehow part of this celebration. Chase was always trying to put everyone at ease.

Not a moment too soon for California, thought Livvy. What a perfect opportunity to rekindle the spark.

.　　.　　.

Ivy Pettibone was drum majorette for life, leading the women of Building 19 in their march from the ward to the cafeteria and back, three times a day. She had been designated as group leader years ago, such that no one working today at Matherville State could remember when it had been any different. Her uniform was usually her favorite daisy-covered dress, and her silky brown hair in a parted pixie with its stubborn cowlick was her topper. She wore a referee whistle. One blast meant walk. Two blasts meant stop.

The ladies walked behind her in single file, with minor variations in spacing from time to time, but with Bertie the last patient bringing up the rear, as far as she could get from Ivy. Two aides loitered behind Bertie, barely paying attention. As the group inched forward, they were reminiscent of a meandering centipede, with legs churning in waves of propulsion.

Ivy's gait was so lop-sided, it was remarkable that she could walk a straight line along the asphalt path. No matter how far she dipped toward the ground, the rocking of her shoulders brought her upright again, completely confident, with a smile for each step that said, "Hah! You didn't think I'd make it back up." She never forgot her father, and how he'd always said, "Practice, practice, practice," and that's what she had done in learning to walk. And that's what she had done for her mother as well who told her to practice, practice, practice, when she was gaining the skill to say the word GOD.

Strange cloudbursts for late June had been toying with Matherville all day. Rather than the solitary front that usually swept through as a single event, with or without tornados, the skies had been dropping bombs of water all day, with the rain lasting only minutes. In between downpours, the sun would sneak out long enough to trick everyone, then it was back to more bombing.

The entourage from 19 was attempting a brisk walk to the cafeteria building during a moment of sunshine, a task too tough for some stragglers with a slow gate. When Ivy realized the group had spread out so far that she could barely see Bertie at the end, she turned around and faced the band, then delivered two short blasts of the whistle that prompted everyone to stop. The stragglers missed the point that they were to close ranks, opting instead to stand their ground.

Ivy began to shout orders in her own language. No one had a clue what she was yelling about. So, using crude sign language, she began motioning with her arms for everyone to catch up and close ranks.

It was then that she spotted Chase walking toward her from the parking lot. He waved, then he smiled. Ivy smiled back. She felt a few sprinkles of rain.

"Wait up, Ivy." He looked first at the sky then started jogging until he reached her. "Glad I caught you on your way to lunch. I've got something to tell you."

He stopped in front of her, ignoring the long line of hungry women strung erratically along the asphalt path.

"I'm going away for a while, Ivy. Do you know what I mean by that?"

She nodded yes.

Some of the more daring women stepped off the confines of the asphalt path and started forming a circle around Ivy and Chase, gesturing to their mouths that hunger was more important than conversation.

"One year. I'll be gone for one year. That means going through this hot summer, then the trees lose their leaves in the fall, then a cold winter, then everything blooms, then it's summer again, and I'll be back in Matherville. Do you know what I mean by all that?"

Again, she nodded yes.

"California is a long way from here, so I won't be dropping by to play the piano with you, and I won't be able to arrange the surgery on your hands. Do you understand that?"

She nodded yes once again, this time adding, "Mesola redoti," which to her meant: "That makes me sad." However, it was more complicated than what her words "meant," because Ivy didn't really hear the sound of "Mesola redoti" when she spoke. Instead, she heard her owns words as, "that makes me sad." These disconnected wires in her brain, providing faulty feedback, is what had made correction nearly impossible, and the speech pathologists had given up years ago.

"I wanted you to know about my leaving so you wouldn't get worried or anything. The time will go by quickly, and I'll be back again. While I'm gone, I want you to play and sing Zanda the Panda every day on the piano."

In her head were the echoes of a little girl who heard, "Practice, practice, practice."

Ivy reached for Chase with both arms. This caught him off guard, but he walked forward, and she enveloped him in a hug. Since Ivy tended to be stand-offish, this hug was something new. As he started to pull away, he felt her tighten the embrace for a few seconds more.

The rain started in again, and Chase backed off, waving good-bye.

"Soti medo," said Ivy.

"I love you, too," he replied.

Ivy started to blast her whistle, but a sob emptied her lungs, and she had to start over. She inhaled deeply, and let the whistle blow at full force, one long signal. Patients were brushing away imaginary cobwebs, a few ran in circles in the rain, others shuffled along, others danced, while still others spoke gibberish to non-existent friends. Still, they managed to reassemble on the black asphalt as the parade resumed its route. At the cafeteria entrance, Ivy stood soaking in the rain while she helped each lady make the shallow step up to the porch and front door.

22

With their worldly possessions jammed into a rental truck, Chase and Olivia Callaway pointed their radiator toward the state line of California, two generations downstream from Steinbeck's Okies. Their journey would end one suburb south of the beach community of Ciena, home to C.C. Chastain, along with celebrities and failed celebrities alike. The Callaways' apartment, only two blocks from the water, did not have an ocean view. Instead, the glass patio door opened to a courtyard, a tropical paradise of lush, flowering plants and ferns of which Chase could identify none. Such bewitching greenery did not exist in west Texas. Before returning in one year, Chase planned to scour the grounds for seeds to take back for experimentation. If *any* of the vegetation could survive the climate at home, it would be worth the try.

Chase and Livvy were overwhelmed by the joy of beachside living, as if a masterful dissection had cut them free from Texas. And strangely, Chase felt perfectly at home. In his limited travels, he'd always felt like a stranger, a tourist, in any location outside of Matherville. Here in Southern California, however, he was curiously moved by the feeling that he could call it home on his first day. He wondered if this familiarity had its origins in a family vacation that had targeted opening day of Disneyland in 1955 when his sister Annie was still alive. How they had gushed as children to hear Walt say, "To all who come to this happy place... welcome."

"Your mother said opening day was a disaster," reminded Livvy. "Talk about selective memory. There was a heat wave at the time, and a plumber's strike left everyone without enough drinking fountains. Then, clogged toilets. I guess someone had printed thousands of fake tickets, so the place was a madhouse. And then, so many people got on the riverboat with your family that it sunk near Tom Sawyer's Island."

"I don't remember much of that, Livvy. Oh, sure, the riverboat thing, that was great fun. The water wasn't deep. I don't recall all that other... "

Chase decided his euphoria was multi-factorial–not simply a break in the routine of surgical training, but the anticipation of reclaiming core passions such as reading novels and writing lyrics, plus living in an apartment without air-conditioning cooled by the ocean breeze, plus the green paradise viewed from their patio doors in such stark contrast to the weed trees that grew in the courtyard of the old Basic Sciences Building. Most of all, there was comfort in knowing that Providence was back in control with a very definite plan–after all, this seaside utopia was a divine selection, the sole acceptance out of 30 queries.

Then, as if paradise weren't enough, three days after they unpacked, Livvy stumbled into show business, simply by rubbing the shoulders of Chase's classmate who had pioneered his way to California already. C.C. Chastain lived in a three-story beachfront home in Ciena, a monument to his burgeoning empire of overseeing indentured emergency room physicians, while he nourished his "other life" as a songwriter-performer at local clubs. A "friend of a friend" needed a gopher at Warner Brothers, which was sharing The Burbank Studios with Columbia Pictures at the time. Livvy's job in the music division was menial labor at first, befitting all gophers. However, her Texas drawl and friendly manner drew such attention that she was soon giving tours to outsiders doing business on the lot, notably the CEOs who were filming their company commercials at nearby Screen Gems. Soon, Livvy was on a first name basis with so many stars and recording artists that Chase's fellowship became secondary, if not outright boring.

For the first time, Livvy's life reigned above his, and Chase looked forward to her return home every evening with yet another story. Ordering a ham and cheese for Leo Sayer, giving Shaun Cassidy's girlfriend a studio tour, loaning a hairbrush to Debby Boone, and the most memorable–Livvy donating a tampon to Streisand. Chase logged it all in a diary to share with his fellow Texans on his return. He was certain they would embrace every detail.

Livvy's access to the recording studios where soundtracks were laid onto film was so tantalizing for Chase that he would sometimes wiggle out of work early and rush to Burbank to listen and watch as full orchestras timed their tunes to match the screen. Although he was studying pathology with intent, he was more inspired than ever to scribble lyrics whenever and wherever, given the outside chance that someone, somewhere, might offer him a new life. Of course, Chase reminded himself that doors were opened and closed by the Lord, and it was merely our job to be available to knock at the right place and the right time.

Music ruled at C.C.'s stucco home, a seaside getaway that had once been the refuge for a long-forgotten star from the silent screen era. Today, recording artists and people "in the business," hearing alluring melodies ooze out the front door and spill onto the boardwalk, wandered inside routinely, passing through the oak-framed door, and into C.C.'s living room where a Steinway grand awaited (with C.C. always at the piano bench), along with guitars, drums, and several microphones.

Chase and C.C. would team up to sing Righteous Brothers songs, but Chase's voice was utterly without distinction, and he knew his place was really at the drawing board–writing lyrics. Still, there was a physical resemblance to the famed duo, as C.C. was short with shaggy blonde hair, and Chase was tall with sad eyes, although not as deep and foreboding as Bill Medley's. On weekends, when the random vocalists and musicians from the boardwalk joined the ever-waiting instruments and microphones, Chase would happily back far away from the spotlight and join Livvy while the jam sessions modulated through genres and finally into silence with the dawn.

Periodically, C.C. would leave the grand piano for a moment to whisper to his naïve friend from Texas a few words to enlighten Chase about the biographies of the rotating revelers: "plays lead guitar for Ronstadt... used to be the drummer for The Hondelles... you've heard of Hamilton, Joe Frank, and Reynolds?... wrote lots of hits for the Fifth Dimension... grew up with Dylan..." Then C.C. would return to his Steinway to commandeer the sessions.

At his work in the pathology lab, Chase played his microscope like a fine musical instrument. It took almost no time for his mentors to realize he had "the gift," the ability to see forms and patterns and the differences therein, allowing accurate diagnoses. After two months, he was offered a full-time position in the pathology residency program. He didn't take this seriously, but it was a nice compliment. After all, as he recalled it at the time, he was happy in the surgery program–happy, that is, as long as he was more than 1,000 miles away.

Pathology was a discipline of pictures. And when he wasn't looking through the microscope, he looked at the textbooks loaded with photographs, memorizing thousands of patterns, compressing a lifetime of experience into a small recess of his brain.

So, when the world-renowned Chairman of the Department of Surgery, doing a late afternoon breast biopsy, called for a frozen section diagnosis, *after the pathology faculty had already gone home,* Chase was it–the solo resident on call.

As a pseudo-pathologist, he performed the quick-freeze, then cut the ice block with the sharp blade of the microtome, mounted the tissue shaving onto the glass slide, then fixed it in preservative and stained it for color through a series of dunks into fluid-filled glasses. The famous surgeon scrubbed out from the operating room and joined Chase at the double-headed microscope.

"What do you think it is, son?"

"Looks malignant to me. It's that rare type of breast cancer–a mucinous carcinoma." Chase lifted his eyes from the scope without moving his head, trying to gauge the surgeon's reaction.

"Are you sure? Sure enough that I can remove this woman's breast?"

"Well, yes, the pattern... it's unusual, very distinctive, and not many things look like it... yes, it's a mucinous carcinoma."

"As a matter of fact, you're correct. I'll be sending you a mastectomy specimen in ninety minutes."

"But—Wait! I'm just a resident. In fact, I'm not even a real path resident. I'm a rotating surgery resident from Far West Texas. I have to get faculty confirmation on all frozens. It'll take twenty minutes for Dr. Bristow to get here. I called him ten minutes ago when the tissue arrived, so—"

"A surgery resident? And at Far West? Well, good for you. Thatcher Taylor is a good friend of mine. I grew up in Texas. Didn't know there were any programs still around that allowed a pathology rotation. Too much emphasis today on technique without knowing why. Don't worry about waiting for your attending on this frozen. You see, I did a year of pathology myself, like we surgeons all did once upon a time, and I can guarantee you this patient, indeed, has a mucinous carcinoma. How'd you recognize a mucinous this early in the academic year? We haven't had one in six months, at least."

"I saw a picture as I was thumbing through a path text. Fooled me for a minute because the header called it a colloid carcinoma, but I remember reading the fine print to see it was one and the same with mucinous."

The Chairman looked at Chase for a moment, then said, "I want you to be assigned to all my cases the rest of the year. I nearly always stop by the path lab to look at my own slides, so I'm going to share with you how pathology impacts my practice. The surgeon who can see with the eyes of a microscope always has the advantage over someone who treats dictated words on a report."

Chase beamed. Oddly, it inspired him, not toward pathology, but toward a return to the operating room where, it appeared, he had been gifted with the "eyes of a microscope."

Autopsies were a snap for Chase. He had undergone desensitization as a medical student working as deaner at Permian Medical Center. Thus, he was well ahead of his co-residents when it came to technique and protocols. His emotional shell extended to the surgical specimens as well, best exemplified by the "products of conception" that he processed every day. Combing through the chorionic villi and decidual tissue in a treasure hunt to find a fragmented arm or leg or torso, or even a tiny face, he felt a sense of Eureka that science bestows upon its practitioners whenever a body part emerged from the purple jelly, confirming conception. To have no feeling in such mundane matters was a confirmatory revelation to Chase that he was emerging as a solid and secure surgeon, unfettered by squandered sentiment.

His greatest revelation in the fellowship, however, came with the realization that the black-and-white world of the sophomore pathology course was often illusory. As it turned out, pathology could be every bit as subjective as the other spheres of medicine—the difference was that the clinicians, admitting "art" in their own practices, seemed oblivious to the "art" of pathology, predicating their treatment plans based on written words backed up by soft calls, controversial calls, and most disturbingly, calls made from personal bias.

Every week, Friday noon, Tough Case Conference attracted all pathology residents and faculty in the department. Indeed, the cases were tough. So tough that votes were tabulated for each patient, and universal agreement among the ten or more faculty members was rare. Chase was dumbstruck the first time he witnessed a "tie"—five votes for Hodgkin's lymphoma, with five dissenting by calling it "atypical reactive lymphoid hyperplasia."

In the cool California evenings, this is how he would describe his day: "My gosh, Livvy, a Reed-Sternberg cell indicating Hodgkin's should be a Reed-Sternberg cell. Or, that's how they taught us. As it turns out, you can't tell for sure sometimes. There are variants that don't quite qualify as Reed-Sternberg cells. Five of them called it cancer, and five called it benign. I can't believe this! What are the oncologists supposed to do? I don't think they even know this goes on."

As the year progressed, the oppressive disillusionment with pathology grew. On one occasion, while pretending to study at his cubicle, Chase eavesdropped on the Chairman of Medicine and the Chairman of Pathology as they dueled, face-to-face, while sitting at a double-headed scope. When the pathologist said, "This is a papillary carcinoma of the thyroid," the internist retorted, "Yes, that's what you boys call it, but there's plenty of evidence to show that some of these are incidental findings, that the behavior is completely benign. Doesn't it strike you odd that the thyroid seems to be the only place in the body where there's not a benign version of papillary pathology? If you and your ilk spot even a micromillimeter of papillary change, you call it a cancer. No wonder our clinical literature is so conflicted here."

Was pathology any different than psychiatry–an obsessive desire for taxonomy, ignoring the natural history of disease? After all, pathology was merely a snapshot in time, tissue stopped dead in its tracks, cut by the microtome and mounted as a trophy for posterity. How were the biologic behaviors, occurring over many years, known for sure if the natural process had been interrupted? Some diagnoses were universally agreed upon, yes, but so were some psychiatric conditions. Back in Texas, Walter had been diagnosed as paranoid schizophrenic by 100% of his psychiatrists over many years, yet there was no agreement about the proper diagnosis for little Ivy Pettibone. The patient, or the tissue, didn't change–only the doctor.

And every week, the docket was full for Tough Case Conference.

When Chase learned that two faculty members detested each other, he was mortified to watch them square off in the Friday conference. They routinely took opposing positions on the diagnoses, with the tissue abnormality in question serving as the rope in a game of tug-of-war. And when Chase expressed his concern to the Chief Resident in Pathology, the answer was: "Sometimes it's better to have diverse viewpoints than what they do in private practice where they simply rubber-stamp each other's work." Chase was not satisfied, however, for it appeared the "diverse viewpoints" that he saw in conference were an impasse based on personality before the slides were ever placed on the microscope.

Subjectivity permeated every aspect of pathology. Even a diagnosis that ought to be as straightforward as cervical cancer was not. There was a "borderline" for many cancers. Chase came to the conclusion that the difference between "severe dysplasia" and "carcinoma in situ" of the cervix was not so much in the pattern on the microscope slide, but based more on the name of the faculty pathologist who was on duty that day. The difference was subjective. And this is where Chase's talent shined brilliantly, to himself. He became so adept at learning each of the ten faculty members' criteria for cervical dysplasia versus carcinoma in situ that he would make his official interpretation based on the attending doctor of the day. For Dr. X, Chase would write his report to indicate "severe dysplasia" (and he would be right), but if Dr. Y was going to be his attending that day, Chase's cleverness delivered the diagnosis as "carcinoma in situ" (and he would be right).

And then came a winter day, sunny of course, when a visiting guru presented Grand Rounds and laid claim to having identified the same "borderline" findings of early breast cancer under the microscope, as was known already to be the case at other sites in the body. Rather than calling it "dysplasia," the guru's term was "atypical hyperplasia," and the distinction between this atypia and carcinoma in situ was a close call, or worse–subjective. In the case of the cervix, the pressure on the pathologist's call was eased by the fact that the gynecologists were going to perform the same procedure–a cervical cone–no matter which label was stuck on the lesion. Not true for the breast.

"So, what do we tell the surgeons?" someone in the audience asked, referencing this new entity of atypical hyperplasia.

The implications were staggering. Unlike the easy cervical cone as treatment for all, the difference with the breast was to do "nothing" for benign disease, but "mastectomy" for all cancers. The concept of atypical hyperplasia as "premalignancy" was new and foreign, and there was no in-between surgical procedure in the repertoire.

"We *don't* tell the surgeons *anything*," came the guru's answer. "They'll be lopping off breasts left and right with this kind of information."

As the only surgeon in the auditorium, Chase felt himself slipping a little lower in his seat. The audience laughed, for there was a pervasive, communal impression that mindless barbarism ruled much of the surgical community. Chase resented this impression of surgeons, and he was becoming more and more convinced that he did not belong among pathologists, these quasi-scientists, no matter how adept he was at the microscope.

"It appears from our work," said the pathology guru, "that these lesions are not committed to become cancer. In fact, the majority probably don't. I contend, however, that the idea of cancer being a continuum that begins with uncommitted pathology is probably beyond the grasp of our surgical colleagues."

A fellow resident poked a teasing finger into Chase's rib, and he felt it all the way to his heart.

During the year, Chase discovered an unusual quality about himself regarding pathology–stamina. He could sit for hours on end, longer than most surgical cases, with his shoulders hunched forward and his eyes glued to the microscope. He felt no fatigue. The pains in the back of his neck were no bother at all. The headaches were of no concern. In fact, he often had to force himself to leave his scope in the evening, long after the other pathology residents had gone home. Each microscope slide, as he slipped it under the lens, was like a miniature revelation, a new and colorful world where Chase could enter and stay as long as he wanted.

His eyes seemed to appreciate more than the other residents. For instance, late in the year, Chase sat across the double-headed scope from an emeritus professor who taught residents only on rare occasion. Chase commented on the supporting stromal cells around a breast duct packed inside with malignant cells, and how this stroma had stained a bluish color rather than the usual pink, and how whenever this happened, Chase had noticed there were more inflammatory cells surrounding the malignant ducts, as if they were "rounding up the wayward cattle." Yet sometimes, the ducts harboring the same sort of cancerous cells would be surrounded by pink stroma and precious few inflammatory cells, as if the body didn't care whether the malignant cells were there or not.

The professor looked up from the scope and said, "Doctor, your professors, all of them just kids compared to me, will teach you to ignore such things. I can't explain what you've observed either, but many have noticed it throughout the years. The bluish change in staining of the stroma is called 'metachromasia', and it happens for a reason. We don't know what that reason is, however. And those inflammatory cells, the lymphocytes, the macrophages, even the rare mast cells that have congregated, why, these things have an explanation as well, not yet defined, but I'll bet it's important.

"Unfortunately, much of traditional training in pathology is the act of putting blinders on you, forcing you to ignore that which you cannot explain, teaching you *not to see*. Keep your child-like wonder intact. Rote memorization of patterns will let you make a living but recognizing new patterns will let you make a difference. The secrets will be unlocked by people like you who see patterns and colors beyond the textbook. Did you know that tradition holds that pathology photos in texts should be black-and-white, to force you to see patterns alone? Yet how could one ever discover something like metachromasia if we force the blinders on? Doctor, I don't know what your plans are in the various fields of pathology, but your place might be in academics, where you can do experimental work. My lab is—"

"Sir, I'm—I'm not a pathology resident. I'm a surgery resident doing a one-year fellowship in path."

The professor gave Chase a quizzical look at first, eyes squinting in disbelief, then opening wide in astonished acceptance. The old man took a deep breath and sighed. He put wire-rimmed spectacles on for a better look at Chase's name tag, then the corners of his eyes seemed to sag after he took the glasses off again. "Then Dr. Callaway, you must change your specialty choice immediately."

. . .

Livvy took samples of Chase's lyrics to the studio on the outside chance she might have an opportunity to plop his words into the hands of someone who could launch a career. And in one bright and brief moment, Livvy's boss, a record producer with several Grammys and one Oscar, the person who had promoted Livvy from gopher to public relations, asked to meet Chase. Chase was ecstatic. Forget his internal debate going on between pathology and surgery, he would give it all up to recreate the joy he'd lost when he left music.

Yet, it turned out that Livvy's boss was simply being polite to the girl from Texas he'd enjoyed so much during the year. In fact, the producer remembered Chase's crossover hit with the New Bloods many years ago and was intrigued, or puzzled, by the song's success. However, he was not interested in today's Chase. "You're lucky to be out of the business, my friend. Steady income. Security. Stick with it." The dream was over before fully resurrected.

As the time grew close to return to Matherville, Chase found himself increasingly consumed with turning back the clock to his world of music. *Just one more chance*, he thought. Surely, C.C. and he could put something together. In truth, C.C. considered Chase's lyrics second-rate. "Good lyrics come only through tragedy, Chase, and frankly, you haven't suffered enough." (C.C. considered his own tragic love affairs over the years to warrant a lifetime of hit tunes.) And, after all, C.C. was already working with a professional, Ted Boone, whose only weakness was his fondness for Oklahoma where the two had first met as fraternity brothers. Ted refused to move to California to collaborate, and it was slowing down the machine, in C.C.'s view. Chase saw it as an opportunity to substitute himself for Ted, but C.C. saw it otherwise. Ted Boone generated "profound and moving" lyrics, and C.C. would wait on Ted to produce.

C.C. needed Chase, all right, but in a different capacity–he wanted Chase to move to California permanently, as soon as he finished his surgical residency, so that Chase could serve as C.C.'s bedrock–a "touchstone to my solid past, so that I can keep my feet on the ground after stardom. You're the only boring guy I know, and I need you to keep things solid for me. I need to have one *normal* person around."

Stardom had come close already for C.C. and Ted Boone, by way of a musical comedy based on a comic strip, *The Sorcerer of Siam*. As it turned out, the cartoonist refused to grant rights for their off-Broadway production, and the dream evaporated. Unfortunately, C.C. had given up his polar-opposite dream of becoming a surgeon, in preparation for the demands of stardom. When the star fizzled, instead of returning to his surgical residency, C.C. began working part-time in emergency rooms in southern California. In short order, he built an empire from scratch, covering 15 hospitals in the Los Angeles area with his doctor-minions.

Toward the end of the year, while serving as C.C.'s temporary bedrock, Chase learned to drink "Bobby Mondavi" on Saturday nights and well into Sunday morning with his old classmate, long after Livvy had returned to their apartment a mile away. During these creative sessions, Chase offered to provide lyrics all the way to the bottom of the wine bottle. Finally, C.C. caved. "Look, this isn't some sophomore skit for medical school, and it's not your so-called Christian music where sales are dependent on the number of times you mention Jesus. I'm talking gut-level, torch-ass lyrics that rip the heart out of your chest, stomp it on the ground, and set it on fire. That said, Chase ol' buddy, word has it that Travolta has gone into production on a cowboy story that's going to bring country music into the mainstream. Some say it's going to explode. So I tell you what–give me your best shot at some country lyrics, and I fully expect to be bawling like a baby when I read 'em, or better yet, slittin' my wrists, partner."

The next weekend, Chase presented C.C. with his song, "Horizon A-Rizin'," and was somewhat surprised that C.C. showed cracks in his stoic cynicism, allowing that Chase might be a halfway decent lyricist. "This is cowboy poetry more than song lyrics, Chase, but it's decent work 'cause it tells a great story, except for your bridge, which sucks big time, if you can even call it a bridge, more of an overpass, but overall, this might work... maybe." One week later, C.C. Chastain had rewritten the chord progression in the bridge, changed some lyrics, and the twosome gave the song its debut to an eclectic crowd that had wandered off the boardwalk into C.C.'s living room on a Saturday afternoon in Ciena, California:

> *I was sittin' at the end of a hopeless dream*
> *Wonderin' what in the world had gone wrong*
> *When I decided to rise and eulogize*
> *The demise of my dream in this song...*

. . .

As the pathology fellowship came to its end in June, Chase slid into a pool of emotions he didn't know existed. The thought of returning to hot and dry west Texas with maximum stress, maximum hours, maximum sleep deprivation, dragged him into despair. Although he had initially scoffed at the offers to stay in pathology here in California, this option had taken root and grown over the course of twelve months. Livvy supported the idea one hundred percent.

"But they're not clinical doctors, Livvy. I wouldn't think of myself as a real doctor. I mean, why would God give me this gift of good hands and communication skills if my purpose was to isolate in the basement of the hospital path lab, doing autopsies and processing detached body parts, all while smelling like formaldehyde? It doesn't make sense. It doesn't feel right."

"Chase. I haven't seen you as happy as you've been here in California for a long time. That's why. Up until this month, at least, you seemed as happy as when you were with the New Bloods."

One week after Chase received next year's academic schedule from Far West Texas (first 3-month rotation–thoracic surgery under Dr. Brick Dagmar), he spotted a flyer at the hospital asking for volunteers for a research project on cystic fibrosis. A scientist on campus was developing a method to detect an abnormal protein in the blood of recessive carriers for the disease. For giving one blood sample and details of his positive family history, Chase would earn 30 bucks.

"Not a bad fee for ten seconds work, so I did it, Livvy. After all, since my sister had it, I'm at a high chance for being a carrier. I've pretty well accepted that."

When the results came in, the researcher was flat-out tickled to reveal to Chase that he was clearly positive, a strong and unequivocal result. "You are a carrier for cystic fibrosis," said the scientist. "I should test your wife now."

This next logical step hadn't really occurred to Chase. "But my wife doesn't have a family history. And how do you know your test really works?"

"Then she'll be a good control. Of course, the gene, being recessive, can pass through several generations undetected, so a family history doesn't mean much, especially if the family is small. And, yes, I think my test is valid, and since it takes two recessive parents to have a CF baby, I'd think you'd want to make sure she's negative." So Livvy complied.

On the day she was to receive her results on the cystic fibrosis test, Livvy was scheduled to host a buffet luncheon for Fleetwood Mac's entourage. However, the lunch turned out to be a surprise party for Livvy, a going away event at the studio for her return to Texas. The decorated cake was inscribed with the words, *Home Is Where the Oil Is*, and a map of Texas in the icing included a big oil rig rising in the far west.

Hours later, back with Chase at the cystic fibrosis research lab, the scientist told her, "You're positive, my dear. Not as strongly positive as your husband, but I believe you're a carrier for CF."

Outside the door of the laboratory, Livvy fell into Chase's arms, crying uncontrollably for the first time since they'd been married.

"Since it's recessive, there's only a twenty-five percent chance it'll happen," said Chase, trying to comfort. "We've got a seventy-five percent chance our first kid will be normal. In fact, the odds are the same for each child, twenty-five percent chance of CF."

Yet, in his own mind, he was visualizing the tormented years his sister Annie had lived, skipping from one bout of pneumonia to the next, never absolutely free of infection, coughing, hacking, connected to oxygen lines throughout the house, the pancreatic insufficiency which left her bound to the bathroom, ostracized by the other kids for her sickly appearance. He saw her purple lips and her sad eyes, and he recalled her frequent allusions to death. Worst of all, he remembered how he'd feigned illness to skip her funeral, totally unable to cope.

Chase cried, too, joining Livvy as passers-by in the hospital hallway diverted their eyes. He felt the hackneyed symbol of the white-picket-fence dissolve, or better yet, explode. Foreign emotions were swirling within teardrops, pulling him away from ever having children, and along with that departure, pulling him away from all things conventional, all things expected. And while he would never admit it, pulling him away from Livvy.

He and Livvy had been planning to conceive as soon as they returned to Texas. Livvy's mother had already picked out a small house, complete with nursery. And Chase had confirmed with the Department of Surgery at Far West that he would be back in uniform July 1st to start on thoracic surgery. It was all scripted, all expected.

They wept together the rest of that night in a closeness they'd never experienced before. Or so it seemed to Livvy. As for Chase, he was coming undone.

Days later, with a rental truck packed for the reverse trip home, with Livvy running last minute errands, Chase gathered seeds from the courtyard flora to carry a bit of California back to Texas. He bought a bottle of Bobby Mondavi and didn't bother to pour the wine into a glass, instead drinking until he fell into the well of a dark dream where he met head-on those tiny products of conception that he'd handled for the past year—miniature hands reaching for life, but embedded in paraffin, then cut into thin slices by the microtome. The shaved fingers of the embryo, stained magnificently in blue and pink, scratched at the glass cover slip, hoping to escape entrapment despite secure mounting in colorful translucency.

The recurrent image of those severed fingers, scratching away, would stick in Chase's memory long after he awoke with a punishing hangover, and long after he had returned home to Texas.

23

Palm trees disappeared in a puff. The tropical courtyard at the oceanside apartment was gone. The landscape changed from paradise into strata of sand and gravel streaming in an alluvial fan from the mountains of Far West Texas. And with the colossal pressure of sleepless nights, life and death decisions, and the stench of commissioned sins, the sedimentary debris turned into metamorphic rock, manifest as concrete hospital walls with many rooms, no views.

While the root of mutiny on H.M.S. Bounty was the crew having grown accustomed to the idyllic life in Tahiti, mutiny occurred with Chase's duty-bound return to Texas. Yet, this was not mutiny of a crew against its captain, but a heart against itself.

Livvy, with stars still swirling from her own California experience, had to face the reality that there was nothing comparable in Matherville for her either. In trekking across country with Chase, she had given up–and lost–her hometown job teaching physical education. Still, her feet were firmly planted, and her pining for Los Angeles was not because she had been star-struck, but because, for the first time, Chase had absorbed himself in *her* life. He had hung on her every word about one celebrity or another, nearly every day. In short, her husband had become every neglected wife's dream–Chase had been totally enthralled by her every utterance.

In Matherville, Livvy tried to cling to that waning memory of the music world by taking a clerical position at the local record store. Ever cheerful, she immersed herself in coordinating private music lessons, stocking sheet music, selling LPs and stereos and cassette tapes and 8-tracks, while ordering instruments for the junior high students entering band programs. Her fingertips danced at the extreme periphery of the music business, though she daydreamed often of her dalliance at the core.

Together, Chase and Livvy made a fragile pact to ignore the cataclysmic results of their cystic fibrosis test results. If the test was indeed valid, marking them as carriers, the chance of a cystic fibrosis baby was only 25%, and if God couldn't cover those odds, then what was the purpose of prayer? Or faith?

Starting the academic year on his least favorite rotation–thoracic surgery–Chase found Dr. Dagmar a less menacing threat than he'd been a year ago, pre-California. In fact, Chase would often test the water simply to see if there was still a boiling point.

Once, Dagmar stated that, as a complication of carotid artery surgery, injury to the hypoglossal nerve would make the patient's protruding tongue deviate to the side *opposite* the injury. Chase challenged the statement, knowing for a fact that Dagmar was dead wrong–the tongue would deviate to the *same* side as the injury.

Instead of quickly correcting himself, Dagmar dug in his heels, drawing on the ferocity of his deep baritone to sway the weak-minded. Chase didn't back down as he knew he was correct, and he was terribly curious to find out how big Dagmar's chest would inflate with hubris before exploding. Dagmar didn't waver, apparently believing he had the power to turn lead into gold. Rather, he somehow looked down at Chase (even though Chase was taller) and snarled in condescension, "Like all *junior* residents, I think you need to read more before you become a Chief."

Chase found the response simultaneously amusing and disturbing. This was the prototypical surgical mind at work–above all, never back down. Did single-minded certainty trump open-minded wisdom in the surgical world? Sometimes, it struck Chase that bluster served as the very backbone for surgeons.

The reason that Dagmar had been discussing carotid surgery in the first place was yet another bizarre story. Dagmar believed that established territories in medicine and surgery were supremely ordained and immutable, that there should be no overlap, that the status quo was fine and dandy, and that he had been appointed as the guardian. And within this construct, at least for Far West Texas University, carotid surgery had been deemed within the divine purview of general surgery.

However, the unthinkable occurred when the *neurosurgeons* requested privileges to begin performing carotid endarterectomies, removing plaques, in order to improve blood flow to the brain. Dagmar blocked the move, launching a war of unprecedented proportion wherein the neurosurgeons went *on strike* at the medical center–no coverage except emergencies. The strike was likely unlawful and unethical, but Dagmar was forced to remember that Harvey Cushing, the "father of neurosurgery" had once been a general surgeon, and that specialties were not static. Instead, dynamic changes forged new specialties and redefined territorial borders. Dagmar buckled. The neurosurgeons won.

The peace that followed, however, did not mean that the neurosurgeons forgave the imperious Dagmar. Rather than split the carotid cases fifty-fifty with general surgery, the neurosurgeons chose to wallow in their victory. After all, they had bridges well-built with their non-surgical counterparts–the neurologists–who generated the cases in the first place. Thereafter, referrals for carotid endarterectomies were steered to the neurosurgeons, leaving the general surgery program bereft of experience, with Chief Residents going into the world untrained in the technique, courtesy of Dagmar's Stand.

Indeed, this was a deep wound to the specialty of general surgery, which was feeling its body carved away piecemeal, a fragmentation well underway nationwide–that is, the birthing of the specialty devoted to the peripheral blood vessels, distinct from general surgery and distinct from cardiac surgery.

If Dagmar had accepted this inevitable trend and established a new section in the department for specialized training, the carotid cases could have been kept in his grip under the all-inclusive "vascular" title. As it was, the neurosurgeons had a good point: "Why are the gut surgeons operating on the blood vessels that go to the brain?" This concept of a new specialty addressing surgery of the blood vessels was repugnant to Dr. Dagmar whose insistence on preserving general surgery–"and that includes peripheral vascular surgery"–only intensified after his defeat by the neurosurgeons.

Chase didn't care much one way or the other. He thought it odd, however, that Dagmar, as a cardiac surgeon, was in a breakaway specialty himself. Sure, peripheral vascular surgery was fun from a technical standpoint. Sewing clean and crisp blood vessels was far more enjoyable than the bacteria-laden ends of jelly-like intestines. However, vascular surgery had one ghastly drawback–the operations gone awry caused the very outcome you were trying to prevent in the first place. In trying to prevent strokes with carotid artery surgery, the primary complication was–a stroke. In trying to improve blood flow to the legs, a primary complication was–gangrene requiring amputation. And so forth. Vascular surgery, for all its rewards in the operating room, was the most punishing "sub-specialty" Chase could imagine. In fact, he wondered if he would bother to include it in his practice after he finished residency. Certainly, the general surgeons in Matherville "did it all," but while in California, Chase noted quite the opposite. There, the vascular work had already been corralled by ex-general surgeons who had anointed themselves with a new title for a new specialty–peripheral vascular surgeons. Fellowships had already been planted, and the harvest of board-certification couldn't be far behind.

. . .

The great incubator in surgical training for converting a mere mortal into a Master of Life and Death was the ICU. Pronouncing people dead– "I'm calling it. Someone note the time"–was as commonplace as announcing, "Let's order pizza." Resurrecting the dead was equally routine–a blast of atropine here, a little shock for V-fib there, and the patient was alive once again. Or, "let's do a *slow* code" was another option, going through the motions for effect, but letting the patient die. These exercises turned the sanctity of life into a profound nothingness, and it transformed the residents into shells of hollow confidence.

Chase knew the shell had already formed, and he deemed it good. He would no longer waste energy looking back at his vacillations. He was not planning to change specialties, or drop out of medicine entirely, as his old classmate Will Glendenning had done several years ago, whining all the way to the laboratories where rat deaths were the greatest concern. In fact, Chase was pleased with himself that he felt no emotion at all during critical care. Still, when it came to breaking the news and comforting the relatives of the newly deceased, he felt clutches around his throat. So his shell was solid, but not rigid.

Judging the plasticity of one's shell was difficult, however, and occasionally Chase wondered if he'd grown too callous. After assisting Dr. Dagmar in "life-extending" neonatal surgery to close a patent ductus–a developmental error with a blood vessel causing heart failure–in a horribly malformed infant (cleft face, microcephaly, and countless other defects prompting the old-fashioned term, "a monster"), Chase helped Dagmar put a feeding tube directly into the stomach of this hideous three-pound blob, not recognizable as human. All physicians involved in the care of nature's error had decided to let the thing go naturally, or at most, perform a "slow code" if anything went wrong. In fact, nothing would have been done in the first place had the parents not insisted on stopping acute heart failure. Everyone, including Dagmar, felt guilty for prolonging the life of this creature whose frog-like face lay divided down the middle, and in whom there would be countless surgeries, simply to save a deformed, non-thinking, non-feeling lump with minimal brain tissue, a ward of the state.

Then, less than 24 hours after placement of the feeding tube, a nurse noted the plastic line had slipped out of the stomach, but remained inside the body, allowing the food to drip, drip, drip into the peritoneal cavity where bacteria could have a field day. Chase, Master of Life and Death, was called when the baby suffered cardiac arrest, and he made the easy decision to let the thing go peacefully. What an easy way out for everyone, he thought. He was wrong.

"You don't let patients die when the cause is a therapeutic misadventure," yelled Dagmar, as he wielded the most ferocious scowl Chase had ever seen. "That baby was post-op, and thanks to you, the immediate cause of death was a wandering feeding tube–a surgical complication, after a procedure *I* performed. Don't you *ever* pull a stunt like that again, Callaway. That baby should have been resuscitated. Nature would have claimed it eventually, but now, you made *me* the executioner!"

Being Master of Life and Death was not always a clear-cut assignment.

· · ·

PG-4 was the last year of in-house call for Chase. Chief residents (PG-5s) slept at home. As a PG-4, Chase tried, on a single occasion, to do the unthinkable–sneak a nap during the day. To his knowledge, it had never been done before, although rumors did exist that, with caution, it was possible.

After rounds one Tuesday, when there was no outpatient clinic, no fresh post-ops in the ICU, no patients to get ready for surgery–a coalescence of liberties rarely experienced–Chase crept to the call quarters on the top floor of the nearby Veteran's Administration Hospital where all residents rotated. He had been up the entire night in the ICU, trying to whip a sick heart into a few more beats for another day, but the veteran had died conveniently in time for Chase to make morning rounds with his team. Sleeping during the day was such an oddity that Chase wondered if it were even legal in the unwritten rules of surgical training. He didn't care.

Before true sleep settled in, however, he was awakened by a wild-haired young man in janitor grays who told Chase he wasn't allowed to sleep during the day.

"Look, I've got eight rooms to clean up here today," said the housekeeper.

Chase felt a frightening rage within, recalling that when the residents tried to shave or shower mid-morning *after* early rounds, they sometimes found a squadron of male housekeepers lounging on the residents' beds watching *I Love Lucy* reruns. "Get the hell out of here," growled Chase, knowing the fury brewing within. "I was up all night with a sick patient in the ICU, who died by the way, so I'm not in the mood for this."

The housekeeper left, and Chase fell into a deep sleep.

A slamming door entered his dreams. When Chase looked up from his pillow, the same housekeeper was back. Only this time, he was hiding behind the epaulets of the Chief of Housekeeping who proclaimed, "If you don't vacate the premises immediately, I'm going to report you to the Administrator." Chase shook away sleep. Wrath erupted. He felt the urge to kill. Sleep was impossible now due to the persistent power of adrenaline and the pseudo-power of housekeepers.

Chase flew from the bed and blitzed the Housekeeping Chief with a litany of profanity, words strung together masterfully, words that had never waggled from his lips before, whirlwind rhetoric so powerful, pouring out over the two housekeepers, that both stepped backwards as Chase brushed by them to exit the room. As he stormed down the hall toward the elevators, Chase heard the Chief Housekeeper call after him: "What's your name, son?"

Chase couldn't believe the empty-headed provocation. *No need to acknowledge an empowered fool*, he thought.

"I said… what's your name?"

You've got to be kidding me. I'm not going to stoop to their level.

"Listen, fella, I demand to know your name. When I ask you a question, you better answer. I'm in charge here."

Chase spun around and marched back toward the head janitor, fingers of both hands flexed tightly into two solid rocks of rage, unbridled, out of control, for the first time in his life. He knew that right now he was capable of maiming, or even killing, and he barely mustered the restraint needed as he pushed his nose within an inch of the janitor's face and yelled, "CALLAWAY. Let me spell it for you, letter for letter, so that you can file it into your report correctly because I'm assuming your report is the most important freakin' thing in your world. C-A-L-L-A-W-A-Y. Did you get that? Let me spell it again. C-A-L-L-A-W-A-Y. But do call me by my first name, if you will. It's DOCTOR. My first name is DOCTOR, you sonuvabitch!" Chase turned his back and walked away, fists still clenched, beyond furious.

Once the elevator made it to the ground floor, after stopping on six of the nine levels, Chase's beeper began wailing. He was summoned to the office—not of the hospital administrator, as expected—but the office of Dr. Brick Dagmar, acting Chief of Surgery since Dr. Thatcher Nolan Taylor was out of town.

Unfortunately for Chase, and unbeknownst to him until enlightened by Dr. Dagmar, one of Chase's co-residents had been using the call quarters regularly during daytime hours for trysts with a bevy of nurses. The Chief of Housekeeping had been delighted with his recent assignment as Chief Detective–seeking clues and pinpointing the culprit–and the burden of guilt now rested squarely on Chase's shoulders.

"Chase, I don't care what you do in your personal life—"

"Dr. Dagmar, I promise you, I have *never* been in those call quarters during the daytime hours until now. Not once. If somebody's been up there with the nurses, it hasn't been me."

"Chase, do you think the faculty is oblivious to what you residents do? Do you think we don't have ears? We hear the nurses talking. Like I said, I don't pass judgment. But on company time… "

Chase could barely contain himself. He'd never been falsely accused of anything in his life, much less something of this magnitude. *What if Livvy were to hear this craziness?*

In the days that followed, Chase discovered the identity of the co-resident who had successfully been bedding nurses in the VA hospital call quarters, a capital offense to the housekeepers. The resident was, in fact, part of the same call rotation with Chase, allowing the luxury of "every third night." Then, a jealous husband broke the hand of this same resident, so with one of three residents lost in the call rotation, Chase was dragged back to the "every other night" cesspool of an intern.

Although he considered his mood to have spiraled a long way down from Southern California to West Texas, and from the ninth floor of the VA Hospital to the office of Dagmar, the continuing spiral into "every other night" taught him that the bottom floor is poorly defined, if it exists at all. He would not enjoy a rested moment again with Livvy for two more months.

His mood took on a darkness foreign to anything in his past, and he began to wonder if he understood himself at all. This alien feeling was magnified after sleep deprivation, which was now the norm. Chase recalled the medical school psychiatry lectures by Dr. Meeker where physiologic and neurologic changes, thus behavioral aberrations, could be correlated directly to the duration of wakefulness, and that the shock to the system overall was so powerful that sleep deprivation had been used in the past as a treatment for schizophrenia. For Chase, he began to feel that sleep deprivation was *causing* a schizoid split–that is, he felt like two different people, one rested, one not. And when not, he felt a Mr. Hyde inside grumbling to be released as a free man from the cohabitating Jekyll.

Near the end of the thoracic rotation, Chase served as second assistant on a triple valve replacement, the probability of survival for the patient being judged at 20%. Since the odds *without* surgery were zero, surgical intervention seemed to be a reasonable option. And, as usual, Dagmar had worked miracles in the operating room, getting the patient off the pump and into the SICU.

Now, it was the post-op care that would make or break all the hard work in the O.R. And, in the "real world," this was the job of board-certified cardiologists and cracker-jack nurses. For Dagmar, however, this was the job of the Master of All Trades–the general surgery resident. So, Chase became the post-op "baby-sitter" as the patient's life straddled the all-too-familiar abyss.

With the maximum number of monitoring tubes in place, and adjustments in multiple cardiotropic medications necessary every few *minutes*, the baby-sitter would be piloting a starship whose flight plan would depend on the speeding up and slowing down of the meds dripping through the IV lines. By juggling afterload and preload and left atrial pressures and peripheral resistance and cardiac output, all the while monitoring oxygenation and making sure the pressors didn't shut down the kidneys, with the ultimate test being to squeeze out the minimal amount of urine needed to reflect vascular perfusion without filling up the lungs with water, the baby-sitter made sure of one thing– that the patient didn't die on his watch.

"I don't want our intern on this one, Chase. You need to be at the bedside all day... and night." Dagmar had spoken.

Chase had already been awake the night before as the on-call resident. He could almost feel the warm sheets at home when Dagmar dictated the plan, a compliment of sorts. So, all afternoon and evening,

Chase opened and closed the valves on the starship, where the pipes were filled with isoproterenol, dopamine pitted against the new dobutamine, digoxin, furosemide, and of course, the usual multi-drug arsenal each time the patient suffered an arrhythmia or, on three occasions, full cardiac arrest. The patient was a living laboratory prep, an experiment in physiology and a wonder of pharmacology, a life being held in the hands of the junior commander.

Dagmar phoned in throughout the day and evening, checking the key stats and lab values, operating from his home base at mission control. As much as Chase loathed the man's bullheadedness, he had to admit that his skill in the operating room was unparalleled, and Dagmar monitored the precarious hours after surgery closer than any other faculty member. So, after many hours of ongoing pharmacologic manipulations, with a mere eight hours to go until daylight, Dagmar said to Chase over the phone, "You're doing an excellent job, Callaway." Chase felt a peculiar lump in his throat. He didn't *want* to be complimented by Dagmar, yet Chase could tell that a younger version of himself was sobbing inside. *I've got to get to sleep. Something is happening to me.*

Chase wasn't sure he could make it the final eight hours. Although he had done "40 straight" on many occasions, rarely had the hours been so intense for so long. Minute-to-minute decisions and countless judgment calls had occupied every second. His vision was blurry. His thoughts muddled. His head throbbed. He remembered the resident last year who fell asleep at the wheel on his way home from "40 straight." Dead at the ripe old age of 24, leaving a would-be physician's wife and a two-year-old behind.

Only eight hours left. He was dealing with only one patient, and this patient was not closer to death under his watch (although not closer to life either). For Chase, the battle would be over in eight hours, and the patient would be in the hands of someone else after that. *He's not going to die on my watch.*

For this final eight hours, a new nurse began her shift in the ICU, that is, new to Chase. She introduced herself, then began scurrying around the patient, stopping only to review the chart for short intervals. She, too, was one-on-one. One nurse for one patient, a staffing arrangement for the most critically ill. With dark brown hair in a bob, short-skirted, fresh and vibrant, she mesmerized Chase in her ability to grasp the total "feel" for the patient's complex status. She was as bright as any resident in training, immediately grasping the treatment plan, the physiology, and the pharmacology.

After a few hours of co-decisions, co-insertions of monitoring lines, co-contemplations, co-reflections, she said to Chase, "I've seen a lot of residents come through the hospital in Galveston where I'm from, but I haven't seen many who can handle things as cool as you. If I didn't know better, I'd think you were a cardiology fellow, or pulmonary. Never seen a surgery resident perform like you do, not in my seven years in the ICU." Chase felt himself blush at the tribute. He wanted to hug her, that is, the sleep-deprived Mr. Hyde wanted to hug her.

When the patient went into full cardiac arrest, unresponsive to the defibrillator, the nurse dropped the bedrails, jumped onto the bed and straddled the man's torso while she pumped the chest, her white skirt riding to the top of her thighs. In an instant, Chase envisioned what the patient might have appreciated from his perspective had he been conscious–what a way to greet death.

With each compression, she rocked forward, spreading her thighs and pushing her hips, allowing more weight to land on the man's chest through her rigid arms, and thus, effecting a rise in circulatory perfusion. Certainly, her unusual approach to CPR delivered deeper compressions than could ever be generated standing at the edge of the bed, feet on the floor.

Chase disconnected the man from the ventilator, so that he could bag the patient, timing the inflations to come between the chest compressions and pelvic thrusts. Amazingly, the nurse was not flustered in the slightest, not embarrassed at all that her skirt was riding high. Instead, she was one of those rare individuals who could stay perfectly calm, allowing her to thrive during crises.

Frustrated that they were getting nowhere, she stopped her rhythmic compressions–"Hold the vents for a second"–then she pounded the sternotomy incision on the chest with such force that a red stain formed on the dressing. "Okay, start the vents again for another few seconds, then let's hit him with some more epi and shock him again." She had taken control. Chase gave the epinephrine as the nurse climbed off the bed and prepared the paddles. Two more shocks were delivered. After the second one, the patient returned to life, first a blip on the screen to disrupt the flatline, then another, and another, then sinus rhythm.

"We did it," she said, patting her hand on his shoulder and holding it there long enough to let him know their relationship was changing.

For the rest of the night, Chase found himself standing close to her at the bedside, merely to get a whiff of her perfume. At 3:10 a.m., he needed to re-start the arterial line, and their thighs touched lightly as she held the patient's wrist for him to stick. At 4:27 a.m., while focused on re-positioning the Swan-Ganz catheter to get a better wedge pressure, he could feel her warm breath against his neck as she assisted him. At 5:02 a.m., after stripping the chest tubes free of clotted blood, the nurse squeezed her body between Chase and the cubicle wall, a tight fit, encircling his waist with her hand as she passed.

"The cardiac output's the best it's been all night," she said with a smile, "I think I'll take my break. I can usually unwind, completely let loose, in five minutes. I'll get Shannon to cover. In fact, she can cover for both of us. Why don't you come with me?"

"Oh… well, no, I better stay and get some charting done. I've barely had time to document any of this." His words did not match the desire of Mr. Hyde, and he looked forward to her return.

.   .   .

Oddly, work stress for Chase dissipated with the realization that skills met challenges, but paradoxically, home stress increased in the form of depression and distance. Chase and Livvy decided their quiet estrangement was due to Post-California Doldrums, and would be self-limited upon completion of the Chief year, if not sooner. They decided to move forward with their plans for children despite the stunning test results from the researcher in L.A.

Clearly, God had placed this specter of cystic fibrosis before them so that they would learn to trust Him, both as a couple and as individuals. The Lord had decreed for all mankind to be fruitful and multiply, so they dedicated themselves to prayer on the matter, while Livvy stopped her birth control pills. As for God's part, there was a 75% chance of a healthy baby based on the science of genetics, so the Lord only needed to pick up the other 25%.

Then–nothing. Nothing again. Or again. Finally, a trip to the fertility clinic.

"You're going to need to think about adoption," came the answer. Chase's mind went blank, and he assumed Livvy's did, too.

The doctor began talking about sperm motility studies as opposed to total counts, and then the number of eggs and premature ovarian failure, and a host of disorders that culminated in: "We don't see this very often, but neither one of you is going to be fertile. I'd place the chances of conception at 1 in 10,000."

God had sealed the deal, making sure that Chase and Livvy didn't waste any more time on frothy prayer. Both were carriers of cystic fibrosis, and both were infertile–it was a match made in Heaven. Had the cystic fibrosis scare been some sort of celestial tease? Was it a prompt to force a leap of faith so that Providence could slap them around later? How did such an answer to prayer reside with the same God who ordered: "Be fruitful."

Of course, there were no answers. Yet, the worn-out phrase, "The Lord works in mysterious ways" became a thorn in his side whenever he heard friends and family use it in response to their test results. Yet, he decided to cling to one abiding thought–"All things work to the good for those who love the Lord"–and he pledged to hang onto this bromide by his fingernails if necessary.

.   .   .

With the abrupt and depressing return to his residency, Chase had been negligent about his promised visits to see Ivy Pettibone. Rather than the "one year" he had explained in advance, the months passed until he was halfway through the academic year before he made the time, on a Saturday afternoon, to visit Ivy. Although buildings and wards were locked, Chase was well-known to the aides and nurses on 19, so all he had to do was knock. To be sure, though, he had called ahead.

"Hi. I came to see how Ivy's doing."

"She's at the piano," said an aide. "Where else? Hardly ever gets stuck in her circles anymore. Now, instead, she drives us all nuts playing

"Chopsticks," among other terrible tunes. We've had to limit her time. See the little clock on top of the piano? She gets twenty minutes, four times a day. She never misses. We had to move the piano as far away from the nurses' station as possible, so that meant out of the Day Room and into the Great Hall to where it is now."

Chase laughed, then walked through the Dutch door into the main TV room, far end, where the upright piano was pushed against one wall. Ivy had her back to him, so he listened a moment to "The Only Lonely Panda in a Tree at Waikiki" as Ivy played. Oddly enough, her technique had improved, with both thumbs targeting the keys nicely. However, what really caught his ear was her singing of the lyrics, wherein her language seemed to have changed ever so slightly.

Chase had heard her version so many times that he had memorized every syllable:

Ladoti solati
Me soti falati
Solaso Dolati
Doti. Fa-la-la-la...

The words had always been the same. Today, however, he was listening to a modulation, one in which he could still hear Ivy's old lyrics, though the staccatos of the consonants had been sanded away, leaving a smooth surface.

Chase inched closer, then reached across the piano bench and began playing with his outstretched arms. "Zanda the Panda, alone in a land-a..." was as far as he got before Ivy turned and grabbed him around the waist, holding tight.

"Soti medo," she cried, "soti medo."

"I've not forgotten you, Ivy. I'll be back in six months or so for another rotation."

.　　.　　.

On the pediatric surgery rotation, Chase prayed for more sleep, but instead, he ended up setting a new record in the program for consecutive hours awake, operating (70). The faculty, of course, had rotated during the 70-hour marathon, as had the intern and junior resident. As the most senior resident on the service, however, Chase's presence was expected on every case during the prolonged onslaught.

A month later, still on the same rotation, Chase was thrilled that Livvy was going to pick him up at the hospital for the most refreshing experience since their return to Texas–a reunion with the New Bloods. The group was still performing with its original members, and they were scheduled for a gig at nearby Midland later in the evening. Livvy had made all the arrangements. The New Bloods would swoop through Matherville first for an early dinner. The window of opportunity would only last two hours. Livvy saw it as her best effort yet to brighten Chase's life.

Standing on the corner near College Hospital, waiting for Livvy to pick him up for the reunion, Chase paused to offer special thanks for this small drop of happiness. At the very moment when he silently said "Amen," his beeper went off. A helicopter was transporting a newborn with a diaphragmatic hernia that would require immediate surgical repair. The faculty surgeon on call told Chase he'd need to give up his night off. He did. But at the same time, he realized how warped his values had become, for he was more concerned with the disruption of his plans than the baby's survival (which would be a toss-up). He longed only for a simple dinner with old friends, a luxury that was apparently unattainable.

Around this time, it dawned on him that no matter what he prayed for, the opposite seemed to occur. Perhaps he had taken a wrong fork in the road long ago, and every prayer from now on would be futile. Perhaps that fork was when he had refused the offer to join a Bible study as a freshman medical student. *Dogs and other philosophers*.

His next three-month rotation was the private surgical service where the faculty performed their own operations, while the surgery residents served as "scut boys." One day, Chase was told to first-assist an older surgeon, a part-time faculty member, who hadn't worked at College Hospital in years. The surgeon was going to perform a hiatal hernia operation. The residents were taught to perform the newer Nissen operation through the abdomen, but the elderly surgeon cracked the patient's chest, proclaiming the need for a good old-fashioned Belsey procedure. It was a matter of opinion, Chase thought, giving the surgeon the benefit of the doubt. However, after the chest was opened, there was no hiatal hernia. Nothing was wrong. Instead of acknowledging an error, the surgeon announced, "Oh, I see the problem now. It's not a hernia, but a lipoma here at the G-E junction."

Chase was nauseous. A small fat pad was *normal* at the gastroesophageal junction.

After removing this normal anatomic feature, the surgeon took one hour to close the chest wall, using catgut combined with sloppy technique. The wound fell apart in the days that followed, the patient developed an abscess in the chest, then he died three weeks post-operatively.

Chase was so upset that he made an appointment with Chairman Thatcher N. Taylor, M.D. who needed to be aware of the horror. To Chase, this was not malpractice—it was assault and battery at a minimum, with negligent homicide as the more appropriate tag.

"Granted, it's terrible, Chase. He probably should have quit operating years ago, and in fact, told me when he scheduled this case that it would be his last. Once a surgeon is at that point in his career, he really needs to hang it up. We as surgeons need to recognize that in ourselves. We're not automatically skilled for life. You'll better understand later in your career how this happens."

Then, nothing.

Dr. Taylor did *nothing*. Chase thought back to the sham surgeries performed at the hospital at Matherville State, removing imagined snakes from the bellies of the delusional, and he began to wonder about the difference between the two institutions. Who defined insanity? And how? Was it a continuum, a subjective subtlety, like the difference between cervical dysplasia and carcinoma in situ? Was it only a matter of opinion? No wonder the public was outraged about the "brotherhood of silence" among physicians. It wasn't malarkey. It wasn't fabricated. The silence was real.

Chase sought refuge with a group of residents and nurses who celebrated evenings off at a nearby bar where pitchers of beer turned horror into humor, as long as the horror had happened to someone else. When Chase took his turn as raconteur and shared the story of the

Murder-by-Belsey (as Chase called it after the first pitcher), it prompted a brief debate as to the role of "policing our own."

Chase espoused the notion that if the reigning leadership wasn't going to act on blatant screw-ups by those already out in practice, then the key to policing in medicine was to identify future transgressors while they were in their infancy, that is, still in residency. "In fact," Chase muttered, "I think our new intern from Arkansas, what's-hiz-name? Covey? Oughta be tossed out of the program."

"You can't ruin a guy's career like that," argued another surgery resident.

"Ruin a career? What are you talking about? Covey's a friggin' intern, for godsakes, with multiple options left–plus, he's a sadist who shouldn't be allowed near patients. He's been reported umpteen times by the nursing staff, especially if he's called out of bed at night. VA nurses caught him trying to force an NG tube down a patient who didn't need one, just because the guy called Covey an asshole. He's pissed off every nurse in the hospital. He's a klutz in the operating room. His post-op care is horrible. C'mon, now."

Chase was shocked to find himself in the minority. While all the guzzlers who were gathered around the sticky oak table agreed that Covey was "bad news," no one other than Chase spoke up in agreement that the intern should be expelled. "The old pyramid system took care of this sort of problem," Chase finally mused. "These days, if a guy gets in, he's in for good." After a few more tallboys, however, the problem didn't seem so bad.

"I agree with Chase," said a nurse at the next table as she scooted over to join the surgery residents. "Covey is as worthless as tits on a boar hog. I can't believe you guys are trying to defend that fool. He has no business being a doctor, much less a surgeon." The residents stared vacantly into their beers. The speaker was the bob-haired nurse from the SICU who now wiggled her way into the vacancy beside Chase. He thanked her for her support and poured her another beer.

One of the Chiefs in general surgery, on his way to cardiac next year, Ronny Foreman, entered the fray. "Chase, the problem is that dang *general* surgery more than the shithead surgeons." Brilliant beyond his gutter-tongue, Ronny Foreman had set the curve in med school one year ahead of Chase. "The badass germs in the GI tract are the great equalizer. You got your general surgery complication rate that's out the wazoo, no matter how good you are. Good surgeon–bad outcome. Bad surgeon–good outcome. The bacteria make the damn decisions, not you. If you're cuttin' out Aunt Bessie's gallbladder, and the sumbitch is gangrenous, and she dies, then it's your ass hanging from the highest tree. 'It was only a freakin' gallbladder, for God's sake,' the relatives say as they call their attorney. Yet, we both know that when I'm doing coronary bypasses next year, the mortality rate will be *lower* than your goldarn gangrenous gallbladder. On the other hand, if I kill someone by trying to fix their hearts, everyone'll say, 'Well, hell. Whaddya expect? It's *freakin' heart surgery*.' So what does it matter if Covey's a worthless bum as an intern? The bugs call the shots. The germs are in control. As for me, I'm countin' the days 'til I can hold the human heart in my hand, dammit, like the sumbitchin' god I was meant to be... Pass me that pitcher."

"Not to worry, my friends," a surgery resident chimed, "haven't you ever noticed how the guys who are dangerous seem to disappear mysteriously from the program? I think T.N.T. still runs a pyramid program secretly. Come July, one bad apple is out, and whaddya know... meet our new PG-4 transferred in from Hopkins where the pyramid is still in play."

The ongoing revelry at the bar several times a week seemed to make all the pain and worry go away – until he got home, which was later and later and later on those nights off. Livvy couldn't believe that her husband was turning into a barfly. "Chase, I don't think you took more than one drink in high school or college. Now, it seems like a regular event. You're making me nervous. Do we need to see someone?"

.   .   .

Toward the end of Chase's PG-4 year, his father Wes was to be honored at a Far West Texas University basketball banquet, marking the arrival of a new coach and new hope for a return to the days of glory. Chase was on call for general surgery, rotating again at the VA hospital, so he couldn't attend, and he made only half-hearted attempts to switch call schedules. Instead, he spent the evening in the hospital library. The wards were quiet. The emergency room was quiet. The SICU was quiet. And, the library was occupied by a lone resident, escaping the fanfare surrounding his father.

His mother had given Chase an advance copy of the program, and he pulled it from his overnight bag to read Wes's biographical sketch, something that sons rarely think about until it's time to write an obituary. He stopped cold at the third paragraph where it gave the date when his father had departed his residency in general surgery to begin private practice–near the end of the fourth year of training, a few months prior to the Chief year, exactly where Chase was right now in the process. In fact, his father had been on the same rotation at the same VA hospital when he had quit residency prematurely to generate income to cover the mounting medical bills for sister Annie with her cystic fibrosis.

Not finishing residency, thus failing to become board-certified, had been Wes Callaway's great regret in life. Chase tried to connect to something inside as to his own motivations, but there was nothing there to feel. Was there a link to his father's story? No. Chase had chosen medical school, then general surgery, of his own free will. The fact that he was surpassing his father's training, at this very moment in time, was merely a benign curiosity.

Then, as Chase finished reading the biographical sketch, a bizarre memory popped into his head, and with it, chills that rippled over the surface of his body.

A ghosted recollection–in a parked car, doors locked, with his older sister Annie–took form in his head. Both were younger than school age, and the only thing he could see out the rear window of the car was a monstrous red-bricked building where his father had disappeared to make rounds, hours ago, it seemed. To Chase, at an age where memories may or may not be real, "making rounds" meant "drawing circles." Why did his dad desert them to draw circles? Chase was crying non-stop. Perhaps, he was screaming. In his mind, the abandonment was permanent. Sister Annie tried to calm him, reminding him they had been instructed to "wait." He cried. She coughed. Finally, their father reappeared, and all was well, it seemed. He said, "I'm going to be longer than I thought, kids, so let's go inside."

He escorted his children into the red-bricked fortress where, in a drab, yellow-walled room, a group of men, all of them dressed in white coats and white pants, were laughing and joking. They seemed to be friends of his father. And then, one of them called out, "Chase... Annie... take a look at this," and the man opened a tall locker. Out popped a pink skeleton, legs and arms dangling in the air. Chase recalled it as a terrible fright, a shocking horror. So why was everyone in the room laughing?

The memory couldn't be real, he thought. How could anything so graphic, so bizarre, stay buried in his head for so long? Yet, the more he replayed the sequence, the more it gelled, the more it took form, the more he realized that the huge, red-bricked building had, indeed, been the very VA hospital where he now sat in the library. And the yellow-walled room? Of course. It was one of the residents' offices, identical rooms, six on each floor, two per ward. Where else would his father and cohorts have gathered? Still, after 30 years, all the offices at the VA had pale yellow walls.

Chase remembered that, during the time his father spent on the orthopedic rotation, the senior Callaway had been assigned to the VA hospital. It certainly fit. Quite possibly, there had once been a skeleton on the orthopedic floor for the residents to study. Pink? Unlikely.

Near midnight, alone in the library and spooking himself with hazy memories and fragile conjecture, Chase decided to explore. In an unchanging environment like the VA, it was likely that the second floor, currently orthopedics, had also been orthopedics back in his father's day. So Chase started there. After checking the two offices on 2-West and finding no lockers, he felt ridiculous as he continued his quest to 2-East. There, with the thrill of an archaeological entry to a centuries-old tomb, he was astonished to discover an old-fashioned locker standing solo in a corner, camouflaged in the same dreary yellow as the rest of the room. The locker was taller and wider than today's models, more of a one-door cabinet. It couldn't be the same one, not after all these years. The memory itself was too fuzzy to be real.

I should leave it shut. The spectral nature of the quest was nothing more than a foolish lark, and Chase considered for a moment that the past should be left alone. Yes, this mystical sense of adventure was fun in an odd way, but it would evaporate should the locker be empty. Yes, better left unopened, preserved as a frivolous game, a romp through time.

He gripped the twisting handle anyway, whereupon a sense of dread settled over him like a shroud. He didn't like to entertain the loony concept of devils and demons roaming carefree in the world, hiding in dark closets. So when he eased the rickety door open to find two jackets, a raincoat, and an umbrella hanging from hooks in the locker, he laughed quietly to himself. *What a fool. I've probably fabricated this entire memory.*

When he tried to shut the door, a pile of crumpled scrub suits, books, manila folders, and drug samples at the bottom of the locker spilled out, halting his efforts. With his toe, he fought back at the mess, trying to close the door at the same time. Then, a bony hand emerged from beneath the pile and reached for his ankle. A flash of terror....

Chase brushed away the scrub suits and trash covering the bones, then lifted out the lonely hand, along with its attached lower arm–radius and ulna–freeing the relics from the locker's junk. The bones were stained with a peculiar shade of salmon, orange bordering on pink. He looked toward the top of the locker where, inside, an extension rack once held a full skeleton, much like the lockers used his freshman year in medical school, allowing the skeleton to slide smoothly out of the closet for examination and study while dangling from the rack. Thirty years removed from the ghastly scare of the hanging skeleton, Chase came face-to-face with his memory. Under the fragile yet pervasive admonition to embrace fear, he interlocked his own right hand with the hand of pink bones, a handshake forming a creepy bridge of emotions long buried.

The curse hath slumbered since heels did hang, he heard himself whispering as he remembered the allegedly prophetic and schizophrenic words uttered by Viola, during her one-night stand in Building 19, years ago. Then he chastened himself against further melodrama, especially the brand fueled by metaphysics.

24

As the clock struck midnight, with June 30 rolling into July 1, the four Chief Surgical Residents, deservedly or not, were filled with certitude and chutzpa with the arrival of the new academic year. The gray-haired surgeons, reminiscing, proclaimed the "chief year experience" as "the best year of your surgical career." Chase found their description dispiriting. As he saw it, the Chief year should be the beginning of a long and satisfying career. Yet, if the gray-hairs were correct, and the best experience was over in one year, then was he in line for a long downhill slide after that? Still, he puffed his chest and pretended supreme confidence, Commander-in-Chiefdom, Master of Life and Death.

Group rounds on the wards were traditionally performed in a flying wedge pattern, with the Chief at the front, flanked by a junior resident and "tern" one step behind, then the flare of the wedge formed by medical students eager to please.

While leading one such wedge only weeks into the new academic year, Chase steered his team toward the double door entry of the SICU. He quizzed the medical students as he walked, turning backwards with the question, spinning forward to await the answer from the flanks.

"Given ulcerative colitis and Crohn's, which of the two diseases has the greatest propensity to develop into colon cancer? And what percentage would you—"

A nurse jumped into his path from the "fresh heart" room. Frantic, she grabbed Chase by the collar of his long white coat, a garment now eight inches longer and commensurate with his new title. "Dr. Callaway, I can't find anyone on the cardiac team, and I've got *pure blood* coming out the chest tubes. Pressure is 60 and dropping. Four-vessel bypass, finished an hour ago. I've paged everyone. Dagmar is off giving a lecture to some civic group at The Colony Club. He'll be here in five minutes, but my patient isn't going to make it that long. We've got four units of packed cells left from surgery, and that's hanging now."

Chase looked through the crack in the door and confirmed that the two chest tubes had turned red with solid columns of blood, sucking life away. "Get the chest set out," he requested, using such a calm voice that he might easily have been saying, "Your turn to deal the cards." In crises, Chase was always calm. Not a phony calm where soft utterance emerges from trembling lips. No, he was truly calm. Later, in bizarre aftermath, as if his adrenal glands were slow to react, he'd shudder at the thought of what he'd done. It was as if terror had to replay itself as a memory over and over before his fight or flight response would kick-start.

While the nurse set up the chest tray, Chase bent over the surprisingly young patient, a man whose wide-eyed stare betrayed active consciousness, although he was unable to speak while on the ventilator. Chase explained, "You're bleeding from your surgery, and I'm going to open your chest and everything will be fine. I won't be able to give you any pain medicine because your blood pressure's too low. No anesthetic. I'm very sorry about that, but we'll get this fixed in a jiffy." With one eye monitoring the nurse who was still ten seconds away from having the tray ready, Chase removed his long white coat, folded it lengthwise with shoulders in apposition, then laid it carefully over the back of a chair. His flying wedge of trainees formed a semi-circle at the open door of the private room.

Chase switched gears, pulling the patient's gown away, pouring a bowl of antiseptic over the man's chest, quickly tossing down sterile drapes, cutting away skin and subcutaneous sutures, then ordering, "wire cutters." "The pressure is fifty systolic," the nurse noted. Chase snipped and pulled out the row of wire loops that held the sternum together, looking at the man's face only once. Eyes had glazed. *He's fading out now, and just in time*. Then, the patient's eyes closed. "Chest spreader," requested Chase. He placed the retractor blades into the gaping sternum and cranked the ratchet open.

Since the pericardium had been left open, the bleeding source was obvious. On the surface of the weakly throbbing heart, a geyser of blood was spurting from a small hole where the saphenous vein had been sutured to the aorta, now partially pulled loose. "Call the O.R. and tell them to get a room ready for the heart team," ordered Chase. "In the meantime, give me a needle driver and 6-0 Prolene." And with a single, ordinary, humdrum, figure-of-eight stitch, he closed the gap in the bleeding anastomosis, avoiding any restriction of blood flow in the graft. The red geyser collapsed as the knot in the suture was secured. Moments later, with blood transfusing and bleeding stopped, the nurse said, "We're back up to eighty on the pressure."

Chase covered the open chest and throbbing heart with a betadine-soaked towel. When he looked up, Dr. Dagmar was pushing his way past the semicircle that blocked the door. "Call the O.R., call anesthesia, get more blood typed and crossed… " Dagmar barked the orders that, of course, had already been done. "As soon as the O.R. calls, rush him over there. No, let's go right now. They'd better be ready."

"There was a hole on the aortic side of the graft," offered Chase. "Single figure-of-eight stopped it."

Dagmar continued, "We'll need to re-do that end of the anastomosis, of course, then clean him out since you've got contamination here, what with opening the chest in the unit, and hopefully, he didn't have an infarct with the pressure being so low."

You're welcome, thought Chase, stepping away from the bedside as Dagmar took over.

Still with no adrenaline sloshing through his bloodstream at all, Chase lifted his white coat from the back of the chair, then slowly worked his way into its sleeves as he nodded to his underlings to follow. As soon as he resumed his position at the front of the wedge, he spun on his heels, walking backward, and picked up mid-sentence where he'd left off– "…so, is it gonna be Crohn's or ulcerative colitis? And, given that propensity for colon cancer, what percentage would you assign as the probability for each?"

At least some of the stunned plebeians *must have known* the answer, but the medical students were speechless. They had witnessed one of the most amazing things they'd ever seen—crisis with aplomb, disaster with equanimity, a chief resident in general surgery casually operating on the open heart while making rounds, without missing a beat. Inside, Chase chuckled to himself, knowing how the scene had played out in the untilled minds of the third-year students. And, at the same time, in this defining moment, Chase realized he could handle *anything*. The bloody red gore sank into his pearly-white bones, dipped in glory. Humility was needless, but it made for a nice veneer. Only later did the juice of adrenaline fire up, prompting restlessness and insomnia.

Ten days later, the brightest student in that troupe of witnesses to Chase's "miraculous deed," Ray Henson, killed himself.

A fellow medical student had approached Chase a few days after the SICU miracle to express her concern that "something" was wrong with her friend, ordinarily a brilliant student. In deference to the "old Chase" who had aspired to a career psychiatry, he assured her that he would "keep a sharp eye" on Ray.

A week later, after simple hernia surgery where Ray Henson had been the student assigned, Chase suggested that Ray write the post-op orders in the recovery room, as was the norm. Ray turned his boyish face toward Chase where there was a vacuous look, every bit as blank as the sheet of paper where Ray was trying to write the orders. "I— I'm having trouble... I don't remember orders... how to write them, I mean. I—I... " The kid looked back down toward the order sheet, then shook his head 'no' as if relinquishing all hope. The pen that was dangling in his fingers fell to the table.

Chief Resident Callaway, assured of his own cautious and wise sensitivity, agreed that something was "stressing out" Ray Henson. Rather than pouncing upon weakness with a primitive force common to some chief residents in the past (Sam Dinwiddie, for one), Chase suggested that Ray go home and "get some sleep" since the student had been on call the night before. "Sleep deprivation can make anyone crazy," said Chase. "Take as much time off as you need, Ray. Do you need to see someone? A counselor, I mean? Do you have someone you can talk to?"

"Jeannie, I guess," he said, referring to the worried medical student who had originally approached Chase.

Instead of sleep, instead of seeking comfort from a friend, Ray Henson walked out of the hospital, traveled two blocks to his apartment, tied a bag over his head and ended his life.

The next day, in reconstructing the sequence of events prior to suicide, Chase had been the last person on earth to see and speak with Ray Henson. No matter how much he exonerated himself from responsibility, no matter how much everyone assured Chase that there was nothing he could have done–"survival of the fittest, you know, Chase"–Chief Resident Callaway felt a chink in his armor. And he couldn't help but wonder whether he had built his own shell too thick to recognize the depth of Ray's suffering.

Medical students, prone to casting easy blame, did not hold Dr. Callaway accountable in the slightest. Later in the year, the junior class of medical students would, in fact, name him recipient of the Outstanding Teaching Resident Award for all clinical departments.

.   .   .

Chase glided through the Chief Year merrily removing stomachs, resecting colon cancers, lopping out diseased gallbladders and retrieving common duct stones. He cured blood disorders by jerking spleens, prevented acid reflux by rearranging the anatomy at the gastroesophageal junction, eradicated thyroid cancers, and brought serum calcium levels back to normal by finding benign tumors of the parathyroid glands. He saved lives after trauma by suturing lacerated vessels, he healed ulcers by cutting vagus nerves, and he released bowel obstructions by dividing adhesions. He amputated the gangrenous legs of neglectful diabetics, once timing an emergency guillotine amputation to fit neatly into halftime of a Far West Texas University basketball game on local TV.

Two particular areas of surgery, however, were deficient at Far West for gaining the proper experience–mastectomies and peripheral vascular surgery. Most all breast cancer patients in the region sought care with the private practice doctors at Permian Medical Center, so the experience at College Hospital was dismal, only thirteen cases split among four Chiefs over the course of one year. For Chase's part, he would enter private practice having performed only three mastectomies.

As for vascular cases, with carotid surgery firmly in the clutches of the neurosurgeons, the case totals were bleak for the Chiefs. Furthermore, when it came to vascular insufficiency of the legs, Dr. Dagmar was a believer that virtually all problems should be addressed first with "inflow correction," so the only procedure where Chase developed vascular skills was abdominal aortic bypass. Remarkably, during his five years of training, he never performed, or even witnessed, an "outflow" correction through what was considered a "common" downstream procedure in the rest of the country–femoral-popliteal bypass. In a way, Dagmar was correct. Few patients who were veterans of high-risk aortic surgery ever returned for more–they either died or danced a jig.

Concerned that the lack of breast cancers and vascular cases could jeopardize board-certification, Chase met with departmental chair, Thatcher Nolan Taylor, M.D., to learn if his fears were justified. After all, the residents were required to log their case experience. For both fem-pops and carotids, staples of vascular surgery, Chase had big fat zeroes.

"Don't worry, Chase. Overall, your numbers will be fine. The Board understands that experience is always thin in some areas when you finish your residency. There's still a lot to learn after you start your practice. That's why it's a good idea to align yourself with other surgeons, master surgeons if possible, so that you continue to develop. And on that note, I'll ask again, one last time–is there a chance that I can talk you into joining the faculty next year?"

"No thanks, sir. I'm pretty set on private practice being the place for me." And as he said these words out loud, his internal answer offered more detail–*and I'd like to do that private practice in Southern California where I can get back to music, a hobby begging to become a second career.*

. . .

C.C. Chastain called him from California.

"Chase, you're not going to believe this. Listen. I'm holding up my cassette recorder to the phone. I taped this from the radio."

Chase couldn't make out the tinny song at first. Then he heard, "...when I decided to rise... and eulogize... the demise of my dream in this song."

"Do you hear it?" asked C.C. as he pulled the phone away from the recorder.

"Barely."

"Here. Listen some more."

Chase couldn't believe it. Surreal.

C.C. returned to the phone. "It's our song. 'Horizon A-Rizin'. Only their title is one word–"Demizin'.""

"What the hell's going on, C.C.?"

"Someone stole it. Had to be someone who wandered in from the boardwalk when we were playing it last year. Remember? The last few weekends before you went back to Texas, we sang it probably ten times a day. And my living room being Grand Central Station and all, I figure someone heard it, then got one of those miniature recorders and tucked it away. Fuggin'-A, buddy, we've been screwed. Country music's exploding right now. You can feel it out here in L.A., what with "Urban Cowboy" being released in a few weeks. Music publishers are buying up country left and right."

"I—I can't even think what to say. I'm... stunned."

"I heard it on the radio earlier. Started to call you, but couldn't believe it myself. It's nearly identical to ours, note for note, word for word. I listened on several channels until I heard it again. Had my recorder ready. Don't know if it's playing anywhere other than L.A. or not."

"Can we sue?" asked Chase.

"What proof do you have of anything? I never put a single note on paper."

Chase said, "I wrote the lyrics on the back of a progress note from the hospital. But I'm sure there's no date on the paper. Even if I had dated it— We don't have anything, do we? Not a freakin' thing."

Both were silent. Chase heard his own breathing in the receiver as he struggled to think of something to say. What was the name of the emotion that arose from anger, depression, frustration, envy, and most of all, intercepted validation of talent? Did this cocktail of passions have a name? The only way Chase could describe it later, after their song became a mega-hit for someone else, was: "I felt like a wonderful, exciting, glorious life was out there with my name plastered on it, then someone came along and chipped off the letters of my name and stuck on their own. Now, for the rest of my life, I get to watch *their* fruits of *their* success."

. . .

When the call came from his old medical school classmate, Amy DeHart, Chase was happy to hear her familiar voice, but the mood turned dark with her opening line: "I've been diagnosed with breast cancer."

While Amy had been serving as Chief Resident in Ob-gyn, her own gynecologist felt a breast lump and biopsy was recommended. The local expert for breast cancer, Chairman Thatcher N. Taylor, was to be her surgeon. He had requested that Amy sign a permit for mastectomy if cancer were found on frozen section. Amy had politely refused. She had done some quick reading and found that a new school of thought was emerging, forcing surgeons to re-evaluate the dictum that "mastectomy must be done at the same operation as the biopsy in order to prevent the spread of cancer cells."

Forever the gentleman, Dr. Taylor honored Amy's request for biopsy alone, even though he considered it a bad choice. The pathology on the biopsy revealed cancer. And now, Amy was on the docket for the newly adopted procedure–*modified* radical mastectomy. At least she didn't have to undergo the Halsted radical. She was thirty-one years old.

In her frantic research, Amy was surprised to find an old copy of a toss-away newspaper in the Department of Surgery library with Dr. Thatcher Taylor's picture on the front cover, holding his hand high in the air to vote for preservation of the traditional Halsted radical mastectomy over the newer "modified" approach. The society's newsletter was dated 1976, so in the past few years, Dr. Taylor had apparently changed his mind. Thank goodness. The lesser surgery allowed her to consider a breast reconstruction. However, she would have to wait the standard two years before entertaining plastic surgery, as she was told she had to prove that she was cancer-free before the surgeons would attempt a reconstruction.

Amy also discovered that a national co-operative group was enrolling patients in a clinical trial for "lumpectomy" as an alternative to mastectomy, but Dr. Taylor had assured her this was a dangerous approach to breast cancer. Amy wanted to do everything possible to live a long and healthy life, and without hesitation, she agreed to undergo modified radical mastectomy.

Yet, facing a mastectomy isn't why she called Chase. She was bothered by something else–the diagnosis. She was disturbed by the fact that she had first felt the lump over a year ago, and it hadn't changed since. It was barely even noticeable. How could it be cancer? She had been so busy at the time, sleep-deprived, rotating on Labor & Delivery, she didn't even think to have it checked. Six months later, the lump hadn't changed so she felt better about doing nothing. Then, on her routine exam, her gynecologist was concerned about the firmness of the lump. Amy was asked to participate in a nationwide study evaluating the effectiveness of a new X-ray called a mammogram, and this X-ray showed a "stellate mass highly suspicious for cancer." How could it be malignant if it wasn't growing? Had she been kidding herself about its unchanging size?

She asked Chase to double-check the pathology slides, and when he did, something didn't look right. In a textbook he recalled from his year in California, one of the photographs showed a cancer next to an abnormality that could mimic breast cancer. He hadn't personally seen such a case, but he remembered the side-by-side patterns in the photo being so similar that it was hard to tell which one was cancer. To his eye, there had been a subtle difference, an orderly appearance, to the benign lesion whereas the malignant lesion was more chaotic. The caption to the photo had also noted that the diagnosis, paradoxically, was easier on lower magnification. By looking too close with high magnification, the two entities were virtually indistinguishable. It was a "can't see the forest for the trees" phenomenon.

An outside opinion on Amy's path slides was certainly a long shot, but worth a try. He asked the pathology department to mail the microscope slides to the same guru who had presented Grand Rounds in Pathology several years ago in California, the expert who was rapidly becoming a "household name" in the exploding art and science of breast pathology.

The Chairman of Pathology at College Hospital refused to send the slides to the expert based on "some *surgery* resident's request." Instead, the pathologist said, "I'll bet my reputation on this being infiltrating ductal carcinoma." So, Chase approached Dr. Taylor whose very initials–TNT–seemed to make things happen, requesting him to go head-to-head with the pathology chairman. The slides were mailed for the outside opinion, and one week later the pathology guru returned a not-guilty verdict of "benign complex sclerosing lesion." No cancer.

Chase was a hero. Dr. Taylor thanked Chase profusely for sparing Amy the mutilation and saving him from an egregious surgical act. "I knew I did the right thing when I sent you off for that year of pathology." Most grateful, of course, was his old foosball partner, Amy, with whom he had served as doubles champion seven years prior when they were medical students. And with her effusive gratitude, in the form of an extended hug, Amy stung Chase with a terrible indictment:

"Chase, I love you like a brother. And I owe my very self to you now. But I want you to be aware that there are rumors out there. That group of hard-living residents and nurses that meet up at the Nautilus to drink beer on their off-nights, well, I think most of the medical center gossip originates about them. I understand how you could be a target for that sort of thing, but I'm afraid Livvy will hear."

Inside, Chase melted. He was embarrassed at the person he was becoming–compartmentalizing his life such that he was medical hero by day and those nights on call. However, during the "off nights," he had made a new set of friends, an underworld of nurses and doctors who laughed at life and its trappings. Somehow, this group rose above worry, levitating. The recent plagiarism of his song, however, seemed to have pushed him over the edge, and he had come to believe that his life needed to unfold in a completely different direction.

"Amy, I appreciate it. Livvy and I have had a rough go of it since we got back from California. That cystic fibrosis thing, you know, then the fertility thing for both of us. A life without children really alters your thinking. The word 'legacy' takes on a new meaning. It's going to work out okay, I think."

"Livvy will help you stay grounded, Chase. You're one of the most talented people I know. I think back on that time I first met you when we were both interviewing for med school. My husband thought you walked on water because of the New Bloods, and I guess I did, too. I'd hate to see you take a bad turn in your life. I've heard you're thinking about going back to California to practice. That can be a dangerous place."

"Don't know what I'm going to do yet. If I end up there, it's not because of medicine. It's because our old module-mate, C.C., is making some headway in the music business, and it might be fun to chase that dream. You and Kyle are going to have your kids here in Matherville, and–well–it's gonna be kind of hard for Livvy and me to watch all that."

"I understand. But hang in there. Livvy has put up with an awful lot during your nine years of training. I worry about her as much as you. And don't forget about adoption."

After Amy finished her sermon, Chase felt as if his face were ablaze. He hoped he hadn't turned bright red in front of her. If he could only make it through this year... but then again, something was wearing away, chipping relentlessly. The more he pulled off heroics at the hospital, the more he seemed alienated from the old Chase. He couldn't figure it out, but the "best year of your surgical career," according to the gray-hairs, needed to end before he became someone else entirely, a total stranger to himself. Considering that he felt minimal stress at the hospital, he wondered if he was living on the edge, that is, generating trouble for himself, as a means to divert what should have been a high-angst transition toward becoming a surgeon. No matter what was beneath it all, he had to get away from College Hospital and the VA Hospital and Far West Texas College of Medicine, and this escape needed to happen soon.

. . .

"I don't know you anymore, Chase. You don't talk. You've buddied up with a bunch of barflies, and I have to hear about it from friends. We used to enjoy things together, but it all seems lost now. I've given *everything* to you. Everything I've done in my life, it seems, was to help you succeed. I feel like I don't even exist anymore. You're obsessed with the fact that someone stole your song. Well, remember the song you wrote for our wedding? Do you? Well, you've stolen that song from me. Let me get to the point–I think one of us needs to move out. Maybe we can get a grip on things and start some counseling. My sisters have told me to let sleeping dogs lie, but I can't."

Livvy's reference to "sleeping dogs" prompted a faint echo from years ago: *The dog awaketh to feel the pain.* Then, for some reason, he thought about "products of conception" and the drunken dream he'd had upon leaving California, wherein the microtome-severed fingers of the fetus scraped at the glass cover slip on the microscope slide, trying to escape.

This moment had been brewing ever since their return from California when communication had collapsed. With only a few months left in his surgical residency, Chase packed his bags. He had mixed feelings about moving out, though relief was stronger than the sadness. As he walked out of their home, he felt he was entering a new world, one without a traditional legacy.

At a pay phone, he called his old classmate, Will Glendenning, who had dropped out of medical school during the third-year surgery rotation. "Will? Chase Callaway here. Listen, I need a place to stay a few nights while I look for an apartment. Or maybe until I end up moving to California. Livvy and I are having some trouble right now. Do you mind if I move in with you and Claudia for a few days? I hear you're studying like a madman right now, but I wouldn't be around much. At the hospital mostly."

"Well, uh, it's not particularly a good time right now, Chase. You're right about my studying and all. I'm defending my dissertation in a few weeks. I got a big fat reject on my first defense. Shoulda been finished with my doctorate years ago. It's not very pleasant around here sometimes. Claudia has lost her patience with me."

"Just tonight, then."

A long pause left Chase dangling, and finally Will said, "Okay, I guess. Maybe things will cool off between you and Livvy. Are y'all going to counseling?"

"Counseling? You gotta be kidding. You remember that I went into *surgery*, right? There's no such thing as time off in general surgery, not for counseling, not for anything."

"Well, come on over. I'll fix you a strong one."

The Master of Life and Death headed for the Glendenning home, fully aware that his life was spinning out of control, without a care in the world.

Back in his car, Chase reached to turn on the radio, but stopped short. What if he were to hear the song that had been ripped from his heart? Not now. He couldn't take it. Instead, he began singing the plagiarized song to himself:

I was sittin' at the end of a hopeless dream
Wonderin' what in the world had gone wrong
When I decided to rise...and eulogize
The demise of my dream in this song.

And he remembered how C.C. had re-worked the bridge, bringing the song to its fruition, only to be stolen...

'T weren't the fall from grace that broke my back
'Twas the chip, chip, chipping away.
Your rain is so fine in a vertical line
It's the sideways flood that's blowin' my mind...

Although written in the genre of tragic country love, the nemesis Chase had in mind for the lyrics was not a person. In fact, he had been inspired by the most destructive force in his life that, unfortunately, was also the most validating force in his life–the making of a surgeon.

Still, everything would be okay. All things worked for the good.

25

Matherville State Mental Hospital, with its link to the showcased Department of Psychiatry at the medical school, had achieved a national reputation for excellence. However, Chief Psychiatrist and Administrator, Dr. Wendall Latimer, sought more. With new psychotropic drugs that could mute madness, the focus on outpatient treatment strategies flourished. When Latimer coupled the development of these wonder drugs to his own grant-writing skills, federal money from D.C. began to flow across the plains of west Texas like foreign oil.

With his new outpatient apartments completed in the fall of 1980, Dr. Latimer appeared on the cover of *News from the World of Mental Health*, plus mainstream publications as well. Readers enjoyed photographs of hard-hatted Dr. Latimer posing in front of the construction site where each apartment appeared slightly catawampus to its neighbor. In the birds-eye view, the Z-shaped floor plans revealed a geometrical arrangement of four radiating spokes of Zs. The front windows (unbreakable) of each apartment could be viewed only by the counselor whose station formed the hub. With each square apartment staggered and angled, the Z-strategy allowed the inhabitant an illusion of privacy, unseen by co-psychotics.

Although communal meals were still required to avoid culinary disasters, the patients would be allowed to have their own refrigerators and snacks. The front Z-line allowed a back Z as well, where plots of ground could be utilized by patients to grow vegetables, flowers, or both. And for those with "pet privileges," the back Z could be fenced with room enough for two dogs per apartment. The therapeutic potential of pets drew journalistic praise as the project was designed as a joint venture with the Matherville city pound where dogs would be "lent" to the patients for compatibility testing before permanent placement.

In multiple interviews with the media, Dr. Latimer revealed how the entire idea had come to him one day as he looked out across the prison-like atmosphere of the asylum. "How in the world," he said to eager reporters, "did the beautiful word 'asylum' take on such hideous connotations? Well, my epiphany was the realization that architecture had only worsened the stigma of mental illness. Why should it be this way? These patients, most of them, understand how to take care of themselves, how to feed themselves, and so forth. Many of them, even those who've lived here most of their lives, whom we call 'institutionalized,' have formed bonds with other patients. Why, it's not unusual to see two patients–one with organic brain syndrome, another with schizophrenia–play a mean game of checkers together. Some of these apartments will hold four individuals, some three, some two, and some will be solo, depending on patient needs. There will be adjustments, of course, as needed. And we're planning a central game room with foosball tables next to the common cafeteria, and there'll be art classes, pottery classes... "

When one of the three main network anchors arrived in Matherville to do a story on this progressive facility, the godfather of College Hospital and the Far West medical center, Hardy Studebaker, son of patriarch Josef, made a rare appearance for a public interview, proudly pointing to the progressive bastion of mental health. That evening, the entire Studebaker clan joined as communal hosts for the network celebrity who gave a lecture on the ethics of journalism in America, a fund-raising event held at The Colony Club. Afterward, the news anchorman adjourned to the inner sanctum–The Smoking Room–along with the privileged men. (The female Studebakers, and wives of Studebakers, were ruffled by this "unliberated" sequestration, many vowing that, someday, women would break the barrier into the Smoking Room.)

"And what will be done with the old mental institution?" asked the celebrated journalist, once he was comfortably seated in his place of honor by a fireplace, cigar lit.

Hardy Studebaker puffed his own cigar and answered, "We still need to hang on to some of the old. For instance, what we call The Tower will still be needed for maximum-security patients. Others will not be suited for outpatient care, especially those in vegetative states. This revolutionary project will only apply to one-third of our population at first, hopefully extending to two-thirds or so eventually. So, yes, some of our buildings will become vacant, probably closed for good. What's nice for our apartment patients is that they will be outside the walls, with a real sense of freedom, some for the first time in their adult lives."

When the anchor left Matherville and presented a glowing story to the nation, the jubilant mayor proclaimed "Dr. Wendall Latimer Day" in the city, based on the visionary genius of "one of the nation's most prominent psychiatrists," fully validated and anointed by the network news where a famous anchor, no less, had opted to visit.

The nearby medical school captured some of the spotlight's overflow. The Chairman of the Psychiatry Department, the colorful Dr. Everett Meeker, considered the publicity as a bonus to his recruitment efforts in attracting new residents and young faculty into Far West's psychiatric training program. Medical students from Ivy League schools applied for positions at the famed Matherville facility with its rich history, dating back to its days as a leader in long-discarded methods of sham surgery, shock therapies of all types, and trail-blazing lobotomies. Then, in the modern era, Matherville State had been a pioneering institution in applying rigid scientific methodology through prospective, randomized, placebo-controlled trials of psychotropic medicines, all accomplished at Building 19. And now, onward to this new and exciting era of outpatient management of the chronically ill, complete with gardens and pets and Z-shaped geometry, all of it serving as a magnet for the greatest psychiatric minds in the country.

One month later, in The Smoking Room at The Colony Club, on a rainy Sunday afternoon, Hardy Studebaker met with city leaders of Matherville–other Studebakers, Studebaker in-laws, and Studebaker cronies.

"Gentlemen, what we're witnessing in the Department of Psychiatry is what I envision happening in every department of the medical school.

One by one, I hope to develop each department, eventually creating a major medical center here in west Texas that will draw in research dollars. And patients. We can't rely on oil forever. The economic boom in health care ventures is going to be tremendous. I've just returned from several jaunts, first to M.D. Anderson, then Memorial Sloan Kettering in New York, and the Mayo Clinic. I had the opportunity to review their data on jobs, real estate values... basically, the overall economic impact that goes far beyond the direct revenues from patient care and research. It's a potential gold mine. I don't need to tell you how depressed the real estate is right now around the health center complex. It's no stretch to call the area a slum. Those good folks living there now will need to be moved out. The Mexicans and Blacks would be better off in new housing anyway. Let's plan ahead. Ten, twenty, at the most thirty years. The future is ours to claim.

"I've instructed the chairmen of all departments, and the Dean himself, to keep their eyes open for stars. By 'stars,' I mean those physicians and scientists who have the talent to create world class pockets of excellence–areas neglected by the other medical centers where we can excel. History is written by great individuals, not committees, not groups, but individual men–I should say 'women' in today's world, of course–who have both the charisma and the ability to forge new trails. Just as psychiatry was neglected by most all the major centers for so many years, while little ol' Matherville recovered the fumble and scored, we can get our foothold in these neglected niche areas, build our reputation further, and finally, the conventional departments will fall into place. We will make sure all of west Texas, if not the world, is flocking to Matherville someday for specific procedures, techniques, expertise. The key is in identifying the forgotten niche. Or niches, if that's a word."

And the men lit their cigars, drank their brandy, and dreamed of the cornucopia as it applied to their individual businesses–be it banking, real estate, construction–if someday, a major medical center stood on the plains of far west Texas, rising well above the lonely oil derricks.

26

As Chase drove to the unnamed hospital at the asylum for his final three-month rotation of surgical residency, he recalled the drudgery of last night's visit to see his parents.

His mother had crumpled into a sobbing heap upon learning that he and Livvy had separated. "I never should have had children," she moaned. "It has broken my heart. It's broken me." His father glared at him with seeming contempt. "You're pathologically self-centered, Chase. I can't believe you'd waltz in here and break your mother's heart, especially after what she went through with your sister. With Annie's passing, Livvy became her daughter, and now you're going to destroy that, too? Even your grandfather has seen the change in you, and it isn't good. Are you even aware that Zeb's cancer has spread? That he's terminal? You haven't seen him in over a month. Nor have you bothered to visit Sukie. You've fallen off the face of the earth, all wrapped up in yourself."

Chase was thankful he'd wolfed down several kamikazes before he'd ventured home with the news of his marital problems. The scene would have been hard to take sober.

Afterward, feeling the pangs of guilt, he ventured to Sukie Spurlock's house near the medical school where she was polite enough to restrain her reaction to bad news. Still haunted by guilt over Sukie losing her job years ago, he reaffirmed his promise of financial payback to her, as soon as he established his practice in California where he was certain now to live, if for no other reason than to avoid the heat of west Texas. Her reaction had been restrained. She barely smiled as he prepared to leave. Then, as he inched down the stairs of her front porch, taking backward steps, he fielded a standard Sukie aphorism as her good-bye: "Don't ever forget, Chase, a clear conscious makes for a soft pillow."

The emotional walls, constructed brick by brick over these past five years, allowed him to cut and slice the human body, anointing him as Master of Life and Death, even though his personal life had unraveled. For Chase, this was powerful testimony to his superlative skill–able to operate on the human body, saving lives, with one hand tied behind his back, so to speak.

Today, at the beginning of the home stretch, the final rotation, Chase drove toward the stone gates at Matherville State, recalling that a full academic year had passed since he had last rotated through the surgical wards at the funny farm. Something was new. On the perimeter of the grounds, outside the stone walls, he was surprised to see what appeared to be an apartment complex under construction. Who would build apartments so close to the crazy folks? He stopped his blue Cutlass, eased backward, and turned onto a dirt road that meandered through the construction zone.

Some of the units had been drywalled, and one apartment even had exterior brick halfway to the roof. Mostly, the piles of brick were still tightly wrapped by ribbons of steel, like Christmas packages lying in wait. One snip through the metal ribbon could send bricks flying in all directions, it seemed. There was no signage to explain the facility. When Chase spotted the jagged footprint of the units in radiating rows, he thought, *That's odd. It's the same floor plan of my old grade school, the way each classroom was angled and staggered. Very 1950s. I haven't seen that style used anywhere since. And, it's the same Z-footprint design I used for my project so long ago on the third-year psych rotation.* Coincidence, I guess.

Chase's world had become so small that he'd missed the national coverage entirely.

· · ·

Besides finishing residency, Chase had a focused mission for his final three months–the repair of Ivy Pettibone's hands. As Chief, he could pull strings that heretofore were not available to him. After confirming that Ivy was still interested in the surgery, Chase began pestering the plastics team to schedule the case. However, the chief resident in plastics, while a friend to Chase, always had an excuse. "Sorry, Chase, we put her on the schedule, but in pencil, of course. I had an opportunity to do a tummy tuck with one of the attendings from Permian that same day, and, well, we'll try to get to your gal next week."

Crooked Creek, separating the medical school from the mental institution, albeit often a dry bed, functioned as raging rapids when trying to get specialty surgeons to cross the waters. The general surgery residency program was an exception by placing full-time residents at the hospital. Other specialties, like plastics, had to "make time." Chase knew he wouldn't give up until the job was done. True, it was probably too late for better function with Ivy's fingers, in that they would still flex together as a single unit after separation. It had become a point of honor, however, and he wasn't going to back down. In fact, he was starting to toy with the idea of doing it himself. After all, how hard could the surgery be, especially for someone who had once performed open heart surgery at the bedside?

With his feet on the desk in the residents' office, his chair rocking gently, Chase read a text on hand surgery that included step-by-step pictures of Z-plasties that allowed for separation of fused fingers. His beeper fired its signal, startling him from the applied geometry of skin flaps. When he answered the call, a nurse said, "We need a gastrostomy feeding tube for one of our patients over here at the Tower." *Oh, sure, you mean one of your vegetables*, he thought. Instead, he said, "Great. I'll send my junior resident, or I'll be there myself to check it out. I'm sure you've already cut through the red tape to get the op permit."

Feeding tubes through the nose, even the smallest ones, were being incriminated by reports of complications, most notably aspiration pneumonia, thus the shift to gastrostomy tubes–poking a hole directly through the abdominal wall and entering the stomach. Chase considered that it would be a nice, simple case for the intern or one of the senior medical students currently on the surgery rotation.

He had not been to the basement of The Tower since his years as a psychiatric aide when he covered vacation time for his compadres. He remembered it as one of the most gruesome spots on earth–no more than two dozen beds, but all occupants either vegetative or rabid. For the latter, with their spasms, seizures, drooling, and paroxysmal wailing, four-point restraints were the norm, around the clock. And while sheepskin padding encircled wrists and ankles, torn flesh was often present at all four points. Leather belts crossed their chests, and some patients sported football helmets to keep them from cracking their skulls as they slammed their heads against the metal bed rails.

Chase remembered the percolating scent of sweat, urine, feces, and liquid food re-emerging as vomitus, stirred together and forming the repugnant bouquet so well-known to employees at mental institutions. However, the worst feature, certainly, was the sound–the harmony of old men crying for their mommies, old women wailing for God's deliverance, and the general lamentations of the lost who screamed in endless repetition, from all four corners: "Help me, help me, help me... "

In his days as an aide, the basement of The Tower was called The Dungeon, but after an administrative decree forbade the insensitive term, the word "Bedlam" had supervened, along with "Bedlamites" for its inhabitants. As a naïve pre-med student with a bent toward psychiatry, Chase had studied the history of mental health, so he knew Bedlam to be a derivative of Bethlem Royal Hospital in London, the world's first psychiatric hospital that, in turn, had its name derived from a nunnery and monastery for the sisters and brethren of the order of the Star of Bethlehem. What a jump from Bethlehem to Bedlam where, after 400 years of operation, someone had the bright idea in the 1800s to charge tourists a penny apiece to peer inside the cells for an endless source of repulsive entertainment. Thousands came.

Pleased that the years of surgical training had thickened his walls and toughened his soul, Chase decided to go to The Tower himself, rather than the intern, to pre-op the patient. In an odd way, he wanted to prove to himself how far he'd come since first witnessing the horrors of Bedlam. Nine years earlier, the Dungeon had, for a moment, made him question the very existence of God.

Descending the concrete steps, made narrow by stark walls that seemed to squeeze inward, Chase was reminded of the stairs leading down to his grandfather's storm cellar. He marveled at the icy temperature when he reached the halfway point. It was the chill of a morgue rather than the flames of Perdition, and he was surprised that he didn't recall such frigid environs. As he approached the bottom of the stairs, the nurses' station appeared from beneath the header of the stairwell, and he saw that the concrete floor was dotted with metal drains that lay in wait to suck human poisons into the heart of the earth.

"I'm here to see one of your patients, a Mr. James Toterrio," Chase said to the lone aide at the nurses' station. "Your head nurse turned in a request for a feeding tube."

"Bed two," said the bald, middle-aged aide without looking up from his *Penthouse*. "He's our newest veggie. Came from College Hospital where something horrible happened to the guy in surgery a few months ago." The aide lowered his magazine and looked at Chase. "Routine gallbladder, they said." The aide pointed a bent finger toward bed two, then aimed his nose back to his literature.

Chase knew the story all too well from Saturday morning Grand Rounds followed by Morbidity and Mortality conference. "It" had happened, in this case, to one of his co-residents who had encountered a gallbladder plastered into the liver so firmly that he couldn't chisel it out. All anatomic boundaries had been lost in concrete. "I'll bet it's cancer," the chief resident had said at the time. Yet, it turned out to be nothing but severe chronic inflammation of an ignored and diseased organ. Nevertheless, given the many anatomic variations that can occur in the gallbladder area, but now obliterated, the resident had cut through an aberrant hepatic artery. By the time the bleeding was under control, a transient drop in blood pressure had caused the patient to suffer a near lethal stroke while anesthetized. Lethal would have been better than a vegetative state, as the extreme agitation of the brain-damaged patient had bought him a ticket to Bedlam. Chase was ever grateful that "It" had happened to someone else.

Since a gastrostomy tube could be inserted under local anesthetic–merely a nick in the skin and a poke through the stomach–there were few contraindications to surgery. And the primary indication was already in place–a signed op permit, approved legally. Chase sat down at the nurses' station to write a brief pre-op note so the staff could prepare for transporting the patient to the O.R. tomorrow morning. As he placed the metal-covered chart back in the rack, he scanned the names of the 20-odd residents to see if any of his former patients were backsliders from Building 19 to Bedlam. One name jumped off the rack and nearly took his breath away: *Jewell Pollard.* How many Jewell Pollards could there possibly be in west Texas?

Jewell Pollard had been Chase's former Sunday School teacher. She had been the one to recognize his knack for lyrics. She had been the one to tell her husband, the choir director, of Chase's skills that eventually launched his brief music career with the New Bloods. And, it was her husband, Jack Pollard, who'd hung himself from the altar cross at the Church of the Driven Nail.

It can't be her. It simply can't be.

Rather than read the chart, Chase forced himself to her bedside, the last bed against the north wall. At first, he was relieved that it wasn't her. Jewell had been a portly woman with a round and jolly face. In contrast, this ghastly figure, tied to the bed in four-point restraints and leather belt across the chest, was skeletal. Wrinkled skin sagged from hollow features, while crazed and frantic eyes tore a hole in the ceiling. The more Chase stared at the death mask, however, the more he was able to pry through the years of her misery, until he finally recognized the once-familiar face of Jewell Pollard embalmed by madness.

With his eyes held firmly on Jewell, Chase backed up slowly to the nurses' station. There, steadying himself with one hand, he found Jewell's chart with the other groping hand, then began to read. He could find nothing more than custodial ramblings written by aides. She had been a patient for so long that her complete records were in a different file cabinet. After convincing the aide to scooch his chair a few inches to allow Chase to access the file cabinet, he readily identified Jewell's complete chart, divided among five thick folders.

From the first file that he pulled, he was shocked to learn that she had been a *voluntary* admission to the acute care wards years ago, and that her diagnosis was "manic-depressive psychosis," a label applied shortly after Chase's time spent in her Sunday School class. In fact, she had been in and out of the mental hospital on multiple occasions, behaving normally during the welcome recesses between "attacks." It took Chase a half-hour to wade through the multiple charts until he finally uncovered the explanation for her one-way trip to Bedlam.

Shortly after she had been transferred from acute care to Building 19 (well before Chase's arrival there as an aide), after volunteering for a clinical trial using a new drug, she had suffered a grand mal seizure, a known side effect of the experimental agent. She would have fared better with placebo. Unfortunately, the seizure had ended with cardiac arrest, and Jewell was resuscitated several minutes too late... or not late enough. The brain damage was both extensive and permanent. Unfortunately, not fatal. She was transferred to Bedlam for the rest of her life, strapped to her bed, with only an occasional need for a protective football helmet.

Chase read through her status reports, noting repeated references to the fact that no aides or nurses had ever witnessed any evidence of communication—words or gestures or eye contact—since her admission to Bedlam. He tried to recall the date when Jewell's husband had killed himself, and the story seemed to fall into place. He also remembered that his grandfather, in discussing the Jack Pollard disaster, had referred to Jack's syndrome as "angry-at-God," a condition perhaps as lethal as any defined psychiatric disorder and certainly fatal for Jack.

Chase was too tough to let things like this get under his skin. After all, he was a Master of Life and Death. Yet, Jewell Pollard was neither life nor death. He returned to Jewell's bedside, intent on making one-way contact at least, having read that vegetative states might still allow—might even welcome—neural input for stimulation to preserved regions of the brain.

He leaned over her bedrail to speak, but she did not look at him. In fact, there was no evidence that she even knew another person was there. Her sunken eyes remained transfixed on the ceiling, shifting vacantly from side to side.

"Jewell. Jewell Pollard. Do you know me? I'm Chase Callaway. You remember? Sunday School? Chase? Callaway? Chase Callaway?"

He continued for a lost amount of time, begging whatever demons that held her in check to let go and allow her to recognize the fact that she was a human being. He talked of old times. Times at the piano. Times at Sunday School. He even talked of her husband as if he were still alive. And finally, he spoke of the old song he'd written in grade school, the words intended to accompany "Chopsticks." He reached for her hand, sliding the sheepskin restraint above her wrist so that he could hold her, flesh to flesh.

"Do you remember the song I wrote, Jewell? I called it, 'The Only Lonely Panda in a Tree at Waikiki.' It was the song about the panda who gets blown across the ocean by a typhoon, from China to the top of a palm tree, and he can't get home. And he thinks if he could only fly, there would be no problem. And then, he decides he'll rock the palm tree back and forth until it catapults him into the air? And then he'll be flying? Remember? Then, just as he catapults, a tidal wave comes along and sweeps him underwater, where he thinks he's flying successfully, only he's really swimming. And—"

Jewell Pollard's eyes broke away from the ceiling and riveted on Chase. He couldn't believe it. He'd read in her chart only moments earlier that she *never* made eye contact. Then her lips began to quiver, and short bursts of air began to puff through. She whispered something. Chase couldn't hear it, so he asked her to repeat. She said it again, something unintelligible.

"Jewell, I know you're trying to talk to me. I'm Chase Callaway. Try it again. Remember? Chase Callaway. Say it again."

Her eyes remained locked on him. Chase had no doubt he was witnessing a vague recognition on her part. Her lips opened again, and she mouthed a silent word. He squeezed her hand and leaned closer to her face, twisting his head so that his ear nearly touched Jewell's cracked and bleeding lips. She said it again, and this time, he heard her.

"Zebulon," she whispered, but with an inflection that turned the word into a question, as if to say, "Is that you?" She repeated: "Zebulon?" Her face turned away from Chase, and her eyes retreated to the barren ceiling. She spoke no more.

He stood frozen, with no measure of time. All of Chase's hard-earned bricks that formed the wall around his heart crumbled to his feet, and he felt like a little kid again in Sunday School, a kid who now wanted to cry. Yet, he held his tears in check. He gathered the wayward bricks back to their place, then he marched up the concrete stairs out of Bedlam and returned to his fellow surgeons at the unnamed hospital where they could joke about the carnival of characters they would be cutting on during these next three months.

27

After the third cancellation of Ivy's surgery by the plastic surgery residents, Chase tossed aside any remaining reverence for specialty boundaries. Time was running out. He would fix Ivy's hands himself. The diagrams and photos in the text were somewhat confusing, but there were no laws against performing surgery with an open book nearby for reference. Simply cut along the dotted lines, then jigsaw the Z-flaps into their new homes. The court-ordered operative permit was about to expire. All clocks were ticking.

Chase had been visiting Ivy several times a week, ever since he started this last rotation in residency, and the last one at Matherville State. And while singing at the piano had been Ivy's focus during these visits, Chase had zeroed in on each step of a geometrically tricky surgery, remembering that the location of underlying nerves and vessels could be variable. He watched her hands as she played, imagining the incisions he would be making, barely noticing that her singing brought with it a subtle evolution in her language.

The Far West residency program in surgery taught early independence. "See one–do one–teach one," was the universal motto for surgical training. In the unnamed hospital at the asylum, however, it was permissible to skip the first step. The surgery residents had remarkable freedom, enabling Chase to take the matter of Ivy's hands into his own.

Chase traveled to Building 19 several times each day as the scheduled operation grew close. There, he would question Ivy as to whether she genuinely wanted her fingers separated. She seemed to understand, perhaps fully, what was about to occur. Chase even tried to scare her out of the procedure using words like, "cut, hurt, ouch, slice, scar" and more complex concepts like, "no feeling or, at best, tingling in certain areas," but Ivy kept nodding her head yes anyway. He had no idea how much she understood, but he further explained that her sore fingers would not work well at first, and that it would take months and months of "exercises" to see if the surgery would really help. When he informed her that playing the piano would be the perfect exercise, Ivy brightened.

On his final visit, the night before his debut as a hand surgeon, Chase drew purple zigzags on Ivy's flippers using a skin marker, matching the photos in the textbook that he brought with him. Although several approaches were possible, Chase had settled on the multiple Z-plasty technique, thought to be the most successful. The procedure itself was low risk, but true success in the form of increased mobility would likely be marginal since the repair was about 40 years overdue, and Ivy's brain might have lost all ability to commandeer her fingers independently.

From the surgeon's standpoint, the hard part was the three-dimensional planning, designing the Z-shaped incisions, up and down the fused fingers, so that the pointed tongues of skin could be wrapped around each digit after separation, the multiple flaps fitting into their respective slots. If he misjudged the reach of the Zs, he could always slip a skin graft onto the open areas, but Chase wanted perfection. He wanted the Zs to embrace each digit, the scars oriented at such an angle that the normal contraction of healing would not restrict motion.

Later that night, back at "home" (he was still living with Will and Claudia Glenndenning, most likely until he moved to California in two months), Chase couldn't sleep. The Chief year had already resurrected his old nemesis–insomnia. By taking call at "home," he could no longer rely on sleep deprivation as his ticket to slumber, paradoxically shifting more hours in bed to more restless hours awake. On this special night before Ivy's surgery, Chase tossed and turned, thinking of puzzles and Zs, perhaps dreaming the same, but sleeping far less than if he were preparing for a major extirpation of a pancreatic cancer.

The liberating surgery lasted five hours. Five hours of mind-numbing tedium. That is, except for one terror-filled minute the exact instant when Chase made the initial incision.

"Chase, we've got malignant hyperthermia here," said the anesthesiologist. "Her temp just now shot up to 105. Pulse is 130, pressure still okay. I'm gonna give dantrolene, and we need to get the cooling blanket going."

"Oh crap," said Chase, after years of planning. "Abort the case."

"Wait a minute, something's crazy here. The dantrolene's not even in yet, but her temp is already back to 99 and her pulse is down to 90, pressure stable."

"What's going on? Let's get the routine lab going," said Chase.

"This is nuts. Malignant hyperthermia doesn't do this."

"What does? Nothing I know of. Let's hold steady for a little while before we abort. I'm gonna deflate the tourniquet while we wait." Chase held pressure on the short incision he'd just made, as blood could now flow with the arm tourniquet released.

After 15 minutes of normal vital signs then normal lab, Chase felt compelled to move ahead with the surgery, knowing that he might be taking a big risk. Malignant hyperthermia could be fatal. It was a decision born of bias.

"Chase, I don't know what this was, but it wasn't malignant hyperthermia. Maybe the monitor wires had a glitch. Then again, her skin sure felt hot. Maybe... we'll, I don't know. I don't have an explanation. Gremlins, I guess."

"Then let's get this done. Tourniquet back up, please."

When the operation was over, Ivy had 10 distinct digits, each bent finger wrapped in a comfy blanket of skin. Over two hundred stitches would be removed later, and physical therapy would be ongoing. Chase felt enormous relief. For him, the score was even. Ivy had saved him from the humiliation of the dirty-dog dancer many years ago, then later from the wrath of Walter that could have been fatal. Now, all was settled.

As Ivy started to emerge from anesthesia, Chase dressed her fingers with long rolls of white gauze covering the strips of Xeroform. In addition to the procedure going well, his current satisfaction was in remembering the years of struggle it took to get Ivy to this point. Relentless effort followed by success was somehow its own reward, even if the victory had been thrust upon Ivy, to a degree. When her eyes opened, Chase pulled the surgeon's mask down from his face and smiled. A groggy Ivy smiled in return, then she shifted her gaze to her mummy-wrapped hands.

After the anesthesiologist rolled her gurney into the recovery room, Chase returned to his office where he dictated the operative note and closed the surgical chart on Ivy, a chapter now complete. When he placed her active hospital chart back with her psychiatric records, Chase spotted the manila folders that he'd opened and read many years ago as an aide. Hospital rules stated that, when mental patients were transferred to the medical hospital, all records, including the psychiatric volumes, were bundled for the trip, even if it took a wheelbarrow.

He had always intended to seek out Ivy's early records at the administrative offices where the archived charts were kept on the lifers, but he'd never made it. As he rummaged through the familiar manila folders, he discovered a white packet with these barely legible words as a return address: "Austin State Colony for the Feeble-minded." A rubber-stamped overlay in bold ink covered most of the faded address, stating: "Austin State School."

As he lifted the tattered package from the bottom of the box and began unwinding the envelope's string from its post, Chase's beeper sounded its alert. His team of residents and students must be ready for their day trip, he thought, with the hospital's van out front. They had scheduled a visit to the Wichita Falls State Hospital where certain psychiatric inmates had been deemed candidates for surgical procedures at Matherville's security hospital.

"Yee-hahhh," yelled Chase's junior resident through the voice beeper, "let's hit the trail and lasso some gallbladders. We're waitin' on you, buddy. Let's grab some hogs and get 'em on the chopping block."

Ivy's archives would stay put for now.

· · ·

Three days passed. The unveiling of Ivy's hands was an anxious moment for Chase. Would the skin flaps survive? Would there be an infection that could destroy all his work and end up making her worse than she'd been? Would the fingers wiggle at all?

Gauze removed, Ivy gawked at her hands for several seconds before she began to giggle. The black stitches were so thick on her fingers that her hands appeared to be covered by ants. And, with only minor skin loss at the tips of some of the triangular skin flaps, no skin grafts would be needed.

Ivy continued to chuckle, uttering her odd words, some of which Chase had not heard before. She bent her fingers into partial fists, though the digits curled as a unit, still believing themselves to be fused. When Chase asked her to wiggle her fingers one by one, he had to imagine that he saw independent movement. Traces of hope could blossom in medicine, so Chase was encouraged.

Then, Ivy pretended she had a piano before her as she sang, "Glow Worm," in her own language, of course, while floating her hands across the imaginary keyboard. She switched tunes to "Baby Face," then finally she sang her favorite, "The Only Lonely Panda."

Several weeks later, with stitches out, Ivy stretched her new hands toward Chase and spread her fingers as best she could, gesturing for him to hold out his hands as well. He gently touched his fingertips to hers, but she pulled away as if he weren't playing the game correctly. He tried again, going palm to palm, but that wasn't what she wanted either. Then, she interdigitated her fingers with his, until their hands were melded together, fingers locked. Despite her healing incisions, she did not seem to be feeling pain.

"Soti medo," Ivy said, the old familiar words for "I love you." Yet, when she repeated it, Ivy sounded more like she was saying, "SoMeLaYu," or even "So Me Love You." He did a double-take, then responded with, "So, I love you, too." She nodded in agreement, leaned toward the clasped hands and kissed several knuckles, both his and hers.

At that moment, Chase felt a flash of warmth and pride, but it turned quickly to a sense of foreboding. For some reason, an old memory struck him, and his face flushed with heat—the recollection of Crazy Viola, the paranoid schizophrenic from years ago, a loony he had seen only once, but a girl who had ranted about demons being released if Ivy's fingers were ever separated. How could he let a thought like that rattle around in his head? For years? He doused the image of Viola to enjoy the sweet success so evident now in Ivy's smile.

Then came another flash–the memory of his hand interdigitated with the bony fingers of the pink skeleton in the old locker at the VA hospital, plus the bizarre preview as a child of that encounter. He had to force himself to stop. "Magical thinking," he said to himself in reprimand, "is the easiest route to some really bad decisions."

His thoughts returned to Ivy and the unexplored medical records from her original admission. An hour later, alone, Chase broke the ancient string from the white envelope, his hands trembling for no reason.

The admitting history from the Austin facility, written in 1937, included the details of her birth and early life near Matherville as the deformed child of Dirk and Neva Pettibone. Chase wondered how this information would have been available to the hospital for a child freshly minted as an orphan, far from home. He assumed the source of the history was from relatives unwilling to assume her care. The narrative went on to describe the novelty of her birth defects and her celebrated status as the archetype of a new complex called – *Callaway's Syndrome*!

"Callaway's Syndrome?" he said aloud to the empty room. Then he saw the name Zebulon Callaway. "What's this about? What's my grandfather's name doing in this chart?"

He read how Dr. Zebulon Callaway had described her unusual birth defects in the medical literature, garnering the syndrome named for himself. Then, after the deadly tornado had destroyed much of Matherville, killing Ivy's parents, Zebulon brought her at age five for admission to the Austin asylum.

Chase had heard the stories growing up, mostly from his mother, how his pharmacist grandfather had once been called "Doc Callaway." However, Ivy's medical records spoke of Dr. Callaway as a true physician. Chase had no idea the ruse had gone that far. Hadn't anyone checked for proof of licensure? Then again, did anyone pay attention to those things in 1937? He flipped to the registration sheet to look at the box marked "Admitting Physician," and there it was again–Dr. Zebulon Callaway. Why had his grandfather taken Ivy all the way to Austin when the Matherville State Hospital was in full swing by then? And what was the story on Callaway's Syndrome?

He thought he knew his grandfather well, but as Chase considered it, simple math told him that Zebulon had been age 57 when Chase was born. Grandpa Zeb had already lived a lifetime by then. So, what exactly had his grandfather done during that initial lifetime?

Chase was long overdue for a visit to his Grandpa Zeb anyway, so now, in a hearty quest for explanations, Chase arranged a cross-town trip to visit "Doc Callaway."

. . .

Ivy had one thing on her mind–how to thank the person who, first as an aide, then as a doctor, had looked deep inside and seen her as a normal person and treated her as such. What could she come up with as a gift for Chase? Or, as they called him now, "Dr. Callaway," the same name as the doctor who had helped her as a child, and used to visit often. This new Dr. Callaway had given her hands that looked like everyone else– other than the bright red zigzags, that is.

Chase had explained that he would be going away soon, this time for good, so she never knew exactly when that last day would come. It made her very sad to think about such things. Still, what could she get for him as a gift? A new song perhaps? No, she didn't know how to make up a new song.

Then she remembered the books. Chase was always reading books, ever since his first time on the ward as an aide. That's it. She would get him a book. And there were plenty of books stacked high in one room at the cafeteria building. Mostly, the aides and nurses would read these books while on break, but they were for the patients, too, at least those who could read. Ivy had never learned to read, and she knew this by watching others convert the scribbles written on the pages into spoken words. While she liked only those books full of pictures, she knew Chase's books were mostly words–written words that held no meaning for Ivy, save one.

Her mother, a tall lady with a pink hand who smelled like flowers, now just a fuzzy memory, had taught her to recognize one word–*GOD*. Ivy had seen several books with that word on the cover, usually mixed with other words. That's it. She would simply pick one of the books with *GOD* on the cover, and that would be that.

She would miss Chase terribly. While it was fun to play and sing by herself, it was much more fun with Chase. Of course, her favorite song, largely because she could play it perfectly with her thumbs, was the panda bear who couldn't find his way home. It made her think about her mother and her dad and her home so long ago when she would go fishing with her father or would sit at the piano, smelling her mother's perfume, being held by her mother, the two of them giggling together, her father standing nearby, always smiling. And whenever she thought of this lost world, now a memory so distant it didn't even seem real, but a memory she kept alive every day and every night for countless days and countless nights, Ivy felt warm tears collect at the bottom of her eyes, sometimes overflowing onto her cheeks, and she wanted to go home.

28

Zebulon Callaway lay perfectly still, allowing his moth-eaten bones to rest. He was no longer allowed out of bed, as his own body weight might be enough to force the scaffolding to implode upon itself. Even the simple stretch for a glass of water caused wrenching pain.

His only hope had come with the recent news from his doctor that the cancer had invaded the lungs, and that Zebulon should "prepare for the worst." Instead, he would prepare for the best, that is, the end to it all. While his body might be riddled with cancer, his soul was riddled with guilt. He had spent much of his lifetime preaching about forgiveness yet had never been able to forgive himself for transgressions long ago.

Wes and Ramona Callaway had closed off the second story of Zebulon's home and hired round-the-clock care, turning Zebulon's library into a sick room where he would die. His magnificent cherry wood desk was gone. The matching credenza was gone. The hospital bed was nothing more than a block of white in the center, but it seemed to fill the entire room. The books that lined three walls served as reminders of the pain-free days, yet these tomes seemed to be creeping to the edge of the shelves, ever vigilant, watching their master, their pupil, die.

When Chase entered the sick room, Zebulon was consumed by a single thought–his grandson might be the last twig on this branch of the

Callaways. Whatever demons were nipping at the heels of Chase, forcing him down a destructive path and wrecking a marriage, Zebulon Callaway loved his grandson more than anything on earth.

He didn't wait for Chase to start the conversation. "Pull up a chair, my boy. Bring me up to date. It's been too long. Your folks already told me about California. And about you and Livvy." He dangled there, waiting for Chase to pick up the lead, but his grandson was quiet, head bowed. "Are you still living with your friends? What are their names? Glenndenning?"

"I'm sorry, Grandpa. I'm sorry this is happening to you. I'm sorry I haven't made it here more often. I'm sor—"

"Don't be sorry. And don't waste your tears on me. You'll be in this same spot yourself someday." Zebulon decided to respect Chase's diversion away from Livvy. "I don't mean you'll have cancer. But we've all been given fair warning that there's a deathbed waiting for us–the covers turned down and the pillow fluffed. We have our whole lives to prepare for it."

"Yeah, sure. I guess."

"You *guess*?"

"I'm around deathbeds every day," said Chase, "and I've seen so many awful things. I've seen mothers fall to their knees in prayer, but their babies still die. I've seen young couples lose their children to drunk drivers, and the tearful prayers of the parents don't change a thing. And when I've been given the chance to save those lives, I've prayed for the strength and power to do so, but I've failed. Not once, but lots of times. If prayer doesn't alter anything, then why? I know what I'm saying sounds awful, but practicing medicine has made me wonder. Not that I don't believe, it's just that now I wonder. I never wondered before."

"It's hard sometimes, Chase, I know. I've heard it said that if doctors are believers, they're either ophthalmologists or blind themselves–the point being that the life-and-death doctors have a tougher time believing in divine intervention. But no matter what happens, or seems to happen, it's impossible to see things from God's perspective, so—"

"And I've seen Jewell Pollard at the asylum, Grandpa. She's basically a vegetable."

Zebulon cringed at the mention of Jewell's name along with the recollection of her husband, Jack, swinging from the cross at the Church of the Driven Nail.

"I'm not sure if I've ever seen anything worse in my life," continued Chase. "I spoke to her. I held her hand. Then, she seemed to recognize the name Callaway, and she spoke your name, even though the chart said she hadn't spoken to anyone in years."

Zebulon revealed what he knew about Jewell and Jack, stuttering his way through the horrors of what had transpired behind closed doors in the Pollard family, realizing that as their guiding pastor, he'd failed miserably. And in such moments of struggle, he had acknowledged only to himself that he, too, had doubts and questions as to why he had failed so many times as a pastor, and how a pastor can have more reasons to doubt than any doctor who only sees the sickness of the body, not the soul. Still, Zebulon knew that the most ardent believer has doubts at times, doubts to be overcome through ongoing prayer and abiding. As he spoke, rambling about the power of faith, the more he sensed skepticism in his grandson's eye.

Chase interrupted. "By all the rules we profess, Jack Pollard ought to be in Hell. But after what I've seen of Jewell, and what I know, and what you've told me now, I can't figure it. I can't see how two of your most devoted flock could end up like this. Their time on Earth was bad enough, and now Hell for Jack? And who knows about Jewell. From what I saw, Hell would be a step up."

Generally able to worm his way through any theological struggle, Zeb felt impotent. "Do you mind, Chase, straightening up that pillow behind my neck so I can see you better?"

The pain felt like a hot poker in his spine as his grandson helped him readjust.

"I have no idea how to explain the Pollards," Zeb admitted finally. "And I know what you're thinking. You're thinking that my excuses are escapist and weak and nothing more than mumbo jumbo that your psychiatrist friends mock."

Chase replied, "In a nutshell, I can't believe Jack Pollard, a wonderful guy, is burning for eternity, or even 'Hell-Lite' where one is merely separated from God. Jack might not have realized it, but when he hooked me up with the New Bloods, why, it's probably the best thing that's ever happened to me. On a bigger scale, a heavenly scale if you must, a huge number of converts came out of those New Blood concerts. Jack was part responsible, indirectly, but still... and so was Jewell. Something doesn't seem right about our theology. That's what I'm trying to say. Too many shades of gray for the black-and-white New Testament to handle. And as for the Old Testament, why, in some places, it's downright scary. There's *got* to be provisions to account for the Jacks and Jewells of the world."

Zebulon knew that some theological cul-de-sacs were best avoided. "Chase, we simply don't have the answers. You can think about it 'til your brain busts, but you're not gonna to make sense of it. Until we die, of course. For some folks, the deepest theological question they have is, 'Why did God create mosquitoes?" They're the lucky ones. Others, like you, are both gifted and plagued by reason. I suspect you'll eventually end up in the lap of Pascal and other highbrows like him who concluded that dedicated reason eventually falls short, and the only thing left is to leap."

He paused while Chase seemed to be struggling with the sermon. Zebulon reflected on his time with Chase dating back to the early days after his own conversion. Back then, as a fervent evangelist, he had asked his grandson to walk the aisles at revivals to motivate the crowd. "You know, Chase, a man mellows with age, and the things he once believed to be justified can sometimes be darn near embarrassing later on. I want you to know that it was wrong of me to use you in those tent meetings like I did. It was my enthusiasm as a new convert. It seems so silly now, I just—"

"I was a kid then, Grandpa. I barely remember it. Seemed more like a game to me at the time. Don't think about it again."

As Zebulon let his neck relax, lowering his head to the pillow, he drifted back to an ancient memory of a hand-carved headboard of an oak bed, oh so many years ago. He contemplated his own conversion and his mountain of guilt that wouldn't wash away after nearly five decades of penance.

He had never told anyone the details of his transformation from pharmacist to preacher, yet now, given death's door, and its way of prying the tongue loose, Zebulon felt the urge, not a total catharsis, but enough to explain the power of his faith to a wavering grandson. Perhaps then, he could shake the final drops of blood from his hands.

"It's easy, Chase, to slip into the belief that the world is a continuum ranging from the incredibly good down through the gray zones, all the way to pure evil, so how can Judgment Day be a simple yes or no? How can it be a dichotomy—like cancer, where you either have it or you don't?"

"Not such a good analogy," Chase interrupted. "There are plenty of intermediate zones in pathology, where you can't say for sure whether it's cancer or not. I know you get a little crazy when someone mentions it, but maybe the Catholics are onto something with their purgatory."

Zebulon ignored his grandson, having gone round and round on this debate many times. "What I'm going to tell you now, Chase, I want you to remember so you'll know why I chose the path that I did. Or, as you'll see, maybe it was not a matter of choice at all."

He recalled the tornado of 1937 and how he'd surfaced from the storm cellar a different man. Then Zebulon said, "That version of things only skimmed the cream from the full story. This is where you're going to think I'm nuts, but visions are real. They still happen. For some people, God chooses to appear in shining raiment so as to rattle their cages. Others, like me, were so cold that Satan himself does the rattling. Understand, I saw the Devil that day with my own eyes. And it wasn't the fires of Hell I felt. It was ice.

"I'd barely made it to the underground cellar when the storm hit. In fact, the door slammed down and hit me in the head, though I never lost consciousness, I don't think. Instead of being in the cellar, however, I found myself in a cave, the place loaded with icicles, coming from both the ceiling and the floor, more like stalactites and stalagmites. When I looked beyond these crystal columns, I saw a three-headed monster I knew to be the Devil himself. No introduction needed. This was no dream. Some sort of altered state, yes, but no dream. Each of the Devil's three heads was chewing up a human body, but all six of his eyes were on me. I didn't convert on the spot, not out of fear. Oh, no. Scared the bejesus out of me, I don't mind saying. The vision disappeared in a flash. I didn't know what it meant until months later when I made a personal vow to start reading the books right here in this library while the floor-to-ceiling glass wall was being repaired. For some strange reason, I was drawn to Dante's *Divine Comedy*.

"Well, you can imagine my shock when I got to the part in the *Inferno* when he encounters Satan, a three-headed beast living in a world of ice where the sinners are frozen stiff. And each of the three heads, according to Dante, are chewing on a body—one head for Brutus, one chomping on Cassius, and one head eating Judas, all three of them traitors to close friends—this being Dante's *vision*, so they say, of the worst sin imaginable... betrayal. A traitor. He believed from his own experience that there was nothing worse, be it a traitor to God, country, family or friend. It was then I realized that the *Inferno* wasn't an allegory like the historians claim. Instead, I believe Dante really traveled to Hell, you see, or at least had the same vision that I did. I'd never read a single word of Dante before this happened in the storm cellar. How could I have seen the same three-headed monster that he described?"

Zebulon waited for a response. His grandson appeared incredulous, bewildered at best, his eyes roaming across the book-laden walls.

"I'm remembering," said Chase, "that back when mother held her own summer school for Annie and me when we were kids, giving us that so-called classical education, that Dante had all those circles of Hell, arranged in levels, a pretty complicated system. Seems to me that Dante had the same trouble with dichotomies that I'm talking about. And hasn't there always been the claim that Dante actually visited Hell? Even in his own day, didn't some believe that to be the case?"

"You're missing my point, Chase. My point is that I saw the Evil One. He's real. He's at work on this planet. And his cleverest lie is that he doesn't exist. My conversion process began in a cave of ice where I caught a glimpse of the very same Devil that Dante saw. And yes, Dante described multiple levels, with Satan living in the ninth and deepest level of Hell."

"Isn't it possible that you saw the same picture of Satan once before, then forgot about it? Maybe years earlier you flipped open the book and saw a picture of the three-headed monster. Or maybe you saw a picture of Dante's vision somewhere else, and it implanted in your brain."

"I'd had the book a long time, yes, but I'd not yet touched any of my collection when this all took place. Except for the medical texts, the books were only for show back when I was younger. I didn't realize 'til much later in life that authors wrote many of these books so they could speak from their graves about what they'd learned in life. I set about a personal study only after I'd survived the tornado. And I believe with my whole heart that the only explanation for my experience is that Dante and I saw the very same Prince of Darkness–that Dante Alighieri actually traveled to Hell. As did I."

As Chase nodded his agreement in a non-believing way, Zebulon wondered if his grandson's doubts were even greater than he was letting on. Oh, the turbulence that such doubts can cause in a life, thought Zebulon. After all, this was the same boy who, beyond his role as songwriter for the New Bloods, was also the emcee, delivering the call to the altar at the end of each concert. Hundreds, no thousands, had become believers through Chase Callaway and the New Bloods. Better to have never believed at all, than to have once believed and fallen away, he thought. Zebulon knew, too, there was room for healthy doubt. It was out of Zebulon's hands now. The grandfather had planted the seeds for the grandson many years ago. Some seeds find rich soil, some find rocky soil, some spring forth but are choked by thorns, and some seeds are devoured by the birds. He who has ears...

"I'm curious, Grandpa. I understand why Satan would be chewing on Judas, but why Brutus and Cassius? There were plenty of folks in history who would be ranked higher on the sin list."

Zebulon sensed an invisible smirk from Chase. Through the pain of the traitorous bones in his cancer-riddled body, he answered cautiously, "Dante believed in two Heavens, one to be realized on Earth and one in the Afterlife. And he believed the one on Earth would've actually come to pass had Julius Caesar been allowed to live. Understand that Dante's time on earth came more than a thousand years after Caesar. Without going into the complicated background of Guelphs and Ghibellines, Dante's world in Italian politics was crushed when he was banished from his beloved Florence for life, condemned to death-by-burning should he ever return. He wrote the *Divine Comedy* only when all hope was lost that he could ever go back to hometown Florence. Many of the greatest books ever written were by men like him, in exile, that is. There's no good word to describe the pain of banishment from your own home, especially when it's the result of a traitor."

Zebulon made a feeble attempt to sweep his hand across the three walls of theology, medicine, and novels as he spoke, but the pain restricted him such that only a few fingers wiggled in fatigue.

Chase said, "It still bothers me that being a traitor would be worse than murder or torture or rape or things in that league."

"Oh, but they did commit murder. All three of them, directly or indirectly. A traitor doesn't have to cause physical death. A psychic death can be worse. After people are betrayed, they rot inside if they can't forgive. Rot with anger to the point that death would be better, *especially* when the traitor is unrepentant. The traitor walks away, prospers according to plan, then laughs while the victim nails themselves to a cross. Betrayal is the sin that keeps on sinning. Only God can offer escape from yourself, once the traitor has done his deed."

Chase stood up, approached the bed, rested one hand on the side rail, while the other hand settled onto his grandfather's forearm. His grandson smiled. "Grandpa, not to change the subject, but I have something to ask you."

"Yes?"

"I recently did some surgery on a patient at Matherville State. Understand, I'd known her from back when I was an aide, and I'd even read her old chart on the ward when I was a freshman med student. Recently, when I operated on her, the original records going back to her admission at another facility in Austin were sent to the O.R., per usual. She had syndactyly, and I corrected it, believe it or not. I know it's been an awful long time, and you may not remember, but you were listed as the admitting doctor. How'd that happen? Her name was—"

"Ivy Pettibone." Zebulon felt the fingers of both hands curl into balls of pain, and he tried to force an unruffled look, wondering how much he would have to reveal. "Of course. Little Ivy. She was a fairly big part of my life back then. And when Sukie started working at the mental hospital, I learned from her that Ivy had been moved to Matherville."

This was not entirely accurate. Zebulon planned to say nothing of how he'd been the one responsible for Ivy's transfer to Matherville, or how he had been the one to finance Sukie's nursing education, or how he had secured Sukie's employment at Building 19 so that she could serve as a guardian for Ivy. He had revealed all to Sukie early on, and she was the only living human who knew the true story about Ivy Pettibone. He had originally met with Ivy every week after her arrival in Matherville, bearing her favorite snacks and taking her on short trips. Sukie secured these secret visitations, a practice he opted to keep from his congregation. Weekly became monthly, however, and over the course of several decades, the frequency of visits simply withered away, with Sukie serving as his ambassador. So when Sukie was dismissed several years ago, covering for Chase's recklessness, Zebulon slithered out of Ivy's life entirely, prompting his shame to mushroom. Yet, serendipitously, or by God's grace, his grandson had waltzed into Ivy's life.

Chase continued, "Well, how'd they let you admit her down at Austin? I mean, without really being a doctor? And why didn't you simply admit her straight to Matherville to begin with?"

Zebulon scrutinized his grandson, and, at the same time, wondered if the final few drops of blood were ready to be shaken from his fingertips after all these many years. He looked at the mantle clock on one of the bookshelves to see that he had only minutes left before he could ask his nurse, Carlotta, for another slug of morphine.

"The tornado left her an orphan, Chase, and I knew nobody would want her. It wasn't her birth defects that kept her from adoption because there's always someone willing to do the Lord's work there. It was her speech. She could never express herself, and that was a hardship only a mother could handle. Her mother was a wonderful woman, and she developed a way of understanding Ivy like no one else could dream of. They loved each other as much as any mother and daughter I've seen."

The big hand on the clock seemed to have stalled, delaying his morphine.

"After Ivy's mother died," continued Zebulon, "those were the years that old man Studebaker was still renovating Matherville State. Austin was clearly the leader in Texas when it came to mentally troubled kids. Ivy really didn't have mental problems, I know, but these institutions were custodial for all types of people with organic problems, not just mental cases. I thought Ivy would have a better chance there at being happy, with friends and all, and maybe even getting some speech therapy. At the time, they had nothing comparable at Matherville State.

"Back to your being the referring doctor for Ivy's admission. Didn't they check on your background? I mean, did they even look at credentials back then?"

"Not for a simple referral for admission. It's not like I was going to be her treating doctor in Austin. To be sure that she'd be admitted, I showed them a publication I wrote about Ivy where I was mistakenly listed as a physician, Zebulon Callaway, *M.D.* Carlotta! Are you out there? Carlotta! It's time for my fix. I need my pain med. Thank goodness the Lord created the poppy."

A middle-aged nurse, her blonde hair grouped into youthful curls held in the clutches of a white nurse's cap, entered the sanctuary long enough to give Zebulon a shot in the thigh.

Relieved even before the drug took effect, he asked Chase, "So how did it go for Ivy, with her surgery, I mean? I can't believe those fingers were never separated in Austin. We'd done some work on her clubfoot before the tornado with some excellent surgeons in Dallas. Then they separated her thumbs as a kid while still at Austin…" He felt a buzz, the first inkling that morphine was coming to the rescue.

"My surgery for Ivy went well," said Chase. "I always got the impression she would do more on the piano if we could get those fingers apart, but I suspect she's stuck with using her thumbs. Those fingers have worked as a single unit her whole life. Probably the worst part about the repair being so delayed is a practical issue. She might have learned sign language better had the repair been done early on. She has her own gestures, of course, but it's very limited. Too bad it wasn't all taken care of forty years ago."

"I guess Ivy would be… what, about ready to turn forty-eight by now?"

"No problem with your memory, is there Grandpa?"

Zeb caught himself. He shouldn't remember a detail like that if Ivy were merely another patient. "Well, I date everything from the tornado, you know. And, of course, I delivered Ivy."

"You what? Gosh, you played the doctor role to the hilt, didn't you? You delivered babies?"

"Yes, quite a few, as a matter of fact. Some folks had trouble getting a doctor back in the Depression, but I was always available, plus most people back then felt there was little difference between a doctor and a pharmacist. Difficult delivery, it was with Ivy. Never thought the girl would make it. Then her mother did miracles with her after that." Zebulon felt beads of sweat breaking out on his forehead. "I can still picture the two of them at that old upright piano. I wonder whatever happened to that thing? Destroyed in the tornado, I guess. It was a black upright, an antique, with built-in candelabra attached in front that rotated over the keyboard, so that you could make music by candlelight. Two silver candelabra on each side, each one with three candles. Neva would light them sometimes in the evenings…"

Zeb felt his eyelids grow heavy, and he barely heard Chase say something about coming back to visit on the weekend.

．　　．　　．

Neva Pettibone. Beautiful Neva–sitting at the upright piano, playing "Moonlight Sonata" by candlelight. The weighty aroma of her special stew would come drifting soon from the kitchen as they prepared for dinner as a couple, while his friend and her husband Dirk Pettibone had traveled to Ft. Worth to look for work. Thinking of it always, talking around it, testing each other with loving words nearly in code, but tonight doing it–kissing Neva first on the cheek, then wherever her allure directed him.

In the kitchen now, standing her up against the icebox, pressing harder, feeling her hand rub against him, his mouth smearing her lipstick over her cheeks, lipstick she rarely wore, but tonight letting him know with crimson that she was ready. Tears dripping from both her eyes that confused him into kissing harder, pressing harder.

Spotting her gold wedding band, alone on her finger, pulling at the ring as she fumbled with the buttons of his shirt. Watching the gold band fly from her hand after he yanked it over her knuckle, losing control.

Then the faint splash of the ring–plop–as it landed in the pot of stew that was not yet simmering.

Neva crying, "Oh no," then groping mindlessly into the stew to retrieve the gold. Her hand ablaze, the stew deceivingly hot, scalding. The ring would wait until later. Neva pouring cold water over her hand in the sink as he latched his hands onto her hips, pressing against her from behind, ignoring her groans of burning pain, then Neva ignoring her own pain, turning to face her lover, mouths locked, moving together as one, upstairs to the bedroom.

On her back, grasping the wooden post of her bed, the backboard of waves and seashells designed so exquisitely by husband Dirk, while Zeb and she merged as one. Curbing the pain in her burned hand by clutching the carved shell atop the post. Both of them moaning in euphoric unison, she squeezing harder on the bedpost to make the fire in her hand go away, then the conch-shaped shell of the bedpost popping off into her red, throbbing fingers–the scarlet hand that would later turn into a pink glove.

Her husband's seed had been faulty for years, but Zebulon's was prime. When it was confirmed, Neva–thrilled. Conception. As for himself, realizing horrible consequences if a child were born, drawing from a pharmacopoeia and his knowledge of herbal chemistry, he bore gifts for Neva of tansy, pennyroyal, and silphion. Yes, he told her that the medicines were vitamins that would nurture her child and its proper growth in utero.

However, the pennyroyal oil made her deathly ill, and tansy, too. As for the silphion, Zebulon's source had seemed dubious about its exact contents, for pure silphion was an extinct fennel that had flourished only in one spot on earth–the hills near Cyrene in North Africa where the most effective abortifacient ever known drove the region's entire economy, that is, 2,000 years ago. "There's a reasonable chance this is pure silphion, I tell you, Zeb," said the source. "There's a secret garden still in Cyrene that few know about."

Oh, sweet silphion, enough to inspire the ancient poet Catullus to ask himself how many kisses his lover and he might enjoy, then answering, "as many grains of sand as there are on Cyrene's silphium shores."

Yet, his malevolent concoctions terminated only the miracle of normal embryonic blossom. The deformities, perhaps all of them, *he* had caused in the child, all the while telling Neva he was bearing gifts of love, a traitor in every sense of the word.

And when the baby was born, there had still been one last chance to end it all. One way to pluck from his memory a rooted sorrow. Out, damned spot!

Indeed, the ugliest sin in the universe was the sin of betrayal. With its inherent evil, a rich and robust life perishes in a living death, while the transgressor emerges like a rose–in this life, at least. Yet, in the Afterlife, betrayal served you as lunch for the Devil.

The morphine escorted Zebulon through many levels of sleep, deeper and deeper, until the fire of a recurrent, haunting dream was frozen by the ice.

29

By the end of the ninth and final year of his medical training, the last five in surgery, the mutations were effective, the metamorphosis complete. As a Master of Life and Death, Chase had sequestered the turmoil of his personal life and had proved the ultimate–that his surgical skills and medical acumen were so solid, so strong, so exemplary, that he was unfazed by the collapse of intimacy and the wake of destruction he had left behind for his wife, his family, his friends. However, the notion that he had performed psychological acupuncture on himself– inducing pain in one location to avoid it in another–never occurred to him.

Popular lyrics on the radio served as anthems, calling him to a charmed mission in California. The music even counseled him to sell his house, buy a ticket to the West Coast, and give them a stand-up routine in L.A. Indeed, when old friend C.C. Chastain had alerted Chase to a job opportunity for a general surgeon in Southern California, Chase acknowledged he couldn't go on with the American Way in Far West Texas.

He still struggled to get over the fact that the song he'd written with C.C. had been stolen, and that the bandits had scored a hit. He simply had to try again, fully understanding that it was C.C. with the true musical talent. Besides, gossip held that Livvy's friends and every doctor's wife in Matherville wanted to tar and feather Chase on his way out of town.

His job in Los Angeles would be modest and unassuming, working in a satellite office of a mammoth medical group, doing surgery at an inland suburb. However, Chase wasn't targeting California for medicine. He was following the music. C.C. Chastain was organizing a country-rock band, and Chase was given the charge to begin cranking out lyrics.

Winning the position as surgeon at the satellite office in L.A. had been no easy feat. Chase was one of 50 applicants for a single position willing to work for half the income he could have enjoyed his first year in West Texas. Fifty new doctors, all searching to practice amidst palm trees, while trying to become something else.

"We had a large number of outstanding surgical applicants," the medical director told Chase at the job offering. "It seems that everyone wants to practice in southern California, but you were the only candidate who had a letter of recommendation from a *non*-surgeon–an internationally known internist, as you know. We thought it remarkable that you would have such a clear endorsement from Dr. Harrod, and his letter is the main reason for our offer to you now."

"I accept."

Chase had been a third-year student under Dr. Harrod, the most famous physician at the medical school at Far West Texas. To ask someone outside your chosen specialty to write a recommendation letter was, admittedly, a novel approach. And Chase was a little surprised that no mention had been made of the glowing letter written by his own Chairman, Thatcher Nolan Taylor, M.D.

Indeed, it had been Dr. Harrod who raised eyebrows when, in recommending Chase, he wrote: "Out of all my years of teaching, I've not had the good fortune to deal with a student who was bound for surgery, yet demonstrated such talent in the other areas of medicine. Dr. Callaway shows unique skills in bridging the chasm between the surgical and non-surgical worlds. The practice of medicine constructs territorial walls to its own discredit and disharmony. If anyone can break down those walls, it is Dr. Chase Callaway."

Still in Texas for a few weeks more, Chase let these words of Dr. Harrod ring in his head over and over to drown out the sound of a choking, coughing, sputtering marriage. He had explained to Livvy that his vacuous turmoil was temporary, and that as soon as he was settled in practice, he would put her on a plane to Los Angeles so they could begin counseling to repair the damage he'd done. And while Livvy wanted nothing less than to strangle him, she kept options and communication open, hoping that she would not add another divorce to the family tally.

· · ·

On a June day that hosted intermittent blushes of summer rain, Chase said his good-byes at College Hospital then prepared to cross Crooked Creek, a final jaunt to Matherville State. As he closed his umbrella and climbed into his Cutlass, he spotted a sports car, gunmetal gray, fishtailing into the parking lot at College Hospital. It was a DeLorean. And when the gull wing lifted, Chase saw a pair of two-toned shoes kicking in the air, the owner struggling to get out. A familiar face finally emerged, hopping out of the car, tossing his tweed sport coat over his shoulder with one hand, while lodging his pipe into the corner of his mouth with the other. It was Porter Piscotel, returning to join the surgical faculty at Far West Texas after five years at the top surgical program back East.

Chase's first impulse was to ignore him completely. While Chase knew his own ego was rich and full as a Master of Life and Death, he figured Piscotel was coming back to academia as a Master of Others, where there would be an everlasting pool of residents and students to impress, and from whom to draw praise. Yes, Porter would fit perfectly where there was always a chain of command, no equals, always someone above to kiss, always someone below to instruct.

Chase admitted that his bias was drawn from old information. As a medical student, Porter had demonstrated the duality so common to academicians—worship and disdain—that is, obsequious devotion to the great heroes, past and present, coupled to the conviction that true medical wisdom was imparted by geography. Specifically, one was charmed by training back East, while the locals would forever remain second-rate, at best. Yet, five years had passed since he'd last seen Porter, and Chase was forced to consider the possibility that he was judging too harshly.

Chase idled in his Cutlass through the parking lot, sneaking closer to Piscotel, observing his confident stride toward the hospital, foregoing an umbrella, undaunted by the sprinkles that danced on his bald and glistening scalp. Porter still had the same hawkish stare coming from beneath hooded brow, a prominence that served well today, keeping the rain out of his eyes.

Just as Porter started to exit the parking lot and cross the street, Chase lowered his window. A quick chat wouldn't be that hard. Besides, Chase was preparing to shake the Texas mud from his shoes forever. He would be finished with Far West and never have to deal with Dr. Brick Dagmar again, nor would he have to deal with Porter, a person who Chase figured had the potential to become more Dagmar than Dagmar himself.

"Hey, Porter, I forget–do Texas Aggies have a thing against umbrellas?"

Porter Piscotel turned to Chase and struck a pose, arms akimbo, with a completely blank stare on his face. Clearly struggling to remember Chase's name, Porter feigned recognition, smiled weakly and waved, turned around, and marched onward to the front doors of College Hospital.

Yes, Chase thought, *he's single-handedly ready to brighten the dismal and backward halls of pathetic West Texas academic medicine. "Hopkins this and Hopkins that" will be the new mottos.* "Oh, who cares?" he said aloud to himself. *Thatcher Nolan Taylor, as he said good-bye just now, told me I might become the most successful surgeon he's ever trained.*

T.N.T.'s parting words were still echoing. "You have it all, Chase. As you know, it's not the hands that make the surgeon, it's the brain connected to the hands. It's an ill-defined connection. Very ill-defined in some surgeons. However, you've got the entire package. If anyone else were headed to Southern California, I'd be a little worried about the doctor glut out there. But Chase, you have the talent to go anywhere you want."

Chase was elated, of course, but especially pleased that Dr. Taylor had not let Chase's crumbling personal life invade such lofty, parting compliments. T.N.T. had chosen his words exactly as Chase had been trying to live—by carving away the ugly and exposing the pure.

After Chase left Porter and his DeLorean behind, he drove across the creek's bridge to Matherville State, still recalling and reliving the awards banquet the night before, once again being named the Outstanding Teaching Resident by the medical students. He had joined the other nominees in a drinking contest, downing shots of whisky while standing on their heads. This gravity-defying stunt left more alcohol in the nasal passages than gullet, but with persistence, the technique could be learned. There had been synchronized choreography to "YMCA" involving medical students, residents, spouses and friends. And there had been the general revelry of knowing that one more year of hell had passed, and that freedom for all was one year closer. For the chief residents in all specialties, however, that freedom could now be tasted and touched.

Katie Roth, the medical student who had served as senior class president, and who had presented Chase with his plaque, approached him during a band break, her table napkin in her hand. "Dr. Callaway, I know it seems silly, but would you mind giving me your autograph on this napkin?" She held out a pen. Chase scrawled his name. "I don't understand... why?" he asked, eyes widening to see if he could read his own signature. "Because we *know*, all of us, that you're going to be famous someday. Whether it's medicine or music, you're going to be a star in California." As comical as it should have been, Chase agreed with her.

Chase had shown up at the awards banquet alone. This was by design. When he saw a particular bob-haired ICU nurse, as the date of one of the medicine residents, he eased her direction until he could pull her into the conga line while the band played Village People's "Hollywood."

In the next dance to "Don't Stop Me Now," Chase was spinning (...*I'm having such a good time...*), arms spread like wings (...*I'm a* rocket ship on my way to Mars...) with his engraved plaque as Outstanding Teaching Resident serving as a landing flap (...*on a collision course...*) in his right hand. Somehow, the plaque slipped from his grasp (...*I am a satellite, I am out of control...*) and flew against the wall where it bounced off and shattered on the floor.

This morning, he had no memory of what happened after that, but somehow he had salvaged the pieces of his plaque. Working through his mental fog now, it all seemed foreign. He was a different person than he once knew.

His performance at the hospital, in the operating room, with patients and their families, had been ideal, award-winning, albeit plaque-busting. His colleagues lived quiet, stable, boring lives that should have allowed them a clear advantage professionally. Yet here he was, after an evening of accolades and debauchery, ripe and ready to make final rounds and still help the junior resident with a gallbladder, his last time to perform surgery in the great state of Texas.

As he drove onto the grounds of the lunatic asylum, he braked his car at one of the crosswalks. A stop sign allowed the passage of inmates, single file, on their way to the cafeteria. The line was all men, all in khaki pants and all with matching khaki shirts. Unlike the disheveled schizos and organics, acutes and chronics, these men had their shirttails tucked in, their hair was combed, and they looked–well–normal. These were not the lunatics. Chase knew from working at Matherville over so many years that these ducks in a row were the alcoholics.

How does anyone get so far down in the gutter that they would end up here in such utter humiliation? I would rather die than be sent to a place like this. He thumped, thumped, thumped on the steering wheel with his anxious palms, waiting for these weak-willed dipsomaniacs to pass.

He parked his car at Building 19 for one final stop at his old haunt before heading to the hospital to hand over the reins to the understudies with the final gallbladder. He had promised Ivy a visit when he saw her last at the clinic, and she had nodded her understanding. In fact, she had seemed unusually excited.

As Chase started to enter the side door of Building 19, he noticed a patient transport van parked out front. An aide was helping three inmates exit onto the sidewalk. Chase recognized all three of the patients as his own post-ops that the team had lassoed from the institution at Wichita Falls. His junior residents had fixed the old catatonic's hernia, they had excised a lipoma from the paranoid shizophrenic's upper back, and they had removed the benign breast lump from the old lobotomized lady who dressed for winter, even in summer, in her red stocking cap, coat, and muff. *What are these post-ops doing here at Building 19?*

Rather than enter the side door of the nurses' station, Chase walked toward the van where he questioned the driver. "Why are these patients coming here? We discharged them to Wichita Falls."

"Permanent transfers, I was told. The rest of the surgical patients in the bus are headed back to Wichita Falls, all right, but my orders were to drop off these three musketeers right here. Administration pulls strings, you know, to keep their numbers up for the almighty dollar. Knowing old Doc Latimer, I'd hazard to guess he dredged up some family ties to Matherville for these three, so's they could be kept here. I suspect that old goat hires detectives to keep this place full. Hard to keep the numbers up when he's cramming chronics into those outpatient apartments at the same time."

It made no difference to Chase. He was *outta here*. Off to California soon. He walked ahead and held the door open for the threesome as they entered the brick building. The first two walked by as if he were invisible, but the tall lady with the stocking cap and muff stared at him with deep-set eyes, vacuous, unsettling. Quite possibly, she remembered him as one of the masked surgeons who had violated her breast a few days earlier.

Beneath her red cap, above her brow on the right, he knew she was hiding a depression in her skull, much larger than standard lobotomies. He had meant to read her old chart while she had been on the surgical unit, but had forgotten. There was no time now. He had studied lobotomy techniques of the past where, prior to nasal and orbital ice picks, a full craniotomy had been used. Yet, to his knowledge, no surgeons ever created such a large crater in the skull for lobotomy. He wondered if, like so many chronics in the system, the patient's history had become an oral tradition, no longer based in fact.

Chase followed the patients through the front door where he saw that the piano bench in the TV room was empty. He maneuvered around the three new patients and headed for the Day room. There, he found Ivy in her daisy-covered dress, walking the same circle as when he began working there as an aide 10 years earlier. When Ivy spotted him, she did not head toward Chase as usual. Instead, she hobbled back to the sleeping room, disappearing for a few seconds. When she returned, she was holding a thin book in her hands, gesturing that it was a present from her to him, by pointing back and forth until he got the message. She had made a decorative bow of sorts out of a paper napkin from the cafeteria. She held out the book to him, a smile on her face.

"Thank you, Ivy. Why, it's a book. What's it about?" he asked, knowing full well Ivy didn't have a clue. Before she released it to him, however, she used both hands to cover up most of the title, leaving only the word *GOD* visible.

Chase wasn't sure what she was trying to do, but she didn't let go of the book until he acknowledged that it was about God. Once he said the word "God," she smiled and gave the present to him. As her hands fell away, he could see the full title and author–*To A God Unknown* by John Steinbeck. He recalled that a temple in Athens had been dedicated to the unknown God, but he was not familiar with this book by Steinbeck.

"Where'd you get this, Ivy?" he asked as he opened the cover and saw *Property of Matherville State Mental Hospital* stamped in black ink. "Oh, I see. Well, thank you very much." He would return the book to the library on the way out. *No, if I return it now, Ivy will see it back on the shelf. Heck, I'll just keep it.*

Ivy held up her fingers, with all the Zs still bright red. She wiggled them as best possible, but they moved mostly in unison. She touched the cover of the book, then pointed up toward the ceiling, or beyond. With her newly released index finger, she wiped away a tear from one cheek.

"Ivy, I'm going to miss your spitting, especially when I need protection in California."

She laughed as if she understood.

"I haven't seen you spit in a long time, but I know you've had to use it on Bertie from time to time."

Ivy backed up a few steps and limped away, heading for the bathroom, then she returned with a handful of paper towels.

What is she doing?

She laid out three towels on the floor, in the middle of her circular path. Then she picked them up, one at a time, rolling her tongue back and squirting something on each towel before laying it down again. Then she picked up the three towels and held them in a row, using her new fingers. The wetness on each towel formed a letter, and when held together, spelled a word: *GOD.*

"Ivy, I don't know which is the better present—this book or that spit. I didn't know you were an artist. I had no idea you could do something like that. *I thought her talent was more like a shotgun.*

She laughed, and it occurred to him for the umpteenth time that she bore no features of mental illness.

Ivy gathered up the three paper towels and walked out to the TV room where she laid them out in the same pattern, on the floor, near the piano bench. She sat down, gesturing for Chase to join her. He did, but began excusing himself right away.

"Ivy, I'm so sorry. I can't stay. I'm late to the operating room. It's my last surgery here. But I want to thank you for all you've done over the years, and I'm going to miss you very much."

"So, me love you," she seemed to mumble, although the words were delivered so quickly it could well have been his imagination, with Ivy twisting her usual, "Soti medo."

"I love you, too, and I won't forget you. I'll probably visit Matherville from time to time, so I'll drop by to see you." He gave Ivy a quick hug that she converted to a long hug, then she waved good-bye with her right hand by wiggling her fingers as best she could. Using both his hands, Chase enveloped Ivy's waving fingers and kissed the tip of each, one by one.

As he spun around on the bench, preparing to stand, Chase was startled by a tall figure looming over them both. It was the lobotomy lady from Wichita Falls.

In her dark overcoat, red knit cap with tufts of gray hair sticking out, hands embedded in a white muff, she appeared at first to be another one of the countless empty souls at the asylum. Her large eyes were simultaneously macabre and alluring, seeming to have once belonged to a thing of beauty. With a damaged mind, however, these same sumptuous eyes were empty caves. She had not been so frightening before, while Chase had her as an in-patient on the surgical unit. The apprehension he felt now was not due simply to her unblinking eyes, but her frozen pose, as if chiseled from ice.

In the subdued light of the TV room, she was a creepy statue, staring relentlessly. However, the old woman was not staring at him. She was staring at Ivy, without expression, at first. Then, the woman saw the paper towels on the floor, and her gaze began bouncing back and forth between Ivy and the floor where the word GOD had nearly dried.

Chase said good-bye to Ivy once again as he eased around the lobotomy lady and walked away from the scene. He looked back over his shoulder expecting Ivy's final good-bye. However, Ivy was not looking at him. She was intently studying the woman in the red cap and white muff.

30

The three-year-old girl sat beside her mother on the bench facing a black upright piano with swinging candelabra. The vagaries of embryology and birth had been brutal to her, leaving footprints of tortured genes that trounced from one end of her body to the other. Yet, save for one minuscule problem, her brain had been spared. The working parts of her mind had been blessed with joy and sadness and fear and hurt and all the emotions that, when bundled, formed her humanity.

The minuscule problem–the only deformity not visible to the world–was a pea-sized mass of twisted arteries and veins, coiled like a snake resting in the middle of a highway. Yet, this highway was a strategic neural path that connected Broca's area of speech articulation to Wernicke's area of speech comprehension. The snake was an arteriovenous malformation, and the nearby neural tract being hammered by this pulsating blob kept the girl from articulating speech, despite the fact that she could understand it. Indeed, she had not spoken one word in the three years since her birth in 1932.

On this exceptional evening, however, while sitting beside her mother who was practicing her scales at the piano, the coiled, pulsating vessels sprung a pinpoint leak, and the malformation collapsed. And for several minutes only, with the direct pressure gone, the tiniest bits of information squeaked by, traveling the highway. And during those vulnerable and receptive minutes, as the mother sang her scales – do-re-mi-fa-so-la-ti-do – over and over, frontward and backward, the alphabet, the syllables, the vocabulary was born for the little girl. And with Broca's area now able to paste and mold words from syllables, a language was born.

However, the hemorrhage from the arteriovenous malformation did not stop until enough pressure developed to tamponade the hole in the vessel. In effect, the roadblock recreated itself within minutes, and the highway was closed again, this time forever, as the escaped blood turned to clot that turned to scar that turned to stone. And yet, "forever" was a long time, and a deeper understanding by science would reveal that the supportive glial cells in the brain could be recruited and converted to shiny new neurons through radical repetition of cognitive exercises.

From the mother's vantage, her daughter slipped into a glassy-eyed stare as the blood first began to leak. The mother slowed and softened the do-re-mi of her scales, her modulations faltering as she sensed something wrong. Then, as the pocket of blood pressed against its boundaries in the brain, her daughter fainted, lying in a spell for several minutes, reawakening with melodic idioms–a language of music.

31

Ivy and the old woman in the red cap tossed their scrutiny back and forth, each lost soul familiar to the other. Neither was sure, so neither moved. Finally, Ivy patted the piano bench beside her, where Dr. Callaway had been moments before. The old woman broke from her frozen pose and shuffled between bench and piano, easing down beside Ivy.

Ivy turned back to the piano keys where she started to play, but then she decided a better check on this person would be to sing acapella in her own language, starting with a few lines of "Baby Face." She stopped, looked at the old woman, then waited for a reaction. The woman's lips, gray and cracked, opened enough for a whisper to pass, but Ivy couldn't understand her. Ivy switched tunes, still acapella, "Shine little glow-worm, glimmer... shine little glow-worm, glimmer... lead us lest too far we wander... love's sweet voice is calling yonder..." At least, those were the words that sounded in Ivy's brain.

Slowly, the old woman who was dressed for a hard winter this June, pulled one hand from its burial place in the white muff. She reached for one of Ivy's hands and began caressing Ivy's fingers with her own. She examined the Z-lined digits, glancing up repeatedly to stare into Ivy's close-set, beaming eyes, as the woman studied her face. Then she reached down and touched Ivy's short leg, moving her fingers down to the black shoe with its thick sole, six extra inches to help minimize Ivy's precarious wobble. Finally, she ran her hand across Ivy's other knee and down to the ankle, whereupon she whispered, "One perfectly good and lovely limb."

Ivy was struggling to confirm her impression, too. A smile broadened across her face when the woman pulled out her other hand from the muff. The skin was precious pink, like a glove, up to the wrist. Ivy said, "Soti medo," and the mother knew those words well, the required neural pathways intact despite resolute damage elsewhere in her brain. She replied, "Soti medo," knowing at a primal level that she was telling Ivy, "I love you."

Decades were lost in a flicker as they put their hands back to the keyboard as a duet. Yet, when Ivy started to pound on the keys, it was clear that her mother's hands were lost. They were like clay, still and cold. All musical talent had been erased. Slowly, the mother pulled her palms from the keyboard, then to her lap where each hand burrowed its way back into the white muff. Then the mother turned to the daughter and spoke words known only to Ivy: "Latido resola me sodo," which, for only two humans on the planet, meant: "Play the piano and sing for me."

Without her mother's skillful playing, Ivy knew only one song where she could hit all the right notes, using only her thumbs. So, she began to play and sing, with these words sounding in her head:

Zanda the panda
Alone in a land-a
Where bears did not live
'Til a storm...blew him out to sea

In a palm tree
He did land
Don't you see
Forever alone at the top.

He cried, boo-hoo, boo-hoo. He wanted bamboo, he only boo-hoo'd
Boo-hoo, bamboo, boo-hoo, I want to go home. I want to go
home...

.   .   .

Joe Davis, Psych Aide-2, had been through orientation with Chase in 1971, and had been assigned to Building 19 ever since. He had stopped pilfering drugs years ago after the sting on Sukie Spurlock, and subsequently considered himself an incredibly lucky man. He was standing at the Dutch door of the nurses' station while Ivy and the new patient were sitting on the far side of the TV room at the piano.

"Oh brother, Ivy has a new audience now, and we're going to have to listen to 'Chopsticks' yet another thousand times." The LPN charting nearby didn't bother to look up.

Joe's hippie locks were long gone, but he had the same style of wire-rimmed glasses, so he looked more like a bank teller than the revolutionary of old. Next year, he figured, he was going back to college. After all, what could another degree hurt?

As Ivy began to play "Chopsticks," however, something was different. Something was wrong. Joe walked slowly across the TV room, approaching the twosome on the bench quietly, so as not to disturb them in their natural habitat.

He knew Ivy's version, with its unintelligible lyrics, as well as Chase's "Zanda" version, sometimes having to smoke at least three joints to get the annoying tune out of his head. And what Joe heard now was too bizarre–Ivy was not singing her own garbled lyrics, but was singing a rough version of Chase's Panda song. It wasn't perfect by a long shot, but clearly, it was not the usual Ivy gibberish. Instead, for the first time, a person could actually understand Ivy.

He muttered to himself, "Boogie down, little Ivy, and keep on truckin'."

.   .   .

Dixie Barnes, R.N., now the gray-haired Chief of Nursing at Matherville State, oversaw the housing assignments for the new outpatient facility. A few would live alone, some in pairs, some in threes or fours. In her heart, she was convinced the experiment would fail. "These patients are completely institutionalized. It'll never work," she had said on many occasions to all who would listen and to others who didn't care. Yet, the orders from the preeminent Dr. Latimer were clear: "Fill the new apartments. I don't care how you do it… but do it." The allure of federal funds for outpatient treatment of mental illness was Dr. Latimer's new love, and his possessiveness of the new outpatient facility was full and complete. It was his legacy.

As Dixie scanned the possible pairings on her metal clipboard melded into the crook of her arm, she came across the name of Jane Dozier in Building 19. She knew every patient in the entire hospital, especially this experimental ward where so many important drug trials had taken place over the years. So who was this?

"Mr. Davis, who is Jane Dozier?" she asked of the charge aide on 19. "I've been off this past week. Is she a new admission? We once used the name Jane Dozier for the female John Doe's, but how could we not know a chronic's name?"

Joe Davis, PA-2 replied, "She's from Wichita Falls. Maybe they didn't know her name either, or maybe it's really Jane Dozier. Anyway, they discharged her from the surgical ward here at Matherville last week. Then somehow, her and two others were transferred here, permanent-like, to us on nineteen. I'm guessing Dr. Latimer is pumpin' the numbers again."

"Now, Joe, Dr. Latimer wouldn't stoop to that. Trust me."

"Yeah, sure. I don't think this woman has got much mojo if you know what I mean. The aides over in surgery were trying to say she's an old lobotomy patient, but dream on. I checked her chart as soon as I saw the front of her skull had a big divot. That ain't no lobotomy."

He continued, "Here's the skinny–her records say she was a court-ordered admission back in 1937. A state trooper picked her up walking along highway 82, north of Abilene. Her head was smashed in, so they took her to a regular hospital first for some sort of brain surgery, then on to Wichita Falls when it came clear she was gonna need custodial care. Her memory was shot, and no one could figure out where she'd come from, especially since there'd been no car wreck, no missing persons, no nothin' in the area, and from her other cuts and scrapes, it didn't look like assault, or anything like that."

"What's her functional level, Joe? Do you see her having any chance in the apartments?"

"Not alone, no way. But it's really funky how she and Ivy Pettibone have buddied up."

"Ivy? She doesn't bond with anyone."

"Well, these two do everything together. Ivy helps her to the cafeteria, carries her tray, even helps feed her. Ivy helps her get dressed, combs her hair, the whole nine yards. And they're always at that piano. Craziest thing, you wouldn't believe it, but I heard Ivy at that piano recently, and she was talking, or actually more like singing—"

"Fine, Joe, yes. Ivy does that a lot. I'm happy to say there will be a new piano in the game room at the apartments, so that's good. I'll start out with the two of them together in Unit A-4."

"One other thing that's pretty far out," Joe said. "Jane Dozier's admission note from Wichita Falls says there were some missing people from the killer tornado in Matherville that year, so they wondered if that's where she came from. But that stretch of road between Abilene and Wichita Falls was almost four hundred miles away from the tornado, so nobody thought it possible. That is, except for a doctor that showed up at Wichita Falls a month or so after her admission. Claimed he was from Matherville, looking to identify people who were missing from the tornado. The records say he examined our Jane Dozier here, but claimed she was *not* one of the Matherville victims, so she stayed in Wichita Falls for the next forty-some-odd years."

Dixie Barnes was only halfway listening as she flipped her pages until she came to the floor plans of the new apartments and wrote "Pettibone/Dozier" in the empty square closest to the game room.

"And what's so... *far out*, as you say, about that?"

"First of all, why would the guy even *think* to look in a mental hospital four hundred miles away? And the second thing, weirder even, is that the doctor's name was Callaway. From Matherville."

Dixie let the floor plans flop down to her side. "Callaway? Dr. Wes Callaway? That can't be." She began counting years by tapping her red fingernails against an imaginary surface in the air. "Wes Callaway would have only been in college back when the tornado hit. Everyone who lived through it remembers where they were at the time. Me, I was in seventh grade English class. Missed my school by only half a mile."

"Must've been another Dr. Callaway then," said Joe. "I looked for a first name, what with knowing Chase and his father and all. The progress notes said a Dr. Callaway showed up one day looking for missing folks from the tornado."

Dixie replied, "Just a coincidence, I suppose. Old Zebulon, Chase's grandfather, was a pharmacist before he became a preacher, I've heard told, but that doesn't make any sense."

"Back to this Ivy deal," Joe persisted, "I about freaked out when I heard her at the piano—"

"She's always at the piano, Joe."

"Yes, but she was speaking English, sorta. I mean she was *singing* English—"

"Oh, my, if you're not careful, they'll be locking *you* up."

32

Dr. Everett Meeker, Chairman of Psychiatry at Far West Texas School of Medicine, had risen to national prominence in recent years, now serving as president of the Society for Behavioral Sciences in Medical Education. His book, *The White Coat: Guard or Prisoner,* was scheduled for a second edition, prompting him to pour over the latest computer printouts, forever searching for the third element, the unknown variable that could help determine which students would succeed versus which would self-destruct.

Identifying the first two parameters–natural empathy coupled with resistance to self-deception–had been a radical leap, in light of the negative implications of paradoxically desirable traits, making his book a best seller in the small market of medical educators. Along with his colleague, Dr. Daryl Crim, they had introduced an objective scale for natural empathy, and another scale for resistance to self-deception. From these two measurements, they created the Meeker-Crim Prognostic Index as a crystal ball that could reasonably predict physician meltdown, years in advance. Modest elevations in the score translated to early burn-out, while very high scores tended to forecast addictions, severe depression, and suicide.

Still, there was room for improvement with the M-C Prognostic Index. A third variable could theoretically be added to the mix, more accurately pinpointing adverse outcomes.

Dr. Meeker was now in his 22nd year of this project, generating profiles on 90 medical students with high index scores out of a pool of nearly 3,000 from Far West. To date, a remarkably high percentage of the 90 had self-destructed in one way or another, a persistent trend noted early in the study. Many more with modestly elevated index scores had suffered career-ending burn-out.

Two rights shouldn't make a wrong–that is, two good qualities for a physician should not translate into a drastic increase in the probability of calamitous self-annihilation. Yet, the numbers were disturbing–60%– that is, 54 out of 90 study participants who met the two criteria as defined in the M-C Prognostic Index had ended up with a major collapse of some sort, compared to only 14% in the control group of 2,991 students. Furthermore, since the first edition of his book, Meeker had documented additional calamities, such that the predictive capability of the index was improving with the passage of time. In the second edition, the 60% would be adjusted to 70%, reflecting an additional 9 physicians whose practices had been interrupted due to a self-destructive pattern or event.

Dr. Meeker opened the report while fumbling for his reading glasses to help decipher the dot matrix print. So far, the mainframe computer had been little help in his research, given that the M-C Prognostic Index had been developed before the university expanded computer access to all faculty members. However, he recognized the potential and tried to keep up with the technology. So far, however, the printed reports seemed more like hieroglyphs.

He was especially curious this afternoon, as he had submitted to the IBM mainframe 3,000-plus questionnaires that medical students had been filling out for the past 22 years. After six months of data entry at the computer lab, the report he got in return was the largest he had ever received, over an inch in thickness, and likely over 30 feet long if the connected pages were completely unfolded.

After his initial study of the report, it was apparent that no particular question was going to earn the title as the third parameter. Then, as Dr. Meeker continued reading through the summary, he stumbled on a curious result that dot matrix had nearly camouflaged through its monotony. He took off his reading glasses and massaged his lambchop sideburns, as if to make sure he wasn't dreaming. "Well, I'll be a left-handed snake oil salesman from the wrong side of the tracks," he said aloud to his empty office. He telephoned his research colleague, Dr. Daryl Crim.

"Daryl, you're not going to believe this, but I think I've found our missing element, that is, the university computer found it. We've had this information for years, but maybe it takes a computer to see the pattern."

"What do you mean, Everett?"

"The questionnaires the students have been filling out before they start on the wards... recall that we asked them to check a box for each of their top three specialty choices. Before, we've only looked at their answers individually, one at a time. But if I'm reading this correctly, it's not a single choice, but a specific combination of three specialties that seems to have hit the mark. It looks like this combination by itself is *as good as our index,* if not better. I'd hate to think we've wasted our time for the past twenty years. After we blend this into our index, though, we could really see some amazing results."

"I give up. What are the three specialties?"

"A very strange grouping–psychiatry, pathology, surgery. Who combines those three? And why? It looks like only one or two students a year pick that triad, or trifecta if you must."

"This might not blend easily into the index," said Dr. Crim. "It might have to stand alone as a separate predictor. It smacks of superficiality, simple taxonomy, or at most, a surrogate risk for something deeper. Our current parameters address underlying psychodynamics—causation, if you will. Not so with this specialty triad thing you're describing."

"Still, regardless of superficiality, what if this rare combination proves to be a helpful predictor whether we understand the underlying psychodynamics or not?"

"That remains to be seen. We certainly have a lot of work to do before that second edition is released. Admittedly, though, this triad of specialties is a bizarre grouping."

Dr. Meeker replied, "It makes no sense, does it? The greatest divergence in specialty choices is represented in this triad, a continuum

from the highly subjective psychiatry to the highly objective pathology–
the two extremes of medicine–with surgery in the middle."

"Regardless, it doesn't tell us anything about why," said Crim. "And
maybe it's not a linear continuum, but instead, some sort of
triangulation, three extremes rather than two. We think of cognitive
dissonance as holding two incompatible beliefs at the same time. Yet,
what if we've discovered a tripartite version where a person holds *three*
incompatible beliefs at the same time, pulling him or her in three
different directions? I suppose the underlying psyche reflected in those
three specialty choices could tear a person apart—"

"Uh-oh, just occurred to me... we have some in our study group
with only short-term follow-up so far, where they've scored high on our
index, but are still doing just fine. What if these individuals also have
the ominous triad?"

"That's the $64,000 question. How does this specialty triad relate
to our index? Check it out, Everett. Are you calling from your office?
Do you have the code book handy?"

Dr. Meeker put his reading glasses back on, then took them off, then
on again. "Yes, I've started going through the list of high index scores
in those who are still doing well... cross-checking with the bizarre triad
list... hmm, that's' odd... doesn't seem to be much overlap... none of
the high index physicians have this triad so far... good thing, I guess...
specialty choices are all over the map. Oh, I stand corrected. Here's one
of our high-indexers who also has the ominous combination—
psychiatry-pathology-surgery. Subject 0002240... looking now in the
code book... I hate it that we have to turn people into numbers... just a
minute, yes, here it is–Chase Callaway. I remember him quite well. We
almost had him talked into a career in psychiatry. Finished his chief year
in surgery this month, so follow-up is too short here for any conclusions.
He's living with a double whammy, though. High index score plus the
bizarre specialty triad. I'll make sure we keep in contact with him."

"Everett, I know you realize what we have here, but the gravity of
this discovery–the full implications–never struck me until now. Maybe I
never believed we would actually come up with such strong predictors."

"Yes, I can guess what you're thinking. In effect, we have a future
diagnosis of a dreadful condition in an individual, yet according to our

Ethics Committee's new rules, we cannot tell the patient. When we started this project, of course, there were few rules, if any.

"We can't break those rules. They've really beefed up that committee, and it's coming down from the national level. Now the committee is called the Institutional Review Board. The IRB is charged with *protecting* patients, no matter what the cost."

"Oh, my. For something like this, such protection could be deadly."

33

Chase's right hand was still throbbing. His knuckles were sinking into the swelling flesh around them. A faint purple was coming into full bloom.

His worldly possessions were locked in a rental trailer behind his Cutlass. It was time to get out of town and never return. The instant this funeral was over, he would be gone. Spurring him on were the comments from co-residents that went something like this: "Good thing you're leaving Matherville. Our wives would rather see you hang, of course. Hope things work out in California because the bridge back to Texas is awful rickety."

He glanced again at his bruised knuckles and slipped his right hand into his pocket where his fingers burned as they surrounded the good luck charm he'd taken from his grandfather's library three nights ago, the evening of Zebulon's death.

On this darkest of days, Chase had not been able to concentrate on the eulogies delivered by members of the Church of the Driven Nail, nor the words offered by the few remaining oldsters who had known him as "Doc" Callaway. The group was at graveside now, and Chase was still struggling to focus.

How had it come this far? How did it get to the point where a father and son no longer speak? How could rage be so powerful as to drive the son's hand into the wall beside his father's face?

Things had never been right. Two years ago, when his father had invited Chase to join him in medical practice, Chase had declined. He was, after all, going to be a board-certified surgeon, and his father's brand of country medicine seemed beneath a specialist. Wes had probably sensed the condescension.

His father had grown increasingly cold ever since, but when he learned that Chase's marriage was dissolving, and that Livvy was not going to California, Wes could barely contain himself. So when Ramona Callaway suffered a heart attack only a week ago, shortly after learning that Livvy was staying behind in Matherville, it was obvious to father Wes that his wife's brush with death had been caused by undue stress, and this stress, in turn, had been caused by a wayward son.

Chase, on the other hand, felt that coronary artery occlusion was the true cause of heart attacks. So, moments earlier, as father and son interchanged their differing theories in an opening salvo before the start of the funeral, with Ramona still recovering in the hospital, with Wes accusing Chase of trying to kill his own mother, Chase had aimed his closed fist at his father, veering at the last minute into a two-by-four stud, camouflaged by drywall, decorated with wallpaper of harvest gold.

Now, Chase lifted his red-rimmed eyes from Zebulon's grave, and he snuck a glance across the mourners to his rental trailer in the distance, marked E-Z Haul, his entire world stored within. Almost his entire world, that is. He was to inherit his grandfather's three-walled library, but Chase had no place for the volumes right now. The books would need to be stored and shipped later. Since his income would be split with Livvy, at least for a while, he would live modestly in a small apartment, no room for such a vast library.

Chase had little in the way of reserve munitions with which to mourn his grandfather's death. There were too many things to cry about. He was alone in the crowd. His heart-damaged mother was in the hospital. His incensed father stood across the grave, opposite Chase. Livvy lingered at the periphery of the crowd, refusing to make eye contact with Chase. And Sukie Spurlock was congregated with the Black members from the Church of the Driven Nail.

His right hand seemed to be expanding with each beat of his heart. The crowd around him faded away as he focused on the casket and the gears of a noisy motor that began their inexorable grind, lowering his grandfather into the chilly clay that lay beneath the sand and gravel surface of the Matherville cemetery.

When the ratcheting sound of the motor stopped, and Zebulon was settled for good, a few clods were tossed, and then the crowd began to disperse. Chase headed toward Sukie, away from Livvy. He felt empowered by clutching the good luck charm in his pocket. The charm, at least he felt it as such, was a wood-carved conch, a little larger than a peach. It had rested for many years on one shelf of his grandfather's library, and Zebulon had told a young Chase that the wooden shell was a symbol of "paradise lost." Those words had intrigued him ever since. Now, the wooden shell was his talisman.

As he approached Sukie, he avoided shaking her outstretched hand, instead, preparing to give her a kiss. She was wearing a black hat that contrasted sharply to her silver hair, and when he lifted the mesh veil to kiss her on the cheek, he saw tears, barely contained.

She wiped her cheeks dry, then said, "Chase, your Grandpa Zeb was a good, good man. I know that you know that. He helped me in ways you don't know. He had some major regrets about his life, though. Someday, maybe I'll tell you all about it. Oh, my dear, dear baby. You're headed for California. Me, oh my." She hugged him briefly. "You are my baby, you know. And I'm so proud you've grown up without hate in your heart. I walk with my chin up around my friends, yes I do, a bit proud, mind you."

Chase answered, "I'll never get over the trouble I caused you way back when, with your job and all, Sukie. I'm going to make it up to you as soon as I get some income going in California."

"Oh, no, baby, I don't need money. You go and forget that now. Wipe that idea plumb clean from your mind." Sukie hugged him again.

From the corner of his eye, Chase spotted Livvy walking away from the grave site. He shifted a little so that Sukie's hat blocked the view, and when Livvy was a safe distance away, he released himself from Sukie's hug. Guilt could be quite the burden.

"Chase, you be careful in California now," said Sukie, as she escorted him toward his blue Cutlass. "There's all sorts of trouble a person can get into out there when you don't know anyone and don't have any touchstones. No roots. You can think you're traveling along a road, straight and narrow-like, but there can be two sets of tracks on that road, running side by side, one track full of grace and blessings, the other side packed with evil. And as your Grandpa used to quote in his sermons, from the Book of James, 'a double-minded man is unstable in all his ways'.

Chase cleared his throat to cover the fact he was not giving Sukie his full attention.

Sukie continued, "You've been given many talents, but you remember the parable of the talents, don't you?"

"Yes, Sukie."

"Bible version or my version?

"Both, I think. Can I give you a ride home, Sukie?"

"No thanks, look, I'm parked right next to you. And Chase, let me refresh your memory."

"About?"

"My version."

He continued to caress the conch as though it were therapeutic for his injury, but the charm was too large to remain in his pocket for the long trip west. Slowly, he withdrew the wooden shell, careful to keep Sukie from spotting his swollen hand. A quick glance at his knuckles shocked him. His hand was a brighter purple than it had been only a half-hour earlier.

Strangely, he heard a whisper that he recognized as his own voice, coming from deep within, yet still alien–*Don't listen to her,* it said, *she's a tough nut with strong opinions, and you'll do better by thinking on your own.*

"When a baby is born, Chase, he or she comes into this world with a key. It might be a brass key, or a silver one, or plain old junk metal. It might even be broken. And that key, no matter what it's made of, or what shape it's in, can open the gates of Heaven. Your key, Chase, why, it's made of gold."

"Yes, Sukie, you've said that ever since I was a kid." He opened the back door of his car and tossed the good luck shell into one of the cardboard boxes in the back seat. Through the open square of the ill-fitting flaps, the shell landed with a gentle thud, spinning on the book, *To A God Unknown*, his present from Ivy Pettibone.

After closing the car door, he turned and kissed Sukie once again on the cheek before sliding into the driver's seat. "Good-bye, Sukie. I'll remember everything you've ever taught me. I promise."

Don't listen to her, he heard once again. *Forget the old Chase. Forget Matherville. Forget Texas. The world awaits.*

A bubbly cumulus cloud passed in front of the sun, dimming the world into a shadow darker than a cloud can usually manage. *Darkness heralds the light,* he thought to himself.

"You haven't forgotten the rest, have you baby?"

Chase turned to face Sukie.

She continued, "The key you're born with..."

"Yes?"

"That key, the one that opens the door to Paradise–why, it's the same key that unlocks the Gates of Perdition."

Although Sukie was both worldly-wise and heavenly-wise, Chase believed that she was naïve to the rigors of surgical training–and, as such, he had already served his sentence in Hell. Now, he was prepared to set the world on fire, without the brimstone. Disregarding the fierce pain in his knuckles, a disembodied set of hands squeezed the life out of the steering wheel as he pulled away.

And so it began.

END

For publishing updates on the adventures of
Dr. Chase Callaway, access the chronicles at:

www.johnalbedo.com

Acknowledgments

For taking the time to read and review an unpublished manuscript, I am grateful for the input from my long-term friend, C.T.T., and my wife, B.J.H. As with prior novels, thanks go to D.C. for listening to my progress on this story over the course of many years. My appreciation also goes to D.B., D.C. and P.H., book club members from "The Booklings" for their review as well. To friends and family and those who might be prone to assuming that this is a true story, keep in mind one definition of fiction as "memory plus imagination," with a strong emphasis on the latter. Please excuse those times when I rope you in with an element of truth, only to use a slip knot of fiction.

Many decades have passed since my encounter with a "chronic" who would emerge as Ivy in this story. The recollection of this patient persisted over time while others faded. I suppose, therefore, that I could claim that *Nutshell* has been a work in progress for over 40 years. In that light, I would like to thank publisher Reagan Rothe and his staff at Black Rose Writing for taking on this story and converting my manuscript to its final form.

ABOUT THE AUTHOR

John Albedo is an award-winning novelist whose stories take place in the south-central U.S., often colored by a decade spent in Los Angeles.

Note from the Publisher

Word-of-mouth is crucial for any author to succeed. If you enjoyed *Nutshell*, please leave a review online—anywhere you are able. Even if it's just a sentence or two. It would make all the difference and would be very much appreciated.

Thanks!
Black Rose Writing

Thank you so much for reading one of our **Medical** novels.
If you enjoyed the experience, please check out
our recommended title for your next great read!

A Surgeon's Knot by William Lynes

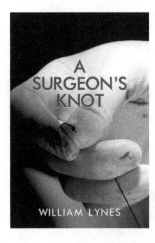

"Heart-pounding tales of a surgical intern that are both
terrifying and profound. This medical thriller will stay with
you long past the final chapter."

–BEST THRILLERS